The Man of Property

and

Indian Summer of a Forsyte

Introduction and Study Guide by

MARSDEN V. DILLENBECK

CHAIRMAN OF THE ENGLISH DEPARTMENT

RYE HIGH SCHOOL

with the assistance, on the study guide, of

MARIAN L. WARREN

ENGLISH DEPARTMENT, RYE HIGH SCHOOL

RYE, NEW YORK

THE MAN
OF
PROPERTY

and

Indian Summer of a Forsyte

JOHN GALSWORTHY

Charles Scribner's Sons • New York

TO
EDWARD GARNETT

CONTENTS

PART THREE

INTERLUDE

INTRODUCTION

IN America in the late 1950's, a new word, *togetherness,* became a common expression with a wide application ranging from the affairs of the family to those of the nation. The fact that it was so commonly used stemmed from a strong prevailing belief that it had been too long absent from many of our ways of living and thinking. It does not necessarily follow that we in America were the only ones to find this true. Representative literature of many countries—novels, short stories, even newspapers and periodicals—underlines that this has been a widespread problem.

As intelligent human beings we want to know more about people, not only those of our time and country, but also those of past eras and other lands. *The Man of Property* presents various aspects of this togetherness, both its presence and absence in varying degrees, in a time not too remote from ours and in a country closely related to us.

The reader will learn much from this novel about family life in England prior to the turn of the twentieth century. How certain people of that era thought and lived should prove interesting, especially when compared to the reader's own experiences. He should be aware of the author's points of view and beliefs, as well as those which he himself will form, or maintain, as he reads.

To obtain a clear understanding of any book and its author, one should know about the writer, as well as the background of his particular work. *The Man of Property,* published in 1906, is Part One of a panoramic novel of the late ninetenth century, *The Forsyte Saga.* Galsworthy, always sharply aware of the tastes of his time, has interpreted upper middle-class Victorian society in true perspective.

John Galsworthy was born in Coombe, Surrey, in England, in 1867, of an old Devonshire family. As a son in a prosperous, established, middle-class English family, his early life was comfortable, calm, and peaceful. He attended Harrow where he made a name for himself as an athlete, and he graduated from New College of Oxford University where the "best" people of his time sent their sons for an education. He then studied law, was admitted to the bar, but rarely practiced, although his legal training is apparent in his writings. Free from financial worry, he traveled widely and read extensively, eventually settling down as a country gentleman in the romantic region of Dartmoor to devote himself to writing. This was a wild, rough area which he loved, that love of countryside so admirably reflected in his ability to describe pastoral scenes in *The Man of Property* and in his other works.

Despite his background, Galsworthy was not a romanticist; he exemplified realism at its best in thought and observation, a trend begun hundreds of years before his time in English literature by Geoffrey Chaucer and emulated since by comparatively few writers. Galsworthy's forte was analyzing, with great perception and insight, upper middle-class life in England. He portrayed human action and character and interpreted motives, drives and behavior of his characters as they actually were, not as a writer or reader might like them to be.

Possessed of an unusually sensitive mind, he detested sham and hypocrisy in people and enjoyed exposing it. However, unlike many writers of protest, he was never bitter toward the people about whom he wrote; his sympathy for them softened the irony and the satire in his writing.

This tolerance for people definitely places him somewhat in the category of a satirist, rather than a propagandist; he was not seriously trying to sell or promote anything or anybody. He was always fair to his characters and maintained an unprejudiced attitude toward them, possibly an end-product of his legal training. When an author shows why his people act as they do, the reader has difficulty blaming any of them for their faults, perversities, and even stupidities. Man has always had his problems, and Galsworthy did not make it easy for any of his characters to extricate themselves from difficult, self-imposed situations.

These few facts and observations about the author indicate that his theme was basically social, and he ranks high among social historians. To write realistically about people, one must know them. Galsworthy, of course, knew the people of his upper middle-class English world, and they became his characters. According to his wife, some of them were even derived from his family or his friends. These characters aroused his absorbing, sympathetic interest. He was opposed to anything that forced people into a pattern of thinking and behaving, but in his writing on this point, he devoted himself basically to the tyrannies of family, of property, and of traditional thinking. In spite of the author's implied criticism of the way his characters thought and lived, he never relinquished his faith in man's potential for being a better person than he is.

Galsworthy's basic conflict of forces is between upper middle-class materialism and the sense of beauty. He stressed the idea that the most precious things are so often common and everyday and that they will not always be obvious. To Galsworthy, the Forsytes were a very real family, and as the author himself stated, this type of family was not uncommon. In this story the characters, even the lesser ones, are fully developed, typifying what has been called "the smugness of the civilized world." The reader can appreciate the likes, the moral standards, and the sense of values of these people who seriously believed that the future of England was almost wholly dependent on them—the investors, the financiers, and their families.

The central character, Soames Forsyte, personifies the materialistic individual whose main purpose in life is to amass property of any value, but who does not realize that one cannot buy everything one wants. This inner tragedy of the outwardly successful Soames runs not only through this novel but also through all three books of *The Forsyte Saga,* published in 1922.

In 1932, Galsworthy was awarded the Nobel Prize in Literature for *The Forsyte Saga.* Originally he had intended to write only *The Man of Property,* and one might well wonder why he did not stop there. However, after reading *The Man of Property,* one can easily understand why the author felt compelled to continue the story of the Forsytes, with all their physical and spiritual meanderings. He particularly wished, as he said, to develop the effect that beauty has on materialistic man, and to offer certain observations on freedom and possessiveness.

In *The Forsyte Saga,* Galsworthy uses the interlude twice to connect, and give unity to, the three basic novels comprising the entire family narrative. One of these interludes, "Indian Summer of a Forsyte," is included in this book, and the reader will find it to be beautifully and sensitively written, but not at all overly emotional or sentimental. The complete novel, in fact, represents the finest in language and phrasing.

INTRODUCTION

One of the many observations one may make about *The Man of Property* is that the author's style seems in many instances to indicate a strong tendency for the dramatic. This is particularly true of Galsworthy, for he wrote seven successful plays, all concerned with social problems. As a result, many of his passages and chapters in the novels resemble scenes from a play.

Perhaps, in some instances, *The Man of Property* might be classed as a story of "manners and morals," in the vein of the seventeenth-century plays of William Wycherly and William Congreve. The latter two, however, were satirists pure and simple; Galsworthy definitely is not.

The Man of Property, then, is the work of a realistic, master novelist. Although it was written many years ago (Galsworthy died in 1933) it will never be outdated or "old hat," for it is concerned with people like those living today and with problems that are relevant to our own times.

In his column, "Speaking of Books," in the "New York Times" Book Review of July 14, 1963, J. Donald Adams noted that Galsworthy has been neglected by the most recent generations. He predicts, "But some day again *The Forsyte Saga* will be accepted for what it is—a sensitive and incisive portrait of the English upper middle-class, with its obsessive concern about property. Whether they know it or not, England's 'angry young men' owe much to his pioneering. Galsworthy, in time, will be read again, not only because he was an artist, but also because he will be invaluable to social historians of twentieth-century England—in his plays as well as in his novels."

MARSDEN V. DILLENBECK

The Forsyte Family

THE FORSYTE FAMILY

1. Jolyon Forsyte (1741-1812) Farmer of Dorset.
2. His son, Jolyon ("Superior Dosset") Forsyte (1770-1850)

The Characters of *"The Man of Property"*

First Generation—the ten children of "Superior Dosset"	Second Generation
1. Ann (1799-1886)	
2. Swithin (1811-1891)	
3. Julia (1814-1905) Aunt Juley *m. Septimus Small*	
4. Hester (1815-1907)	
5. Timothy (1819-1920)	
6. Roger (1813-1899) *m. 1853 Mary Monk*	Young Roger, 1853 George, 1856 Francie, 1858 Eustace, 1859 Thomas, 1862
7. Nicholas (1817-1908) *m. 1848 Elizabeth Blaine (Fanny)*	Young Nicholas, 1849 *m. 1877 Dorothy Boxton* Ernest, 1853 Archibald, 1857 Marian, 1859 *m. Tweetyman* Florence, 1861 Euphemia, 1862
8. Susan (1821-1895) *m. Hayman*	St. John Augustus Annabel *m. Spender* Giles ⎫ Jesse ⎭ "The Dromios"

First Generation (CONTINUED)	Second Generation (CONTINUED)	Third Generation
9. James (1811-1901) m. 1852 Emily Golding (1831-1910)	Soames 1855 m. 1885 first wife, Irene Heron div. 1900 m. 1901 second wife, Annette Lamotte, 1880	
	Winifred, 1858 m. 1879 Montague Dartie	Val, 1880 m. 1900 Holly Forsyte Imogen, 1882 Maud, 1884 Benedict, 1886
	Rachel, 1861 Cicely, 1865	
10. Jolyon. "Old Jolyon" (1806-1892) m. 1846 Edith Moor	Jolyon. "Young Jolyon" (1847-1920) m. 1868 first wife, Frances Crisson, d. 1880	June 1869. Engaged to Philip Bosinney. Never married.
	m. 1880 second wife, Helene Hilmer, d. 1894	Jolyon ("Jolly") (1879-1900) Holly, 1881 m. 1900 Val Dartie
	m. 1901 third wife, Irene Heron, divorced wife of Soames	

The Man of Property

"... You will answer
The slaves are ours. ..."
—*Merchant of Venice.*

'AT HOME' AT OLD JOLYON'S

THOSE privileged to be present at a family festival of the For-sytes have seen that charming and instructive sight—an upper middle-class family in full plumage. But whosoever of these favoured persons has possessed the gift of psychological analysis (a talent without monetary value and properly ignored by the Forsytes), has witnessed a spectacle, not only delightful in itself, but illustrative of an obscure hu-man problem. In plainer words, he has gleaned from a gathering of this family—no branch of which had a liking for the other, between no three members of whom existed anything worthy of the name of sympathy—evidence of that mysterious concrete tenacity which renders a family so formidable a unit of society, so clear a reproduction of society in mini-ature. He has been admitted to a vision of the dim roads of social prog-ress, has understood something of patriarchal life, of the swarmings of savage hordes, of the rise and fall of nations. He is like one who, having watched a tree grow from its planting—a paragon of tenacity, insula-tion, and success, amidst the deaths of a hundred other plants less fibrous, sappy, and persistent—one day will see it flourishing with bland, full foliage, in an almost repugnant prosperity, at the summit of its efflor-escence.

On June 15, eighteen eighty-six, about four of the afternoon, the ob-server who chanced to be present at the house of old Jolyon Forsyte in Stanhope Gate, might have seen the highest efflorescence of the Forsytes.

This was the occasion of an 'at home' to celebrate the engagement of Miss June Forsyte, old Jolyon's granddaughter, to Mr. Philip Bosinney. In the bravery of light gloves, buff waistcoats, feathers and frocks, the family were present—even Aunt Ann, who now but seldom left the corner of her brother Timothy's green drawing-room, where, under the aegis of a plume of dyed pampas grass in a light blue vase, she sat all day reading and knitting, surrounded by the effigies of three generations of Forsytes. Even Aunt Ann was there; her inflexible back, and the dignity

3

of her calm old face personifying the rigid possessiveness of the family idea.

When a Forsyte was engaged, married, or born, the Forsytes were present; when a Forsyte died—but no Forsyte had as yet died; they did not die; death being contrary to their principles, they took precautions against it, the instinctive precautions of highly vitalized persons who resent encroachments on their property.

About the Forsytes mingling that day with the crowd of other guests, there was a more than ordinarily groomed look, an alert, inquisitive assurance, a brilliant respectability, as though they were attired in defiance of something. The habitual sniff on the face of Soames Forsyte had spread through their ranks; they were on their guard.

The subconscious offensiveness of their attitude has constituted old Jolyon's 'at home' the psychological moment of the family history, made it the prelude of their drama.

The Forsytes were resentful of something, not individually, but as a family; this resentment expressed itself in an added perfection of raiment, an exuberance of family cordiality, an exaggeration of family importance, and—the sniff. Danger—so indispensable in bringing out the fundamental quality of any society, group, or individual—was what the Forsytes scented; the premonition of danger put a burnish on their armour. For the first time, as a family, they appeared to have an instinct of being in contact with some strange and unsafe thing.

Over against the piano a man of bulk and stature was wearing two waistcoats on his wide chest, two waistcoats and a ruby pin, instead of the single satin waistcoat and diamond pin of more usual occasions, and his shaven, square, old face, the colour of pale leather, with pale eyes, had its most dignified look, above his satin stock. This was Swithin Forsyte. Close to the window, where he could get more than his fair share of fresh air, the other twin, James—the fat and the lean of it, old Jolyon called these brothers—like the bulky Swithin, over six feet in height, but very lean, as though destined from his birth to strike a balance and maintain an average, brooded over the scene with his permanent stoop; his grey eyes had an air of fixed absorption in some secret worry, broken at intervals by a rapid, shifting scrutiny of surrounding facts; his cheeks, thinned by two parallel folds, and a long, clean-shaven upper lip, were framed within Dundreary whiskers. In his hands he

4

turned and turned a piece of china. Not far off, listening to a lady in brown, his only son Soames, pale and well-shaved, dark-haired, rather bald, had poked his chin up sideways, carrying his nose with that aforesaid appearance of 'sniff,' as though despising an egg which he knew he could not digest. Behind him his cousin, the tall George, son of the fifth Forsyte, Roger, had a Quilpish look on his fleshy face, pondering one of his sardonic jests.

Something inherent to the occasion had affected them all.

Seated in a row close to one another were three ladies—Aunts Ann, Hester (the two Forsyte maids), and Juley (short for Julia), who not in first youth had so far forgotten herself as to marry Septimus Small, a man of poor constitution. She had survived him for many years. With her elder and younger sister she lived now in the house of Timothy, her sixth and youngest brother, on the Bayswater Road. Each of these ladies held fans in their hands, and each with some touch of colour, some emphatic feather or brooch, testified to the solemnity of the opportunity.

In the centre of the room, under the chandelier, as became a host, stood the head of the family, old Jolyon himself. Eighty years of age, with his fine, white hair, his dome-like forehead, his little, dark grey eyes and an immense white moustache, which drooped and spread below the level of his strong jaw, he had a patriarchal look, and in spite of lean cheeks and hollows at his temples, seemed master of perennial youth. He held himself extremely upright, and his shrewd, steady eyes had lost none of their clear shining. Thus he gave an impression of superiority to the doubts and dislikes of smaller men. Having had his own way for innumerable years, he had earned a prescriptive right to it. It would never have occurred to old Jolyon that it was necessary to wear a look of doubt or of defiance.

Between him and the four other brothers who were present, James, Swithin, Nicholas, and Roger, there was much difference, much similarity. In turn, each of these four brothers was very different from the other, yet they, too, were alike.

Through the varying features and expression of those five faces could be marked a certain steadfastness of chin, underlying surface distinctions, marking a racial stamp, too prehistoric to trace, too remote and permanent to discuss—the very hall-mark and guarantee of the family fortunes.

Among the younger generation, in the tall, bull-like George, in pallid strenuous Archibald, in young Nicholas with his sweet and tentative obstinacy, in the grave and foppishly determined Eustace, there was this same stamp—less meaningful perhaps, but unmistakable—a sign of something ineradicable in the family soul.

At one time or another during the afternoon, all these faces, so dissimilar and so alike, had worn an expression of distrust, the object of which was undoubtedly the man whose acquaintance they were thus assembled to make.

Philip Bosinney was known to be a young man without fortune, but Forsyte girls had become engaged to such before, and had actually married them. It was not altogether for this reason, therefore, that the minds of the Forsytes misgave them. They could not have explained the origin of a misgiving obscured by the mist of family gossip. A story was undoubtedly told that he had paid his duty call to Aunts Ann, Juley, and Hester, in a soft grey hat—a soft grey hat, not even a new one—a dusty thing with a shapeless crown. "So extraordinary, my dear—so odd!" Aunt Hester, passing through the little, dark hall (she was rather short-sighted), had tried to 'shoo' it off a chair, taking it for a strange, disreputable cat—Tommy had such disgraceful friends! She was disturbed when it did not move.

Like an artist for ever seeking to discover the significant trifle which embodies the whole character of a scene, or place, or person, so those unconscious artists—the Forsytes—had fastened by intuition on this hat; it was their significant trifle, the detail in which was embedded the meaning of the whole matter; for each had asked himself: "Come, now, should I have paid that visit in that hat?" and each had answered "No!" and some, with more imagination than others, had added: "It would never have come into my head!"

George, on hearing the story, grinned. The hat had obviously been worn as a practical joke! He himself was a connoisseur of such.

"Very haughty!" he said, "the wild Buccaneer!"

And this _mot_, 'the Bucaneer,' was bandied from mouth to mouth, till it became the favourite mode of alluding to Bosinney.

Her aunts reproached June afterwards about the hat.

"We don't think you ought to let him, dear!" they had said.

June had answered in her imperious brisk way, like the little embodiment of will she was:

"Oh! what does it matter? Phil never knows what he's got on!"

No one had credited an answer so outrageous. A man not to know what he had on? No, no!

What indeed was this young man, who, in becoming engaged to June, old Jolyon's acknowledged heiress, had done so well for himself? He was an architect, not in itself a sufficient reason for wearing such a hat. None of the Forsytes happened to be architects, but one of them knew two architects who would never have worn such a hat upon a call of ceremony in the London season. Dangerous—ah, dangerous!

June, of course, had not seen this, but, though not yet nineteen, she was notorious. Had she not said to Mrs. Soames—who was always so beautifully dressed—that feathers were vulgar? Mrs. Soames had actually given up wearing feathers, so dreadfully downright was dear June!

These misgivings, this disapproval and perfectly genuine distrust, did not prevent the Forsytes from gathering to old Jolyon's invitation. An 'at home' at Stanhope Gate was a great rarity; none had been held for twelve years, not indeed, since old Mrs. Jolyon died.

Never had there been so full an assembly, for, mysteriously united in spite of all their differences, they had taken arms against a common peril. Like cattle when a dog comes into the field, they stood head to head and shoulder to shoulder, prepared to run upon and trample the invader to death. They had come, too, no doubt, to get some notion of what sort of presents they would ultimately be expected to give; for though the question of wedding gifts was usually graduated in this way —"What are *you* givin'? Nicholas is givin' spoons!"—so very much depended on the bridegroom. If he were sleek, well-brushed, prosperous-looking, it was more necessary to give him nice things; he would expect them. In the end each gave exactly what was right and proper, by a species of family adjustment arrived at as prices are arrived at on the Stock Exchange—the exact niceties being regulated at Timothy's commodious, redbrick residence in Bayswater, overlooking the Park, where dwelt Aunts Ann, Juley, and Hester.

The uneasiness of the Forsyte family has been justified by the simple mention of the hat. How impossible and wrong would it have been for any family, with the regard for appearances which should ever characterize the great upper middle-class, to feel otherwise than uneasy!

The author of the uneasiness stood talking to June by the further door; his curly hair had a rumpled appearance, as though he found what was going on around him unusual. He had an air, too, of having a joke all to himself.

George, speaking aside to his brother Eustace, said:

"Looks as if he might make a bolt of it—the dashing Buccaneer!"

This 'very singular-looking man,' as Mrs. Small afterwards called him, was of medium height and strong build, with a pale, brown face, a dust-coloured moustache, very prominent cheek-bones, and hollow cheeks. His forehead sloped back towards the crown of his head, and bulged out in bumps over the eyes, like foreheads seen in the lion-house at the Zoo. He had sherry-coloured eyes, disconcertingly inattentive at times. Old Jolyon's coachman, after driving June and Bosinney to the theatre, had remarked to the butler:

"I dunno what to make of 'im. Looks to me for all the world like an 'alf-tame leopard."

And every now and then a Forsyte would come up, sidle round, and take a look at him.

June stood in front, fending off this idle curiosity—a little bit of a thing, as somebody once said, 'all hair and spirit,' with fearless blue eyes, a firm jaw, and a bright colour, whose face and body seemed too slender for her crown of red-gold hair.

A tall woman, with a beautiful figure, which some member of the family had once compared to a heathen goddess, stood looking at these two with a shadowy smile.

Her hands, gloved in French grey, were crossed one over the other, her grave, charming face held to one side, and the eyes of all men near were fastened on it. Her figure swayed, so balanced that the very air seemed to set it moving. There was warmth, but little colour, in her cheeks; her large, dark eyes were soft. But it was at her lips—asking a question, giving an answer, with that shadowy smile—that men looked; they were sensitive lips, sensuous and sweet, and through them seemed to come warmth and perfume like the warmth and perfume of a flower.

The engaged couple thus scrutinized were unconscious of this passive goddess. It was Bosinney who first noticed her, and asked her name.

June took her lover up to the woman with the beautiful figure.

"Irene is my greatest chum," she said: "Please be good friends, you two!"

8

At the little lady's command they all three smiled; and while they were smiling, Soames Forsyte, silently appearing from behind the woman with the beautiful figure, who was his wife, said:

"Ah! introduce me too!"

He was seldom, indeed, far from Irene's side at public functions, and even when separated by the exigencies of social intercourse, could be seen following her about with his eyes, in which were strange expressions of watchfulness and longing.

At the window his father, James, was still scrutinizing the marks on the piece of china.

"I wonder at Jolyon's allowing this engagement," he said to Aunt Ann. "They tell me there's no chance of their getting married for years. This young Bosinney" (he made the word a dactyl in opposition to general usage of a short o) "has got nothing. When Winifred married Dartie, I made him bring every penny into settlement—lucky thing, too —they'd ha' had nothing by this time!"

Aunt Ann looked up from her velvet chair. Grey curls banded her forehead, curls that, unchanged for decades, had extinguished in the family all sense of time. She made no reply, for she rarely spoke, husbanding her aged voice; but to James, uneasy of conscience, her look was as good as an answer.

"Well," he said, "I couldn't help Irene's having no money. Soames was in such a hurry; he got quite thin dancing attendance on her."

Putting the bowl pettishly down on the piano, he let his eyes wander to the group by the door.

"It's my opinion," he said unexpectedly, "that it's just as well as it is."

Aunt Ann did not ask him to explain this strange utterance. She knew what he was thinking. If Irene had no money she would not be so foolish as to do anything wrong; for they said—they said—she had been asking for a separate room; but, of course, Soames had not——

James interrupted her reverie:

"But where," he asked, "was Timothy? Hadn't he come with them?"

Through Aunt Ann's compressed lips a tender smile forced its way:

"No, he didn't think it wise, with so much of this diphtheria about; and he so liable to take things."

James answered:

9

"Well, *he* takes good care of himself. I can't afford to take the care of myself that he does."

Nor was it easy to say which, of admiration, envy, or contempt, was dominant in that remark.

Timothy, indeed, was seldom seen. The baby of the family, a publisher by profession, he had some years before, when business was at full tide, scented out the stagnation which, indeed, had not yet come, but which ultimately, as all agreed, was bound to set in, and, selling his share in a firm engaged mainly in the production of religious books, had invested the quite conspicuous proceeds in three per cent. consols. By this act he had at once assumed an isolated position, no other Forsyte being content with less than four per cent. for his money; and this isolation had slowly and surely undermined a spirit perhaps better than commonly endowed with caution. He had become almost a myth—a kind of incarnation of security haunting the background of the Forsyte universe. He had never committed the imprudence of marrying, or encumbering himself in any way with children.

James resumed, tapping the piece of china.

"This isn't real old Worcester. I s'pose Jolyon's told you something about the young man. From all *I* can learn, he's got no business, no income, and no connection worth speaking of; but then, I know nothing— nobody tells me anything."

Aunt Ann shook her head. Over her square-chinned, aquiline old face a trembling passed; the spidery fingers of her hands pressed against each other and interlaced, as though she were subtly recharging her will.

The eldest by some years of all the Forsytes, she held a peculiar position amongst them. Opportunists and egotists one and all—though not, indeed, more so than their neighbours—they quailed before her incorruptible figure, and, when opportunities were too strong, what could they do but avoid her!

Twisting his long, thin legs, James went on:

"Jolyon, he will have his own way. He's got no children——" and stopped, recollecting the continued existence of old Jolyon's son, young Jolyon, June's father, who had made such a mess of it, and done for himself by deserting his wife and child and running away with that foreign governess. "Well," he resumed hastily, "if he likes to do these things, I s'pose he can afford to. Now, what's he going to give her? I

10

against each other, were busy again with the recharging of her will against that inevitable ultimate departure of her own.

'Yes,' she thought, 'everybody's been most kind; quite a lot of people come to congratulate her. She ought to be very happy.'

Amongst the throng of people by the door—the well-dressed throng drawn from the families of lawyers and doctors, from the Stock Exchange, and all the innumerable avocations of the upper middle class—there were only some twenty per cent. of Forsytes; but to Aunt Ann they seemed all Forsytes—and certainly there was not much diffrence—she saw only her own flesh and blood. It was her world, this family, and she knew no other, had never perhaps known any other. All their little secrets, illnesses, engagements, and marriages, how they were getting on, and whether they were making money—all this was her property, her delight, her life; beyond this only a vague, shadowy mist of facts and persons of no real significance. This it was that she would have to lay down when it came to her turn to die; this which gave to her that importance, that secret self-importance, without which none of us can bear to live; and to this she clung wistfully, with a greed that grew each day. If life were slipping away from her, *this* she would retain to the end.

She thought of June's father, young Jolyon, who had run away with that foreign girl. Ah! what a sad blow to his father and to them all. Such a promising young fellow! A sad blow, though there had been no public scandal, most fortunately, Jo's wife seeking for no divorce! A long time ago! And when June's mother died, six years ago, Jo had married that woman, and they had two children now, so she had heard. Still, he had forfeited his right to be there, had cheated her of the complete fulfilment of her family pride, deprived her of the rightful pleasure of seeing and kissing him of whom she had been so proud, such a promising young fellow! The thought rankled with the bitterness of a long-inflicted injury in her tenacious old heart. A little water stood in her eyes. With a handkerchief of the finest lawn she wiped them stealthily.

"Well, Aunt Ann?" said a voice behind.

Soames Forsyte, flat-shouldered, clean-shaven, flat-cheeked, flat-waisted, yet with something round and secret about his whole appearance, looked downwards and aslant at Aunt Ann, as though trying to see through the side of his own nose.

"And what do *you* think of the engagement?" he asked.

Aunt Ann's eyes rested on him proudly; of all the nephews since young Jolyon's departure from the family nest, he was now her favourite, for she recognised in him a sure trustee of the family soul that must so soon slip beyond her keeping.

"Very nice for the young man," she said; "and he's a good-looking young fellow; but I doubt if he's quite the right lover for dear June."

Soames touched the edge of a gold-lacquered lustre.

"She'll tame him," he said, stealthily wetting his finger and rubbing it on the knobby bulbs. "That's genuine old lacquer; you can't get it nowadays. It'd do well in a sale at Jobson's." He spoke with relish, as though he felt that he was cheering up his old aunt. It was seldom he was so confidential. "I wouldn't mind having it myself," he added; "you can always get your price for old lacquer."

"You're so clever with all those things," said Aunt Ann. "And how is dear Irene?"

Soames's smile died.

"Pretty well," he said. "Complains she can't sleep; she sleeps a great deal better than I do," and he looked at his wife, who was talking to Bosinney at the door.

Aunt Ann sighed.

"Perhaps," she said, "it will be just as well for her not to see so much of June. She's such a decided character, dear June!"

Soames flushed; his flushes passed rapidly over his flat cheeks and centred between his eyes, where they remained, the stamp of disturbing thoughts.

"I don't know what she sees in that little flibbertigibbet," he burst out, but noticing that they were no longer alone, he turned and again began examining the lustre.

"They tell me Jolyon's bought another house," said his father's voice close by; "he must have a lot of money—he must have more money than he knows what to do with! Montpellier Square, they say; close to Soames! They never told me—Irene never tells me anything!"

"Capital position, not two minutes from me," said the voice of Swithin, "and from my rooms I can drive to the Club in eight."

The position of their houses was of vital importance to the Forsytes, nor was this remarkable, since the whole spirit of their success was embodied therein.

Their father, of farming stock, had come from Dorsetshire near the beginning of the century.

14

'Superior Dosset Forsyte,' as he was called by his intimates, had been a stonemason by trade, and risen to the position of a master-builder. Towards the end of his life he moved to London, where, building on until he died, he was buried at Highgate. He left over thirty thousand pounds between his ten children. Old Jolyon alluded to him, if at all, as 'A hard, thick sort of man; not much refinement about him.' The second generation of Forsytes felt indeed that he was not greatly to their credit. The only aristocratic trait they could find in his character was a habit of drinking Madeira.

Aunt Hester, an authority on family history, described him thus:

"I don't recollect that he ever did anything; at least, not in *my* time. He was er—an owner of houses, my dear. His hair about your Uncle Swithin's colour; rather a square build. Tall? No-ot very tall" (he had been five feet five, with a mottled face); "a fresh-coloured man. I re-member he used to drink Madeira; but ask your Aunt Ann. What was *his* father? He—er—had to do with the land down in Dorsetshire, by the sea."

James once went down to see for himself what sort of place this was that they had come from. He found two old farms, with a cart track rutted into the pink earth, leading down to a mill by the beach; a little grey church with a buttressed outer wall, and a smaller and greyer chapel. The stream which worked the mill came bubbling down in a dozen rivulets, and pigs were hunting round that estuary. A haze hovered over the prospect. Down this hollow, with their feet deep in the mud and their faces towards the sea, it appeared that the primeval Forsytes had been content to walk Sunday after Sunday for hundreds of years.

Whether or no James had cherished hopes of an inheritance, or of something rather distinguished to be found down there, he came back to town in a poor way, and went about with a pathetic attempt at making the best of a bad job.

"There's very little to be had out of that," he said; "regular country little place, old as the hills."

Its age was felt to be a comfort. Old Jolyon, in whom a desperate honesty welled up at times, would allude to his ancestors as: "Yeomen—I suppose very small beer." Yet he would repeat the word 'yeomen' as if it afforded him consolation.

They had all done so well for themselves, these Forsytes, that they

were all what is called 'of a certain position.' They had shares in all
sorts of things, not as yet—with the exception of Timothy—in consols,
for they had no dread in life like that of 3 per cent. for their money.
They collected pictures, too, and were supporters of such charitable
institutions as might be beneficial to their sick domestics. From their
father, the builder, they inherited a talent for bricks and mortar.
Originally, perhaps, members of some primitive sect, they were now in
the natural course of things members of the Church of England, and
caused their wives and children to attend with some regularity the more
fashionable churches of the Metropolis. To have doubted their Christi-
anity would have caused them both pain and surprise. Some of them
paid for pews, thus expressing in the most practical form their sympathy
with the teachings of Christ.

Their residences, placed at stated intervals round the park, watched
like sentinels, lest the fair heart of this London, where their desires were
fixed, should slip from their clutches, and leave them lower in their
own estimations.

There was old Jolyon in Stanhope Place; the Jameses in Park Lane;
Swithin in the lonely glory of orange and blue chambers in Hyde Park
Mansions—he had never married, not he!—the Soameses in their nest
off Knightsbridge; the Rogers in Prince's Gardens (Roger was that
remarkable Forsyte who had conceived and carried out the notion of
bringing up his four sons to a new profession. 'Collect house property—
nothing like it!' he would say; '*I* never did anything else!').

The Haymans again—Mrs. Hayman was the one married Forsyte sister—in a house high up on Campden Hill, shaped like a giraffe, and so
tall that it gave the observer a crick in the neck; the Nicholases in
Ladbroke Grove, a spacious abode and a great bargain; and last, but not
least, Timothy's on the Bayswater Road, where Ann, and Juley, and
Hester, lived under his protection.

But all this time James was musing, and now he inquired of his host
and brother what he had given for that house in Montpellier Square.
He himself had had his eye on a house there for the last two years, but
they wanted such a price.

Old Jolyon recounted the details of his purchase.

"Twenty-two years to run?" repeated James; "the very house I was
after—you've given too much for it!"

Old Jolyon frowned.

"It's not that I want it," said James hastily; "wouldn't suit my purp
at that price. Soames knows the house, well—he'll tell you it's too dea
his opinion's worth having."

"I don't," said old Jolyon, "care a fig for his opinion."

"Well," murmured James, "you *will* have your own way—it's a go
opinion. Good-bye! We're going to drive down to Hurlingham. Th
tell me June's going to Wales. You'll be lonely tomorrow. What'll y
do with yourself? You'd better come and dine with us!"

Old Jolyon refused. He went down to the front door and saw the
into their barouche, and twinkled at them, having already forgotten l
spleen—Mrs. James facing the horses, tall and majestic with aubu
hair; on her left, Irene—the two husbands, father and son, sitting fo
ward, as though they expected something, opposite their wives. Bo
bing and bounding upon the spring cushions, silent, swaying to eac
motion of their chariot, old Jolyon watched them drive away under th
sunlight.

During the drive the silence was broken by Mrs. James.

"Did you ever see such a collection of rumty-too people?"

Soames, glancing at her beneath his eyelids, nodded, and he saw Iren
steal at him one of her unfathomable looks. It is likely enough that eac
branch of the Forsyte family made that remark as they drove away from
old Jolyon's 'at home.'

Amongst the last of the departing guests the fourth and fifth brothers
Nicholas and Roger, walked away together, directing their steps along
side Hyde Park towards the Praed Street Station of the Underground
Like all other Forsytes of a certain age they kept carriages of thei
own, and never took cabs if by any means they could avoid it.

The day was bright, the trees of the Park in the full beauty of
mid-June foliage; the brothers did not seem to notice phenomena, which
contributed, nevertheless, to the jauntiness of promenade and conversation.

"Yes," said Roger, "she's a good-lookin' woman, that wife of Soames's.
I'm told they don't get on."

This brother had a high forehead, and the freshest colour of any of the
Forsytes; his light grey eyes measured the street frontage of the houses
by the way, and now and then he would level his umbrella and take a
'lunar,' as he expressed it, of the varying heights.

"She'd no money," replied Nicholas.

He himself had married a good deal of money, of which, it being then the golden age before the Married Women's Property Act, he had mercifully been enabled to make a successful use.

"What was her father?"

"Heron was his name, a Professor, so they tell me."

Roger shook his head.

"There's no money in that," he said.

"They say her mother's father was cement."

Rogers face brightened.

"But he went bankrupt," went on Nicholas.

"Ah!" exclaimed Roger, "Soames will have trouble with her; you mark my words, he'll have trouble—she's got a foreign look."

Nicholas licked his lips.

"Shes a pretty woman," and he waved aside a crossing-sweeper.

"How did he get hold of her?" asked Roger presently. "She must cost him a pretty penny in dress!"

"Ann tells me," replied Nicholas, "he was half-cracked about her. She refused him five times. James, he's nervous about it, I can see."

"Ah!" said Roger again; "I'm sorry for James; he had trouble with Dartie." His pleasant colour was heightened by exercise, he swung his umbrella to the level of his eye more frequently than ever. Nicholas's face also wore a pleasant look.

"Too pale for me," he said, "but her figure's capital!"

Roger made no reply.

"I call her distinguished-looking," he said at last—it was the highest praise in the Forsyte vocabulary. "That young Bosinney will never do any good for himself. They say at Burkitt's he's one of these artistic chaps—got an idea of improving English architecture; there's no money in that! I should like to hear what Timothy would say to it."

They entered the station.

"What class are you going? I go second."

"No second for me," said Nicholas; "you never know what you may catch."

He took a first-class ticket to Notting Hill Gate; Roger a second to South Kensington. The train coming in a minute later, the two brothers parted and entered their respective compartments. Each felt aggrieved that the other had not modified his habits to secure his society a little longer; but as Roger voiced it in his thoughts:

18

'Always a stubborn beggar, Nick!'

And as Nicholas expressed it to himself:

'Cantankerous chap Roger—always was!'

There was little sentimentality about the Forsytes. In that great London, which they had conquered and become merged in, what time had they to be sentimental?

Chapter II

OLD JOLYON GOES TO THE OPERA

AT five o'clock the following day old Jolyon sat alone, a cigar between his lips, and on a table by his side a cup of tea. He was tired, and before he had finished his cigar he fell asleep. A fly settled on his hair, his breathing sounded heavy in the drowsy silence, his upper lip under the white moustache puffed in and out. From between the fingers of his veined and wrinkled hand the cigar, dropping on the empty hearth, burned itself out.

The gloomy little study, with windows of stained glass to exclude the view, was full of dark green velvet and heavily carved mahogany— a suite of which old Jolyon was wont to say: 'Shouldn't wonder if it made a big price some day!'

It was pleasant to think that in the after life he could get more for things than he had given.

In the rich brown atmosphere peculiar to back rooms in the mansion of a Forsyte, the Rembrandtesque effect of his great head, with its white hair, against the cushion of his high-backed seat, was spoiled by the moustache, which imparted a somewhat military look to his face. An old clock that had been with him since before his marriage forty years ago kept with its ticking a jealous record of the seconds slipping away for ever from its old master.

He had never cared for this room, hardly going into it from one year's end to another, except to take cigars from the Japanese cabinet in the corner, and the room now had its revenge.

His temples, curving like thatches over the hollows beneath, his cheek-bones and chin, all were sharpened in his sleep, and there had come upon his face the confession that he was an old man.

He woke. June had gone! James had said he would be lonely. James had always been a poor thing. He recollected with satisfaction that he had bought that house over James's head. Serve him right for

20

sticking at the price; the only thing the fellow thought of was money. Had he given too much, though? It wanted a lot of doing to—— He dared say he would want all his money before he had done with this affair of June's. He ought never to have allowed the engagement. She had met this Bosinney at the house of Baynes—Baynes and Bilde-boy, the architects. He believed that Baynes, whom he knew—a bit of an old woman—was the young man's uncle by marriage. After that she'd been always running after him; and when she took a thing into her head there was no stopping her. She was continually taking up with 'lame ducks' of one sort or another. This fellow had no money, but she must needs become engaged to him—a harum-scarum, un-practical chap, who would get himself into no end of difficulties.

She had come to him one day in her slap-dash way and told him; and, as if it were any consolation, she had added:

"He's so splendid; he's often lived on cocoa for a week!"

"And he wants you to live on cocoa too?"

"Oh no; he is getting into the swim now."

Old Jolyon had taken his cigar from under his white moustaches, stained by coffee at the edge, and looked at her, that little slip of a thing who had got such a grip of his heart. He knew more about 'swims' than his granddaughter. But she, having clasped her hands on his knees, rubbed her chin against him, making a sound like a purring cat. And, knocking the ash off his cigar, he had exploded in nervous desperation:

"You're all alike: you won't be satisfied till you've got what you want. If you must come to grief, you must; *I* wash my hands of it."

So, he had washed his hands of it, making the condition that they should not marry until Bosinney had at least four hundred a year.

"*I* shan't be able to give you very much," he had said, a formula to which June was not unaccustomed. "Perhaps this What's-his-name will provide the cocoa."

He had hardly seen anything of her since it began. A bad business! He had no notion of giving her a lot of money to enable a fellow he knew nothing about to live on in idleness. He had seen that sort of thing before; no good ever came of it. Worst of all, he had no hope of shaking her resolution; she was as obstinate as a mule, always had

21

been from a child. He didn't see where it was to end. They must cut their coat according to their cloth. He would not give way till he saw young Bosinney with an income of his own. That June would have trouble with the fellow was as plain as a pikestaff; he had no more idea of money than a cow. As to this rushing down to Wales to visit the young man's aunts, he fully expected they were old cats.

And, motionless, old Jolyon stared at the wall; but for his open eyes, he might have been asleep . . . . The idea of supposing that young cub Soames could give him advice! He had always been a cub, with his nose in the air! He would be setting up as a man of property next, with a place in the country! A man of property! H'mph! Like his father, he was always nosing out bargains, a cold-blooded young beggar!

He rose, and, going to the cabinet, began methodically stocking his cigar-case from a bundle fresh in. They were not bad at the price, but you couldn't get a good cigar nowadays, nothing to hold a candle to those old Superfinos of Hanson and Bridger's. *That* was a cigar!

The thought, like some stealing perfume, carried him back to those wonderful nights at Richmond when after dinner he sat smoking on the terrace of the Crown and Sceptre with Nicholas Treffry and Traquair and Jack Herring and Anthony Thornworthy. How good his cigars were then! Poor old Nick!—dead, and Jack Herring—dead, and Traquair—dead of that wife of his, and Thornworthy—awfully shaky (no wonder, with his appetite).

Of all the company of those days he himself alone seemed left, except Swithin, of course, and *he* so outrageously big there was no doing anything with him.

Difficult to believe it was so long ago; he felt young still! Of all his thoughts, as he stood there counting his cigars, this was the most poignant, the most bitter. With his white head and his loneliness he had remained young and green at heart. And those Sunday afternoons on Hampstead Heath, when young Jolyon and he went for a stretch along the Spaniard's Road to Highgate, to Child's Hill, and back over the Heath again to dine at Jack Straw's Castle—how delicious his cigars were then! And such weather! There was no weather now.

When June was a toddler of five, and every other Sunday he took her to the Zoo, away from the society of those two good women, her mother and her grandmother, and at the top of the bear-den baited his umbrella with buns for her favourite bears, how sweet his cigars were then!

Cigars! He had not even succeeded in outliving his palate—the famous palate that in the fifties men swore by, and speaking of him, said: "Forsyte—the best palate in London!" The palate that in a sense had made his fortune—the fortune of the celebrated tea men, Forsyte and Treffry, whose tea, like no other man's tea, had a romantic aroma, the charm of a quite singular genuineness. About the house of Forsyte and Treffry in the City had clung an air of enterprise and mystery, of special dealings in special ships, at special ports, with special Orientals.

He had worked at that business! Men did work in those days! these young pups hardly knew the meaning of the word. He had gone into every detail, known everything that went on, sometimes sat up all night over it. And he had always chosen his agents himself, prided himself on it. His eye for men, he used to say, had been the secret of his success, and the exercise of this masterful power of selection had been the only part of it all that he had really liked. Not a career for a man of his ability. Even now, when the business had been turned into a Limited Liability Company, and was declining (he had got out of his shares long ago), he felt a sharp chagrin in thinking of that time. How much better he might have done! He would have succeeded splendidly at the Bar! He had even thought of standing for Parliament. How often had not Nicholas Treffry said to him: "You could do anything, Jo, if you weren't so d-damned careful of yourself!" Dear old Nick! Such a good fellow, but a racketty chap! The notorious Treffry! *He* had never taken any care of himself! So he was dead. Old Jolyon counted his cigars with a steady hand, and it came into his mind to wonder if perhaps he had been *too* careful of himself.

He put the cigar-case in the breast of his coat, buttoned it in, and walked up the long flights to his bedroom, leaning on one foot and the other, and helping himself by the bannister. The house was too big. After June was married, if she ever did marry this fellow, as he supposed she would, he would let it and go into rooms. What was the use of keeping half a dozen servants eating their heads off?

The butler came to the ring of his bell—a large man with a beard,

23

a soft tread, and a peculiar capacity for silence. Old Jolyon told him to put his dress clothes out; he was going to dine at the Club.

How long had the carriage been back from taking Miss June to the station? Since two? Then let him come round at half-past six!

The Club which old Jolyon entered on the stroke of seven was one of those political institutions of the upper middle class which have seen better days. In spite of being talked about, perhaps in consequence of being talked about, it betrayed a disappointing vitality. People had grown tired of saying that the 'Disunion' was on its last legs. Old Jolyon would say it, too, yet disregarded the fact in a manner truly irritating to well-constituted Clubmen.

"Why do you keep your name on?" Swithin often asked him with profound vexation. "Why don't you join the 'Polyglot'? You can't get a wine like our Heidsieck under twenty shillin' a bottle anywhere in London;" and, dropping his voice, he added: "There's only five hundred dozen left. I drink it every night of my life."

"I'll think of it," old Jolyon would answer; but when he did think of it there was always the question of fifty guineas entrance fee, and it would take him four or five years to get in. He continued to think of it.

He was too old to be a Liberal, had long ceased to believe in the political doctrines of his Club, had even been known to allude to them as 'wretched stuff,' and it afforded him pleasure to continue a member in the teeth of principles so opposed to his own. He had always had a contempt for the place, having joined it many years ago when they refused to have him at the 'Hotch Potch' owing to his being 'in trade.' As if he were not as good as any of them! He naturally despised the Club that *did* take him. The members were a poor lot, many of them in the City—stockbrokers, solicitors, auctioneers, what not! Like most men of strong character but not too much originality, old Jolyon set small store by the class to which he belonged. Faithfully he followed their customs, social and otherwise, and secretly he thought them 'a common lot.'

Years and philosophy, of which he had his share, had dimmed the recollection of his defeat at the 'Hotch Potch'; and now in his thoughts it was enshrined as the Queen of Clubs. He would have been a member all these years himself, but, owing to the slipshod way his proposer, Jack Herring, had gone to work, they had not known what they were doing in keeping him out. Why! they had taken his son Jo at once, and he believed the boy was still a member; he had received a letter dated from there eight years ago.

He had not been near the 'Disunion' for months, and the house had undergone the piebald decoration which people bestow on old houses and old ships when anxious to sell them.

'Beastly colour, the smoking-room!' he thought. 'The dining-room is good.'

Its gloomy chocolate, picked out with light green, took his fancy.

He ordered dinner, and sat down in the very corner, at the very table perhaps (things did not progress much at the 'Disunion,' a Club of almost Radical principles) at which he and young Jolyon used to sit twenty-five years ago, when he was taking the latter to Drury Lane, during his holidays.

The boy had loved the theatre, and old Jolyon recalled how he used to sit opposite, concealing his excitement under a careful but transparent nonchalance.

He ordered himself, too, the very dinner the boy had always chosen —soup, whitebait, cutlets, and a tart. Ah! if he were only opposite now!

The two had not met for fourteen years. And not for the first time during those fourteen years old Jolyon wondered whether he had been a little to blame in the matter of his son. An unfortunate love-affair with that precious flirt Danäe Thornworthy (now Danäe Pellew), Anthony Thornworthy's daughter, had thrown him on the rebound into the arms of June's mother. He ought perhaps to have put a spoke in the wheel of their marriage; they were too young; but after that experience of Jo's susceptibility he had been only too anxious to see him married. And in four years the crash had come! To have approved his son's conduct in that crash was, of course, impossible; reason and training—that combination of potent factors which stood for his principles—told him of this impossibility, and his heart cried out. The grim remorselessness of that business had no pity for hearts. There was June, the atom with flaming hair, who had climbed all over him, twined and twisted herself about him— about his heart that was made to be the plaything and beloved resort of tiny, helpless things. With characteristic insight he saw he must part with one or with the other; no half-measures could serve in such a situation. In that lay its tragedy. And the tiny, helpless thing prevailed. He would not run with the hare and hunt with the hounds, and so to his son he said good-bye.

That good-bye had lasted until now.

He had proposed to continue a reduced allowance to young Jolyon, but this had been refused, and perhaps that refusal had hurt him more than anything, for with it had gone the last outlet of his penned-in affection; and there had come such tangible and solid proof of rupture as only a transaction in property, a bestowal or refusal of such, could supply.

His dinner tasted flat. His pint of champagne was dry and bitter stuff, not like the Veuve Clicquots of old days.

Over his cup of coffee, he bethought him that he would go to the opera. In the *Times,* therefore—he had a distrust of other papers— he read the announcement for the evening. It was 'Fidelio.'

Mercifully not one of those new-fangled German pantomimes by that fellow Wagner.

Putting on his ancient opera hat, which, with its brim flattened by use, and huge capacity, looked like an emblem of greater days, and pulling out an old pair of very thin lavender kid gloves smelling strongly of Russia leather, from habitual proximity to the cigar-case in the pocket of his overcoat, he stepped into a hansom.

The cab rattled gaily along the streets, and old Jolyon was struck by their unwonted animation.

'The hotels must be doing a tremendous business,' he thought. A few years ago there had been none of these big hotels. He made a satisfactory reflection on some property he had in the neighbourhood. It must be going up in value by leaps and bounds! What traffic!

But from that he began indulging in one of those strange impersonal speculations, so uncharacteristic of a Forsyte, wherein lay, in part, the secret of his supremacy amongst them. What atoms men were, and what a lot of them! And what would become of them all?

He stumbled as he got out of the cab, gave the man his exact fare, walked up to the ticket office to take his stall, and stood there with his purse in his hand—he always carried his money in a purse, never having approved of that habit of carrying it loosely in the

26

pockets, as so many young men did nowadays. The official leaned out, like an old dog from a kennel.

"Why," he said in a surprised voice, "it's Mr. Jolyon Forsyte! So it is! Haven't seen you, sir, for years. Dear me! Times aren't what they were. Why! you and your brother, and that auctioneer—Mr. Traquair, and Mr. Nicholas Treffry—you used to have six or seven stalls here regular every season. And how are *you* sir? We don't get younger!"

The colour in old Jolyon's eyes deepened; he paid his guinea. They had not forgotten him. He marched in, to the sounds of the overture, like an old war-horse to battle.

Folding his opera hat, he sat down, drew out his lavender gloves in the old way, and took up his glasses for a long look round the house. Dropping them at last on his folded hat, he fixed his eyes on the curtain. More poignantly than ever he felt that it was all over and done with him. Where were all the women, the pretty women, the house used to be so full of? Where was that old feeling in the heart as he waited for one of those great singers? Where that sensation of the intoxication of life and of his own power to enjoy it all?

The greatest opera-goer of his day! There was no opera now! That fellow Wagner had ruined everything; no melody left, nor any voices to sing it. Ah! the wonderful singers! Gone! He sat watching the old scenes acted, a numb feeling at his heart.

From the curl of silver over his ear to the pose of his foot in its elastic-sided patent boot, there was nothing clumsy or weak about old Jolyon. He was as upright—very nearly—as in those old times when he came every night; his sight was as good—almost as good. But what a feeling of weariness and disillusion!

He had been in the habit all his life of enjoying things, even imperfect things—and there had been many imperfect things—he had enjoyed them all with moderation, so as to keep himself young. But now he was deserted by his power of enjoyment, by his philosophy, and left with this dreadful feeling that it was all done with. Not even the Prisoners' Chorus, nor Florian's Song, had the power to dispel the gloom of his loneliness.

If Jo were only with him! The boy must be forty by now. He had wasted fourteen years out of the life of his only son. And Jo was no longer a social pariah. He was married. Old Jolyon had been unable to refrain from marking his appreciation of the action by enclosing his son a cheque for £500. The cheque had been returned in a letter from the 'Hotch Potch,' couched in these words:

'MY DEAREST FATHER,

'Your generous gift was welcome as a sign that you might think worse of me. I return it, but should you think fit to invest it for the benefit of the little chap (we call him Jolly), who bears our Christian and, by courtesy, our surname, I shall be very glad.

'I hope with all my heart that your health is as good as ever.

'Your loving son,

'Jo.'

The letter was like the boy. He had always been an amiable chap. Old Jolyon had sent this reply:

'MY DEAR JO,

'The sum (£500) stands in my books for the benefit of your boy, under the name of Jolyon Forsyte, and will be duly credited with interest at 5 per cent. I hope that you are doing well. My health remains good at present.

'With love, I am,

'Your affectionate Father,

'JOLYON FORSYTE.'

And every year on the 1st of January he had added a hundred and the interest. The sum was mounting up—next New Year's Day it would be fifteen hundred and odd pounds! And it is difficult to say how much satisfaction he had got out of that yearly transaction. But the correspondence had ended.

In spite of his love for his son, in spite of an instinct, partly constitutional, partly the result, as in thousands of his class, of the continual handling and watching of affairs, prompting him to judge conduct by results rather than by principle, there was at the bottom of his heart a sort of uneasiness. His son ought, under the circumstances, to have gone to the dogs; that law was laid down in all the novels, sermons, and plays he had ever read, heard, or witnessed.

After receiving the cheque back there seemed to him to be something wrong somewhere. Why had his son not gone to the dogs? But, then, who could tell?

He had heard, of course—in fact, he had made it his business to find out—that Jo lived in St. John's Wood, that he had a little house in Wistaria Avenue with a garden, and took his wife about with him into society—a queer sort of society, no doubt—and that they had two children—the little chap they called Jolly (considering the circumstances the name struck him as cynical, and old Jolyon both feared and disliked cynicism), and a girl called Holly, born since the marriage. Who could tell what his son's circumstances really were? He had capitalized the income he had inherited from his mother's father and joined Lloyd's as an underwriter; he painted pictures, too—water-colours. Old Jolyon knew this, for he had surreptitiously bought them from time to time, after chancing to see his son's name signed at the bottom of a representation of the river Thames in a dealer's window. He thought them bad, and did not hang them because of the signature; he kept them locked up in a drawer.

In the great opera-house a terrible yearning came on him to see his son. He remembered the days when he had been wont to slide him, in a brown holland suit, to and fro under the arch of his legs; the times when he ran beside the boy's pony, teaching him to ride; the day he first took him to school. He had been a loving, lovable little chap! After he went to Eton he had acquired, perhaps, a little too much of that desirable manner which old Jolyon knew was only to be obtained at such places and at great expense; but he had always been companionable. Always a companion, even after Cambridge— a little far off, perhaps, owing to the advantages he had received. Old Jolyon's feeling towards our public schools and 'Varsities never wavered, and he retained touchingly his attitude of admiration and mistrust towards a system appropriate to the highest in the land, of which he had not himself been privileged to partake. ... Now that June had gone and left, or as good as left him, it would have been

29

a comfort to see his son again. Guilty of this treason to his family, his principles, his class, old Jolyon fixed his eyes on the singer. A poor thing—a wretched poor thing! And the Florian a perfect stick!

It was over. They were easily pleased nowadays!

In the crowded street he snapped up a cab under the very nose of a stout and much younger gentleman, who had already assumed it to be his own. His route lay through Pall Mall, and at the corner, instead of going through the Green Park, the cabman turned to drive up St. James's Street. Old Jolyon put his hand through the trap (he could not bear being taken out of his way); in turning, however, he found himself opposite the 'Hotch Potch,' and the yearning that had been secretly with him the whole evening prevailed. He called to the driver to stop. He would go in and ask if Jo still belonged there.

He went in. The hall looked exactly as it did when he used to dine there with Jack Herring, and they had the best cook in London; and he looked round with the shrewd, straight glance that had caused him all his life to be better served than most men.

"Mr. Jolyon Forsyte still a member here?"

"Yes, sir; in the Club now, sir. What name?"

Old Jolyon was taken aback.

"His father," he said.

And having spoken, he took his stand, back to the fireplace.

Young Jolyon, on the point of leaving the Club, had put on his hat, and was in the act of crossing the hall, as the porter met him. He was no longer young, with hair going grey, and face—a narrower replica of his father's, with the same large drooping moustache—decidedly worn. He turned pale. This meeting was terrible after all those years, for nothing in the world was so terrible as a scene. They met and crossed hands without a word. Then, with a quaver in his voice, the father said:

"How are you, my boy?"

The son answered:

"How are you, Dad?"

Old Jolyon's hand trembled in its thin lavender glove.

"If you're going my way," he said, "I can give you a lift."

And as though in the habit of taking each other home every night they went out and stepped into the cab.

To old Jolyon it seemed that his son had grown. 'More of a man altogether,' was his comment. Over the natural amiability of that son's face had come a rather sardonic mask, as though he had found in the circumstances of his life the necessity for armour. The features were certainly those of a Forsyte, but the expression was more the introspective look of a student or philosopher. He had no doubt been obliged to look into himself a good deal in the course of those fifteen years.

To young Jolyon the first sight of his father was undoubtedly a shock—he looked so worn and old. But in the cab he seemed hardly to have changed, still having the calm look so well remembered, still being upright and keen-eyed.

"You look well, Dad."

"Middling," old Jolyon answered.

He was the prey of an anxiety that he found he must put into words. Having got his son back like this, he felt he must know what was his financial position.

"Jo," he said, "I should like to hear what sort of water you're in. I suppose you're in debt?"

He put it this way that his son might find it easier to confess.

Young Jolyon answered in his ironical voice:

"No! I'm not in debt!"

Old Jolyon saw that he was angry, and touched his hand. He had run a risk. It was worth it, however, and Jo had never been sulky with him. They drove on, without speaking again, to Stanhope Gate. Old Jolyon invited him in, but young Jolyon shook his head.

"June's not here," said his father hastily: "went off to-day on a visit. I suppose you know that she's engaged to be married?"

"Already?" murmured young Jolyon.

Old Jolyon stepped out, and, in paying the cab fare, for the first time in his life gave the driver a sovereign in mistake for a shilling.

Placing the coin in his mouth, the cabman whipped his horse secretly on the underneath and hurried away.

Old Jolyon turned the key softly in the lock, pushed open the door, and beckoned. His son saw him gravely hanging up his coat, with an expression on his face like that of a boy who intends to steal cherries.

The door of the dining-room was open, the gas turned low; a spirit-urn hissed on a tea-tray, and close to it a cynical-looking cat had fallen asleep on the dining-table. Old Jolyon 'shoo'd' her off at once. The incident was a relief to his feelings; he rattled his opera hat behind the animal.

"She's got fleas," he said, following her out of the room. Through the door in the hall leading to the basement he called "Hssst!" several times, as though assisting the cat's departure, till by some strange coincidence the butler appeared below.

"You can go to bed, Parfitt," said old Jolyon. "I will lock up and put out."

When he again entered the dining-room the cat unfortunately preceded him, with her tail in the air, proclaiming that she had seen through this manoeuvre for suppressing the butler from the first.

A fatality had dogged old Jolyon's domestic stratagems all his life.

Young Jolyon could not help smiling. He was very well versed in irony, and everything that evening seemed to him ironical. The episode of the cat; the announcement of his own daughter's engagement. So he had no more part or parcel in her than he had in the Puss! And the poetical justice of this appealed to him.

"What is June like now?" he asked.

"She's a little thing," returned old Jolyon; "they say she's like me, but that's their folly. She's more like your mother—the same eyes and hair."

"Ah! and she is pretty?"

Old Jolyon was too much of a Forsyte to praise anything freely; especially anything for which he had a genuine admiration.

"Not bad looking—a regular Forsyte chin. It'll be lonely here when she's gone, Jo."

The look on his face again gave young Jolyon the shock he had felt on first seeing his father.

"What will you do with yourself, Dad? I suppose she's wrapped up in him?"

"Do with myself?" repeated old Jolyon with an angry break in his voice. "It'll be miserable work living here alone. I don't know how it's to end. I wish to goodness——" He checked himself, and added: "The question is, what had I better do with this house?"

Young Jolyon looked round the room. It was peculiarly vast and dreary, decorated with the enormous pictures of still life that he remembered as a boy—sleeping dogs with their noses resting on bunches of carrots, together with onions and grapes lying side by side in mild surprise. The house was a white elephant, but he could not conceive of his father living in a smaller place; and all the more did it all seem ironical.

In his great chair with the book-rest sat old Jolyon, the figurehead of his family and class and creed, with his white head and dome-like forehead, the representative of moderation, and order, and love of property. As lonely an old man as there was in London.

There he sat in the gloomy comfort of the room, a puppet in the power of great forces that cared nothing for family or class or creed, but moved, machine-like, with dread processes to inscrutable ends. This was how it struck young Jolyon, who had the impersonal eye.

The poor old Dad! So this was the end, the purpose to which he had lived with such magnificent moderation! To be lonely, and grow older and older, yearning for a soul to speak to!

In his turn old Jolyon looked back at his son. He wanted to talk about many things that he had been unable to talk about all these years. It had been impossible to seriously confide in June his conviction that property in the Soho quarter would go up in value; his uneasiness about that tremendous silence of Pippin, the superintendent of the New Colliery Company, of which he had so long been chairman; his disgust at the steady fall in American Golgothas, or even to discuss how, by some sort of settlement, he could best avoid the payment of those death duties which would follow his decease. Under the influence, however, of a cup of tea, which he seemed to stir indefinitely, he began to speak at last. A new vista of life was thus opened up, a promised land of talk, where he could find a harbour against the waves of anticipation and regret; where he could soothe his soul with the opium of devising how to round off his property and make eternal the only part of him that was to remain alive.

Young Jolyon was a good listener; it was his great quality. He kept his eyes fixed on his father's face, putting a question now and then.

The clock struck one before old Jolyon had finished, and at the sound of its striking his principles came back. He took out his watch with a look of surprise:

"I must go to bed, Jo," he said.

Young Jolyon rose and held out his hand to help his father up. The old face looked worn and hollow again; the eyes were steadily averted.

"Good-bye, my boy; take care of yourself."

A moment passed, and young Jolyon, turning on his heel, marched out at the door. He could hardly see; his smile quavered. Never in all the fifteen years since he had first found out that life was no simple business, had he found it so singularly complicated.

Chapter III

DINNER AT SWITHIN'S

IN Swithin's orange and light-blue dining-room, facing the Park, the round table was laid for twelve.

A cut-glass chandelier filled with lighted candles hung like a giant stalactite above its centre, radiating over large gilt-framed mirrors, slabs of marble on the tops of side-tables, and heavy gold chairs with crewel-worked seats. Everything betokened that love of beauty so deeply implanted in each family which has had its own way to make into Society, out of the more vulgar heart of Nature. Swithin had indeed an impatience of simplicity, a love of ormolu, which had always stamped him amongst his associates as a man of great, if somewhat luxurious taste; and out of the knowledge that no one could possibly enter his rooms without perceiving him to be a man of wealth, he had derived a solid and prolonged happiness such as perhaps no other circumstance in life had afforded him.

Since his retirement from land agency, a profession deplorable in his estimation, especially as to its auctioneering department, he had abandoned himself to naturally aristocratic tastes.

The perfect luxury of his latter days had embedded him like a fly in sugar; and his mind, where very little took place from morning till night, was the junction of two curiously opposite emotions, a lingering and sturdy satisfaction that he had made his own way and his own fortune, and a sense that a man of his distinction should never have been allowed to soil his mind with work.

He stood at the sideboard in a white waistcoat with large gold and onyx buttons, watching his valet screw the necks of three champagne bottles deeper into ice-pails. Between the points of his stand-up collar, which—though it hurt him to move—he would on no account have had altered, the pale flesh of his under chin remained immovable. His eyes roved from bottle to bottle. He was debating, and he argued like this: Jolyon drinks a glass, perhaps two, he's so careful of himself. James, he can't take his wine nowadays. Nicholas—Fanny and he would swill water he shouldn't wonder! Soames didn't count; these young nephews —Soames was thirty-one—couldn't drink! But Bosinney? Encountering in the name of this stranger something outside the range of his philosophy, Swithin paused. A misgiving arose within him! It was impossible to tell! June was only a girl, in love too! Emily (Mrs. James) liked a good glass of champagne. It was too dry for Juley, poor old soul, she had no palate. As to Hatty Chessman! The thought of this old friend caused a cloud of thought to obscure the perfect glassiness of his eyes: He shouldn't wonder if she drank half a bottle!

But in thinking of his remaining guest, an expression like that of a cat who is just going to purr stole over his old face: Mrs. Soames! She mightn't take much, but she would appreciate what she drank; it was a pleasure to give her good wine! A pretty woman—and sympathetic to him!

The thought of her was like champagne itself! A pleasure to give a good wine to a young woman who looked so well, who knew how to dress, with charming manners, quite distinguished—a pleasure to entertain her. Between the points of his collar he gave his head the first small, painful oscillation of the evening.

"Adolf!" he said. "Put in another bottle."

He himself might drink a good deal, for, thanks to that p—prescription of Blight's, he found himself extremely well, and he had been careful to take no lunch. He had not felt so well for weeks. Puffing out his lower lip, he gave his last instructions:

"Adolf, the least touch of the West India when you come to the ham."

Passing into the anteroom, he sat down on the edge of a chair, with his knees apart; and his tall, bulky form was wrapped at once in an expectant, strange, primeval immobility. He was ready to rise at a moment's notice. He had not given a dinner-party for months. This dinner in honour of June's engagement had seemed a bore at first (among Forsytes the custom of solemnizing engagements by feasts was religiously observed), but the labours of sending invitations and ordering the repast over, he felt pleasantly stimulated.

And thus sitting, a watch in his hand, fat, and smooth, and golden, like a flattened globe of butter, he thought of nothing.

A long man, with side whiskers, who had once been in Swithin's service, but was now a green-grocer, entered and proclaimed:

"Mrs. Chessman, Mrs. Septimus Small!"

Two ladies advanced. The one in front, habited entirely in red, had large, settled patches of the same colour in her cheeks, and a hard, dashing eye. She walked at Swithin, holding out a hand cased in a long, primrose-coloured glove:

"Well, Swithin," she said, "I haven't seen you for ages. How are you? Why, my dear boy, how stout you're getting!"

The fixity of Swithin's eye alone betrayed emotion. A dumb and grumbling anger swelled his bosom. It was vulgar to be stout, to talk of being stout; he had a chest, nothing more. Turning to his sister, he grasped her hand, and said in a tone of command:

"Well, Juley."

Mrs. Septimus Small was the tallest of the four sisters; her good, round old face had gone a little sour; an innumerable pout clung all over it, as if it had been encased in an iron wire mask up to that evening, which, being suddenly removed, left little rolls of mutinous flesh all over her countenance. Even her eyes were pouting. It was thus that she recorded her permanent resentment at the loss of Septimus Small.

She had quite a reputation for saying the wrong thing, and, tenacious like all her breed, she would hold to it when she had said it, and add to it another wrong thing, and so on. With the decease of her husband the family tenacity, the family matter-of-factness, had gone sterile within her. A great talker, when allowed, she would converse without the faintest animation for hours together, relating, with epic monotony, the innumerable occasions on which Fortune had misused her; nor did she ever perceive that her hearers sympathized with Fortune, for her heart was kind.

Having sat, poor soul, long by the bedside of Small (a man of poor constitution) she had acquired the habit, and there were countless subsequent occasions when she had sat immense periods of time to amuse sick people, children, and other helpless persons, and she could never divest herself of the feeling that the world was the most ungrateful place anybody could live in. Sunday after Sunday she sat at the feet of that extremely witty preacher, the Rev. Thomas Scoles, who exercised a great influence over her; but she succeeded in convincing everybody that even this was a misfortune. She had passed into a proverb in the family, and when anybody was observed to be peculiarly distressing, he was known as 'a regular Juley.' The habit of her mind would have killed anybody but a Forsyte at forty; but she was seventy-two, and had never looked better. And one felt that there were capacities for enjoyment about her which might yet come out. She owned three canaries, the cat Tommy, and half a parrot—in common with her sister Hester; and these poor creatures (kept carefully out of Timothy's way—he was nervous about animals), unlike human beings, recognising that she could not help being blighted, attached themselves to her passionately.

She was sombrely magnificent this evening in black bombazine, with a mauve front cut in a shy triangle, and crowned with a black velvet ribbon round the base of her thin throat; black and mauve for evening wear was esteemed very chaste by nearly every Forsyte.

Pouting at Swithin, she said:

"Ann has been asking for you. You haven't been near us for an age!"

Swithin put his thumbs within the armholes of his waistcoat, and replied:

"Ann's getting very shaky; she ought to have a doctor!"

"Mr. and Mrs. Nicholas Forsyte!"

Nicholas Forsyte, cocking his rectangular eyebrows, wore a smile. He had succeeded during the day in bringing to fruition a scheme for the employment of a tribe from Upper India in the gold-mines of Ceylon. A pet plan, carried at last in the teeth of great difficulties—he was justly pleased. It would double the output of his mines, and, as he had often forcibly argued, all experience tended to show that a man must die; and whether he died of a miserable old age in his own country, or prematurely of damp in the bottom of a foreign mine, was surely of little consequence, provided that by a change in his mode of life he benefited the British Empire.

His ability was undoubted. Raising his broken nose towards his listener, he would add:

"For want of a few hundred of these fellows we haven't paid a dividend for years, and look at the price of the shares. I can't get ten shillings for them."

He had been at Yarmouth, too, and had come back feeling that he had added at least ten years to his own life. He grasped Swithin's hand, exclaiming in a jocular voice:

"Well, so here we are again!"

Mrs. Nicholas, an effete woman, smiled a smile of frightened jollity behind his back.

"Mr. and Mrs. James Forsyte! Mr. and Mrs. and Mrs. Soames Forsyte!"
Swithin drew his heels together, his deportment ever admirable.

"Well, James, well Emily! How are you, Soames? How do you *do?*"

His hand enclosed Irene's, and his eyes swelled. She was a pretty
woman—a little too pale, but her figure, her eyes, her teeth! Too good
for that chap Soames!

The gods had given Irene dark brown eyes and golden hair, that
strange combination, provocative of men's glances, which is said to be
the mark of a weak character. And the full, soft pallor of her neck and
shoulders, above a gold-coloured frock, gave to her personality an allur-
ing strangeness.

Soames stood behind, his eyes fastened on his wife's neck. The hands
of Swithin's watch, which he still held open in his hand, had left eight
behind; it was half an hour beyond his dinner-time—he had had no
lunch—and a strange primeval impatience surged up within him.

"It's not like Jolyon to be late!" he said to Irene, with uncontrollable
vexation. "I suppose it'll be June keeping him!"

"People in love are always late," she answered.

Swithin stared at her; a dusky orange dyed his cheeks.

"They've no business to be. Some fashionable nonsense!"

And behind this outburst the inarticulate violence of primitive generations seemed to mutter and grumble.

"Tell me what you think of my new star, Uncle Swithin," said Irene
softly.

Among the lace in the bosom of her dress was shining a five-pointed
star, made of eleven diamonds.

Swithin looked at the star. He had a pretty taste in stones; no question
could have been more sympathetically devised to distract his attention.

"Who gave you that?" he asked.

"Soames."

There was no change in her face, but Swithin's pale eyes bulged as
though he might suddenly have been afflicted with insight.

"I dare say you're dull at home," he said. "Any day you like to come
and dine with me, I'll give you as good a bottle of wine as you'll get in
London."

"Miss June Forsyte—Mr. Jolyon Forsyte! . . . Mr. Boswainey! . . ."

Swithin moved his arm, and said in a rumbling voice:

"Dinner, now—dinner!"

He took in Irene, on the ground that he had not entertained her since she was a bride. June was the portion of Bosinney, who was placed between Irene and his fiancée. On the other side of June was James with Mrs. Nicholas, then old Jolyon with Mrs. James, Nicholas with Hatty Chessman, Soames with Mrs. Small completing the circle to Swithin again.

Family dinners of the Forsytes observe certain traditions. There are, for instance, no *hors d'oeuvres*. The reason for this is unknown. Theory among the younger members traces it to the disgraceful price of oysters; it is more probably due to a desire to come to the point, to a good practical sense deciding at once that *hors d'oeuvres* are but poor things. The Jameses alone, unable to withstand a custom almost universal in Park Lane, are now and then unfaithful.

A silent, almost morose, inattention to each other succeeds to the subsidence into their seats, lasting till well ino the first entrée, but interspersed with remarks such as, "Tom's bad again; I can't tell what's the matter with him!"—"I suppose Ann doesn't come down in the mornings?"—"What's the name of your doctor, Fanny? Stubbs? He's a quack!"—"Winifred? She's got too many children. Four, isn't it? She's as thin as a lath!"—"What d'you give for this sherry, Swithin? Too dry for me!"

With the second glass of champagne, a kind of hum makes itself heard, which, when divested of casual accessories and resolved into its primal element, is found to be James telling a story, and this goes on for a long time, encroaching sometimes even upon what must universally be recognised as the crowning point of a Forsyte feast—'the saddle of mutton.'

No Forsyte has given a dinner without providing a saddle of mutton. There is something in its succulent solidity which makes it suitable to people 'of a certain position.' It is nourishing and—tasty; the sort of thing a man remembers eating. It has a past and a future, like a deposit paid into a bank; and it is something that can be argued about.

Each branch of the family tenaciously held to a particular locality— old Jolyon swearing by Dartmoor, James by Welsh, Swithin by Southdown, Nicholas maintaining that people might sneer, but there was nothing like New Zealand. As for Roger, the 'original' of the brothers, he had been obliged to invent a locality of his own, and with an ingenuity worthy of a man who had devised a new profession for his sons, he had discovered a shop where they sold German; on being remonstrated with, he had proved his point by producing a butcher's bill, which showed that he paid more than any of the others. It was on this occasion that old Jolyon, turning to June, had said in one of his bursts of philosophy:

"You may depend upon it, they're a cranky lot, the Forsytes—and you'll find it out, as you grow older!"

Timothy alone held apart, for though he ate saddle of mutton heartily, he was, he said, afraid of it.

To anyone interested psychologically in Forsytes, this great saddle-of-mutton trait is of prime importance; not only does it illustrate their tenacity, both collectively and as individuals, but it marks them as belonging in fibre and instincts to that great class which believes in nourishment and flavour, and yields to no sentimental craving for beauty.

Younger members of the family indeed would have done without a joint altogether, preferring guinea-fowl, or lobster salad—something which appealed to the imagination, and had less nourishment—but these were females; or, if not, had been corrupted by their wives, or by mothers, who having been forced to eat saddle of mutton throughout their married lives, had passed a secret hostility towards it into the fibre of their sons.

The great saddle-of-mutton controversy at an end, a Tewkesbury ham commenced, together with the least touch of West India—Swithin was so long over this course that he caused a block in the progress of the dinner. To devote himself to it with better heart, he paused in his conversation.

From his seat by Mrs. Septimus Small, Soames was watching. He had a reason of his own connected with a pet building scheme, for observing Bosinney. The architect might do for his purpose; he looked clever, as he sat leaning back in his chair, moodily making little ramparts with bread-crumbs. Soames noted his dress clothes to be well cut, but too small, as though made many years ago.

He saw him turn to Irene and say something, and her face sparkle as he often saw it sparkle at other people—never at himself. He tried to catch what they were saying, but Aunt Juley was speaking.

Hadn't that always seemed very extraordinary to Soames? Only last Sunday dear Mr. Scoles had been so witty in his sermon, so sarcastic: " 'For what,' he had said, 'shall it profit a man if he gain his own soul, but lose all his property?' " That, he had said, was the motto of the middle-class; now, what *had* he meant by that? Of course, it might be what middle-class people believed—she didn't know; what did Soames think?

He answered abstractedly: "How should I know? Scoles is a humbug, though, isn't he?" For Bosinney was looking round the table, as if pointing out the peculiarities of the guests, and Soames wondered what he was saying. By her smile Irene was evidently agreeing with his remarks. She seemed always to agree with other people.

Her eyes were turned on himself; Soames dropped his glance at once. The smiled had died off her lips.

A humbug? But what did Soames mean? If Mr. Scoles was a humbug, a clergyman—then anybody might be—it was frightful!

"Well, and so they are!" said Soames.

During Aunt Juley's momentary and horrified silence he caught some words of Irene's that sounded like: 'Abandon hope, all ye who enter here!'

But Swithin had finished his ham.

"Where do you go for your mushrooms?" he was saying to Irene in a voice like a courtier's; "you ought to go to Snileybob's—he'll give 'em you fresh. These *little* men, they won't take the trouble!"

Irene turned to answer him, and Soames saw Bosinney watching her and smiling to himself. A curious smile the fellow had. A half-simple arrangement, like a child who smiles when he is pleased. As for George's nickname—'The Buccaneer'—he did not think much of that. And, seeing Bosinney turn to June, Soames smiled too, but sardonically—he did not like June, who was not looking too pleased.

This was not surprising, for she had just held the following conversation with James:

"I stayed on the river on my way home, Uncle James, and saw a beautiful site for a house."

James, a slow and thorough eater, stopped the process of mastication. "Eh?" he said. "Now where was that?"

"Close to Pangbourne."

James placed a piece of ham in his mouth, and June waited.

"I suppose *you* wouldn't know whether the land about there was free-hold?" he asked at last. *"You* wouldn't know anything about the price of land about there?"

"Yes," said June; "I made inquiries." Her little resolute face under its copper crown was suspiciously eager and aglow.

James regarded her with the air of an inquisitor.

"What? You're not thinking of buying land!" he ejaculated, dropping his fork.

June was greatly encouraged by his interest. It had long been her pet plan that her uncles should benefit themselves and Bosinney by building country-houses.

"Of course not," she said. "I thought it would be such a splendid place for—you or—someone to build a country-house!"

James looked at her sideways, and placed a second piece of ham in his mouth.

"Land ought to be very dear about there," he said.

What June had taken for personal interest was only the impersonal excitement of every Forsyte who hears of something eligible in danger of passing into other hands. But she refused to see the disappearance of her chance, and continued to press her point.

"You ought to go into the country, Uncle James. I wish I had a lot of money, I wouldn't live another day in London."

James was stirred to the depths of his long thin figure; he had no idea his niece held such downright views.

"Why don't you go into the country?" repeated June; "it would do you a lot of good."

"Why?" began James in a fluster. "Buying land—what good d'you suppose I can do buying land, building houses?—I couldn't get four per cent. for my money!"

"What does that matter? You'd get fresh air."

"Fresh air!" exclaimed James; "what should I do with fresh air——"

"I should have thought anybody liked to have fresh air," said June scornfully.

James wiped his napkin all over his mouth.

"You don't know the value of money," he said, avoiding her eye.

"No! and I hope I never shall!" and biting her lip with inexpressible mortification, poor June was silent.

Why were her own relations so rich, and Phil never knew where the money was coming from for to-morrow's tobacco. Why couldn't they do something for him? But they were so selfish. Why couldn't they build country-houses? She had all that naïve dogmatism which is so pathetic, and sometimes achieves such great results. Bosinney, to whom she turned in her discomfiture, was talking to Irene, and a chill fell on June's spirit. Her eyes grew steady with anger, like old Jolyon's when his will was crossed.

James, too, was much disturbed. He felt as though someone had threatened his right to invest his money at five per cent. Jolyon had spoiled her. None of *his* girls would have said such a thing. James had always been exceedingly liberal to his children, and the consciousness of this made him feel it all the more deeply. He trifled moodily with his strawberries, then, deluging them with cream, he ate them quickly; they, at all events, should not escape him.

No wonder he was upset. Engaged for fifty-four years (he had been admitted a solicitor on the earliest day sanctioned by the law) in arranging mortgages, preserving investments at a dead level of high and safe interest, conducting negotiations on the principle of securing the utmost possible out of other people compatible with safety to his clients and himself, in calculations as to the exact pecuniary possibilities of all the relations of life, he had come at last to think purely in terms of money. Money was now his light, his medium for seeing, that without which he was really unable to see, really not cognisant of phenomena; and to have this thing, "I hope I shall never know the value of money!" said to his face, saddened and exasperated him. He knew it to be nonsense, or it would have frightened him. What was the world coming to! Suddenly recollecting the story of young Jolyon, however, he felt a little comforted, for what could you expect with a father like that! This turned his thoughts into a channel still less pleasant. What was all this talk about Soames and Irene?

As in all self-respecting families, an emporium had been established where family secrets were battered, and family stock priced. It was known on Forsyte 'Change that Irene regretted her marriage. Her regret was disapproved of. She ought to have known her own mind; no dependable woman made these mistakes.

44

James reflected sourly that they had a nice house (rather small) in an excellent position, no children, and no money troubles. Soames was reserved about his affairs, but he must be getting a very warm man. He had a capital income from the business—for Soames, like his father, was a member of that well-known firm of solicitors, Forsyte, Bustard and Forsyte—and had always been very careful. He had done quite unusually well with some mortgages he had taken up, too—a little timely foreclosure—most lucky hits!

There was no reason why Irene should not be happy, yet they said she'd been asking for a separate room. He knew where that ended. It wasn't as if Soames drank.

James looked at his daughter-in-law. That unseen glance of his was cold and dubious. Appeal and fear were in it, and a sense of personal grievance. Why should he be worried like this? It was very likely all nonsense; women were funny things! They exaggerated so, you didn't know what to believe; and then, nobody told him anything, he had to find out everything for himself. Again he looked furtively at Irene, and across from her to Soames. The latter, listening to Aunt Juley, was looking up under his brows in the direction of Bosinney.

'He's fond of her, I know,' thought James. 'Look at the way he's always giving her things.'

And the extraordinary unreasonableness of her disaffection struck him with increased force. It was a pity, too, she was a taking little thing, and he, James, would be really quite fond of her if she'd only let him. She had taken up lately with June; *that* was doing her no good, that was certainly doing her no good. She was getting to have opinions of her own. He didn't know what she wanted with anything of the sort. She'd a good home, and everything she could wish for. He felt that her friends ought to be chosen for her. To go on like this was dangerous.

June, indeed, with her habit of championing the unfortunate, had dragged from Irene a confession, and, in return, had preached the necessity of facing the evil, by separation, if need be. But in the face of these exhortations, Irene had kept a brooding silence, as though she found terrible the thought of this struggle carried through in cold blood. He would never give her up, she had said to June.

"Who cares?" June cried; "let him do what he likes—you've only to stick to it!" And she had not scrupled to say something of this sort at Timothy's; James, when he heard of it, had felt a natural indignation and horror.

What if Irene were to take it into her head to—he could hardly frame the thought—to leave Soames? But he felt this thought so unbearable that he at once put it away; the shady visions it conjured up, the sound of family tongues buzzing in his ears, the horror of the conspicuous happening so close to him, to one of his own children! Luckily, she had no money—a beggarly fifty pound a year! And he thought of the deceased Heron, who had had nothing to leave her, with contempt. Brooding over his glass, his long legs twisted under the table, he quite omitted to rise when the ladies left the room. He would have to speak to Soames —would have to put him on his guard; they could not go on like this, now that such a contingency had occurred to him. And he noticed with sour disfavour that June had left her wine-glasses full of wine.

'That little thing's at the bottom of it all,' he mused; 'Irene'd never have thought of it herself.' James was a man of imagination.

The voice of Swithin roused him from his reverie.

"I gave four hundred pounds for it," he was saying. "Of course it's a regular work of art."

"Four hundred! H'm! that's a lot of money!" chimed in Nicholas.

The object alluded to was an elaborate group of statuary in Italian marble, which, placed upon a lofty stand (also of marble), diffused an atmosphere of culture throughout the room. The subsidiary figures, of which there were six, female, nude, and of highly ornate workmanship, were all pointing towards the central figure, also nude, and female, who was pointing at herself; and all this gave the observer a very pleasant sense of her extreme value. Aunt Juley, nearly opposite, had had the greatest difficulty in not looking at it all the evening.

Old Jolyon spoke; it was he who had started the discussion.

"Four hundred fiddlesticks! Don't tell me you gave four hundred for *that?*"

Between the points of his collar Swithin's chin made the second painful oscillatory movement of the evening. "Four—hundred—pounds, of English money; not a farthing less. I don't regret it. It's not common English—it's genuine modern Italian!"

Soames raised the corner of his lip in a smile, and looked across at

Bosinney. The architect was grinning behind the fumes of his cigarette. Now, indeed, he looked more like a buccaneer.

"There's a lot of work about it," remarked James hastily, who was really moved by the size of the group. "It'd sell well at Jobson's."

"The poor foreign dey-vil that made it," went on Swithin, "asked me five hundred—I gave him four. It's worth eight. Looked half-starved, poor dey-vil!"

"Ah!" chimed in Nicholas suddenly, "poor, seedy-lookin' chaps, these artists; it's a wonder to me how they live. Now, there's young Flageoletti, that Fanny and the girls are always havin' in, to play the fiddle; if he makes a hundred a year it's as much as ever he does!"

James shook his head. "Ah!" he said, "I don't know how they live!"

Old Jolyon had risen, and, cigar in mouth, went to inspect the group at close quarters.

"Wouldn't have given two for it!" he pronounced at last.

Soames saw his father and Nicholas glance at each other anxiously; and, on the other side of Swithin, Bosinney, still shrouded in smoke.

'I wonder what *he* thinks of it?' thought Soames, who knew well enough that this group was hopelessly *vieux jeu;* hopelessly of the last generation. There was no longer any sale at Jobson's for such works of art.

Swithin's answer came at last. "You never know anything about a statue. You've got your pictures, and that's all!"

Old Jolyon walked back to his seat, puffing his cigar. It was not likely that he was going to be drawn into an argument with an obstinate beggar like Swithin, pig-headed as a mule, who had never known a statue from a—straw hat.

"Stucco!" was all he said.

It had long been physically impossible for Swithin to start; his fist came down on the table.

"Stucco! I should like to see anything you've got in your house half as good!"

And behind his speech seemed to sound again that rumbling violence of primitive generations.

It was James who saved the situation.

"Now, what do *you* say, Mr. Bosinney? You're an architect; you ought to know all about statues and things!"

Every eye was turned upon Bosinney; all waited with a strange, suspicious look for his answer.

And Soames, speaking for the first time, asked:

"Yes, Bosinney, what do you say?"

Bosinney replied coolly:

"The work is a remarkable one."

His words were addressed to Swithin, his eyes smiled slyly at old Jolyon; only Soames remained unsatisfied.

"Remarkable for what?"

"For its naïveté."

The answer was followed by an impressive silence; Swithin alone was not sure whether a compliment was intended.

Chapter IV

PROJECTION OF THE HOUSE

S OAMES FORSYTE walked out of his green-painted front door
three days after the dinner at Swithin's, and looking back from
across the Square, confirmed his impression that the house wanted
painting.

He had left his wife sitting on the sofa in the drawing-room, her
hands crossed in her lap, manifestly waiting for him to go out. This was
not unusual. It happened, in fact, every day.

He could not understand what she found wrong with him. It was not
as if he drank! Did he run into debt, or gamble, or swear; was he violent;
were his friends rackety; did he stay out at night? On the contrary.

The profound, subdued aversion which he felt in his wife was a
mystery to him, and a source of the most terrible irritation. That she
had made a mistake, and did not love him, had tried to love him and
could not love him, was obviously no reason.

He that could imagine so outlandish a cause for his wife's not getting
on with him was certainly no Forsyte.

Soames was forced, therefore, to set the blame entirely down to his
wife. He had never met a woman so capable of inspiring affection. They
could not go anywhere without his seeing how all the men were attracted by her; their looks, manners, voices, betrayed it; her behaviour
under this attention had been beyond reproach. That she was one of
those women—not too common in the Anglo-Saxon race—born to be
loved and to love, who when not loving are not living, had certainly
never even occurred to him. Her power of attraction he regarded as
part of her value as his property; but it made him, indeed, suspect that
she could give as well as receive; and she gave him nothing! 'Then why
did she marry me?' was his continual thought. He had forgotten his
courtship; that year and a half when he had besieged and lain in wait
for her, devising schemes for her entertainment, giving her presents,

proposing to her periodically, and keeping her other admirers away with his perpetual presence. He had forgotten the day when, adroitly taking advantage of an acute phase of her dislike to her home surroundings, he crowned his labours with success. If he remembered anything, it was the dainty capriciousness with which the gold-haired, dark-eyed girl had treated him. He certainly did not remember the look on her face— strange, passive, appealing—when suddenly one day she had yielded, and said that she would marry him.

It had been one of those real devoted wooings which books and people praise, when the lover is at length rewarded for hammering the iron till it is malleable, and all must be happy ever after as the wedding bells.

Soames walked eastwards, mousing doggedly along on the shady side.

The house wanted doing up, unless he decided to move into the country, and build.

For the hundredth time that month he turned over this problem. There was no use in rushing into things! He was very comfortably off, with an increasing income getting on for three thousand a year; but his invested capital was not perhaps so large as his father believed—James had a tendency to expect that his children should be better off than they were. 'I can manage eight thousand easily enough,' he thought, 'without calling in either Robertson's or Nicholl's.'

He had stopped to look in at a picture shop, for Soames was an 'amateur' of pictures, and had a little room in No. 62 Montpellier Square, full of canvases, stacked against the wall, which he had no room to hang. He brought them home with him on his way back from the City, generally after dark, and would enter this room on Sunday afternoons, to spend hours turning the pictures to the light, examining the marks on their backs, and occasionally making notes.

They were nearly all landscapes with figures in the foreground, a sign of some mysterious revolt against London, its tall houses, its interminable streets, where his life and the lives of his breed and class were passed. Every now and then he would take one or two pictures away with him in a cab, and stop at Jobson's on his way into the City.

He rarely showed them to anyone; Irene, whose opinion he secretly respected and perhaps for that reason never solicited, had only been into the room on rare occasions, in discharge of some wifely duty. She was not asked to look at the pictures, and she never did. To Soames this was another grievance. He hated that pride of hers, and secretly dreaded it.

In the plate-glass window of the picture shop his image stood and looked at him.

His sleek hair under the brim of the tall hat had been a sheen like the hat itself; his cheeks, pale and flat, the line of his clean-shaven lips, his firm chin with its greyish shaven tinge, and the buttoned strictness of his black cut-away coat, conveyed an appearance of reserve and secrecy, of imperturbable, enforced composure; but his eyes, cold, grey, strained-looking, with a line in the brow between them, examined him wistfully, as if they knew of a secret weakness.

He noted the subjects of the pictures, the names of the painters, made a calculation of their values, but without the satisfacion he usually derived from this inward appraisement, and walked on.

No. 62 would do well enough for another year, if he decided to build! The times were good for building, money had not been so dear for years; and the site he had seen at Robin Hill, when he had gone down there in the spring to inspect the Nicholl mortgage—what could be better! Within twelve miles of Hyde Park Corner, the value of the land certain to go up, would always fetch more than he gave for it; so that a house, if built in really good style, was a first-class investment.

The notion of being the one member of his family with a country house weighed but little with him; for to a true Forsyte, sentiment, even the sentiment of social position, was a luxury only to be indulged in after his appetite for more material pleasure had been satisfied.

To get Irene out of London, away from opportunities of going about and seeing people, away from her friends and those who put ideas into her head! That was the thing! She was too thick with June! June disliked him. He returned the sentiment. They were of the same blood.

It would be everything to get Irene out of town. The house would please her, she would enjoy messing about with the decoration, she was very artistic!

The house must be in good style, something that would always be certain to command a price, something unique, like that last house of Parkes, which had a tower; but Parkes had himself said that his architect was ruinous. You never knew where you were with those fellows; if

51

they had a name they ran you into no end of expense and were conceited into the bargain.

And a common architect was no good—the memory of Parkes' tower precluded the employment of a common architect.

This was why he had thought of Bosinney. Since the dinner at Swithin's he had made enquiries, the result of which had been meagre, but encouraging: "One of the new school."

"Clever?"

"As clever as you like,—a bit—a bit up in the air!"

He had not been able to discover what houses Bosinney had built, nor what his charges were. The impression he gathered was that he would be able to make his own terms. The more he reflected on the idea, the more he liked it. It would be keeping the thing in the family, with Forsytes almost an instinct; and he would be able to get 'favoured-nation,' if not nominal terms—only fair, considering the chance to Bosinney of displaying his talents, for this house must be no common edifice.

Soames reflected complacently on the work it would be sure to bring the young man; for, like every Forsyte, he could be a thorough optimist when there was anything to be had out of it.

Bosinney's office was in Sloane Street, close at hand, so that he would be able to keep his eye continually on the plans.

Again, Irene would not be so likely to object to leave London if her greatest friend's lover were given the job. June's marriage might depend on it. Irene could not decently stand in the way of June's marriage; she would never do that, he knew her too well. And June would be pleased; of this he saw the advantage.

Bosinney looked clever, but he had also—and it was one of his great attractions—an air as if he did not quite know on which side his bread were buttered; he should be easy to deal with in money matters. Soames made this reflection in no defrauding spirit; it was the natural attitude of his mind—of the mind of any good business man—of all those thousands of good business men through whom he was threading his way up Ludgate Hill.

Thus he fulfilled the inscrutable laws of his great class—of human nature itself—when he reflected, with a sense of comfort, that Bosinney would be easy to deal with in money matters.

While he elbowed his way on, his eyes, which he usually kept fixed on the ground before his feet, were attracted upwards by the dome of St. Paul's. It had a peculiar fascination for him, that old dome, and not once, but twice or three times a week, would he halt in his daily pilgrimage to enter beneath and stop in the side aisles for five or ten minutes, scrutinizing the names and epitaphs on the monuments. The attraction for him of this great church was inexplicable, unless it enabled him to concentrate his thoughts on the business of the day. If any affair of particular moment, or demanding peculiar acuteness, was weighing on his mind, he invariably went in, to wander with mouse-like attention from epitaph to epitaph. Then retiring in the same noiseless way, he would hold steadily on up Cheapside, a thought more of dogged purpose in his gait, as though he had seen something which he had made up his mind to buy.

He went in this morning, but, instead of stealing from monument to monument, turned his eyes upwards to the columns and spacings of the walls, and remained motionless.

His uplifted face, with the awed and wistful look which faces take on themselves in church, was whitened to a chalky hue in the vast building. His gloved hands were clasped in front over the handle of his umbrella. He lifted them. Some sacred inspiration perhaps had come to him.

'Yes,' he thought, 'I must have room to hang my pictures.'

That evening, on his return from the City, he called at Bosinney's office. He found the architect in his shirt-sleeves, smoking a pipe, and ruling off lines on a plan. Soames refused a drink, and came at once to the point.

"If you've nothing better to do on Sunday, come down with me to Robin Hill, and give me your opinion on a building site."

"Are you going to build?"

"Perhaps," said Soames; "but don't speak of it. I just want your opinion."

"Quite so," said the architect.

Soames peered about the room.

"You're rather high up here," he remarked.

Any information he could gather about the nature and scope of Bosinney's business would be all to the good.

"It does well enough for me so far," answered the architect. "You're accustomed to the swells."

He knocked out his pipe, but replaced it empty between his teeth; it assisted him perhaps to carry on the conversation. Soames noted a hollow in each cheek, made as it were by suction .

"What do you pay for an office like this?" said he.

"Fifty too much," replied Bosinney.

This answer impressed Soames favourably.

"I suppose it is dear," he said. "I'll call for you on Sunday about eleven."

The following Sunday therefore he called for Bosinney in a hansom, and drove him to the station. On arriving at Robin Hill, they found no cab, and started to walk the mile and a half to the site.

It was the 1st of August—a perfect day, with a burning sun and cloudless sky—and in the straight, narrow road leading up the hill their feet kicked up a yellow dust.

"Gravel soil," remarked Soames, and sideways he glanced at the coat Bosinney wore. Into the side-pockets of this coat were thrust bundles of papers, and under one arm was carried a queer-looking stick. Soames noted these and other peculiarities.

No one but a clever man, or, indeed, a buccaneer, would have taken such liberties with his appearance; and though these eccentricities were revolting to Soames, he derived a certain satisfaction from them, as evidence of qualities by which he must inevitably profit. If the fellow could build houses, what did his clothes matter?

"I told you," he said, "that I want this house to be a surprise, so don't say anything about it. I never talk of my affairs until they're carried through."

Bosinney nodded.

"Let women into your plans," pursued Soames, "and you never know where it'll end."

"Ah!" said Bosinney, "women are the devil!"

This feeling had long been at the bottom of Soames's heart; he had never, however, put it into words.

"Oh!" he muttered, "so you're beginning to——" He stopped, but added, with an uncontrollable burst of spite: "June's got a temper of her own—always had."

"A temper's not a bad thing in an angel."

Soames had never called Irene an angel. He could not so have violated his best instincts, letting other people into the secret of her value, and giving himself away. He made no reply.

They had struck into a half-made road across a warren. A cart-track led at right-angles to a gravel pit, beyond which the chimneys of a cottage rose amongst the clump of trees at the border of a thick wood. Tussocks of feathery grass covered the rough surface of the ground, and out of these the larks soared into the haze of sunshine. On the far horizon, over a countless succession of fields and hedges, rose a line of downs.

Soames led till they had crossed to the far side, and there he stopped. It was the chosen site; but now that he was about to divulge the spot to another he had become uneasy.

"The agent lives in that cottage," he said; "he'll give us some lunch—we'd better have lunch before we go into this matter."

He again took the lead to the cottage, where the agent, a tall man named Oliver, with a heavy face and grizzled beard, welcomed them. During lunch, which Soames hardly touched, he kept looking at Bosinney, and once or twice passed his silk handkerchief stealthily over his forehead. The meal came to an end at last, and Bosinney rose.

"I dare say you've got business to talk over," he said; "I'll just go and nose about a bit." Without waiting for a reply he strolled out.

Soames was soliictor to this estate, and he spent nearly an hour in the agent's company, looking at ground-plans and discussing the Nicholl and other mortgages; it was as it were by an afterthought that he brought up the question of the building site.

"Your people," he said, "ought to come down in their price to *me,* considering that I shall be the first to build."

Oliver shook his head.

"The site you've fixed on, sir," he said, "is the cheapest we've got. Sites at the top of the slope are dearer by a good bit."

"Mind," said Soames, "I've not decided; it's quite possible I shan't build at all. The ground-rent's very high."

"Well, Mr. Forsyte, I shall be sorry if you go off, and I think you'll make a mistake, sir. There's not a bit of land near London with such a view as this, nor one that's cheaper, all things considered; we've only to advertise, to get a mob of people after it."

They looked at each other. Their faces said very plainly: 'I respect you as a man of business; and you can't expect me to believe a word you say.'

"Well," repeated Soames, "I haven't made up my mind; the thing will very likely go off!" With these words, taking up his umbrella, he put his chilly hand into the agent's, withdrew it without the faintest pressure, and went out into the sun.

He walked slowly back towards the site in deep thought. His instinct told him that what the agent had said was true. A cheap site. And the beauty of it was, that he knew the agent did not really think it cheap; so that his own intuitive knowledge was a victory over the agent's.

'Cheap or not, I mean to have it,' he thought.

The larks sprang up in front of his feet, the air was full of butterflies, a sweet fragrance rose from the wild grasses. The sappy scent of the bracken stole forth from the wood, where, hidden in the depths, pigeons were cooing, and from afar on the warm breeze came the rhythmic chiming of church bells.

Soames walked with his eyes on the ground, his lips opening and closing as though in anticipation of a delicious morsel. But when he arrived at the site, Bosinney was nowhere to be seen. After waiting some little time, he crossed the warren in the direction of the slope. He would have shouted, but dreaded the sound of his voice.

The warren was as lonely as a prairie, its silence only broken by the rustle of rabbits bolting to their holes, and the song of the larks.

Soames, the pioneer-leader of the great Forsyte army advancing to the civilization of this wilderness, felt his spirit daunted by the loneliness, by the invisible singing, and the hot, sweet air. He had begun to retrace his steps when he at last caught sight of Bosinney.

The architect was sprawling under a large oak tree, whose trunk, with a huge spread of bough and foliage, ragged with age, stood on the verge of the rise.

Soames had to touch him on the shoulder before he looked up.

"Hallo! Forsyte," he said, "I've found the very place for your house! Look here!"

Soames stood and looked, then he said, coldly:

"You may be very clever, but this site will cost me half as much again."

"Hang the cost, man. Look at the view!"

Almost from their feet stretched ripe corn, dipping to a small dark copse beyond. A plain of fields and hedges spread to the distant grey-blue downs. In a silver streak to the right could be seen the line of the river.

The sky was so blue, and the sun so bright, that an eternal summer seemed to reign over this prospect. Thistledown floated round them, enraptured by the serenity of the ether. The heat danced over the corn, and, pervading all, was a soft, insensible hum, like the murmur of bright minutes holding revel between earth and heaven.

Soames looked. In spite of himself, something swelled in his breast. To live here in sight of all this, to be able to point it out to his friends, to talk of it, to possess it! His cheeks flushed. The warmth, the radiance, the glow, were sinking into his senses as, four years before, Irene's beauty had sunk into his senses and made him long for her. He stole a glance at Bosinney, whose eyes, the eyes of the coachman's 'half-tame leopard,' seemed running wild over the landscape. The sunlight had caught the promontories of the fellow's face, the bumpy cheekbones, the point of his chin, the vertical ridges above his brow; and Soames watched this rugged, enthusiastic, careless face with an unpleasant feeling.

A long, soft ripple of wind flowed over the corn, and brought a puff of warm air into their faces.

"I could build you a teaser here," said Bosinney, breaking the silence at last.

"I dare say," replied Soames, drily. "You haven't got to pay for it."

"For about eight thousand I could build you a palace."

Soames had become very pale—a struggle was going on within him. He dropped his eyes, and said stubbornly:

"I can't afford it."

And slowly, with his mousing walk, he led the way back to the first site.

They spent some time there going into particulars of the projected house, and then Soames returned to the agent's cottage.

He came out in about half an hour, and, joining Bosinney, started for the station.

"Well," he said, hardly opening his lips, "I've taken that site of yours, after all."

And again he was silent, confusedly debating how it was that this fellow, whom by habit he despised, should have overborne his own decision.

Chapter V

A FORSYTE MÉNAGE

LIKE the enlightened thousands of his class and generation in this great city of London, who no longer believe in red velvet chairs, and know that groups of modern Italian marble are *vieux jeu*, Soames Forsyte inhabited a house which did what it could. It owned a copper door knocker of individual design, windows which had been altered to open outwards, hanging flower boxes filled with fuchsias, and at the back (a great feature) a little court tiled with jade-green tiles, and surrounded by pink hydrangeas in peacock-blue tubs. Here, under a parchment-coloured Japanese sunshade covering the whole end, inhabitants or visitors could be screened from the eyes of the curious while they drank tea and examined at their leisure the latest of Soames's little silver boxes.

The inner decoration favoured the First Empire and William Morris. For its size, the house was commodious; there were countless nooks resembling birds' nests, and little things made of silver were deposited like eggs.

In this general perfection two kinds of fastidiousness were at war. There lived here a mistress who would have dwelt daintily on a desert island; a master whose daintiness was, as it were, an investment, cultivated by the owner for his advancement, in accordance with the laws of competition. This competitive daintiness had caused Soames in his Marlborough days to be the first boy into white waistcoats in summer, and corduroy waistcoats in winter, had prevented him from ever appearing in public with his tie climbing up his collar, and induced him to dust his patent leather boots before a great multitude assembled on Speech Day to hear him recite Molière.

Skin-like immaculateness had grown over Soames, as over many Londoners; impossible to conceive of him with a hair out of place, a tie deviating one-eighth of an inch from the perpendicular, a collar unglossed! He would not have gone without a bath for worlds—it was the fashion to take baths; and how bitter was his scorn of pepole who omitted them!

But Irene could be imagined, like some nymph, bathing in wayside streams, for the joy of the freshness and of seeing her own fair body.

In this conflict throughout the house the woman had gone to the wall. As in the struggle between Saxon and Celt still going on within the nation, the more impressionable and receptive temperament had forced on it a conventional superstructure.

Thus the house had acquired a close resemblance to hundreds of other houses with the same high aspirations, having become: 'That very charming little house of the Soames Forsytes, quite individual, my dear —really elegant!'

For Soames Forsyte—read James Peabody, Thomas Atkins, or Emmanuel Spagnoletti, the name in fact of any upper-middle class Englishman in London with any pretensions to taste; and though the decoration be different, the phrase is just.

On the evening of August 8, a week after the expedition to Robin Hill, in the dining-room of this house—'quite individual, my dear— really elegant!'—Soames and Irene were seated at dinner. A hot dinner on Sundays was a little distinguishing elegance common to this house and many others. Early in married life Soames had laid down the rule: 'The servants must give us hot dinner on Sundays—they've nothing to do but play the concertina.'

The custom had produced no revolution. For—to Soames a rather deplorable sign—servants were devoted to Irene, who, in defiance of all safe tradition, appeared to recognize their right to a share in the weaknesses of human nature.

The happy pair were seated, not opposite each other, but rectangularly, at the handsome rosewood table; they dined without a cloth—a distinguishing elegance—and so far had not spoken a word.

Soames liked to talk during dinner about business, or what he had been buying, and so long as he talked Irene's silence did not distress him. This evening he had found it impossible to talk. The decision to build had been weighing on his mind all the week, and he had made up his mind to tell her.

His nervousness about this disclosure irritated him profoundly; she had no business to make him feel like that—a wife and a husband being one person. She had not looked at him once since they sat down; and he wondered what on earth she had been thinking about all the time. It was hard, when a man worked as he did, making money for her—yes, and with an ache in his heart—that she should sit there, looking—looking as if she saw the walls of the room closing in. It was enough to make a man get up and leave the table.

The light from the rose-shaded lamp fell on her neck and arms— Soames liked her to dine in a low dress, it gave him an inexpressible feeling of superiority to the majority of his acquaintance, whose wives were contented with their best high frocks or with tea-gowns, when they dined at home. Under that rosy light her amber-coloured hair and fair skin made strange contrast with her dark brown eyes.

Could a man own anything prettier than this dining-table with its deep tints, the starry, soft-petalled roses, the ruby-coloured glass, and quaint silver furnishing; could a man own anything prettier than the woman who sat at it? Gratitude was no virtue among Forsytes, who, competitive, and full of common-sense, had no occasion for it; and Soames only experienced a sense of exasperation amounting to pain, that he did not own her as it was his right to own her, that he could not, as by stretching out his hand to that rose, pluck her and sniff the very secrets of her heart.

Out of his other property, out of all the things he had collected, his silver, his pictures, his houses, his investments, he got a secret and intimate feeling; out of her he got none.

In this house of his there was writing on every wall. His business-like temperament protested against a mysterious warning that she was not made for him. He had married this woman, conquered her, made her his own, and it seemed to him contrary to the most fundamental of all laws, the law of possession, that he could do no more than own her body—if indeed he could do that, which he was beginning to doubt. If any one had asked him if he wanted to own her soul, the question would have seemed to him both ridiculous and sentimental. But he did so want, and the writing said he never would.

She was ever silent, passive, gracefully averse; as though terrified lest by word, motion, or sign she might lead him to believe that she was fond of him; and he asked himself: Must I always go on like this?

Like most novel readers of his generation (and Soames was a great novel reader), literature coloured his view of life; and he had imbibed the belief that it was only a question of time. In the end the husband always gained the affection of his wife. Even in those cases—a class of book he was not very fond of—which ended in tragedy, the wife always died with poignant regrets on her lips, or if it were the husband who died—unpleasant thought—threw herself on his body in an agony of remorse.

He often took Irene to the theatre, instinctively choosing the modern Society plays with the modern Society conjugal problem, so forunately different from any conjugal problem in real life. He found that they too always ended in the same way, even when there was a lover in the case. While he was watching the play Soames often sympathized with the lover; but before he reached home again, driving with Irene in a han-som, he saw that this would not do, and he was glad the play had ended as it had. There was one class of husband that had just then come into fashion, the strong, rather rough, but extermely sound man, who was peculiarly successful at the end of the play; with this person Soames was really not in sympathy, and had it not been for his own position, would have expressed his disgust with the fellow. But he was so conscious of how vital to himself was the necessity for being a successful, even a 'strong,' husband, that he never spoke of a distaste born perhaps by the perverse processes of Nature out of a secret fund of brutality in himself.

But Irene's silence this evening was exceptional. He had never before seen such an expression on her face. And since it is always the unusual which alarms, Soames was alarmed. He ate his savoury, and hurried the maid as she swept off the crumbs with the silver sweeper. When she had left the room, he filled his glass with wine and said:

"Anybody been here this afternoon?"

"June."

"What did *she* want?" It was an axiom with the Forsytes that people did not go anywhere unless they wanted something. "Came to talk about her lover, I suppose?"

Irene made no reply.

"It looks to me," continued Soames, "as if she were sweeter on him than he is on her. She's always following him about."

Irene's eyes made him feel uncomfortable.

"You've no business to say such a thing!" she exclaimed.

"Why not? Anybody can see it."

"They cannot. And if they could, it's disgraceful to say so."

Soames's composure gave way.

"You're a pretty wife!" he said. But secretly he wondered at the heat of her reply; it was unlike her. "You're cracked about June! I can tell you one thing: now that she has the Buccaneer in tow, she doesn't care twopence about you, and you'll find it out. But you won't see so much of her in future; we're going to live in the country."

He had been glad to get his news out under cover of this burst of irritation. He had expected a cry of dismay; the silence with which his pronouncement was received alarmed him.

"You don't seem interested," he was obliged to add.

"I knew it already."

He looked at her sharply.

"Who told you?"

"June."

"How did she know?"

Irene did not answer. Baffled and uncomfortable, he said:

"It's a fine thing for Bosinney; it'll be the making of him. I suppose she's told you all about it?"

"Yes."

There was another pause, and then Soames said:

"I suppose you don't *want* to go?"

Irene made no reply.

"Well, I can't tell what you want. You never seem contented here."

"Have my wishes anything to do with it?"

She took the vase of roses and left the room. Soames remained seated. Was it for this that he had signed that contract? Was it for this that he was going to spend some ten thousand pounds? Bosinney's phrase came back to him: "Women are the devil!"

But presently he grew calmer. It might have been worse. She might have flared up. He had expected something more than this. It was lucky, after all, that June had broken the ice for him. She must have wormed it out of Bosinney; he might have known she would.

He lighted his cigarette. After all, Irene had not made a scene! She

63

would come round—that was the best of her; she was cold, but not sulky. And, puffing the cigarette smoke at a lady-bird on the shining table, he plunged into a reverie about the house. It was no good worrying; he would go and make it up presently. She would be sitting out there in the dark, under the Japanese sunshade, knitting. A beautiful, warm night. . . .

In truth, June had come in that afternoon with shining eyes, and the words: "Soames is a brick! It's splendid for Phil—the very thing for him!"

Irene's face remaining dark and puzzled, she went on:

"Your new house at Robin Hill, of course. What? Don't you know?"

Irene did not know.

"Oh! then, I suppose I oughtn't to have told you!" Looking impatiently at her friend, she cried: "You look as if you didn't care. Don't you see, it's what I've been praying for—the very chance he's been wanting all this time. Now you'll see what he can do;" and thereupon she poured out the whole story.

Since her own engagement she had not seemed much interested in her friend's position; the hours she spent with Irene were given to confidences of her own; and at times, for all her affectionate pity, it was impossible to keep out of her smile a trace of compassionate contempt for the woman who had made such a mistake in her life—such a vast, ridiculous mistake.

"He's to have all the decorations as well—a free hand. It's perfect——" June broke into laughter, her little figure quivered gleefully; she raised her hand, and struck a blow at a muslin curtain. "Do you know I even asked Uncle James——" But, with a sudden dislike to mentioning that incident, she stopped; and presently, finding her friend so unresponsive, went away. She looked back from the pavement, and Irene was still standing in the doorway. In response to her farewell wave, Irene put her hand to her brow, and, turning slowly, shut the door. . . .

Soames went to the drawing-room presently, and peered at her through the window.

Out in the shadow of the Japanese sunshade she was sitting very still, the lace on her white shoulders stirring with the soft rise and fall of her bosom.

But about this silent creature sitting there so motionless, in the dark, there seemed a warmth, a hidden fervour of feeling, as if the whole of her being had been stirred, and some change were taking place in its very depths.

He stole back to the dining-room unnoticed.

Chapter VI

JAMES AT LARGE

IT was not long before Soames's determination to build went the round of the family, and created the flutter that any decision connected with property should make among Forsytes.

It was not his fault, for he had been determined that no one should know. June, in the fulness of her heart, had told Mrs. Small, giving her leave only to tell Aunt Ann—she thought it would cheer her, the poor old sweet! for Aunt Ann had kept her room now for many days.

Mrs. Small told Aunt Ann at once, who, smiling as she lay back on her pillows, said in her distinct, trembling old voice:

"It's very nice for dear June; but I hope they will be careful—it's rather dangerous!"

When she was left alone again, a frown, like a cloud presaging a rainy morrow, crossed her face.

While she was lying there so many days the process of recharging her will went on all the time; it spread to her face, too, and tightening movements were always in action at the corners of her lips.

The maid Smither, who had been in her service since girlhood, and was spoken of as "Smither—a good girl—but so slow!"—the maid Smither performed every morning with extreme punctiliousness the crowning ceremony of that ancient toilet. Taking from the recesses of their pure white hand-box those flat, grey curls, the insignia of personal dignity, she placed them securely in her mistress's hands, and turned her back.

And every day Aunts Juley and Hester were required to come and report on Timothy; what news there was of Nicholas; whether dear June had succeeded in getting Jolyon to shorten the engagement, now that Mr. Bosinney was building Soames a house; whether young Roger's wife was really—expecting; how the operation on Archie had succeeded; and what Swithin had done about that empty house in Wigmore Street, where the tenant had lost all his money and treated him so badly; above all, about Soames; was Irene still—still asking for a separate room? And every morning Smither was told: "I shall be coming down this after-noon, Smither, about two o'clock. I shall want your arm, after all these days in bed!"

After telling Aunt Ann, Mrs. Small had spoken of the house in the strictest confidence to Mrs. Nicholas, who in her turn had asked Wini-fred Dartie for confirmation, supposing, of course, that, being Soames's sister, she would know all about it. Through her it had in due course come round to the ears of James. He had been a good deal agitated.

"Nobody," he said, "told him anything." And, rather than go direct to Soames himself, of whose taciturnity he was afraid, he took his um-brella and went round to Timothy's.

He found Mrs. Septimus and Hester (who had been told—she was so safe, she found it tiring to talk) ready, and indeed eager, to discuss the news. It was very good of dear Soames, they thought, to employ Mr. Bosinney, but rather risky. What had George named him? 'The Buc-caneer!' How droll! But George was always droll! However, it would be all in the family—they supposed they must really look upon Mr. Bosinney as belonging to the family, though it seemed strange.

James here broke in:

"Nobody knows anything about him. I don't see what Soames wants with a young man like that. I shouldn't be surprised if Irene had put her oar in. I shall speak to——"

"Soames," interposed Aunt Juley, "told Mr. Bosinney that he didn't wish it mentioned. He wouldn't like it to be talked about, I'm sure, and if Timothy knew he would be very vexed, I——"

James put his hand behind his ear:

"What?" he said. "I'm getting very deaf. I suppose I don't hear peo-ple. Emily's got a bad toe. We shan't be able to start for Wales till the end of the month. There's always something!" And, having got what he wanted, he took his hat and went away.

It was a fine afternoon, and he walked across the Park towards Soames's, where he intended to dine, for Emily's toe kept her in bed, and Rachel and Cicely were on a visit to the country. He took the slant-ing path from the Bayswater side of the Row to the Knightsbridge Gate, across a pasture of short, burnt grass, dotted with blackened sheep, strewn with seated couples and strange waifs lying prone on their faces, like corpses on a field over which the wave of battle has rolled.

He walked rapidly, his head bent, looking neither to right nor left.

The appearance of this park, the centre of his own battle-field, where he had all his life been fighting, excited no thought or speculation in his mind. These corpses flung down there from out the press and turmoil of the struggle, these pairs of lovers sitting cheek by jowl for an hour of idle Elysium snatched from the monotony of their treadmill, awakened no fancies in his mind; he had outlived that kind of imagination; his nose, like the nose of a sheep, was fastened to the pastures on which he browsed.

One of his tenants had lately shown a disposition to be behind-hand in his rent, and it had become a grave question whether he had not better turn him out at once, and so run the risk of not re-letting before Christmas. Swithin had just been let in very badly, but it had served him right—he had held on too long.

He pondered this as he walked steadily, holding his umbrella carefully by the wood, just below the crook of the handle, so as to keep the ferule off the ground, and not fray the silk in the middle. And, with his thin, high shoulders stooped, his long legs moving with swift mechanical precision, this passage through the Park, where the sun shone with a clear flame on so much idleness—on so many human evidences of the remorseless battle of Property raging beyond its ring—was like the flight of some land bird across the sea.

He felt a touch on the arm as he came out at Albert Gate.

It was Soames, who, crossing from the shady side of Piccadilly, where he had been walking home from the office, had suddenly appeared alongside.

"Your mother's in bed," said James; "I was just coming to you, but I suppose I shall be in the way."

The outward relations between James and his son were marked by a lack of sentiment peculiarly Forsytean, but for all that the two were by no means unattached. Perhaps they regarded one another as an investment; certainly they were solicitous of each other's welfare, glad of each other's company. They had never exchanged two words upon the more intimate problems of life, or revealed in each other's presence the existence of any deep feeling.

Something beyond the power of word-analysis bound them together, something hidden deep in the fibre of nations and families—for blood, they say, is thicker than water—and neither of them was a cold-blooded man. Indeed, in James love of his children was now the prime motive of his existence. To have creatures who were parts of himself, to whom he might transmit the money he saved, was at the root of his saving; and, at seventy-five, what was left that could give him pleasure, but—saving? The kernel of life was in this saving for his children.

Than James Forsyte, notwithstanding all his 'Jonah-isms,' there was no saner man (if the leading symptom of sanity, as we are told, is self-preservation, though without doubt Timothy went too far) in all this London, of which he owned so much, and loved with such a dumb love, as the centre of his opportunities. He had the marvellous instinctive sanity of the middle class. In him—more than in Jolyon, with his masterful will and his moments of tenderness and philosophy—more than in Swithin, the martyr to crankiness—Nicholas, the sufferer from ability—and Roger, the victim of enterprise—beat the true pulse of compromise; of all the brothers he was least remarkable in mind and person, and for that reason more likely to live for ever.

To James, more than to any of the others, was 'the family' significant and dear. There had always been something primitive and cosy in his attitude towards life; he loved the family hearth, he loved gossip, and he loved grumbling. All his decisions were formed of a cream which he skimmed off the family mind; and, through that family, off the minds of thousands of other families of similar fibre. Year after year, week after week, he went to Timothy's, and in his brother's front drawing-room—his legs twisted, his long white whiskers framing his clean-shaven mouth—would sit watching the family pot simmer, the cream rising to the top; and he would go away sheltered, refreshed, comforted, with an indefinable sense of comfort.

Beneath the adamant of his self-preserving instinct there was much real softness in James; a visit to Timothy's was like an hour spent in the lap of a mother; and the deep craving he himself had for the protection of the family wing reacted in turn on his feelings towards his own children; it was a nightmare to him to think of them exposed to the treatment of the world, in money, health, or reputation. When his old friend John Street's son volunteered for special service, he shook his head querulously, and wondered what John Street was about to allow it; and when young Street was assagaied, he took it so much to heart that he made a point of calling everywhere with the special object of saying: He knew how it would be—he'd no patience with them!

When his son-in-law Dartie had that financial crisis, due to speculation in Oil Shares, James made himself ill worrying over it; the knell of all prosperity seemed to have sounded. It took him three months and a visit to Baden-Baden to get better; there was something terrible in the idea that but for his, James's, money, Dartie's name might have appeared in the Bankruptcy List.

Composed of a physiological mixture so sound that if he had an earache he thought he was dying, he regarded the occasional ailments of his wife and children as in the nature of personal grievances, special interventions of Providence for the purpose of destroying his peace of mind; but he did not believe at all in the ailments of people outside his own immediate family, affirming them in every case to be due to neglected liver.

His universal comment was: "What can they expect? I have it myself, if I'm not careful!"

When he went to Soames's that evening he felt that life was hard on him: There was Emily with a bad toe, and Rachel gadding about in the country; he got no sympathy from anybody; and Ann, she was ill—he did not believe she would last through the summer; he had called there three times now without her being able to see him! And this idea of Soames's, building a house, *that* would have to be looked into. As to the trouble with Irene, he didn't know what was to come of that—anything might come of it!

He entered 62, Montpellier Square with the fullest intentions of being miserable.

It was already half-past seven, and Irene, dressed for dinner, was seated in the drawing-room. She was wearing her gold-coloured frock—for, having been displayed at a dinner-party, a soirée, and a dance, it was now to be worn at home—and she had adorned the bosom with a cascade of lace, on which James's eyes riveted themselves at once.

"Where do you get your things?" he said in an aggravated voice. "I never see Rachel and Cicely looking half so well. That rose-point, now—that's not real!"

Irene came close, to prove to him that he was in error.

And, in spite of himself, James felt the influence of her deference, of the faint seductive perfume exhaling from her. No self-respecting Forsyte surrendered at a blow; so he merely said: He didn't know—he expected she was spending a pretty penny on dress.

The gong sounded, and, putting her white arm within his, Irene took

him into the dining-room. She seated him in Soames's usual place, round
the corner on her left. The light fell softly there, so that he would not
be worried by the gradual dying of the day; and she began to talk to him
about himself.

Presently, over James came a change, like the mellowing that steals
upon a fruit in the sun; a sense of being caressed, and praised, and
petted, and all without the bestowal of a single caress or word of praise.
He felt that what he was eating was agreeing with him; he could not
get that feeling at home; he did not know when he had enjoyed a glass
of champagne so much, and, on inquiring the brand and price, was
surprised to find that it was one of which he had a large stock himself,
but could never drink; he instantly formed the resolution to let his
wine merchant know that he had been swindled.

Looking up from his food, he remarked:

"You've a lot of nice things about the place. Now, what did you give
for that sugar-sifter? Shouldn't wonder if it was worth money!"

He was particularly pleased with the appearance of a picture on the
wall opposite, which he himself had given them:

"I'd no idea it was so good!" he said.

They rose to go into the drawing-room, and James followed Irene
closely.

"That's what I call a capital little dinner," he murmured, breathing
pleasantly down on her shoulder; "nothing heavy—and not too Frenchified. But *I* can't get it at home. I pay my cook sixty pounds a year, but
she can't give me a dinner like that!"

He had as yet made no allusion to the building of the house, nor did
he when Soames, pleading the excuse of business, betook himself to the
room at the top, where he kept his pictures.

James was left alone with his daughter-in-law. The glow of the wine,
and of an excellent liqueur, was still within him. He felt quite warm
towards her. She was really a taking little thing; she listened to you, and
seemed to understand what you were saying; and, while talking, he kept
examining her figure, from her bronze-coloured shoes to the waved gold
of her hair. She was leaning back in an Empire chair, her shoulders
poised against the top—her body, flexibly straight and unsupported
from the hips, swaying when she moved, as though giving to the arms
of a lover. Her lips were smiling, her eyes half-closed.

It may have been a recognition of danger in the very charm of her

71

attitude, or a twang of digestion, that caused a sudden dumbness to fall on James. He did not remember ever having been quite alone with Irene before. And, as he looked at her, an odd feeling crept over him, as though he had come across something strange and foreign.

Now what was she thinking about—sitting back like that?

Thus when he spoke it was in a sharper voice, as if he had been awakened from a pleasant dream.

"What d'you do with yourself all day?" he said. "You never come round to Park Lane!"

She seemed to be making very lame excuses, and James did not look at her. He did not want to believe that she was really avoiding them— it would mean too much.

"I expect the fact is, you haven't time," he said; "you're always about with June. I expect you're useful to her with her young man, chaperoning, and one thing and another. They tell me she's never at home now; your Uncle Jolyon he doesn't like it, I fancy, being left so much alone as he is. They tell me she's always hanging about for this young Bosinney; I suppose he comes here every day. Now, what do *you* think of him? D'you think he knows his own mind? He seems to me a poor thing. I should say the grey mare was the better horse!"

The colour deepened in Irene's face; and James watched her suspiciously.

"Perhaps you don't quite understand Mr. Bosinney," she said.

"Don't understand him!" James hurried out: "Why not?—you can see he's one of these artistic chaps. They say he's clever—they all think they're clever. You know more about him than I do," he added; and again his suspicious glance rested on her.

"He is designing a house for Soames," she said softly, evidently trying to smooth things over.

"That brings me to what I was going to say," continued James; "I don't know what Soames wants with a young man like that; why doesn't he go to a first-rate man?"

"Perhaps Mr. Bosinney is first-rate!"

James rose, and took a turn with bent head.

"That's it," he said, "you young people, you all stick together; you all think you know best!"

Halting his tall, lank figure before her, he raised a finger, and levelled it at her bosom, as though bringing an indictment against her beauty:

"All I can say is, these artistic people, or whatever they call themselves, they're as unreliable as they can be; and my advice to *you* is, don't you have too much to do with him!"

Irene smiled; and in the curve of her lips was a strange provocation. She seemed to have lost her deference. Her breast rose and fell as though with secret anger; she drew her hands inwards from their rest on the arms of her chair until the tips of her fingers met, and her dark eyes looked unfathomably at James.

The latter gloomily scrutinized the floor.

"I tell you my opinion," he said, "it's a pity you haven't got a child to think about, and occupy you!

A brooding look came instantly on Irene's face, and even James became conscious of the rigidity that took possession of her whole figure beneath the softness of its silk and lace clothing.

He was frightened by the effect he had produced, and, like most men with but little courage, he sought at once to justify himself by bullying.

"You don't seem to care about going about. Why don't you drive down to Hurlingham with us? And go to the theatre now and then. At your time of life you ought to take an interest in things. You're a young woman!"

The brooding look darkened on her face; he grew nervous.

"Well, I know nothing about it," he said; "nobody tells me anything. Soames ought to able to take care of himself. If he can't take care of himself he mustn't look to me—that's all——"

Biting the corner of his forefinger he stole a cold, sharp look at his daughter-in-law.

He encountered her eyes fixed on his own, so dark and deep, that he stopped, and broke into a gentle perspiration.

"Well, I must be going," he said after a short pause, and a minute later rose, with a slight appearance of surprise, as though he had expected to be asked to stop. Giving his hand to Irene, he allowed himself to be conducted to the door, and let out into the street. He would not have a cab, he would walk, Irene was to say good-night to Soames for him, and if she wanted a little gaiety, well, he would drive her down to Richmond any day.

He walked home, and going upstairs, woke Emily out of the first sleep she had had for four and twenty hours, to tell her that it was his impression things were in a bad way at Soames's; on this theme he descanted for half an hour, until at last, saying that he would not sleep a wink, he turned on his side and instantly began to snore.

In Montpellier Square Soames, who had come from the picture room, stood invisible at the top of the stairs, watching Irene sort the letters brought by the last post. She turned back into the drawing-room; but in a minute came out, and stood as if listening. Then she came stealing up the stairs, with a kitten in her arms. He could see her face bent over the little beast, which was purring against her neck. Why couldn't she look at him like that?

Suddenly she saw him, and her face changed.

"Any letters for me?" he said.

"Three."

He stood aside, and without another word she passed on into the bedroom.

Chapter VII

OLD JOLYON'S PECCADILLO

O LD JOLYON came out of Lord's cricket ground that same afternoon with the intention of going home. He had not reached
Hamilton Terrace before he changed his mind, and hailing a cab, gave
the driver an address in Wistaria Avenue. He had taken a resolution.

June had hardly been at home at all that week; she had given him
nothing of her company for a long time past, not, in fact, since she had
become engaged to Bosinney. He never asked her for her company. It
was not his habit to ask people for things! She had just that one idea
now—Bosinney and his affairs—and she left him stranded in his great
house, with a parcel of servants, and not a soul to speak to from morning to night. His Club was closed for cleaning; his Boards in recess;
there was nothing, therefore, to take him into the City. June had
wanted him to go away; she would not go herself, because Bosinney
was in London.

But where was he to go by himself? He could not go abroad alone;
the sea upset his liver; he hated hotels. Roger went to a hydropathic—
he was not going to begin that at his time of life, those new-fangled
places were all humbug!

With such formulas he clothed to himself the desolation of his spirit;
the lines down his face deepening, his eyes day by day looking forth
with the melancholy which sat so strangely on a face wont to be strong
and serene.

And so that afternoon he took this journey through St. John's Wood,
in the golden light that sprinkled the rounded green bushes of the
acacias before the little houses, in the summer sunshine that seemed
holding a revel over the little gardens; and he looked about him with
interest; for this was a district which no Forsyte entered without open
disapproval and secret curiosity.

His cab stopped in front of a small house of that peculiar buff colour which implies a long immunity from paint. It had an outer gate, and a rustic approach.

He stepped out, his bearing extremely composed; his massive head, with its drooping moustache and wings of white hair, very upright, under an excessively large top hat; his glance firm, a little angry. He had been driven into this!

"Mrs. Jolyon Forsyte at home?"

"Oh, yes, sir!—what name shall I say, if you please, sir?"

Old Jolyon could not help twinkling at the little maid as he gave his name. She seemed to him such a funny little toad!

And he followed her through the dark hall, into a small double drawing-room, where the furniture was covered in chintz, and the little maid placed him in a chair.

"They're all in the garden, sir; if you'll kindly take a seat, I'll tell them."

Old Jolyon sat down in the chintz-covered chair, and looked around him. The whole place seemed to him, as he would have expressed it, pokey; there was a certain—he could not tell exactly what—air of shab-biness, or rather of making two ends meet, about everything. As far as he could see, not a single piece of furniture was worth a five-pound note. The walls, distempered rather a long time ago, were decorated with water-colour sketches; across the ceiling meandered a long crack.

These little houses were all old, second-rate concerns; he should hope the rent was under a hundred a year; it hurt him more than he could have said, to think of a Forsyte—his own son—living in such a place.

The little maid came back. Would he please to go down into the garden?

Old Jolyon marched out through the French windows. In descending the steps he noticed that they wanted painting.

Young Jolyon, his wife, his two children, and his dog, Balthasar, were all out there under a pear-tree.

This walk towards them was the most courageous act of old Jolyon's life; but no muscle of his face moved, no nervous gesture betrayed him. He kept his deep-set eyes steadily on the enemy.

In those two minutes he demonstrated to perfection all that uncon-scious soundness, balance, and vitality of fibre that made of him and so many others of his class the core of the nation. In the unostentatious

conduct of their own affairs, to the neglect of everything else, they typi-
fied the essential individualism, born in the Briton from the natural
isolation of his country's life.

The dog Balthasar sniffed round the edges of his trousers; this
friendly and cynical mongrel—offspring of a liaison between a Russian
poodle and a fox-terrier—had a nose for the unusual.

The strange greetings over, old Jolyon seated himself in a wicker
chair, and his two grandchildren, one on each side of his knees, looked
at him silently, never having seen so old a man.

They were unlike, as though recognizing the difference set between
them by the circumstances of their births. Jolly, the child of sin, pudgy-
faced, with his tow-coloured hair brushed off his forehead, and a dimple
in his chin, had an air of stubborn amiability, and the eyes of a Forsyte;
little Holly, the child of wedlock, was a dark-skinned, solemn soul, with
her mother's grey and wistful eyes.

The dog Balthasar, having walked round the three small flowerbeds,
to show his extreme contempt for things at large, had also taken a seat
in front of old Jolyon, and, oscillating a tail curled by Nature tightly
over his back, was staring up with eyes that did not blink.

Even in the garden, that sense of things being pokey haunted old
Jolyon; the wicker chair creaked under his weight; the garden-beds
looked 'daverdy'; on the far side, under the smut-stained wall, cats had
made a path.

While he and his grandchildren thus regarded each other with the
peculiar scrutiny, curious yet trustful, that passes between the very
young and the very old, young Jolyon watched his wife.

The colour had deepened in her thin, oval face, with its straight
brows, and large, grey eyes. Her hair, brushed in fine, high curves back
from her forehead, was going grey, like his own, and this greyness made
the sudden vivid colour in her cheeks painfully pathetic.

The look on her face, such as he had never seen before, such as
she had always hidden from him, was full of secret resentments, and
longings, and fears. Her eyes, under their twitching brows, stared painfully. And she was silent.

Jolly alone sustained the conversation; he had many possessions, and
was anxious that his unknown friend with extremely large moustaches,
and hands all covered with blue veins, who sat with legs crossed like

his own father (a habit he was himself trying to acquire), should know it; but being a Forsyte, though not yet quite eight years old, he made no mention of the thing at the moment dearest to his heart—a camp of soldiers in a shop-window, which his father had promised to buy. No doubt it seemed to him too precious; a tempting of Providence to mention it yet.

And the sunlight played through the leaves on that little party of the three generations grouped tranquilly under the pear-tree, which had long borne no fruit.

Old Jolyon's furrowed face was reddening patchily, as old men's faces redden in the sun. He took one of Jolly's hands in his own; the boy climbed on to his knee; and little Holly, mesmerized by this sight, crept up to them; the sound of the dog Balthasar's scratching arose rhythmically.

Suddenly young Mrs. Jolyon got up and hurried indoors. A minute later her husband muttered an excuse, and followed. Old Jolyon was left alone with his grandchildren.

And Nature with her quaint irony began working in him one of her strange revolutions, following her cyclic laws into the depths of his heart. And that tenderness for little children, that passion for the beginnings of life which had once made him forsake his son and follow June, now worked in him to forsake June and follow these littler things. Youth, like a flame, burned ever in his breast, and to youth he turned, to the round little limbs, so reckless, that wanted care, to the small round faces so unreasonably solemn or bright, to the treble tongues, and the shrill, chuckling laughter, to the insistent tugging hands, and the feel of small bodies against his legs, to all that was young and young, and once more young. And his eyes grew soft, his voice, and thin, veined hands soft, and soft his heart within him. And to those small creatures he became at once a place of pleasure, a place where they were secure, and could talk and laugh and play; till, like sunshine, there radiated from old Jolyon's wicker chair the perfect gaiety of three hearts.

But with young Jolyon following to his wife's room it was different.

He found her seated on a chair before her dressing-glass, with her hands before her face.

Her shoulders were shaking with sobs. This passion of hers for suffering was mysterious to him. He had been through a hundred of these moods; how he had survived them he never knew, for he could never believe they *were* moods, and that the last hour of his partnrship had not struck.

In the night she would be sure to throw her arms round his neck and say: "Oh! Jo, how I make you suffer!" as she had done a hundred times before.

He reached out his hand, and, unseen, slipped his razor-case into his pocket.

'I can't stay here,' he thought, 'I must go down!' Without a word he left the room, and went back to the lawn.

Old Jolyon had little Holly on his knee; she had taken possession of his watch; Jolly, very red in the face, was trying to show that he could stand on his head. The dog Balthasar, as close as he might be to the tea-table, had fixed his eyes on the cake.

Young Jolyon felt a malicious desire to cut their enjoyment short.

What business had his father to come and upset his wife like this? It was a shock, after all these years! He ought to have known; he ought to have given them warning; but when did a Forsyte ever imagine that his conduct could upset anybody! And in his thoughts he did old Jolyon wrong.

He spoke sharply to the children, and told them to go in to their tea. Greatly surprised, for they had never heard their father speak sharply before, they went off, hand in hand, little Holly looking back over her shoulder.

Young Jolyon poured out the tea.

"My wife's not the thing today," he said, but he knew well enough that his father had penetrated the cause of that sudden withdrawal, and almost hated the old man for sitting there so calmly.

"You've got a nice little house here," said old Jolyon with a shrewd look; "I suppose you've taken a lease of it!"

Young Jolyon nodded.

"I don't like the neighborhood," said old Jolyon; "a ramshackle lot."

Young Jolyon replied: "Yes, we're a ramshackle lot."

The silence was now only broken by the sound of the dog Balthasar's scratching.

Old Jolyon said simply: "I suppose I oughtn't have come here, Jo; but I get so lonely!"

At these words young Jolyon got up and put his hand on his father's shoulder.

In the next house someone was playing over and over again: 'La Donna è mobile' on an untuned piano; and the little garden had fallen into shade, the sun now only reached the wall at the end, whereon basked a crouching cat, her yellow eyes turned sleepily down on the dog Balthasar. There was a drowsy hum of very distant traffic; the creepered trellis round the garden shut out everything but sky, and house, and pear-tree, with its top branches still gilded by the sun.

For some time they sat there, talking but little. Then old Jolyon rose to go, and not a word was said about his coming again.

He walked away very sadly. What a poor miserable place; and he thought of the great, empty house in Stanhope Gate, fit residence for a Forsyte, with its huge billiard-room and drawing-room that no one entered from one week's end to another.

That woman, whose face he had rather liked, was too thin-skinned by half; she gave Jo a bad time he knew! And those sweet children! Ah! what a piece of awful folly!

He walked towards the Edgware Road, between rows of little houses, all suggesting to him (erroneously no doubt, but the prejudices of a Forsyte are sacred) shady histories of some sort or kind.

Society, forsooth, the chattering hags and jackanapes—had set themselves up to pass judgment on *his* flesh and blood! A parcel of old women! He stumped his umbrella on the ground, as though to drive it into the heart of that unfortunate body, which had dared to ostracize his son and his son's son, in whom he could have lived again!

He stumped his umbrella fiercely; yet he himself had followed Society's behaviour for fifteen years—had only to-day been false to it!

He thought of June, and her dead mother, and the whole story, with all his old bitterness. A wretched business!

He was a long time reaching Stanhope Gate, for, with native perversity, being extremely tired, he walked the whole way.

After washing his hands in the lavatory downstairs, he went to the dining-room to wait for dinner, the only room he used when June was out—it was less lonely so. The evening paper had not yet come; he had finished the *Times,* there was therefore nothing to do.

The room faced the backwater of traffic, and was very silent. He disliked dogs, but a dog even would have been company. His gaze, travelling round the walls, rested on a picture entitled: 'Group of Dutch fishing boats at sunset'; the *chef d'oeuvre* of his collection. It gave him no pleasure. He closed his eyes. He was lonely! He oughtn't to complain, he knew, but he couldn't help it: He was a poor thing—had always been a poor thing—no pluck! Such was his thought.

The butler came to lay the table for dinner, and seeing his master apparently asleep, exercised extreme caution in his movements. This bearded man also wore a moustache, which had given rise to grave doubts in the minds of many members of the family—especially those who, like Soames, had been to public schools, and were accustomed to niceness in such matters. Could he really be considered a butler? Playful spirits alluded to him as 'Uncle Jolyon's Nonconformist'; George, the acknowledged wag, had named him: 'Sankey.'

He moved to and fro between the great polished sideboard and the great polished table inimitably sleek and soft.

Old Jolyon watched him, feigning sleep. The fellow was a sneak—he had always thought so—who cared about nothing but rattling through his work, and getting out to his betting or his woman or goodness knew what! A slug! Fat too! And didn't care a pin about his master!

But then against his will, came one of those moments of philosophy which made old Jolyon different from the other Forsytes:

After all why should the man care? He wasn't paid to care, and why expect it? In this world people couldn't look for affection unless they paid for it. It might be different in the next—he didn't know—couldn't tell! And again he shut his eyes.

Relentless and stealthy, the butler pursued his labours, taking things from the various compartments of the sideboard. His back seemed always turned to old Jolyon; thus, he robbed his operations of the unseemliness of being carried on in his master's presence; now and then he furtively breathed on the silver, and wiped it with a piece of chamois leather. He appeared to pore over the quantities of wine in the decanters, which he carried carefully and rather high, letting his beard droop over them protectingly. When he had finished, he stood for over a minute watching his master, and in his greenish eyes there was a look of contempt:

After all, this master of his was an old buffer, who hadn't much left in him!

Soft as a tom-cat, he crossed the room to press the bell. His orders were 'dinner at seven.' What if his master were asleep; he would soon have him out of that; there was the night to sleep in! He had himself to think of, for he was due at his Club at half-past eight!

In answer to the ring, appeared a page boy with a silver soup toureen. The butler took it from his hands and placed it on the table, then, standing by the open door, as though about to usher company into the room, he said in a solemn voice:

"Dinner is on the table, sir!"

Slowly old Jolyon got up out of his chair, and sat down at the table to eat his dinner.

Chapter VIII

PLANS OF THE HOUSE

A LL FORSYTES, as is generally admitted, have shells, like that extremely useful little animal which is made into Turkish delight; in other words, they are never seen, or if seen would not be
recognised, without habitats, composed of circumstance, property, acquaintances, and wives, which seem to move along with them in their
passage through a world composed of thousands of other Forsytes with
their habitats. Without a habitat a Forsyte is inconceivable—he would
be like a novel without a plot which is well-known to be an anomaly.

To Forsyte eyes Bosinney appeared to have no habitat, he seemed
one of those rare and unfortunate men who go through life surrounded
by circumstance, property, acquaintances, and wives that do not belong
to them.

His rooms in Sloane Street, on the top floor, outside which, on a
plate, was his name, 'Philip Baynes Bosinney, Architect,' were not those
of a Forsyte. He had no sitting-room apart from his office, but a large
recess had been screened off to conceal the necessaries of life—a couch,
an easy chair, his pipes, spirit case, novels, and slippers. The business
part of the room had the usual furniture; an open cupboard with
pigeon-holes, a round oak table, a folding wash-stand, some hard chairs,
a standing desk of large dimensions covered with drawings and designs.
June had twice been to tea there under the chaperonage of his aunt.

He was believed to have a bedroom at the back.

As far as the family had been able to ascertain his income, it con-
sisted of two consulting appointments at twenty pounds a year, together
with an odd fee once in a while, and—more worthy item—a private
annuity under his father's will of one hundred and fifty pounds a year.

What had transpired concerning that father was not so reassuring. It
appeared that he had been a Lincolnshire country doctor of Cornish
extraction, striking appearance, and Byronic tendencies—a well-known
figure, in fact, in his country. Bosinney's uncle by marriage, Baynes, of

Baynes and Bildeboy, a Forsyte in instincts if not in name, had but little that was worthy to relate of his brother-in-law.

"An odd fellow!" he would say: "always spoke of his three eldest boys as 'good creatures, but so dull'; they're all doing capitally in the Indian Civil! Philip was the only one *he* liked. I've heard him talk in the queerest way; he once said to me: 'My dear fellow, never let your poor wife know what you're thinking of!' But I didn't follow his advice; not I! An eccentric man! He would say to Phil: 'Whether you live like a gentleman or not, my boy, be sure you die like one!' and he had himself embalmed in a frock coat suit, with a satin cravat and a diamond pin. Oh, quite an original, I can assure you!"

Of Bosinney himself Baynes would speak warmly, with a certain compassion: "He's got a streak of his father's Byronism. Why, look at the way he threw up his chances when he left my office; going off like that for six months with a knapsack, and all for what?—to study foreign architecture—foreign! What could he expect? And there he is—a clever young fellow—doesn't make his hundred a year! Now this engagement is the best thing that could have happened—keep him steady; he's one of those that go to bed all day and stay up all night, simply because they've no method; but no vice about him—not an ounce of vice. Old Forsyte's a rich man!"

Mr. Baynes made himself extremely pleasant to June, who frequently visited his house in Lowndes Square at this period.

"This house of your cousin's—what a capital man of business—is the very thing for Philip," he would say to her; "you mustn't expect to see too much of him just now, my dear young lady. The good cause—the good cause! The young man must make his way. When I was his age I was at work day and night. My dear wife used to say to me, 'Bobby, don't work too hard, think of your health'; but I never spared myself!"

June had complained that her lover found no time to come to Stanhope Gate.

The first time he came again they had not been together a quarter of an hour before, by one of those coincidences of which she was a mistress, Mrs. Septimus Small arrived. Thereon Bosinney rose and hid himself, according to previous arrangement, in the little study, to wait for her departure.

"My dear," said Aunt Juley, "how thin he is! I've often noticed it with engaged people; but you mustn't let it get worse. There's Barlow's extract of veal; it did your Uncle Swithin a lot of good."

June, her little figure erect before the hearth, her small face quivering grimly, for she regarded her aunt's untimely visit in the light of a personal injury, replied with scorn:

"It's because he's busy; people who can do anything worth doing are never fat!"

Aunt Juley pouted; she herself had always been thin, but the only pleasure she derived from the fact was the opportunity of longing to be stouter.

"I don't think," she said mournfully, "that you ought to let them call him 'The Buccaneer'; people might think it odd, now that he's going to build a house for Soames. I do hope he will be careful; it's so important for him. Soames has such good taste!"

"Taste!" cried June, flaring up at once; "I wouldn't give that for his taste, or any of the family's!"

Mrs. Small was taken aback.

"Your Uncle Swithin," she said, "always had beautiful taste! And Soames's little house is lovely; you don't mean to say you don't think so!"

"H'mph!" said June, "that's only because Irene's there!"

Aunt Juley tried to say something pleasant:

"And how will dear Irene like living in the country?"

June gazed at her intently, with a look in her eyes as if her conscience had suddenly leaped up into them; it passed; and an even more intent look took its place, as if she had stared that conscience out of countenance. She replied imperiously:

"Of course she'll like it; why shouldn't she?"

Mrs. Small grew nervous.

"I didn't know," she said; "I thought she mightn't like to leave her friends. Your Uncle James says she doesn't take enough interest in life. *We* think—I mean Timothy thinks—she ought to go out more. I expect you'll miss her very much!"

June clasped her hands behind her neck.

"I do wish," she cried, "Uncle Timothy wouldn't talk about what doesn't concern him!"

Aunt Juley rose to the full height of her tall figure.

"He never talks about what doesn't concern him," she said.

June was instantly compunctuous; she ran to her aunt and kissed her. "I'm very sorry, auntie; but I wish they'd let Irene alone."

Aunt Juley, unable to think of anything further on the subject that would be suitable, was silent; she prepared for departure, hooking her black silk cape across her chest, and, taking up her green reticule:

"And how is your dear grandfather?" she asked in the hall, "I expect he's very lonely now that all your time is taken up with Mr. Bosinney." She bent and kissed her niece hungrily, and with little, mincing steps passed away.

The tears sprang up in June's eyes; running into the little study, where Bosinney was sitting at the table drawing birds on the back of an envelope, she sank down by his side and cried:

"Oh, Phil! it's all so horrid!" Her heart was as warm as the colour of her hair.

On the following Sunday morning, while Soames was shaving, a message was brought him to the effect that Mr. Bosinney was below, and would be glad to see him. Opening the door into his wife's room, he said:

"Bosinney's downstairs. Just go and entertain him while I finish shaving. I'll be down in a minute. It's about the plans, I expect."

Irene looked at him, without reply, put the finishing touch to her dress and went downstairs.

He could not make her out about this house. She had said nothing against it, and, as far as Bosinney was concerned, seemed friendly enough.

From the window of his dressing-room he could see them talking together in the little court below.

He hurried on with his shaving, cutting his chin twice. He heard them laugh, and thought to himself: "Well, they get on all right, anyway!"

As he expected, Bosinney had come round to fetch him to look at the plans.

He took his hat and went over.

The plans were spread on the oak table in the architect's room; and pale, imperturbable, inquiring, Soames bent over them for a long time without speaking.

He said at last with a puzzled voice:

"It's an odd sort of house!"

A rectangular house of two stories was designed in a quadrangle round a covered-in court. This court, encircled by a gallery on the upper floor, was roofed with a glass roof, supported by eight coulmns running up from the ground.

It was indeed, to Forsyte eyes, an odd house.

"There's a lot of room cut to waste," pursued Soames.

Bosinney began to walk about, and Soames did not like the expression on his face.

"The principle of this house," said the architect, "was that you should have room to breathe—like a gentleman!"

Soames extended his finger and thumb, as if measuring the extent of the distinction he should acquire, and replied:

"Oh! yes; I see."

The peculiar look came into Bosinney's face which marked all his enthusiasms.

"I've tried to plan you a house with some self-respect of its own. If you don't like it, you'd better say so. It's certainly the last thing to be considered—who wants self-respect in a house, when you can squeeze in an extra lavatory?" He put his finger suddenly down on the left division of the centre oblong: "You can swing a cat here. This is for your pictures, divided from this court by curtains; draw them back and you'll have a space of fifty-one by twenty-three six. This double-face stove in the centre, here, looks one way towards the court, one way towards the picture room; this end wall is all window; you've a south-east light from that, a north light from the court. The rest of your pictures you can hang round the gallery upstairs, or in the other rooms. In architecture," he went on—and though looking at Soames he did not seem to see him, which gave Soames an unpleasant feeling—"as in life, you'll get no self-respect without regularity. Fellows tell you that's old fashioned. It appears to be peculiar any way; it never occurs to us to embody the main principle of life in our buildings; we load our houses with decoration, gimcracks, corners, anything to distract the eye. On the contrary the eye should rest; get your effects with a few strong lines. The whole thing is regularity—there's no self-respect without it."

Soames, the unconscious ironist, fixed his gaze on Bosinney's tie, which was far from being in the perpendicular; he was unshaven too, and his dress not remarkable for order. Architecture appeared to have exhausted his regularity.

"Won't it look like a barrack?" he inquired.

He did not at once receive a reply.

"I can see what it is," said Bosinney, "you want one of Littlemaster's houses—one of the pretty and commodious sort, where the servants will live in garrets, and the front door be sunk so that you may come up again. By all means try Littlemaster, you'll find him a capital fellow, I've known him all my life!"

Soames was alarmed. He had really been struck by the plans, and the concealment of his satisfaction had been merely instinctive. It was difficult for him to pay a compliment. He despised people who were lavish with their praises.

He found himself now in the embarrassing position of one who must pay a compliment or run the risk of losing a good thing. Bosinney was just the fellow who might tear up the plans and refuse to act for him; a kind of grown-up child!

This grown-up childishness, to which he felt so superior, exercised a peculiar and almost mesmeric effect on Soames, for he had never felt anything like it in himself.

"Well," he stammered at last, "it's—it's certainly original."

He had such a private distrust and even dislike of the word 'original' that he felt he had not really given himself away by this remark.

Bosinney seemed pleased. It was the sort of thing that *would* please a fellow like that! And his success encouraged Soames.

"It's—a big place," he said.

"Space, air, light," he heard Bosinney murmur, "you can't live like a gentleman in one of Littlemaster's—he builds for manufacturers."

Soames made a deprecating movement; he had been identified with a gentleman; not for a good deal of money now would he be classed with manufacturers. But his innate distrust of general principles revived. What the deuce was the good of talking about regularity and self-respect? It looked to him as if the house would be cold.

"Irene can't stand the cold!" he said.

"Ah!" said Bosinney sarcastically. "Your wife? She doesn't like the cold? I'll see to that; she shan't be cold. Look here!" he pointed to four marks at regular intervals on the walls of the court. "I've given you hot-water pipes in aluminum casings; you can get them with very good designs."

Soames looked suspiciously at these marks.

"It's all very well, all this," he said, "but what's it going to cost?"

The architect took a sheet of paper from his pocket.

"The house, of course, should be built entirely of stone, but, as I thought you wouldn't stand that, I've compromised for a facing. It ought to have a copper roof, but I've made it green slate. As it is, including metal work, it'll cost you eight thousand five hundred."

"Eight thousand five hundred?" said Soames. "Why, I gave you an outside limit of eight!"

"Can't be done for a penny less," replied Bosinney coolly. "You must take it or leave it!"

It was the only way, probably, that such a proposition could have been made to Soames. He was nonplussed. Conscience told him to throw the whole thing up. But the design was good, and he knew it—there was completeness about it, and dignity; the servants' apartments were excellent too. He would gain credit by living in a house like that—with such individual features, yet perfectly well-arranged.

He continued poring over the plans, while Bosinney went into his bedroom to shave and dress.

The two walked back to Montpellier Square in silence, Soames watching him out of the corner of his eye.

The Buccaneer was rather a good-looking fellow—so he thought—when he was properly got up.

Irene was bending over her flowers when the two men came in.

She spoke of sending across the Park to fetch June.

"No, no," said Soames, "we've still got business to talk over!"

At lunch he was almost cordial, and kept pressing Bosinney to eat. He was pleased to see the architect in such high spirits, and left him to spend the afternoon with Irene, while he stole off to his pictures, after his Sunday habit. At tea-time he came down to the drawing-room, and found them talking, as he expressed it, nineteen to the dozen.

Unobserved in the doorway, he congratulated himself that things were taking the right turn. It was lucky she and Bosinney got on; she seemed to be falling into line with the idea of the new house.

Quiet meditation among his pictures had decided him to spring the five hundred if necessary; but he hoped that the afternoon might have softened Bosinney's estimates. It was so purely a matter which Bosinney could remedy if he liked; there must be a dozen ways in which he could cheapen the production of a house without spoiling the effect.

He awaited, therefore, his opportunity till Irene was handing the architect his first cup of tea. A chink of sunshine through the lace of the blinds warmed her cheek, shone in the gold of her hair, and in her soft eyes. Possibly the same gleam deepened Bosinney's colour, gave the rather startled look to his face.

Soames hated sunshine, and he at once got up to draw the blind. Then he took his own cup of tea from his wife, and said, more coldly than he had intended:

"Can't you see your way to do it for eight thousand after all? There must be a lot of little things you could alter."

Bosinney drank off his tea at a gulp, put down his cup, and answered:

"Not one!"

Soames saw that his suggestion had touched some unintelligible point of personal vanity.

"Well," he agreed, with sulky resignation; "you must have it your own way, I suppose."

A few minutes later Bosinney rose to go, and Soames rose too, to see him off the premises. The architect seemed in absurdly high spirits. After watching him walk away at a swinging pace, Soames returned moodily to the drawing-room, where Irene was putting away the music, and, moved by an uncontrollable spasm of curiosity, he asked:

"Well, what do you think of 'The Buccaneer'?"

He looked at the carpet while waiting for her answer, and he had to wait some time.

"I don't know," she said at last.

"Do you think he's good-looking?"

Irene smiled. And it seemed to Soames that she was mocking him.

"Yes," she answered; "very."

Chapter IX

DEATH OF AUNT ANN

THERE came a morning at the end of September when Aunt Ann was unable to take from Smither's hands the insignia of personal dignity. After one look at the old face, the doctor, hurriedly sent for, announced that Miss Forsyte had passed away in her sleep.

Aunts Juley and Hester were overwhelmed by the shock. They had never imagined such an ending. Indeed, it is doubtful whether they had ever realized that an ending was bound to come. Secretly they felt it unreasonable of Ann to have left them like this without a word, without even a struggle. It was unlike her.

Perhaps what really affected them so profoundly was the thought that a Forsyte should have let go her grasp on life. If one, then why not all!

It was a full hour before they could make up their minds to tell Timothy. If only it could be kept from him! If only it could be broken to him by degrees!

And long they stood outside his door whispering together. And when it was over they whispered together again.

He would feel it more, they were afraid, as time went on. Still, he had taken it better than could have been expected. He would keep his bed, of course!

They separated, crying quietly.

Aunt Juley stayed in her room, prostrated by the blow. Her face, discoloured by tears, was divided into compartments by the little ridges of pouting flesh which had swollen with emotion. It was impossible to conceive of life without Ann, who had lived with her for seventy-three years, broken only by the short interregnum of her married life, which seemed now so unreal. At fixed intervals she went to her drawer, and took from beneath the lavender bags a fresh pocket-handkerchief. Her warm heart could not bear the thought that Ann was lying there so cold.

Aunt Hester, the silent, the patient, that backwater of the family energy, sat in the drawing-room, where the blinds were drawn; and she, too, had wept at first, but quietly, without visible effect. Her guiding principle, the conservation of energy, did not abandon her in sorrow. She sat, slim, motionless, studying the grate, her hands idle in the lap of her black silk dress. They would want to rouse her into doing something, no doubt. As if there were any good in that! Doing something would not bring back Ann! Why worry her?

Five o'clock brought three of the brothers, Jolyon and James and Swithin; Nicholas was at Yarmouth, and Roger had a bad attack of gout. Mrs. Hayman had been by herself earlier in the day, and, after seeing Ann, had gone away, leaving a message for Timothy—which was kept from him—that she ought to have been told sooner. In fact, there was a feeling amongst them all that they ought to have been told sooner, as though they had missed something; and James said:

"I knew how it'd be; I told you she wouldn't last through the summer."

Aunt Hester made no reply; it was nearly October, but what was the good of arguing; some people were never satisfied.

She sent up to tell her sister that the brothers were there. Mrs. Small came down at once. She had bathed her face, which was still swollen, and though she looked severely at Swithin's trousers, for they were of light blue—he had come straight from the club, where the news had reached him—she wore a more cheerful expression than usual, the instinct for doing the wrong thing being even now too strong for her.

Presently all five went up to look at the body. Under the pure white sheet a quilted counterpane had been placed, for now, more than ever, Aunt Ann had need of warmth; and, the pillows removed, her spine and head rested flat, with the semblance of their life-long inflexibility; the coif banding the top of her brow was drawn on either side to the level of the ears, and between it and the sheet her face, almost as white, was turned with closed eyes to the faces of her brothers and sisters. In its extraordinary peace the face was stronger than ever, nearly all bone now under the scarce-wrinkled parchment of skin—square jaw and chin, cheekbones, forehead with hollow temples, chiselled nose—the fortress of an unconquerable spirit that had yielded to death, and in its upward sightlessness seemed trying to regain that spirit, to regain the guardianship it had just laid down.

Swithin took but one look at the face, and left the room; the sight, he said afterwards, made him very queer. He went downstairs shaking the whole house, and, seizing his hat, clambered into his brougham, without giving any direction to the coachman. He was driven home, and all the evening sat in his chair without moving.

He could take nothing for dinner but a partridge, with an imperial pint of champagne. . . .

Old Jolyon stood at the bottom of the bed, his hands folded in front of him. He alone of those in the room remembered the death of his mother, and though he looked at Ann, it was of that he was thinking. Ann was an old woman, but death had come to her at last—death came to all! His face did not move, his gaze seemed travelling from very far.

Aunt Hester stood beside him. She did not cry now, tears were exhausted—her nature refused to permit a further escape of force; she twisted her hands, looking, not at Ann, but from side to side, seeking some way of escaping the effort of realization.

Of all the brothers and sisters James manifested the most emotion. Tears rolled down the parallel furrows of his thin face; where he should go now to tell his troubles he did not know; Juley was no good, Hester worse than useless! He felt Ann's death more than he had ever thought he should; this would upset him for weeks!

Presently Aunt Hester stole out, and Aunt Juley began moving about, doing 'what was necessary,' so that twice she knocked against something. Old Jolyon, roused from his reverie, that reverie of the long, long past, looked sternly at her, and went away. James alone was left by the bedside; glancing stealthily round, to see that he was not observed, he twisted his long body down, placed a kiss on the dead forehead, then he, too, hastily left the room. Encountering Smither in the hall, he began to ask her about the funeral, and, finding that she knew nothing, complained bitterly that, if they didn't take care, everything would go wrong. She had better send for Mr. Soames—he knew all about that sort of thing; her master was very much upset, he supposed— he would want looking after; as for her mistresses, they were no good— they had no gumption! They would be ill too, he shouldn't wonder. She had better send for the doctor; it was best to take things in time. He didn't think his sister Ann had had the best opinion; if she'd had Blank she would have been alive now. Smither might send to Park Lane any time she wanted advice. Of course, his carriage was at their service for the funeral. He supposed she hadn't such a thing as a glass of claret and a biscuit—he had had no lunch!

The days before the funeral passed quietly. It had long been known, of course, that Aunt Ann had left her little property to Timothy. There was, therefore, no reason for the slightest agitation. Soames, who was sole executor, took charge of all arrangements, and in due course sent out the following invitation to every male member of the family:

'To ——

'*Your presence is requested at the funeral of Miss Ann Forsyte, in Highgate Cemetery, at noon of Oct. 1st. Carriages will meet at "The Bower," Bayswater Road, at 10:45. No flowers by request.*

'*R.S.V.P.*'

The morning came, cold, with a high, grey, London sky, and at half-past ten the first carriage, that of James, drove up. It contained James and his son-in-law Dartie, a fine man, with a square chest, buttoned very tightly into a frock coat, and a sallow, fattish face adorned with dark, well-curled moustaches, and that incorrigible commencement of whisker which, eluding the strictest attempts at shaving, seems the mark of something deeply ingrained in the personality of the shaver, being especially noticeable in men who speculate.

Soames, in his capacity of executor, received the guests, for Timothy still kept his bed; he would get up after the funeral; and Aunts Juley and Hester would not be coming down till all was over, when it was understood there would be lunch for anyone who cared to come back. The next to arrive was Roger, still limping from the gout, and encircled by three of his sons—young Roger, Eustace, and Thomas. George, the remaining son, arrived almost immediately afterwards in a hansom, and paused in the hall to ask Soames how he found undertaking pay.

They disliked each other.

Then came the two Haymans—Giles and Jesse—perfectly silent, and very well dressed, with special creases down their evening trousers. Then old Jolyon alone. Next, Nicholas, with a healthy colour in his face, and a carefully veiled sprightliness in every movement of his head and body. One of his sons followed him, meek and subdued. Swithin Forsyte, and Bosinney arrived at the same moment, and stood bowing precedence to each other, but on the door opening they tried to enter together; they renewed their apologies in the hall, and Swithin, settling his stock, which had become disarranged in the struggle, very slowly mounted the stairs. The other Hayman; two married sons of Nicholas, together with Tweetyman, Spender, and Warry, the husbands of married Forsyte and Hayman daughters. The company was then complete, twenty-one in all, not a male member of the family being absent but Timothy and young Jolyon.

Entering the scarlet and green drawing-room, whose apparel made so vivid a setting for their unaccustomed costumes, each tried nervously to find a seat, desirous of hiding the emphatic blackness of his trousers. There seemed a sort of indecency in that blackness and in the colour of their gloves—a sort of exaggeration of the feelings; and many cast shocked looks of secret envy at 'The Buccaneer,' who had no gloves, and was wearing grey trousers. A subdued hum of conversation rose, no one speaking of the departed, but each asking after the other, as though thereby casting an indirect libation to this event, which they had come to honour.

And presently James said:

"Well, I think we ought to be starting."

They went downstairs, and, two and two, as they had been told off in strict precedence, mounted the carriages.

The hearse started at a foot's pace; the carriages moved slowly after. In the first went old Jolyon with Nicholas; in the second, the twins, Swithin and James; in the third, Roger and young Roger; Soames, young Nicholas, George, and Bosinney followed in the fourth. Each of the other carriages, eight in all, held three or four of the family; behind them came the doctor's brougham; then, at a decent interval, cabs containing family clerks and servants; and at the very end, one containing nobody at all, but bringing the total cortège up to the number of thirteen.

So long as the procession kept to the highway of the Bayswater Road, it retained the foot's pace, but, turning into less important thoroughfares, it soon broke into a trot, and so proceeded, with intervals of walking in the more fashionable streets, until it arrived. In the first carriage old Jolyon and Nicholas were talking of their wills. In the second the twins, after a single attempt, had lapsed into complete silence; both were rather deaf, and the exertion of making themselves heard was too great. Only once James broke this silence:

"I shall have to be looking about for some ground somewhere. What arrangements have you made, Swithin?"

And Swithin, fixing him with a dreadful stare, answered:

"Don't talk to me about such things!"

In the third carriage a disjointed conversation was carried on in the intervals of looking out to see how far they had got, George remarking, "Well, it was really time that the poor old lady 'went.'" He didn't believe in people living beyond seventy. Young Nicholas replied mildly that the rule didn't seem to apply to the Forsytes. George said he himself intended to commit suicide at sixty. Young Nicholas, smiling and stroking a long chin, didn't think *his* father would like that theory; he had made a lot of money since he was sixty. Well, seventy was the outside limit; it was then time, George said, for them to go and leave their money to their children. Soames, hitherto silent, here joined in; he had not forgotten the remark about the 'undertaking,' and, lifting his eyelids almost imperceptibly, said it was all very well for people who never made money to talk. He himself intended to live as long as he could. This was a hit at George, who was notoriously hard up. Bosinney muttered abstractedly "Hear, hear!" and, George yawning, the conversation dropped.

Upon arriving, the coffin was borne into the chapel, and, two by two, the mourners filed in behind it. This guard of men, all attached to the dead by the bond of kinship, was an impressive and singular sight in the great city of London, with its overwhelming diversity of life, its innumerable vocations, pleasures, duties, its terrible hardness, its terrible call to individualism.

The family had gathered to triumph over all this, to give a show of tenacious unity, to illustrate gloriously that law of property underlying the growth of their tree, by which it had thriven and spread, trunk and branches, the sap flowing through all, the full growth reached at the appointed time. The spirit of the old woman lying in her last sleep had called them to this demonstration. It was her final appeal to that unity which had been their strength—it was her final triumph that she had died while the tree was yet whole.

She was spared the watching of the branches jut out beyond the point of balance. She could not look into the hearts of her followers. The same law that had worked in her, bringing her up from a tall, straight-back slip of a girl to a woman strong and grown, from a woman grown to a woman old, angular, feeble, almost witch-like, with individuality all sharpened and sharpened, as all rounding from the world's contact fell off from her—that same law would work, was working, in the family she had watched like a mother.

She had seen it young, and growing, she had seen it strong and grown, and before her old eyes had time or strength to see any more, she died. She would have tried, and who knows but she might have kept it young and strong, with her old fingers, her trembling kisses—a little longer; alas! not even Aunt Ann could fight with Nature.

'Pride comes before a fall!' In accordance with this, the greatest of Nature's ironies, the Forsyte family had gathered for a last proud pageant before they fell. Their faces to right and left, in single lines, were turned for the most part impassively toward the ground, guardians of their thoughts; but here and there, one looking upward, with a line between his brows, seemed to see some sight on the chapel walls too much for him, to be listening to something that appalled. And the responses, low-muttered, in voices through which rose the same tone, the same unseizable family ring, sounded weird, as though murmured in hurried duplication by a single person.

The service in the chapel over, the mourners filed up again to guard the body to the tomb. The vault stood open, and, round it, men in black were waiting.

From that high and sacred field, where thousands of the upper middle class lay in their last sleep, the eyes of the Forsytes travelled down across the flocks of graves. There—spreading to the distance, lay London, with no sun over it, mourning the loss of its daughter, mourning with this family, so dear, the loss of her who was mother and guardian. A hundred thousand spires and houses, blurred in the great grey web of property, lay there like prostrate worshippers before the grave of this, the oldest Forsyte of them all.

A few words, a sprinkle of earth, the thrusting of the coffin home, and Aunt Ann had passed to her last rest.

Round the vault, trustees of that passing, the five brothers stood, with white heads bowed; they would see that Ann was comfortable where she was going. Her little property must stay behind, but otherwise, all that could be should be done.

Then severally, each stood aside, and putting on his hat, turned back to inspect the new inscription on the marble of the family vault:

SACRED TO THE MEMORY OF
ANN FORSYTE,

THE DAUGHTER OF THE ABOVE
JOLYON AND ANN FORSYTE,
WHO DEPARTED THIS LIFE THE 27TH DAY OF SEPTEMBER, 1886,
AGED EIGHTY-SEVEN YEARS AND FOUR DAYS

Soon perhaps, someone else would be wanting an inscription. It was strange and intolerable, for they had not thought somehow, that Forsytes could die. And one and all they had a longing to get away from this painfulness, this ceremony which had reminded them of things they could not bear to think about—to get away quickly and go about their business and forget.

It was cold, too; the wind, like some slow, disintegrating force, blowing up the hill over the graves, struck them with its chilly breath, they began to split into groups, and as quickly as possible to fill the waiting carriages.

Swithin said he should go back to lunch at Timothy's, and he offered to take anybody with him in his brougham. It was considered a doubtful privilege to drive with Swithin in his brougham, which was not a large one; nobody accepted, and he went off alone. James and Roger followed immediately after; they also would drop in to lunch. The others gradually melted away, old Jolyon taking three nephews to fill up his carriage; he had a want of those young faces.

Soames, who had to arrange some details in the cemetery office, walked away with Bosinney. He had much to talk over with him, and, having finished his business, they strolled to Hampstead, lunched together at the Spaniard's Inn, and spent a long time in going into practical details connected with the building of the house; they then proceeded to the tram-line, and came as far as the Marble Arch, where Bosinney went off to Stanhope Gate to see June.

Soames felt in excellent spirits when he arrived home, and confided to Irene at dinner that he had had a good talk with Bosinney, who really seemed a sensible fellow; they had a capital walk too, which had done his liver good—he had been short of exercise for a long time—and altogether a very satisfactory day. If only it hadn't been for poor Aunt Ann, he would have taken her to the theatre; as it was, they must make the best of an evening at home.

"The Buccaneer asked after you more than once," he said suddenly. And moved by some inexplicable desire to assert his proprietorship, he rose from his chair and planted a kiss on his wife's shoulder.

Part II · *Chapter* I

PROGRESS OF THE HOUSE

THE winter had been an open one. Things in the trade were slack; and as Soames had reflected before making up his mind, it had been a good time for building. The shell of the house at Robin Hill was thus completed by the end of April.

Now that there was something to be seen for his money, he had been coming down once, twice, even three times a week, and would mouse about among the débris for hours, careful never to soil his clothes, moving silently through the unfinished brickwork of doorways, or circling round the columns in the central court.

And he would stand before them for minutes together, as though peering into the real quality of their substance.

On April 30 he had an appointment with Bosinney to go over the accounts, and five minutes before the proper time he entered the tent which the architect had pitched for himself close to the old oak tree.

The accounts were already prepared on a folding table, and with a nod Soames sat down to study them. It was some time before he raised his head.

"I can't make them out," he said at last; "they come to nearly seven hundred more than they ought!"

After a glance at Bosinney's face, he went on quickly:

"If you only make a firm stand against these builder chaps you'll get them down. They stick you with everything if you don't look sharp. Take ten per cent. off all round. I shan't mind its coming out a hundred or so over the mark!"

Bosinney shook his head:

"I've taken off every farthing I can!"

Soames pushed back the table with a movement of anger, which sent the account sheets fluttering to the ground.

"Then all I can say is," he flustered out, "you've made a pretty mess of it!"

"I've told you a dozen times," Bosinney answered sharply, "that there'd be extras. I've pointed them out to you over and over again!"

"I know that," growled Soames: "I shouldn't have objected to a ten pound note here and there. How was I to know that by 'extras' you meant seven hundred pounds?"

The qualities of both men had contributed to this not inconsiderable discrepancy. On the one hand, the architect's devotion to his idea, to the image of a house which he had created and believed in—had made him nervous of being stopped, or forced to the use of makeshifts; on the other, Soames's not less true and whole-hearted devotion to the very best article that could be obtained for the money, had rendered him averse to believing that things worth thirteen shillings could not be bought with twelve.

"I wish I'd never undertaken your house," said Bosinney suddenly. "You come down here worrying me out of my life. You want double the value for your money anybody else would, and now that you've got a house that for its size is not to be beaten in the county, you don't want to pay for it. If you're anxious to be off your bargain, I daresay I can find the balance above the estimates myself, but I'm d——d if I do another stroke of work for you!"

Soames regained his composure. Knowing that Bosinney had no capital, he regarded this as a wild suggestion. He saw, too, that he would be kept indefinitely out of this house on which he had set his heart, and just at the crucial point when the architect's personal care made all the difference. In the meantime there was Irene to be thought of! She had been very queer lately. He really believed it was only because she had taken to Bosinney that she tolerated the idea of the house at all. It would not do to make an open breach with her.

"You needn't get into a rage," he said. "If I'm willing to put up with it, I suppose *you* needn't cry out. All I meant was that when you tell me a thing is going to cost so much, I like to—well, in fact, I—like to know where I am."

"Look here!" said Bosinney, and Soames was both annoyed and surprised by the shrewdness of his glance. "You've got my services dirt cheap. For the kind of work I've put into this house, and the amount of time I've given to it, you'd have had to pay Littlemaster or some other fool four times as much. What you want, in fact, is a first-rate man for a fourth-rate fee, and that's exactly what you've got!"

Soames saw that he really meant what he said, and, angry though he was, the consequences of a row rose before him too vividly. He saw his house unfinished, his wife rebellious, himself a laughing-stock.

"Let's go over it," he said sulkily, "and see how the money's gone."

"Very well," assented Bosinney. "But we'll hurry up, if you don't mind. I have to get back in time to take June to the theatre."

Soames cast a stealthy look at him, and said: "Coming to our place, I suppose to meet her?" He was always coming to their place!

There had been rain the night before—a spring rain, and the earth smelt of sap and wild grasses. The warm, soft breeze swung the leaves and the golden buds of the old oak tree, and in the sunshine the black-birds were whistling their hearts out.

It was such a spring day as breathes into a man an ineffable yearning, a painful sweetness, a longing that makes him stand motionless, looking at the leaves or grass, and fling out his arms to embrace he knows not what. The earth gave forth a fainting warmth, stealing up through the chilly garment in which winter had wrapped her. It was her long caress of invitation, to draw men down to lie within her arms, to roll their bodies on her, and put their lips to her breast.

On just such a day as this Soames had got from Irene the promise he had asked her for so often. Seated on the fallen trunk of a tree, he had promised for the twentieth time that if their marriage were not a success, she should be as free as if she had never married him!

"Do you swear it?" she had said. A few days back she had reminded him of that oath. He had answered: "Nonsense! I couldn't have sworn any such thing!" By some awkward fatality he remembered it now. What queer things men would swear for the sake of women! He would have sworn it at any time to gain her! He would swear it now, if thereby he could touch her—but nobody could touch her, she was cold-hearted!

And memories crowded on him with the fresh, sweet savour of the spring wind—memories of his courtship.

In the spring of the year 1881 he was visiting his old school-fellow and client, George Liversedge, of Branksome, who, with the view of de-veloping his pine-woods in the neighbourhood of Bournemouth, had placed the formation of the company necessary to the scheme in Soames's hands. Mrs. Liversedge, with a sense of the fitness of things, had given a musical tea in his honour. Later in the course of this function, which

Soames, no musician, had regarded as an unmitigated bore, his eye had been caught by the face of a girl dressed in mourning, standing by herself. The lines of her tall, as yet rather thin figure, showed through the wispy, clinging stuff of her black dress, her black-gloved hands were crossed in front of her, her lips slightly parted, and her large, dark eyes wandered from face to face. Her hair, done low on her neck, seemed to gleam above her black collar like coils of shining metal. And as Soames stood looking at her, the sensation that most men have felt at one time or another went stealing through him—a peculiar saisfaction of the senses, a peculiar certainty, which novelists and old ladies call love at first sight. Still stealthily watching her, he at once made his way to his hostess, and stood doggedly waiting for the music to cease.

"Who is that girl with yellow hair and dark eyes?" he asked.

"That—oh! Irene Heron. Her father, Professor Heron, died this year. She lives with her stepmother. She's a nice girl, a pretty girl, but no money!"

"Introduce me, please," said Soames.

It was very little that he found to say, nor did he find her responsive to that little. But he went away with the resolution to see her again. He effected his object by chance, meeting her on the pier with her stepmother, who had the habit of walking there from twelve to one of a forenoon. Soames made this lady's acquaintance with alacrity, nor was it long before he perceived in her the ally he was looking for. His keen scent for the commercial side of family life soon told him that Irene cost her stepmother more than the fifty pounds a year she brought her; it also told him that Mrs. Heron, a woman yet in the prime of life, desired to be married again. The strange ripening beauty of her step-daughter stood in the way of this desirable consummation. And Soames, in his stealthy tenacity, laid his plans.

He left Bournemouth without having given himself away, but in a month's time came back, and this time he spoke, not to the girl, but to her stepmother. He had made up his mind, he said; he would wait any time. And he had long to wait, watching Irene bloom, the lines of her young figure softening, the stronger blood deepening the gleam of her eyes, and warming her face to a creamy glow; and at each visit he proposed to her, and when that visit was at an end, took her refusal away with him, back to London, sore at heart, but steadfast and silent as the grave. He tried to come at the secret springs of her resistance; only once had he a gleam of light. It was at one of those assembly dances, which afford the only outlet to the passions of the population of seaside watering-places. He was sitting with her in an embrasure, his senses tingling with the contact of the waltz. She had looked at him over her slowly waving fan; and he had lost his head. Seizing that moving wrist, he pressed his lips to the flesh of her arm. And she had shuddered—to this day he had not forgotten that shudder—nor the look so passionately averse she had given him.

A year after that she had yielded. What had made her yield he could never make out; and from Mrs. Heron, a woman of some diplomatic talent, he learnt nothing. Once after they were married he asked her, "What made you refuse me so often?" She had answered by a strange silence. An enigma to him from the day that he first saw her, she was an enigma to him still. . . .

Bosinney was waiting for him at the door; and on his rugged, good-looking face was a queer, yearning, yet happy look, as though he too saw a promise of bliss in the spring sky, sniffed a coming happiness in the spring air. Soames looked at him waiting there. What was the matter with the fellow that he looked so happy? What was he waiting for with that smile on his lips and in his eyes? Soames could not see that for which Bosinney was waiting as he stood there drinking in the flower-scented wind. And once more he felt baffled in the presence of this man whom by habit he despised. He hastened on to the house.

"The only colour for those tiles," he heard Bosinney say, "is ruby with a grey tint in the stuff, to give a transparent effect. I should like Irene's opinion. I'm ordering the purple leather curtains for the doorway of this court; and if you distemper the drawing-room ivory cream over paper, you'll get an illusive look. You want to aim all through the decorations at what I call—charm."

Soames said: "You mean that my wife has charm!"

Bosinney evaded the question.

"You should have a clump of iris plants in the centre of that court."

Soames smiled superciliously.

"I'll look into Beech's some time," he said, "and see what's appropriate!"

They found little else to say to each other, but on the way to the Station Soames asked:

"I suppose you find Irene very artistic?"

"Yes." The abrupt answer was as distinct a snub as saying: "If you want to discuss her you can do it with someone else!"

And the slow, sulky anger Soames had felt all the afternoon burned the brighter within him.

Neither spoke again till they were close to the Station, then Soames asked:

"When do you expect to have finished?"

"By the end of June, if you really wish me to decorate as well."

Soames nodded. "But you quite understand," he said, "that the house is costing me a lot beyond what I contemplated. I may as well tell you that I should have thrown it up, only I'm not in the habit of giving up what I've set my mind on.!"

Bosinney made no reply. And Soames gave him askance a look of dogged dislike—for in spite of his fastidious air and that supercilious, dandified taciturnity, Soames, with his set lips and his squared chin, was not unlike a bulldog. . . .

When, at seven o'clock that evening, June arrived at 62, Montpellier Square, the maid Bilson told her that Mr. Bosinney was in the drawing-room; the mistress—she said—was dressing, and would be down in a minute. She would tell her that Miss June was here.

June stopped her at once.

"All right, Bilson," she said, "I'll just go in. You needn't hurry Mrs. Soames."

She took off her cloak, and Bilson, with an understanding look, did not even open the drawing-room door for her, but ran downstairs.

June paused for a moment to look at herself in the little old-fashioned silver mirror above the oaken rug chest—a slim, imperious young figure, with a small resolute face, in a white frock, cut moon-shaped at the base of a neck too slender for her crown of twisted red-gold hair.

She opened the drawing-room door softly, meaning to take him by surprise. The room was filled with a sweet hot scent of flowering azaleas.

She took a long breath of the perfume, and heard Bosinney's voice, not in the room, but quite close, saying:

"Ah! there were such heaps of things I wanted to talk about, and now we shan't have time!"

Irene's voice answered: "Why not at dinner?"

"How can one talk——"

June's first thought was to go away, but instead she crossed to the long window opening on the little court. It was from there that the scent of the azaleas came, and, standing with their backs to her, their faces buried in the golden-pink blossoms, stood her lover and Irene.

Silent but unashamed, with flaming cheeks and angry eyes, the girl watched.

"Come on Sunday by yourself—we can go over the house to-gether——"

June saw Irene look up at him through her screen of blossoms. It was not the look of a coquette, but—far worse to the watching girl—of a woman fearful lest that look should say too much.

"I've promised to go for a drive with Uncle——"

"The big one! Make him bring you; it's only ten miles—the very thing for his horses."

"Poor old Uncle Swithin!"

A wave of the azalea scent drifted into June's face; she felt sick and dizzy.

"Do! ah! do!"

"But why?"

"I must see you there—I thought you'd like to help me——"

The answer seemed to the girl to come softly, with a tremble from amongst the blossoms: "So I do!"

And she stepped into the open space of the window.

"How stuffy it is here!" she said; "I can't bear this scent!"

Her eyes, so angry and direct, swept both their faces.

"Were you talking about the house? *I* haven't seen it yet, you know—shall we all go on Sunday?"

From Irene's face the colour had flown.

"I am going for a drive that day with Uncle Swithin," she answered.

"Uncle Swithin! What does he matter? You can throw him over!"

"I am not in the habit of throwing people over!"

There was a sound of footsteps and June saw Soames standing just behind her.

"Well! if you are all ready," said Irene, looking from one to the other with a strange smile, "dinner is too!"

Chapter II

JUNE'S TREAT

DINNER began in silence; the women facing one another, and the men.

In silence the soup was finished—excellent, if a little thick; and fish was brought. In silence it was handed.

Bosinney ventured: "It's the first spring day."

Irene echoed softly: "Yes—the first spring day."

"Spring!" said June: "there isn't a breath of air!" No one replied.

The fish was taken away, a fine fresh sole from Dover. And Bilson brought champagne, a bottle swathed around the neck with white.

Soames said: "You'll find it dry."

Cutlets were handed, each pink-frilled about the legs. They were refused by June, and silence fell.

Soames said: "You'd better take a cutlet, June; there's nothing coming."

But June again refused, so they were borne away. And then Irene asked: "Phil, have you heard my blackbird?"

Bosinney answered: "Rather—he's got a hunting-song. As I came round I heard him in the Square."

"He's such a darling!"

"Salad, sir?" Spring chicken was removed.

But Soames was speaking: "The asparagus is very poor. Bosinney, glass of sherry with your sweet? June, you're drinking nothing!"

June said: "You know I never do. Wine's such horrid stuff!"

An apple charlotte came upon a silver dish. And smilingly Irene said: "The azaleas are so wonderful this year!"

To this Bosinney murmured: "Wonderful! The scent's extraordinary!"

June said: "How *can* you like the scent? Sugar, please, Bilson."

Sugar was handed her, and Soames remarked: "This charlotte's good!"

The charlotte was removed. Long silence followed. Irene, beckoning, said: "Take out the azalea, Bilson. Miss June can't bear the scent."

"No; let it stay," said June.

Olives from France, with Russian caviare, were placed on little plates. And Soames remarked: "Why can't we have the Spanish?" But no one answered.

The olives were removed. Lifting her tumbler June demanded: "Give me some water, please." Water was given her. A silver tray was brought, with German plums. There was a lengthy pause. In perfect harmony all were eating them.

Bosinney counted up the stones: "This year—next year—some time——"

Irene finished softly: "Never. There was such a glorious sunset. The sky's all ruby still—so beautiful!"

He answered: "Underneath the dark."

Their eyes had met, and June cried scornfully: "A London sunset!"

Egyptian cigarettes were handed in a silver box. Soames, taking one, remarked: "What time's your play begin?"

No one replied, and Turkish coffee followed in enamelled cups.

Irene, smiling quietly, said: "If only——"

"Only what?" said June.

"If only it could always be the spring!"

Brandy was handed; it was pale and old.

Soames said: "Bosinney, better take some brandy."

Bosinney took a glass; they all arose.

"You want a cab?" asked Soames.

June answered: "No. My cloak, please, Bilson." Her cloak was brought.

Irene, from the window, murmured: "Such a lovely night! The stars are coming out!"

Soames added: "Well, I hope you'll both enjoy yourselves."

From the door June answered: "Thanks. Come, Phil."

Bosinney cried: "I'm coming."

Soames smiled a sneering smile, and said: "I wish you luck!"

And at the door Irene watched them go.

Bosinney called: "Good night!"

"Good night!" she answered softly. . . .

June made her lover take her on the top of a 'bus, saying she wanted air, and there sat silent, with her face to the breeze.

The driver turned once or twice, with the intention of venturing a remark, but thought better of it. They were a lively couple! The spring had got into his blood, too; he felt the need for letting steam escape, and clucked his tongue, flourishing his whip, wheeling his horses, and even they, poor things, had smelled the spring, and for a brief half-hour spurned the pavement with happy hoofs.

The whole town was alive; the boughs, curled upward with their decking of young leaves, awaited some gift the breeze could bring. New-lighted lamps were gaining mastery, and the faces of the crowd showed pale under that glare, while on high the great white clouds slid swiftly, softly, over the purple sky.

Men in evening dress had thrown back overcoats, stepping jauntily up the steps of Clubs; working folk loitered; and women—those women who at that time of night are solitary—solitary and moving eastward in a stream—swung slowly along, with expectation in their gait, dreaming of good wine and a good supper, or, for an unwonted minute, of kisses given for love.

Those countless figures, going their ways under the lamps and the moving sky, had one and all received some restless blessing from the stir of spring. And one and all, like those clubmen with their opened coats, had shed something of caste, and creed, and custom, and by the cock of their hats, the pace of their walk, their laughter, or their silence, revealed their common kinship under the passionate heavens.

Bosinney and June entered the theatre in silence, and mounted to their seats in the upper boxes. The piece had just begun, and the half-darkened house, with its rows of creatures peering all one way, resembled a great garden of flowers turning their faces to the sun.

June had never before been in the upper boxes. From the age of fifteen she had habitually accompanied her grandfather to the stalls, and not common stalls, but the best seats in the house, towards the centre of the third row, booked by old Jolyon, at Grogan and Boyne's, on his way home from the City, long before the day; carried in his overcoat pocket, together with his cigar-case and his old kid gloves, and handed to June to keep till the appointed night. And in those stalls—an erect old figure with a serene white head, a little figure, strenuous and eager, with a red-gold head—they would sit through every kind of play, and on the way home old Jolyon would say of the principal actor: "Oh, he's a poor stick! You should have seen little Bobson!"

109

She had looked forward to this evening with keen delight; it was stolen, chaperone-less, undreamed of at Stanhope Gate, where she was supposed to be at Soames's. She had expected reward for her subterfuge, planned for her lover's sake; she had expected it to break up the thick, chilly cloud, and make the relations between them—which of late had been so puzzling, so tormenting—sunny and simple again as they had been before the winter. She had come with the intention of saying something definite; and she looked at the stage with a furrow beween her brows, seeing nothing, her hands squeezed together in her lap. A swarm of jealous suspicions stung and stung her.

If Bosinney was conscious of her trouble he made no sign.

The curtain dropped. The first act had come to an end.

"It's awfully hot here!" said the girl; "I should like to go out."

She was very white, and she knew—for with her nerves thus sharpened she saw everything—that he was both uneasy and compunctious.

At the back of the theatre an open balcony hung over the street; she took possession of this, and stood leaning there without a word, waiting for him to begin.

At last she could bear it no longer.

"I want to say something to you, Phil," she said.

"Yes?"

The defensive tone of his voice brought the colour flying to her cheek, the words flying to her lips: "You don't give me a chance to be nice to you; you haven't for ages now!"

Bosinney stared down at the street. He made no answer.

June cried passionately: "You know I want to do everything for you —that I want to be everything to you——"

A hum rose from the street, and, piercing it with a sharp 'ping,' the bell sounded for the raising of the curtain. June did not stir. A desperate struggle was going on within her. Should she put everything to the proof? Should she challenge directly that influence, that attraction which was drawing him away from her? It was her nature to challenge, and she said: "Phil, take me to see the house on Sunday!"

With a smile quivering and breaking on her lips, and trying, how hard! not to show that she was watching, she searched his face, saw it waver and hesitate, saw a troubled line come between his brows, the blood rush into his face. He answered: "Not Sunday, dear; some other day!"

110

"Why not Sunday? I shouldn't be in the way on Sunday."

He made an evident effort, and said: "I have an engagement."

"You are going to take——"

His eyes grew angry; he shrugged his shoulders, and answered: "An engagement that will prevent my taking you to see the house!"

June bit her lip till the blood came, and walked back to her seat without another word, but she could not help the tears of rage rolling down her face. The house had been mercifully darkened for a crisis, and no one could see her trouble.

Yet in this world of Forsytes let no man think himself immune from observation.

In the third row behind, Euphemia, Nicholas's youngest daughter, with her married sister, Mrs. Tweetyman, were watching.

They reported at Timothy's, how they had seen June and her fiancé at the theatre.

"In the stalls?" "No, not in the——" "Oh! in the dress circle, of course. That seemed to be quite fashionable nowadays with young people!"

Well—not exactly. In the— Anyway, *that* engagement wouldn't last long. They had never seen anyone look so thunder and lightningy as that little June! With tears of enjoyment in their eyes, they related how she had kicked a man's hat as she returned to her seat in the middle of an act, and how the man had looked. Euphemia had a noted, silent laugh, terminating most disappointingly in squeaks; and when Mrs. Small, holding up her hands, said: "My dear! Kicked a ha-at?" she let out such a number of these that she had to be recovered with smelling-salts. As she went away she said to Mrs. Tweetyman: " 'Kicked a ha-at!' Oh! I shall die."

For 'that little June' this evening, that was to have been 'her treat,' was the most miserable she had ever spent. God knows she tried to stifle her pride, her suspicion, her jealousy!

She parted from Bosinney at old Jolyon's door without breaking down; the feeling that her lover must be conquered was strong enough to sustain her till his retiring footsteps brought home the true extent of her wretchedness.

The noiseless 'Sankey' let her in. She would have slipped up to her own room, but old Jolyon, who had heard her entrance, was in the dining-room doorway.

"Come in and have your milk," he said. "It's been kept hot for you. You're very late. Where have you been?"

June stood at the fireplace, with a foot on the fender and an arm on the mantelpiece, as her grandfather had done when he came in that night of the opera. She was too near a breakdown to care what she told him.

"We dined at Soames's."

"H'm! the man of property! His wife there—and Bosinney?"

"Yes."

Old Jolyon's glance was fixed on her with the penetrating gaze from which it was difficult to hide; but she was not looking at him, and when she turned her face, he dropped his scrutiny at once. He had seen enough, and too much. He bent down to lift the cup of milk for her from the hearth, and, turning away, grumbled: "You oughtn't to stay out so late; it makes you fit for nothing."

He was invisible now behind his paper, which he turned with a vicious crackle; but when June came up to kiss him, he said: "Goodnight, my darling," in a tone so tremulous and unexpected, that it was all the girl could do to get out of the room without breaking into the fit of sobbing which lasted her well on into the night.

When the door was closed, old Jolyon dropped his paper, and stared long and anxiously in front of him.

'The beggar!' he thought. 'I always knew she'd have trouble with him!'

Uneasy doubts and suspicions, the more poignant that he felt himself powerless to check or control the march of events, came crowding upon him.

Was the fellow going to jilt her? He longed to go and say to him: "Look here, you sir! Are you going to jilt my granddaughter?" But how could he? Knowing little or nothing, he was yet certain, with his unerring astuteness, that there was something going on. He suspected Bosinney of being too much at Montpellier Square.

'This fellow,' he thought, 'may not be a scamp; his face is not a bad one, but he's a queer fish. I don't know what to make of him. I shall never know what to make of him! They tell me he works like a nigger, but I see no good coming of it. He's unpractical, he has no method. When he comes here, he sits as glum as a monkey. If I ask him what wine he'll have, he says: "Thanks, any wine." If I offer him a cigar, he smokes it as if it were a twopenny German thing. I never see him looking at June as he ought to look at her; and yet, he's not after her money. If she were to make a sign, he'd be off his bargain to-morrow. But she won't—not she! She'll stick to him! She's as obstinate as fate—she'll never let go!'

Sighing deeply, he turned the paper; in its columns perchance he might find consolation.

And upstairs in her room June sat at her open window, where the spring wind came, after its revel across the Park, to cool her hot cheeks and burn her heart.

Chapter III

DRIVE WITH SWITHIN

T WO lines of a certain song in a certain famous old school's song-
book run as follows:

'How the buttons on his blue frock shone, tra-la-la!
How he carolled and he sang, like a bird! ...'

Swithin did not exactly carol and sing like a bird, but he felt almost
like endeavouring to hum a tune, as he stepped out of Hyde Park
Mansions, and contemplated his horses drawn up before the door.

The afternoon was as balmy as a day in June, and to complete the
simile of the old song, he had put on a blue frock-coat, dispensing with
an overcoat, after sending Adolf down three times to make sure that
there was not the least suspicion of east in the wind; and the frock-coat
was buttoned so tightly around his personable form, that, if the buttons
did not shine, they might pardonably have done so. Majestic on the
pavement he fitted on a pair of dog-skin gloves; with his large bell-
shaped top hat, and his great stature and bulk he looked too primeval
for a Forsyte. His thick white hair, on which Adolf had bestowed a
touch of pomatum, exhaled the fragrance of opopomax and cigars—the
celebrated Swithin brand, for which he paid one hundred and forty
shillings the hundred, and of which old Jolyon had unkindly said, he
wouldn't smoke them as a gift; they wanted the stomach of a horse! ...

"Adolf!"

"Sare!"

"The new plaid rug!"

He would never teach that fellow to look smart; and Mrs. Soames he
felt sure, had an eye!

"The phaeton hood down; I am going—to—drive—a—lady!"

A pretty woman would want to show off her frock; and well—he
was going to drive a lady! It was like a new beginning to the good
old days.

Ages since he had driven a woman! That last time, if he remembered, it had been Juley; the poor old soul had been as nervous as a cat the whole time, and so put him out of patience that, as he dropped her in the Bayswater Road, he had said: "Well I'm d——d if I ever drive you again!" And he never had, not he!

Going up to his horses' heads, he examined their bits; not that he knew anything about bits—he didn't pay his coachman sixty pounds a year to do his work for him, that had never been his principle. Indeed, his reputation as a horsey man rested mainly on the fact that once, on Derby Day, he had been welshed by some thimble-riggers. But some one at the Club, after seeing him drive his greys up to the door—he always drove grey horses, you got more style for the money, some thought—had called him 'Four-in-hand Forsyte.' The name having reached his ears through that fellow Nicholas Treffrey, old Jolyon's dead partner, the great driving man—notorious for more carriage accidents than any man in the kingdom—Swithin had ever after conceived it right to act up to it. The name had taken his fancy, not because he had ever driven four-in-hand, or was ever likely to, but because of something distinguished in the sound. Four-in-hand Forsyte! Not bad! Born too soon, Swithin had missed his vocation. Coming upon London twenty years later, he could not have failed to have become a stockbroker, but at the time when he was obliged to select, this great profession had not as yet became the chief glory of the upper middle-class. He had literally been forced into land agency.

Once in the driving seat, with the reins handed to him, and blinking over his pale old cheeks in the full sunlight, he took a slow look round. Adolf was already up behind; the cockaded groom at the horses' heads stood ready to let go; everything was prepared for the signal, and Swithin gave it. The equipage dashed forward, and before you could say Jack Robinson, with a rattle and flourish drew up at Soames's door.

Irene came out at once, and stepped in—he afterward described it at Timothy's—"as light as—er—Taglioni, no fuss about it, no wanting this or wanting that;" and above all, Swithin dwelt on this, staring at Mrs. Septimus in a way that disconcerted her a good deal, "no silly nervousness!" To Aunt Hester he portrayed Irene's hat. "Not one of your great flopping things, sprawling about, and catching the dust, that women are so fond of nowadays, but a neat little——" he made a circular motion of his hand, "white veil—capital taste."

"What was it made of?" inquired Aunt Hester, who manifested a languid but permanent excitement at any mention of dress.

"Made of?" returned Swithin; "now how should *I* know?"

He sank into silence so profound that Aunt Hester began to be afraid he had fallen into a trance. She did not try to rouse him herself, it not being her custom.

'I wish somebody would come,' she thought; 'I don't like the look of him!'

But suddenly Swithin returned to life. "Made of?" he wheezed out slowly, "what should it be made of?"

They had not gone four miles before Swithin received the impression that Irene liked driving with him. Her face was so soft behind that white veil, and her dark eyes shone so in the spring light, and whenever he spoke she raised them to him and smiled.

On Saturday morning Soames had found her at her writing-table with a note written to Swithin, putting him off. Why did she want to put him off? he asked. She might put her own people off when she liked, he would not have her putting off *his* people!

She had looked at him intently, had torn up the note, and said: "Very well!"

And then she began writing another. He took a casual glance presently, and saw that it was addressed to Bosinney.

"What are you writing to *him* about?" he asked.

Irene, looking at him again with that intent look, said quietly: "Something he wanted me to do for him!"

"Humph!" said Soames. "Commissions! You'll have your work cut out if you begin that sort of thing!" He said no more.

Swithin opened his eyes at the mention of Robin Hill; it was a long way for his horses, and he always dined at half-past seven, before the rush at the Club began; the new chef took more trouble with an early dinner—a lazy rascal!

He would like to have a look at the house, however. A house appealed to any Forsyte, and especially to one who had been an auctioneer. After all he said the distance was nothing. When he was a younger man he had had rooms at Richmond for many years, kept his carriage and pair there, and drove them up and down to business every day of his life. Four-in-hand Forsyte they called him! His T-cart, his horses had been known from Hyde Park Corner to the Star and Garter. The Duke of Z—— wanted to get hold of them, would have given him double the money, but he had kept them; know a good thing when you have it, eh? A look of solemn pride came portentiously on his shaven square old face, he rolled his head in his stand-up collar, like a turkey-cock preening himself.

She was really a charming woman! He enlarged upon her frock afterwards to Aunt Juley, who held up her hands at his way of putting it.

Fitted her like a skin—tight as a drum; that was how he liked 'em, all of a piece, none of your daverdy, scarecrow women! He gazed at Mrs. Septimus Small, who took after James—long and thin.

"There's style about her," he went on, "fit for a king! And she's so quiet with it too!"

"She seems to have made quite a conquest of you, any way," drawled Aunt Hester from her corner.

Swithin heard extremely well when anybody attacked him.

"What's that?" he said. "I know a—pretty—woman when I see one, and all I can say is, I don't see the young man about that's fit for her; but perhaps—you—do, come, perhaps—you—do!"

"Oh?" murmured Aunt Hester, "ask Juley!"

Long before they reached Robin Hill, however, the unaccustomed airing had made him terribly sleepy; he drove with his eyes closed, a life-time of deportment alone keeping his tall and bulky form from falling askew.

Bosinney, who was watching, came out to meet them, and all three entered the house together; Swithin in front making play with a stout gold-mounted Malacca cane, put into his hand by Adolf, for his knees were feeling the effects of their long stay in the same position. He had assumed his fur coat, to guard against the draughts of the unfinished house.

The staircase—he said—was handsome! the baronial style! They would want some statuary about! He came to a standstill between the columns of the doorway into the inner court, and held out his cane inquiringly.

What was this to be—this vestibule, or whatever they called it? But gazing at the skylight, inspiration came to him.

"Ah! the billiard-room!"

When told it was to be a tiled court with plants in the centre, he turned to Irene:

"Waste this on plants? You take my advice and have a billiard table here!"

Irene smiled. She had lifted her veil, banding it like a nun's coif across her forehead, and the smile of her dark eyes below this seemed to Swithin more charming than ever. He nodded. She would take his advice he saw.

He had little to say of the drawing or dining-rooms, which he described as 'spacious'; but fell into such raptures as he permitted to a man of his dignity, in the wine-cellar, to which he descended by stone steps, Bosinney going first with a light.

"You'll have room here," he said, "for six or seven hundred dozen— a very pooty little cellar!"

Bosinney having expressed the wish to show them the house from the copse below, Swithin came to a stop.

"There's a fine view from here," he remarked; "you haven't such a thing as a chair?"

A chair was brought him from Bosinney's tent.

"You go down," he said blandly; "you two! I'll sit here and look at the view."

He sat down by the oak tree, in the sun; square and upright, with one hand stretched out, resting on the nob of his cane, the other planted on his knee; his fur coat thrown open, his hat, roofing with its flat top the pale square of his face; his stare, very blank, fixed on the landscape.

He nodded to them as they went off down through the fields. He was, indeed, not sorry to be left thus for a quiet moment of reflection. The air was balmy, not too much heat in the sun; the prospect a fine one, a remarka—. His head fell a little to one side; he jerked it up and thought: Odd! He—ah! They were waving to him from the bottom! He put up his hand, and moved it more than once. They were active—the prospect was remar—. His head fell to the left, he jerked it up at once; it fell to the right. It remained there; he was asleep.

And asleep, a sentinel on the top of the rise, he appeared to rule over this prospect—remarkable—like some image blocked out by the special artist of primeval Forsytes in pagan days, to record the domination of mind over matter!

118

And all the unnumbered generations of his yeoman ancestors, wont of a Sunday to stand akimbo surveying their little plots of land, their grey unmoving eyes hiding their instinct with its hidden roots of violence, their instinct for possession to the exclusion of all the world—all these unnumbered generations seemed to sit there with him on top of the rise.

But from him, thus slumbering, his jealous Forsyte spirit travelled far, into God-knows-what jungle of fancies; with those two young people, to see what they were doing down there in the copse—in the copse where the spring was running riot with the scent of sap and bursting buds, the song of birds innumerable, a carpet of blue-bells and sweet growing things, and the sun caught like gold in the tops of the trees; to see what they were doing, walking along there so close together on the path that was too narrow; walking along there so close that they were always touching; to watch Irene's eyes, like dark thieves, stealing the heart out of the spring. And a great unseen chaperon, his spirit was there, stopping with them to look at the little furry corpse of a mole, not dead an hour, with his mushroom and silver coat untouched by the rain or dew; watching over Irene's bent head, and the soft look of her pitying eyes; and over that young man's head, gazing at her so hard, so strangely. Walking on with them, too, across the open space where a woodcutter had been at work, where the bluebells were trampled down, and a trunk had swayed and staggered down from its gashed stump. Climbing it with them, over, and on to the very edge of the copse, whence there stretched an undiscovered country, from far away in which came the sounds, 'Cuckoo—cuckoo!'

Silent, standing with them there, and uneasy at their silence! Very queer, very strange!

Then back again, as though guilty, through the wood—back to the cutting, still silent, amongst the songs of birds that never ceased, and the wild scent—hum! what was it—like that herb they put in—back to the log across the path.

And then unseen, uneasy, flapping above them, trying to make noises, his Forsyte spirit watched her balanced on the log, her pretty figure swaying, smiling down at that young man gazing up with such strange, shining eyes; slipping now—a-ah! falling, o-oh! sliding—down his breast; her soft, warm body clutched, her head bent back from his lips;

his kiss; her recoil; his cry: "You must know—I love you!" Must know —indeed, a pretty——? Love! Hah!

Swithin awoke; virtue had gone out of him. He had a taste in his mouth. Where was he?

Damme! He had been asleep!

He had dreamed something about a new soup, with a taste of mint in it.

Those young people—where had they got to? His left leg had pins and needles.

"Adolf!" The rascal was not there; the rascal was asleep somewhere.

He stood up, tall, square, bulky in his fur, looking anxiously down over the fields, and presently he saw them coming.

Irene was in front; that young fellow—what had they nicknamed him—'The Buccaneer?'—looked precious hangdog there behind her; had got a flea in his ear, he shouldn't wonder. Serve him right, taking her down all that way to look at the house! The proper place to look at a house from was the lawn.

They saw him. He extended his arm, and moved it spasmodically to encourage them. But they had stopped. What were they standing there for, talking—talking? They came on again. She had been giving him a rub, he had not the least doubt of it, and no wonder, over a house like that—a great ugly thing, not the sort of house *he* was accustomed to.

He looked intently at their faces, with his pale, immovable stare. That young man looked very queer!

"You'll never make anything of this!" he said tartly, pointing at the mansion; "too new-fangled!"

Bosinney gazed at him as though he had not heard; and Swithin afterwards described him to Aunt Hester as "an extravagant sort of fellow—very odd way of looking at you—a bumpy beggar!"

What gave rise to this sudden piece of psychology he did not state; possibly Bosinney's prominent forehead and cheekbones and chin, or something hungry in his face, which quarrelled with Swithin's conception of the calm satiety that should characterize the perfect gentleman.

He brightened up at the mention of tea. He had a contempt for tea— his brother Jolyon had been in tea; made a lot of money by it—but he was so thirsty, and had such a taste in his mouth, that he was prepared to drink anything. He longed to inform Irene of the taste in his mouth— she was so sympathetic—but it would not be a distinguished thing to

120

do; he rolled his tongue round, and faintly smacked it against his palate.

In a far corner of the tent Adolf was bending his cat-like moustaches over a kettle. He left it at once to draw the cork of a pint bottle of champagne. Swithin smiled, and, nodding at Bosinney, said: "Why, you're quite a Monte Cristo!" This celebrated novel—one of the half-dozen he had read—had produced an extraordinary impression on his mind.

Taking his glass from the table, he held it away from him to scrutin-ize the colour; thirsty as he was, it was not likely that he was going to drink trash! Then, placing it to his lips, he took a sip.

"A very nice wine," he said at last, passing it before his nose; "not the equal of my Heidsieck!"

It was at this moment that the idea came to him which he afterwards imparted at Timothy's in this nutshell: "I shouldn't wonder a bit if that architect chap were sweet upon Mrs. Soames!"

And from this moment his pale, round eyes never ceased to bulge with the interest of his discovery.

"The fellow," he said to Mrs. Septimus, "follows her about with his eyes like a dog—the bumpy beggar! I don't wonder at it—she's a very charming woman, and, I should say, the pink of discretion!" A vague consciousness of perfume clinging about Irene, like that from a flower · with half-closed petals and a passionate heart, moved him to the creation of this image. "But I wasn't sure of it," he said, "till I saw him pick up her handkerchief."

Mrs. Small's eyes bulged with excitement.

"And did he give it her back?" she asked.

"Give it back?" said Swithin: "I saw him slobber on it when he thought I wasn't looking!"

Mrs. Small gasped—too interested to speak.

"But *she* gave him no encouragement," went on Swithin; he stopped, and stared for a minute or two in the way that alarmed Aunt Hester so —he had suddenly recollected that, as they were starting back in the phaeton, she had given Bosinney her hand a second time, and let it stay there too. . . . He had touched his horses smartly with the whip, anxious to get her all to himself. But she had looked back, and she had not answered his first question; neither had he been able to see her face—she had kept it hanging down.

There is somewhere a picture, which Swithin has not seen, of a man sitting on a rock, and by him, immersed in the still, green water, a sea-nymph lying on her back, with her hand on her naked breast. She has a half-smile on her face—a smile of hopeless surrender and of secret joy. Seated by Swithin's side, Irene may have been smiling like that.

When, warmed by champagne, he had her all to himself, he unbosomed himself of his wrongs; of his smothered resentment against the new chef at the club; his worry over the house in Wigmore Street, where the rascally tenant had gone bankrupt through helping his brother-in-law—as if charity did not begin at home; of his deafness, too, and that pain he sometimes got in his right side. She listened, her eyes swimming under their lids. He thought she was thinking deeply of his troubles, and pitied himself terribly. Yet in his fur coat, with frogs across the breast, his top hat aslant, driving this beautiful woman, he had never felt more distinguished.

A coster, however, taking his girl for a Sunday airing, seemed to have the same impression about himself. This person had flogged his donkey into a gallop alongside, and sat, upright as a waxwork, in his shallopy chariot, his chin settled pompously on a red handkerchief, like Swithin's on his full cravat; while his girl, with the ends of a fly-blown boa floating out behind, aped a woman of fashion. Her swain moved a stick with a ragged bit of string dangling from the end, reproducing with strange fidelity the circular flourish of Swithin's whip, and rolled his head at his lady with a leer that had a weird likeness to Swithin's primeval stare.

Though for a time unconscious of the lowly ruffian's presence, Swithin presently took it into his head that he was being guyed. He laid his whip-lash across the mare's flank. The two chariots, however, by some unfortunate fatality continued abreast. Swithin's yellow, puffy face grew red; he raised his whip to lash the costermonger, but was saved from so far forgetting his dignity by a special intervention of Providence. A carriage driving out through a gate forced phaeton and donkey-cart into proximity; the wheels grated, the lighter vehicle skidded, and was overturned.

Swithin did not look round. On no account would he have pulled up to help the ruffian. Serve him right if he had broken his neck!

But he could not if he would. The greys had taken alarm. The phaeton swung from side to side, and people raised frightened faces as they

122

went dashing past. Swithin's great arms, stretched at full length, tugged at the reins. His cheeks were puffed, his lips compressed, his swollen face was of a dull, angry red.

Irene had her hand on the rail, and at every lurch she gripped it tightly. Swithin heard her ask:

"Are we going to have an accident, Uncle Swithin?"

He gasped out between his pants: "It's nothing; a—little fresh!"

"I've never been in an accident."

"Don't you move!" He took a look at her. She was smiling, perfectly calm. "Sit still," he repeated. "Never fear, I'll get you home!"

And in the midst of all his terrible efforts, he was surprised to hear her answer in a voice not like her own:

"I dont care if I never get home!"

The carriage giving a terrific lurch, Swithin's exclamation was jerked back into his throat. The horses, winded by the rise of a hill, now steadied to a trot, and finally stopped of their own accord.

"When"—Swithin described it at Timothy's—"I pulled 'em up, there she was as cool as myself. God bless my soul! she behaved as if she didn't care whether she broke her neck or not! What was it she said: 'I don't care if I never get home!'" Leaning over the handle of his cane, he wheezed out, to Mrs. Small's terror: "And I'm not altogether surprised, with a finickin' feller like young Soames for a husband!"

It did not occur to him to wonder what Bosinney had done after they had left him there alone; whether he had gone wandering about like the dog to which Swithin had compared him; wandering down to that copse where the spring was still in riot, the cuckoo still calling from afar; gone down there with her handkerchief pressed to his lips, its fragrance mingling with the scent of mint and thyme. Gone down there with such a wild, exquisite pain in his heart that he could have cried out among the trees. Or what, indeed, the fellow had done. In fact, till he came to Timothy's, Swithin had forgotten all about him.

Chapter IV

JAMES GOES TO SEE FOR HIMSELF

THOSE ignorant of Forsyte 'Change would not, perhaps, foresee all the stir made by Irene's visit to the house.

After Swithin had related at Timothy's the full story of his memorable drive, the same, with the least suspicion of curiosity, the merest touch of malice, and a real desire to do good, was passed on to June.

"And what a *dreadful* thing to say, my dear!" ended Aunt Juley; "that about not going home. What did she mean?"

It was a strange recital for the girl. She heard it flushing painfully, and, suddenly, with a curt handshake, took her departure.

"Almost rude!" Mrs. Small said to Aunt Hester, when June was gone.

The proper construction was put on her reception of the news. She was upset. Something was therefore very wrong. Odd! She and Irene had been such friends!

It all tallied too well with whispers and hints that had been going about for some time past. Recollections of Euphemia's account of the visit to the theatre—Mr. Bosinney always at Soames's? Oh, indeed! Yes, of course, he *would* be—about the house! Nothing open. Only upon the greatest, the most important provocation was it necessary to say anything open on Forsyte 'Change. This machine was too nicely adjusted; a hint, the merest trifling expression of regret or doubt, sufficed to set the family soul—so sympathetic—vibrating. No one desired that harm should come of these vibrations—far from it; they were set in motion with the best intentions, with the feeling that each member of the family had a stake in the family soul.

And much kindness lay at the bottom of the gossip; it would frequently result in visits of condolence being made, in accordance with the customs of Society, thereby conferring a real benefit upon the sufferers, and affording consolation to the sound, who felt pleasantly that someone at all events was suffering from that from which they themselves were not suffering. In fact, it was simply a desire to keep things well-aired, the desire which animates the Public Press, that brought James, for instance, into communication with Mrs. Septimus, Mrs. Septimus with the little Nicholases, the little Nicholases with who-knows-whom, and so on. That great class to which they had risen, and now belonged, demanded a certain candour, a still more certain reticence. This combination guaranteed their membership.

Many of the younger Forsytes felt, very naturally, and would openly declare, that they did not want their affairs pried into; but so powerful was the invisible, magnetic current of family gossip, that for the life of them they could not help knowing all about everything. It was felt to be hopeless.

One of them (young Roger) had made an heroic attempt to free the rising generation, by speaking of Timothy as an 'old cat.' The effort had justly recoiled upon himself; the words, coming round in the most delicate way to Aunt Juley's ears, were repeated by her in a shocked voice to Mrs. Roger, whence they returned again to young Roger.

And, after all, it was only the wrong-doers who suffered; as, for instance, George, when he lost all that money playing billiards; or young Roger himself, when he was so dreadfully near to marrying the girl to whom, it was whispered, he was already married by the laws of Nature; or again Irene, who was thought, rather than said, to be in danger.

All this was not only pleasant but salutary. And it made so many hours go lightly at Timothy's in the Bayswater Road; so many hours that must otherwise have been sterile and heavy to those three who lived there; and Timothy's was but one of hundreds of such homes in this City of London—the homes of neutral persons of the secure classes, who are out of the battle themselves, and must find their reason for existing, in the battles of others.

But for the sweetness of family gossip, it must indeed have been lonely there. Rumours and tales, reports, surmises—were they not the children of the house, as dear and precious as the prattling babes the brother and sisters had missed in their own journey? To talk about them, was as near as they could get to the possession of all those children and grandchildren after whom their soft hearts yearned. For though it is doubtful whether Timothy's heart yearned, it is indubitable that at the arrival of each fresh Forsyte child he was quite upset.

Useless for young Roger to say, "Old cat!"—for Euphemia to hold up her hands and cry: "Oh! those three!" and break into her silent laugh with the squeak at the end. Useless, and not too kind.

The situation which at this stage might seem, and especially to Forsyte eyes, strange—not to say 'impossible'—was, in view of certain facts, not so strange after all.

Some things had been lost sight of.

And first, in the security bred of many harmless marriages, it had been forgotten that Love is no hot-house flower, but a wild plant, born of a wet night, born of an hour of sunshine; sprung from wild seed, blown along the road by a wild wind. A wild plant that, when it blooms by chance within the hedge of our gardens, we call a flower; and when it blooms outside we call a weed; but, flower or weed, whose scent and colour are always wild!

And further—the facts and figures of their own lives being against the perception of this truth—it was not generally recognised by Forsytes that, where this wild plant springs, men and women are but moths around the pale, flame-like blossom.

It was long since young Jolyon's escapade—there was danger of a tradition again arising that people in their position never cross the hedge to pluck that flower; that one could reckon on having love, like measles, once in due season, and getting over it comfortably for all time—as with measles, on a soothing mixture of butter and honey—in the arms of wedlock.

Of all those whom this strange rumour about Bosinney and Mrs. Soames reached, James was the most affected. He had long forgotten how he had hovered, lanky and pale, in side whiskers of chestnut hue, round Emily, in the days of his own courtship. He had long forgotten the small house in the purlieus of Mayfair, where he had spent the early days of his married life, or rather, he had long forgotten the early days, not the small house,—a Forsyte never forgot a house—he had afterwards sold it at a clear profit of four hundred pounds.

He had long forgotten those days, with their hopes and fears and doubts about the prudence of the match (for Emily, though pretty, had nothing, and he himself at that time was making a bare thousand a year), and that strange, irresistible attraction which had drawn him on, till he felt he must die if he could not marry the girl with the fair hair, looped so neatly back, the fair arms emerging from a skin-tight bodice, the fair form decorously shielded by a cage of really stupendous circumference.

James had passed through the fire, but he had passed also through the river of years which washes out the fire; he had experienced the saddest experience of all—forgetfulness of what it was like to be in love.

Forgotten! Forgotten so long, that he had forgotten even that he had forgotten.

And now this rumour had come upon him, this rumour about his son's wife; very vague, a shadow dodging among the palpable, straightforward appearances of things, unreal, unintelligible as a ghost, but carrying with it, like a ghost, inexplicable terror.

He tried to bring it home to his mind, but it was no more use than trying to apply to himself one of these tragedies he read of daily in his evening paper. He simply could not. There could be nothing in it. It was all their nonsense. She didn't get on with Soames as well as she might, but she was a good little thing—a good little thing!

Like the not inconsiderable majority of men, James relished a nice little bit of scandal, and would say, in a matter-of-fact tone, licking his lips, "Yes, yes—she and young Dyson; they tell me they're living at Monte Carlo!"

But the significance of an affair of this sort—of its past, its present, or its future—had never struck him. What it meant, what torture and raptures had gone to its construction, what slow, overmastering fate had lurked within the facts, very naked, sometimes sordid, but generally spicy, presented to his gaze. He was not in the habit of blaming, praising, drawing deductions, or generalizing at all about such things; he simply listened rather greedily, and repeated what he was told, finding considerable benefit from the practice, as from the consumption of a sherry and bitters before a meal.

Now, however, that such a thing—or rather the rumour, the breath of it—had come near him personally, he felt as in a fog, which filled his mouth full of a bad, thick flavour, and made it difficult to draw breath.

A scandal! A possible scandal!

To repeat this word to himself thus was the only way in which he

127

could focus or make it thinkable. He had forgotten the sensations necessary for understanding the progress, fate, or meaning of any such business; he simply could no longer grasp the possibilities of people running any risk for the sake of passion.

Amongst all those persons of his acquaintance, who went into the City day after day and did their business there, whatever it was, and in their leisure moments bought shares, and houses, and ate dinners, and played games, as he was told, it would have seemed to him ridiculous to suppose that there were any who would run risks for the sake of anything so recondite, so figurative, as passion.

Passion! He seemed, indeed, to have heard of it, and rules such as 'A young man and a young woman ought never to be trusted together' were fixed in his mind as the parallels of latitude are fixed on a map (for all Forsytes, when it comes to 'bed-rock' matters of fact, have quite a fine taste in realism); but as to anything else—well, he could only appreciate it at all through the catch-word 'scandal.'

Ah! but there was no truth in it—could not be. He was not afraid; she was really a good little thing. But there it was when you got a thing like that into your mind. And James was of a nervous temperament—one of those men whom things will not leave alone, who suffer tortures from anticipation and indecision. For fear of letting something slip that he might otherwise secure, he was physically unable to make up his mind until absolutely certain that, by not making it up, he would suffer loss.

In life, however, there were many occasions when the business of making up his mind did not even rest with himself, and this was one of them.

What could he do? Talk it over with Soames? That would only make matters worse. And, after all, there was nothing in it, he felt sure.

It was all that house. He had mistrusted the idea from the first. What did Soames want to go into the country for? And, if he must go spending a lot of money building himself a house, why not have a first-rate man, instead of this young Bosinney, whom nobody knew anything about? He had told them how it would be. And he had heard that the house was costing Soames a pretty penny beyond what he had reckoned on spending.

This fact, more than any other, brought home to James the real danger of the situation. It was always like this with these 'artistic' chaps; a sensible man should have nothing to say to them. He had warned Irene, too. And see what had come of it!

And it suddenly sprang into James's mind that he ought to go and see for himself. In the midst of that fog of uneasiness in which his mind was enveloped the notion that he could go and look at the house afforded him inexplicable satisfaction. It may have been simply the decision to do something—more possibly the fact that he was going to look at a house—that gave him relief.

He felt that in staring at an edifice of bricks and mortar, of wood and stone, built by the suspected man himself, he would be looking into the heart of that rumour about Irene.

Without saying a word, therefore, to anyone, he took a hansom to the station and proceeded by train to Robin Hill; thence—there being no 'flies,' in accordance with the custom of the neighbourhood—he found himself obliged to walk.

He started slowly up the hill, his angular knees and high shoulders bent complainingly, his eyes fixed on his feet, yet, neat for all that, in his high hat and his frock-coat, on which was the speckless gloss imparted by perfect superintendence. Emily saw to that; that is, she did not, of course, see to it—people of good position not seeing to each other's buttons, and Emily was of good position—but she saw that the butler saw to it.

He had to ask his way three times; on each occasion he repeated the directions given him, got the man to repeat them, then repeated them a second time, for he was naturally of a talkative disposition, and one could not be too careful in a new neighbourhood.

He kept assuring them that it was a *new* house he was looking for; it was only, however, when he was shown the roof through the trees that he could feel really satisfied that he had not been directed entirely wrong.

A heavy sky seemed to cover the world with the grey whiteness of a whitewashed ceiling. There was no freshness or fragrance in the air. On such a day even British workmen scarcely cared to do more than they were obliged, and moved about their business without the drone of talk which whiles away the pangs of labour.

Through spaces of the unfinished house, shirt-sleeved figures worked slowly, and sounds arose—spasmodic knockings, the scraping of metal, the sawing of wood, with the rumble of wheel-barrows along boards; now and again the foreman's dog, tethered by a string to an oaken beam, whimpered feebly, with a sound like the singing of a kettle.

The fresh-fitted window-panes, daubed each with a white patch in the centre, stared out at James like the eyes of a blind dog.

And the building chorus went on, strident and mirthless under the grey-white sky. But the thrushes, hunting amongst the fresh-turned earth for worms, were silent quite.

James picked his way among the heaps of gravel—the drive was being laid—till he came opposite the porch. Here he stopped and raised his eyes. There was but little to see from this point of view, and that little he took in at once; but he stayed in this position many minutes, and who shall know of what he thought.

His china-blue eyes under white eyebrows that jutted out in little horns, never stirred; the long upper lip of his wide mouth, between the fine white whiskers, twitched once or twice; it was easy to see from that anxious rapt expression, whence Soames derived the handicapped look which sometimes came upon his face. James might have been saying to himself: 'I don't know—life's a tough job.'

In this position Bosinney surprised him.

James brought his eyes down from whatever bird's-nest they had been looking for in the sky to Bosinney's face, on which was a kind of humorous scorn.

"How do you do, Mr. Forsyte? Come down to see for yourself?"

It was exactly what James, as we know, *had* come for, and he was made correspondingly uneasy. He held out his hand, however, saying:

"How are you?" without looking at Bosinney.

The latter made way for him with an ironical smile.

James scented something suspicious in this courtesy. "I should like to walk around the outside first," he said, "and see what you've been doing!"

A flagged terrace of rounded stones with a list of two or three inches to port had been laid round the south-east and south-west sides of the house, and ran with a bevelled edge into mould, which was in preparation for being turfed; along this terrace James led the way.

"Now what did *this* cost?" he asked, when he saw the terrace extending round the corner.

"What should you think?" inquired Bosinney.

"How should I know?" replied James somewhat nonplussed; "two or three hundred, I dare say!"

"The exact sum!"

James gave him a sharp look, but the architect appeared unconscious, and he put the answer down to mishearing.

On arriving at the garden entrance, he stopped to look at the view.

"That ought to come down," he said, pointing to the oak-tree.

"You think so? You think that with the tree there you don't get enough view for your money?"

Again James eyed him suspiciously—this young man had a peculiar way of putting things: "Well," he said, with a perplexed, nervous emphasis, "I don't see what you want with a tree."

"It shall come down to-morrow," said Bosinney.

James was alarmed. "Oh," he said, "don't go saying I said it was to come down; *I* know nothing about it!"

"No?"

James went on in a fluster: "Why, what should I know about it? It's nothing to do with me! You do it on your own responsibility."

"You'll allow me to mention your name?"

James grew more and more alarmed: "I don't know what you want mentioning my name for," he muttered; "you'd better leave the tree alone. It's not your tree!"

He took out a silk handkerchief and wiped his brow. They entered the house. Like Swithin, James was impressed by the inner court-yard.

"You must have spent a deuce of a lot of money here," he said, after staring at the columns and gallery for some time. "Now, what did it cost to put up those columns?"

"I can't tell you off-hand," thoughtfully answered Bosinney, "but I know it was a deuce of a lot!"

"I should think so," said James. "I should—" He caught the architect's eye, and broke off. And now, whenever he came to anything of which he desired to know the cost, he stifled that curiosity.

Bosinney appeared determined that he should see everything, and had not James been of too 'noticing' a nature, he would certainly have found himself going round the house a second time. He seemed so anxious to be asked questions, too, that James felt he must be on his

131

guard. He began to suffer from his exertions, for, though wiry enough for a man of his long build, he was seventy-five years old.

He grew discouraged; he seemed no nearer to anything, had not obtained from his inspection any of the knowledge he had vaguely hoped for. He had merely increased his dislike and mistrust of this young man, who had tired him out with his politeness, and in whose manner he now certainly detected mockery.

The fellow was sharper than he had thought, and better-looking than he had hoped. He had a 'don't care' apearance that James, to whom risk was the most intolerable thing in life, did not appreciate; a peculiar smile, too, coming when least expected; and very queer eyes. He reminded James, as he said afterwards, of a hungry cat. This was as near as he could get, in conversation with Emily, to a description of the peculiar exasperation, velvetiness, and mockery, of which Bosinney's manner had been composed.

At last, having seen all that was to be seen, he came out again at the door where he had gone in; and now, feeling that he was wasting time and strength and money, all for nothing, he took the courage of a Forsyte in both hands, and, looking sharply at Bosinney, said:

"I dare say you see a good deal of my daughter-in-law; now, what does *she* think of the house? But she hasn't seen it, I suppose?"

This he said, knowing all about Irene's visit—not, of course, that there was anything in the visit, except that extraordinary remark she had made about 'not caring to get home'—and the story of how June had taken the news!

He had determined, by this way of putting the question, to give Bosinney a chance, as he said to himself.

The latter was long in answering, but kept his eyes with uncomfortable steadiness on James.

"She *has* seen the house, but I can't tell you what she thinks of it."

Nervous and baffled, James was constitutionally prevented from letting the matter drop.

"Oh!" he said, "she has seen it? Soames brought her down, I suppose?"

Bosinney smilingly replied: "Oh, no!"

"What, did she come down alone?"

"Oh, no!"

132

"Then—who brought her?"

"I really don't know whether I ought to tell you who brought her."

To James, who knew that it was Swithin, this answer appeared incomprehensible.

"Why!" he stammered, "you know that——" but he stopped, suddenly perceiving his danger.

"Well," he said, "if you don't want to tell me, I suppose you won't! Nobody tells me anything."

Somewhat to his surprise Bosinney asked him a question.

"By the by," he said, "could you tell me if there are likely to be any more of you coming down? I should like to be on the spot!"

"Any more?" said James bewildered, "who should there be more? I don't know of any more. Good-bye."

Looking at the ground he held out his hand, crossed the palm of it with Bosinney's, and taking his umbrella just above the silk, walked away along the terrace.

Before he turned the corner he glanced back, and saw Bosinney following him slowly—'slinking along the wall' as he put it to himself, 'like a great cat.' He paid no attention when the young fellow raised his hat.

Outside the drive, and out of sight, he slackened his pace still more. Very slowly, more bent than when he came, lean, hungry, and disheartened, he made his way back to the station.

The Buccaneer, watching him go so sadly home, felt sorry perhaps for his behaviour to the old man.

Chapter V

SOAMES AND BOSINNEY CORRESPOND

JAMES said nothing to his son of this visit to the house; but, having occasion to go to Timothy's one morning on a matter connected with a drainage scheme which was being forced by the
sanitary authorities on his brother, he mentioned it there.

It was not, he said, a bad house. He could see that a good deal could
be made of it. The fellow was clever in his way, though what it was
going to cost Soames before it was done with he didn't know.

Euphemia Forsyte, who happened to be in the room—she had come
round to borrow the Rev. Mr. Scoles' last novel, 'Passion and Paregoric,'
which was having such a vogue—chimed in.

"I saw Irene yesterday at the Stores; she and Mr. Bosinney were having a nice little chat in the Groceries."

It was thus, simply, that she recorded a scene which had really made
a deep and complicated impression on her. She had been hurrying to the
silk department of the Church and Commercial Stores—that Institution
than which, with its admirable system, admitting only guaranteed persons on a basis of payment before delivery, no emporium can be more
highly recommended to Forsytes—to match a piece of prunella silk for
her mother, who was waiting in the carriage outside.

Passing through the Groceries her eye was unpleasantly attracted by
the back view of a very beautiful figure. It was so charmingly propor-
tioned, so balanced, and so well clothed, that Euphemia's instinctive
propriety was at once alarmed; such figures, she knew, by intuition
rather than experience, were rarely connected with virtue—certainly
never in her mind, for her own back was somewhat difficult to fit.

Her suspicions were fortunately confirmed. A young man coming
from the Drugs had snatched off his hat, and was accosting the lady with
the unknown back.

It was then that she saw with whom she had to deal; the lady was
undoubtedly Mrs. Soames, the young man Mr. Bosinney. Concealing

134

herself rapidly over the purchase of a box of Tunisian dates, for she was impatient of awkwardly meeting people with parcels in her hands, and at the busy time of the morning, she was quite unintentionally an interested observer of their little interview.

Mrs. Soames, usually somewhat pale, had a delightful colour in her cheeks; and Mr. Bosinney's manner was strange, though attractive (she thought him rather a distinguished-looking man, and George's name for him, 'The Buccaneer'—about which there was something romantic— quite charming). He seemed to be pleading. Indeed, they talked so earnestly—or, rather, he talked so earnestly, for Mrs. Soames did not say much—that they caused, inconsiderately, an eddy in the traffic. One nice old General, going towards Cigars, was obliged to step quite out of the way, and chancing to look up and see Mrs. Soames's face, he actually took off his hat, the old fool! So like a man!

But it was Mrs. Soames's eyes that worried Euphemia. She never once looked at Mr. Bosinney until he moved on, and then she looked after him. And, oh, that look!

On that look Euphemia had spent much anxious thought. It is not too much to say that it had hurt her with its dark, lingering softness, for all the world as though the woman wanted to drag him back, and unsay something she had been saying.

Ah, well, she had had no time to go deeply into the matter just then, with that prunella silk on her hands; but she was 'very *intriguée*—very!' She had just nodded to Mrs. Soames, to show her that she had seen; and, as she confided, in talking it over afterwards, to her chum Francie (Roger's daughter), "Didn't she look caught out just? . . ."

James, most averse at the first blush to accepting any news confirmatory of his own poignant suspicions, took her up at once.

"Oh," he said, "they'd be after wall-papers no doubt."

Euphemia smiled. "In the Groceries?" she said softly; and, taking 'Passion and Paregoric' from the table, added: "And so you'll lend me this, dear Auntie? Good-bye!" and went away.

James left almost immediately after; he was late as it was.

When he reached the office of Forsyte, Bustard and Forsyte, he found Soames sitting in his revolving chair, drawing up a defence. The latter greeted his father with a curt good-morning, and, taking an envelope from his pocket, said:

"It may interest you to look through this."

James read as follows:

'309D, SLOANE STREET,
May 15.

'DEAR FORSYTE,

'The construction of your house being now completed, my duties as architect have come to an end. If I am to go on with the business of decoration, which at your request I undertook, I should like you to clearly understand that I must have a free hand.

'You never come down without suggesting something that goes counter to my scheme. I have here three letters from you, each of which recommends an article I should never dream of putting in. I had your father here yesterday afternoon, who made further valuable suggestions.

'Please make up your mind, therefore, whether you want me to decorate for you, or to retire, which on the whole I should prefer to do.

'But understand that, if I decorate, I decorate alone, without inter-ference of any sort.

'If I do the thing, I will do it thoroughly, but I must have a free hand.

'Yours truly,

'PHILIP BOSINNEY.'

The exact and immediate cause of this letter cannot, of course, be told, though it is not improbable that Bosinney may have been moved by some sudden revolt against his position towards Soames—that eternal position of Art towards Property—which is so admirably summed up, on the back of the most indispensable of modern appliances, in a sen-tence comparable to the very finest in Tacitus:

THOS. T. SORROW,
Inventor.

BERT M. PADLAND,
Proprietor.

"What are you going to say to him?" James asked.

Soames did not even turn his head. "I haven't made up my mind," he said, and went on with his defence.

A client of his, having put some buildings on a piece of ground that did not belong to him, had been suddenly and most irritatingly warned to take them off again. After carefully going into the facts, however, Soames had seen his way to advise that his client had what was known as a title by possession, and that, though undoubtedly the ground did not belong to him, he was entitled to keep it, and had better do so; and he was now following up this advice by taking steps to—as the sailors say—'make it so.'

He had a distinct reputation for sound advice; people saying of him: "Go to young Forsyte—a long-headed fellow!" and he prized this reputation highly.

His natural taciturnity was in his favour; nothing could be more calculated to give people, especially people with property (Soames had no other clients), the impression that he was a safe man. And he *was* safe. Tradition, habit, education, inherited aptitude, native caution, all joined to form a solid professional honesty, superior to temptation from the very fact that it was built on an innate avoidance of risk. How could he fall, when his soul abhorred circumstances which render a fall possible—a man cannot fall off the floor!

And those countless Forsytes, who, in the course of innumerable transactions concerned with property of all sorts (from wives to water rights), had occasion for the services of a safe man, found it both reposeful and profitable to confide in Soames. That slight superciliousness of his, combined with an air of mousing amongst precedents, was in his favour too—a man would not be supercilious unless he knew!

He was really at the head of the business, for though James still came nearly every day to see for himself, he did little now but sit in his chair, twist his legs, slightly confuse things already decided, and presently go away again, and the other partner, Bustard, was a poor thing, who did a great deal of work but whose opinion was never taken.

So Soames went steadily on with his defence. Yet it would be idle to say that his mind was at ease. He was suffering from a sense of impending trouble, that had haunted him for some time past. He tried to think it physical—a condition of his liver—but knew that it was not.

He looked at his watch. In a quarter of an hour he was due at the General Meeting of the New Colliery Company—one of Uncle Jolyon's concerns; he should see Uncle Jolyon there, and say something to him about Bosinney—he had not made up his mind what, but something—

in any case he should not answer this letter until he had seen Uncle Jolyon. He got up and methodically put away the draft of his defence. Going into a dark little cupboard, he turned up the light, washed his hands with a piece of brown Windsor soap, and dried them on a roller towel. Then he brushed his hair, paying strict attention to the parting, turned down the light, took his hat, and saying he would be back at half-past two, stepped into the Poultry.

It was not far to the Offices of the New Colliery Company in Iron-monger Lane, where, and not at the Cannon Street Hotel, in accordance with the more ambitious practice of other companies, the General Meeting was always held. Old Jolyon had from the first set his face against the Press. What business—he said—had the Public with his concerns!

Soames arrived on the stroke of time, and took his seat alongside the Board, who, in a row, each Director behind his own ink-pot, faced their Shareholders.

In the centre of this row old Jólyon, conspicuous in his black, tightly-buttoned frock-coat and his white moustaches, was leaning back with finger tips crossed on a copy of the Directors' report and accounts.

On his right hand, always a little larger than life, sat the Secretary, 'Down-by-the-starn' Hemmings; an all-too-sad sadness beaming in his fine eyes; his iron-grey beard, in mourning like the rest of him, giving the feeling of an all-too-black tie behind it.

The occasion indeed was a melancholy one, only six weeks having elapsed since that telegram had come from Scorrier, the mining expert, on a private mission to the Mines, informing them that Pippin, their Superintendent, had committed suicide in endeavouring, after his extra-ordinary two years' silence, to write a letter to his Board. That letter was on the table now; it would be read to the Shareholders, who would of course be put into possession of all the facts.

Hemmings had often said to Soames, standing with his coat-tails divided before the fireplace:

"What our Shareholders don't know about our affairs isn't worth knowing. You may take that from me, Mr. Soames."

On one occasion, old Jolyon being present, Soames recollected a little unpleasantness. His uncle had looked up sharply and said: "Don't talk nonsense, Hemmings! You mean that what they *do* know isn't worth knowing!" Old Jolyon detested humbug.

Hemmings, angry-eyed, and wearing a smile like that of a trained poodle, had replied in an outburst of artificial applause: "Come, now, that's good, sir—that's very good. Your uncle *will* have his joke!"

The next time he had seen Soames he had taken the opportunity of saying to him: "The chairman's getting very old—I can't get him to understand things; and he's so wilful—but what can you expect, with a chin like his?"

Soames had nodded.

Everyone knew that Uncle Jolyon's chin was a caution. He was looking worried to-day, in spite of his General Meeting look; he (Soames) should certainly speak to him about Bosinney.

Beyond old Jolyon on the left was little Mr. Booker, and he, too, wore his General Meeting look, as though searching for some particularly tender shareholder. And next him was the deaf director, with a frown; and beyond the deaf director again, was old Mr. Bleedham, very bland, and having an air of conscious virtue—as well he might, knowing that the brown-paper parcel he always brought to the Board-room was concealed behind his hat (one of that old-fashioned class of flat-brimmed top-hats which go with very large bow ties, clean-shaven lips, fresh cheeks, and neat little white whiskers).

Soames always attended the General Meeting; it was considered better that he should do so, in case 'anything should arise!' He glanced round with his close, supercilious air at the walls of the room, where hung plans of the mine and harbour, together with a large photograph of a shaft leading to a working which had proved quite remarkably unprofitable. This photograph—a witness to the eternal irony underlying commercial enterprise—still retained its position on the wall, an effigy of the directors' pet, but dead, lamb.

And now old Jolyon rose, to present the report and accounts.

Veiling under a Jove-like serenity that perpetual antagonism deepseated in the bosom of a director towards his shareholders, he faced them calmly. Soames faced them too. He knew most of them by sight. There was old Scrubsole, a tar man, who always came, as Hemmings would say, 'to make himself nasty,' a cantankerous-looking old fellow with a red face, a jowl, and an enormous low-crowned hat reposing on his knee. And the Rev. Mr. Boms, who always proposed a vote of thanks to the chairman, in which he invariably expressed the hope that the

Board would not forget to elevate their employees, using the word with a double e, as being more vigorous and Anglo-Saxon (he had the strong Imperialistic tendencies of his cloth). It was his salutary custom to buttonhole a director afterwards, and ask him whether he thought the coming year would be good or bad; and, according to the trend of the answer, to buy or sell three shares within the ensuing fortnight.

And there was that military man, Major O'Bally, who could not help speaking, if only to second the re-election of the auditor, and who sometimes caused serious consternation by taking toasts—proposals rather—out of the hands of persons who had been flattered with little slips of paper, entrusting the said proposals to their care.

These made up the lot, together with four or five strong, silent shareholders, with whom Soames could sympathize—men of business, who liked to keep an eye on their affairs for themselves, without being fussy—good, solid men, who came to the City every day and went back in the evening to good, solid wives.

Good, solid wives! There was something in that thought which roused the nameless uneasiness in Soames again.

What should he say to his uncle? What answer should he make to this letter?

. . . "If any shareholder has any question to put, I shall be glad to answer it." A soft thump. Old Jolyon had let the report and accounts fall, and stood twisting his tortoise-shell glasses between thumb and forefinger.

The ghost of a smile appeared on Soames's face. They had better hurry up with their questions! He well knew his uncle's method (the ideal one) of at once saying: "I propose, then, that the report and accounts be adopted!" Never let them get their wind—shareholders were notoriously wasteful of time!

A tall, white-bearded man, with a gaunt, dissatisfied face, arose:

"I believe I am in order, Mr. Chairman, in raising a question on this figure of £5,000 in the accounts. 'To the widow and family' " (he looked sourly round), " 'of our late superintendent,' who so—er—ill-advisedly (I say—ill-advisedly) committed suicide, at a time when his services were of the utmost value to this Company. You have stated that the agreement which he has so unfortunately cut short with his own hand was for a period of five years, of which one only had expired—I——"

Old Jolyon made a gesture of impatience.

"I believe I am in order, Mr. Chairman—I ask whether this amount paid, or proposed to be paid, by the Board to the—er—deceased—is for services which might have been rendered to the Company had he not committed suicide?"

"It is in recognition of past services, which we all know—you as well as any of us—to have been of vital value."

"Then, sir, all I have to say is, that the services being past, the amount is too much."

The shareholder sat down.

Old Jolyon waited a second and said: "I now propose that the report and——"

The shareholder rose again: "May I ask if the Board realizes that it is not their money which—I don't hesitate to say that if it were their money——"

A second shareholder, with a round, dogged face, whom Soames recognised as the late superintendent's brother-in-law, got up and said warmly: "In my opinion, sir, the sum is not enough!"

The Rev. Mr. Boms now rose to his feet. "If I may venture to express myself," he said, "I should say that the fact of the—er—deceased having committed suicide should weigh very heavily—*very* heavily with our worthy chairman. I have no doubt it has weighed with him, for—I say this for myself and I think for everyone present (hear, hear)—he enjoys our confidence in a high degree. We all desire, I should hope, to be charitable. But I feel sure" (he looked severely at the late superintendent's brother-in-law) "that he will in some way, by some written expression, or better perhaps by reducing the amount, record our grave disapproval that so promising and valuable a life should have been thus impiously removed from a sphere where both its own interests and—if I may say so—*our* interests so imperatively demanded its continuance. We should not—nay, we may not—countenance so grave a dereliction of all duty, both human and divine."

The reverend gentleman resumed his seat. The late superintendent's brother-in-law again rose: "What I have said I stick to," he said: "the amount is not enough!"

The first shareholder struck in: "I challenge the legality of the payment. In my opinion this payment is not legal. The Company's solicitor is present; I believe I am in order in asking him the question."

All eyes were now turned upon Soames. Something had arisen!

He stood up, close-lipped and cold; his nerves inwardly fluttered, his attention tweaked away at last from contemplation of that cloud looming on the horizon of his mind.

"The point," he said in a low, thin voice, "is by no means clear. As there is no possibility of future consideration being received, it is doubtful whether the payment is strictly legal. If it is desired, the opinion of the court could be taken."

The superintendent's brother-in-law frowned, and said in a meaning tone: "We have no doubt the opinion of the court could be taken. May I ask the name of the gentleman who has given us that striking piece of information? Mr. Soames Forsyte? Indeed!" He looked from Soames to old Jolyon in a pointed manner.

A flush coloured Soames's pale cheeks, but his superciliousness did not waver. Old Jolyon fixed his eyes on the speaker.

"If," he said, "the late superintendent's *brother-in-law* has nothing more to say, I propose that the report and accounts——"

At this moment, however, there rose one of those five silent, stolid shareholders, who had excited Soames's sympathy. He said:

"I deprecate the proposal altogether. We are expected to give charity to this man's wife and children, who, you tell us, were dependent on him. They may have been; I do not care whether they were or not. I object to the whole thing on principle. It is high time a stand was made against this sentimental humanitarianism. The country is eaten up with it. I object to my money being paid to these people of whom I know nothing, who have done nothing to earn it. I object *in toto;* it is not business. I now move that the report and accounts be put back, and amended by striking out the grant altogether."

Old Jolyon had reminded standing while the strong, silent man was speaking. The speech awoke an echo in all hearts, voicing, as it did, the worship of strong men, the movement against generosity, which had at that time already commenced among the saner members of the community.

The words 'it is not business' had moved even the Board; privately everyone felt that indeed it was not. But they knew also the chairman's domineering temper and tenacity. He, too, at heart must feel that it was not business; but he was committed to his own proposition. Would he go back upon it? It was thought to be unlikely.

All waited with interest. Old Jolyon held up his hand; dark-rimmed glasses depending between his finger and thumb quivered slightly with a suggestion of menace.

He addressed the strong, silent shareholder.

"Knowing, as you do, the efforts of our late superintendent upon the occasion of the explosion at the mines, do you seriously wish me to put that amendment, sir?"

"I do."

Old Jolyon put the amendment.

"Does anyone second this?" he asked, looking calmly round.

And it was then that Soames, looking at his uncle, felt the power of will that was in that old man. No one stirred. Looking straight into the eyes of the strong, silent shareholder, old Jolyon said:

"I now move, 'That the report and accounts for the year 1886 be received and adopted.' You second that? Those in favour signify the same in the usual way. Contrary—no. Carried. The next business, gentlemen——"

Soames smiled. Certainly Uncle Jolyon had a way with him!

But now his attention relapsed upon Bosinney. Odd how that fellow haunted his thoughts, even in business hours.

Irene's visit to the house—but there was nothing in that, except that she might have told him; but then, again, she never did tell him anything. She was more silent, more touchy, every day. He wished to God the house were finished, and they were in it, away from London. Town did not suit her; her nerves were not strong enough. That nonsense of the separate room had cropped up again!

The meeting was breaking up now. Underneath the photograph of the lost shaft Hemmings was buttonholed by the Rev. Mr. Boms. Little Mr. Booker, his bristling eyebrows wreathed in angry smiles, was having a parting turn-up with old Scrubsole. The two hated each other like poison. There was some matter of a tar-contract between them, little Mr. Booker having secured it from the Board for a nephew of his, over old Scrubsole's head. Soames had heard that from Hemmings, who liked a gossip, more especially about his directors, except, indeed, old Jolyon, of whom he was afraid.

Soames awaited his opportunity. The last shareholder was vanishing through the door, when he approached his uncle, who was putting on his hat.

"Can I speak to you for a minute, Uncle Jolyon?"

143

It is uncertain what Soames expected to get out of this interview.

Apart from that somewhat mysterious awe in which Forsytes in general held old Jolyon, due to his philosophical twist, or perhaps—as Hemmings would doubtless have said—to his chin, there was, and always had been, a subtle antagonism between the younger man and the old. It had lurked under their dry manner of greeting, under their noncommittal allusions to each other, and arose perhaps from old Jolyon's perception of the quiet tenacity ('obstinacy,' he rather naturally called it) of the young man, of a secret doubt whether he could get his own way with him.

Both these Forsytes, wide asunder as the poles in many respects, possessed in their different ways—to a greater degree than the rest of the family—that essential quality of tenacious and prudent insight into 'affairs,' which is the high-water mark of their great class. Either of them, with a little luck and opportunity, was equal to a lofty career; either of them would have made a good financier, a great contractor, a statesman, though old Jolyon, in certain of his moods—when under the influence of a cigar or of Nature—would have been capable of, not perhaps despising, but certainly of questioning, his own high position, while Soames, who never smoked cigars, would not.

Then, too, in old Jolyon's mind there was always the secret ache, that the son of James—of James, whom he had always thought such a poor thing, should be pursuing the paths of success, while his own son——!

And last, not least—for he was no more outside the radiation of family gossip than any other Forsyte—he had now heard the sinister, indefinite, but none the less disturbing rumour about Bosinney, and his pride was wounded to the quick.

Characteristically, his irritation turned not against Irene but against Soames. The idea that his nephew's wife (why couldn't the fellow take better care of her—oh! quaint injustice! as though Soames could possibly take more care!)—should be drawing to herself June's lover, was intolerably humiliating. And seeing the danger, he did not, like James, hide it away in sheer nervousness, but owned with the dispassion of his broader outlook, that it was not unlikely; there was something very attractive about Irene!

He had a presentiment on the subject of Soames's communication as they left the Board Room together, and went out into the noise and hurry of Cheapside. They walked together a good minute without speaking, Soames with his mousing, mincing step, and old Jolyon upright and using his umbrella languidly as a walking-stick.

They turned presently into comparative quiet, for old Jolyon's way to a second Board led him in the direction of Moorgate Street.

Then Soames, without lifting his eyes, began: "I've had this letter from Bosinney. You see what he says; I thought I'd let you know. I've spent a lot more than I intended on this house, and I want the position to be clear."

Old Jolyon ran his eyes unwillingly over the letter: "What he says is clear enough," he said.

"He talks about 'a free hand,' " replied Soames.

Old Jolyon looked at him. The long-suppressed irritation and antagonism towards this young fellow, whose affairs were beginning to intrude upon his own, burst from him.

"Well, if you don't trust him, why do you employ him?"

Soames stole a sideway look: "It's much too late to go into that," he said, "I only want it to be quite understood that if I give him a free hand, he doesn't let me in. I thought if you were to speak to him, it would carry more weight!"

"No," said old Jolyon abruptly; "I'll have nothing to do with it!"

The words of both uncle and nephew gave the impression of unspoken meanings, far more important, behind. And the look they interchanged was like a revelation of this consciousness.

"Well," said Soames; "I thought, for June's sake, I'd tell you, that's all; I thought you'd better know I shan't stand any nonsense!"

"What is that to me?" old Jolyon took him up.

"Oh! I don't know," said Soames, and flurried by that sharp look he was unable to say more. "Don't say I didn't tell you," he added sulkily, recovering his composure.

"Tell me!" said old Jolyon; "I don't know what you mean. You come worrying me about a thing like this. _I_ don't want to hear about your affairs; you must manage them yourself!"

"Very well," said Soames immovably, "I will!"

"Good-morning, then," said old Jolyon, and they parted.

Soames retraced his steps, and going into a celebrated eating-house, asked for a plate of smoked salmon and a glass of Chablis; he seldom ate much in the middle of the day, and generally ate standing, finding the position beneficial to his liver, which was very sound, but to which he desired to put down all his troubles.

When he had finished he went slowly back to his office, with bent head, taking no notice of the swarming thousands on the pavements, who in their turn took no notice of him.

The evening post carried the following reply to Bosinney:

'FORSYTE, BUSTARD AND FORSYTE,
'Commissioners for Oaths,
'2001, BRANCH LANE, POULTRY, E.C.,
'*May* 17, 1887.

'DEAR BOSINNEY,

'I have received your letter, the terms of which not a little surprise me. I was under the impression that you had, and have had all along, a "free hand"; for I do not recollect that any suggestions I have been so unfortunate as to make, have met with your approval. In giving you, in accordance with your request, this "free hand," I wish you to clearly understand that the total cost of the house as handed over to me completely decorated, inclusive of your fee (as arranged between us), must not exceed twelve thousand pounds—£12,000. This gives you an ample margin, and, as you know, is far more than I originally contemplated.

'I am,
'Yours truly,
'SOAMES FORSYTE.'

On the following day he received a note from Bosinney:

'PHILIP BAYNES BOSINNEY,
'Architect,
'309D, SLOANE STREET, S.W.,
'*May* 18.

'DEAR FORSYTE,

'If you think that in such a delicate matter as decoration I can bind myself to the exact pound, I am afraid you are mistaken. I can see that you are tired of the arrangement, and of me, and I had better, therefore, resign.

'Yours faithfully,
'PHILIP BAYNES BOSINNEY.'

Soames pondered long and painfully over his answer, and late at night in the dining-room, when Irene had gone to bed, he composed the following:

'62, MONTPELLIER SQUARE, S.W.,
'*May* 19, 1887.

'DEAR BOSINNEY,

'I think that in both our interests it would be extremely undesirable that matters should be so left at this stage. I did not mean to say that if you should exceed the sum named in my letter to you by ten or twenty or even fifty pounds, there would be any difficulty between us. This being so, I should like you to reconsider your answer. You have a "free hand" in the terms of this correspondence, and I hope you will see your way to completing the decorations, in the matter of which I know it is difficult to be absolutely exact.

'Yours truly,

'SOAMES FORSYTE.'

Bosinney's answer, which came in the course of the next day, was:

'*May* 20.

'DEAR FORSYTE,
  'Very well.

'PH. BOSINNEY.'

Chapter VI

OLD JOLYON AT THE ZOO

OLD JOLYON disposed of his second Meeting—an ordinary Board—summarily. He was so dictatorial that his fellow directors were left in cabal over the increasing domineeringness of old Forsyte, which they were far from intending to stand much longer, they said.

He went out by Underground to Portland Road Station, whence he took a cab and drove to the Zoo.

He had an assignation there, one of those assignations that had lately been growing more frequent, to which his increasing uneasiness about June and the 'change in her,' as he expressed it, was driving him.

She buried herself away, and was growing thin; if he spoke to her he got no answer, or had his head snapped off, or she looked as if she would burst into tears. She was as changed as she could be, all through this Bosinney. As for telling him about anything, not a bit of it!

And he would sit for long spells brooding, his paper unread before him, a cigar extinct between his lips. She had been such a companion to him ever since she was three years old! And he loved her so!

Forces regardless of family or class or custom were beating down his guard; impending events over which he had no control threw their shadows on his head. The irritation of one accustomed to have his way was roused against he knew not what.

Chafing at the slowness of his cab, he reached the Zoo door; but, with his sunny instinct for seizing the good of each moment, he forgot his vexation as he walked towards the tryst.

From the stone terrace above the bear-pit his son and his two grand-children came hastening down when they saw old Jolyon coming, and led him away towards the lion-house. They supported him on either side, holding one to each of his hands, whilst Jolly, perverse like his father, carried his grandfather's umbrella in such a way as to catch people's legs with the crutch of the handle.

148

Young Jolyon followed.

It was as good as a play to see his father with the children, but such a play as brings smiles with tears behind. An old man and two small children walking together can be seen at any hour of the day; but the sight of old Jolyon, with Jolly and Holly seemed to young Jolyon a special peep-show of the things that lie at the bottom of our hearts. The complete surrender of that erect old figure to those little figures on either hand was too poignantly tender, and, being a man of an habitual reflex action, young Jolyon swore softly under his breath. The show affected him in a way unbecoming to a Forsyte, who is nothing if not undemonstrative.

Thus they reached the lion-house.

There had been a morning fête at the Botanical Gardens, and a large number of Forsy—that is, of well-dressed people who kept carriages—had brought them on to the Zoo, so as to have more, if possible, for their money, before going back to Rutland Gate or Bryanston Square.

"Let's go on to the Zoo," they had said to each other; "it'll be great fun!" It was a shilling day; and there would not be all those horrid common people.

In front of the long line of cages they were collected in rows, watching the tawny, ravenous beasts behind the bars await their only pleasure of the four-and-twenty hours. The hungrier the beast, the greater the fascination. But whether because the spectators envied his appetite, or more humanely, because it was so soon to be satisfied, young Jolyon could not tell. Remarks kept falling on his ears: "That's a nasty-looking brute, that tiger!" "Oh, what a love! Look at his little mouth!" "Yes, he's rather nice! Don't go too near, mother."

And frequently, with little pats, one or another would clap their hands to their pockets behind and look round, as though expecting young Jolyon or some disinterested-looking person to relieve them of the contents.

A well-fed man in a white waistcoat said slowly through his teeth: "It's all greed; they can't be hungry. Why, they take no exercise." At these words a tiger snatched a piece of bleeding liver, and the fat man laughed. His wife, in a Paris-model frock and gold nose-nippers, reproved him: "How can you laugh, Harry? Such a horrid sight!"

Young Jolyon frowned.

149

The circumstances of his life, though he had ceased to take a too personal view of them, had left him subject to an intermittent contempt; and the class to which he had belonged—the carriage class—especially excited his sarcasm.

To shut up a lion or tiger in confinement was surely a horrible barbarity. But no cultivated person would admit this.

The idea of its being barbarous to confine wild animals had probably never even occurred to his father for instance; he belonged to the old school, who considered it at once humanizing and educational to confine baboons and panthers, holding the view, no doubt, that in course of time they might induce these creatures not so unreasonably to die of misery and heart-sickness against the bars of their cages, and put the society to the expense of getting others! In his eyes, as in the eyes of all Forsytes, the pleasure of seeing these beautiful creatures in a state of captivity far outweighed the inconvenience of imprisonment to beasts whom God had so improvidently placed in a state of freedom! It was for the animals' good, removing them at once from the countless dangers of open air and exercise, and enabling them to exercise their functions in the guaranteed seclusion of a private compartment! Indeed, it was doubtful what wild animals were made for but to be shut up in cages!

But as young Jolyon had in his constitution the elements of impartiality, he reflected that to stigmatize as barbarity that which was merely lack of imagination must be wrong; for none who held these views had been placed in a similar position to the animals they caged, and could not, therefore, be expected to enter into their sensations.

It was not until they were leaving the gardens—Jolly and Holly in a state of blissful delirium—that old Jolyon found an opportunity of speaking to his son on the matter next his heart. "I don't know what to make of it," he said; "if she's to go on as she's going on now, I can't tell what's to come. I wanted her to see the doctor, but she won't. She's not a bit like me. She's your mother all over. Obstinate as a mule! If she doesn't want to do a thing, she won't, and there's an end of it!"

Young Jolyon smiled; his eyes had wandered to his father's chin. 'A pair of you,' he thought, but he said nothing.

"And then," went on old Jolyon, "there's this Bosinney. I should like to punch the fellow's head, but I can't, I suppose, though—I don't see why you shouldn't," he added doubtfully.

"What has he done? Far better that it should come to an end, if they don't hit it off!"

Old Jolyon looked at his son. Now they had actually come to discuss a subject connected with the relations between the sexes he felt distrustful. Jo would be sure to hold some loose view or other.

"Well, I don't know what *you* think," he said; "I dare say your sympathy's with him—shouldn't be surprised; but *I* think he's behaving precious badly, and if he comes my way I shall tell him so." He dropped the subject.

It was impossible to discuss with his son the true nature and meaning of Bosinney's defection. Had not his son done the very same thing (worse, if possible) fifteen years ago? There seemed no end to the consequences of that piece of folly!

Young Jolyon also was silent; he had quickly penetrated his father's thought, for, dethroned from the high seat of an obvious and uncomplicated view of things, he had become both perceptive and subtle.

The attitude he had adopted towards sexual matters fifteen years before, however, was too different from his father's. There was no bridging the gulf.

He said coolly: "I suppose he's fallen in love with some other woman?"

Old Jolyon gave him a dubious look: "I can't tell," he said; "they say so!"

"Then, it's probably true," remarked young Jolyon unexpectedly; "and I suppose *they've* told you who she is?"

"Yes," said old Jolyon—"Soames's wife!"

Young Jolyon did not whistle. The circumstances of his own life had rendered him incapable of whistling on such a subject, but he looked at his father, while the ghost of a smile hovered over his face.

If old Jolyon saw, he took no notice.

"She and June were bosom friends!" he muttered.

"Poor little June!" said young Jolyon softly. He thought of his daughter still as a babe of three.

Old Jolyon came to a sudden halt.

"I don't believe a word of it," he said, "it's some old woman's tale. Get me a cab, Jo, I'm tired to death!"

They stood at a corner to see if an empty cab would come along, while carriage after carriage drove past, bearing Forsytes of all descriptions from the Zoo. The harness, the liveries, the gloss on the horses' coats, shone and glittered in the May sunlight, and each equipage, landau, sociable, barouche, Victoria, or brougham, seemed to roll out proudly from its wheels:

> 'I and my horses and my men you know,
> Indeed the whole turn-out have cost a pot.
> But we were worth it every penny. Look
> At Master and at Missis now, the dawgs!
> Ease with security—ah! that's the ticket!'

And such, as everyone knows, is fit accompaniment for a perambulating Forsyte.

Amongst these carriages was a barouche coming at a greater pace than the others, drawn by a pair of bright bay horses. It swung on its high springs, and the four people who filled it seemed rocked as in a cradle.

This chariot attracted young Jolyon's attention; and suddenly, on the back seat, he recognised his Uncle James, unmistakable in spite of the increased whiteness of his whiskers; opposite, their backs defended by sunshades, Rachel Forsyte and her elder but married sister, Winifred Dartie, in irreproachable toilettes, had posed their heads haughtily, like two of the birds they had been seeing at the Zoo; while by James's side reclined Dartie, in a brand-new frock-coat buttoned tight and square, with a large expanse of carefully shot linen protruding below each wristband.

An extra, if subdued, sparkle, an added touch of the best gloss or varnish characterized this vehicle, and seemed to distinguish it from all the others, as though by some happy extravagance—like that which marks out the real 'work of art' from the ordinary 'picture'—it were designated as the typical car, the very throne of Forsytedom.

Old Jolyon did not see them pass; he was petting poor Holly who was tired, but those in the carriage had taken in the little group; the ladies' heads tilted suddenly, there was a spasmodic screening movement of parasols; James's face protruded naïvely, like the head of a long bird, his mouth slowly opening. The shield-like rounds of the parasols grew smaller and smaller, and vanished.

Young Jolyon saw that he had been recognised, even by Winifred, who could not have been more than fifteen when he had forfeited the right to be considered a Forsyte.

There was not much change in *them!* He remembered the exact look of their turn-out all that time ago: Horses, men, carriage—all different now, no doubt—but of the precise stamp of fifteen years before; the same neat display, the same nicely calculated arrogance—ease with security! The swing exact, the pose of the sunshades exact, exact the spirit of the whole thing.

And in the sunlight, defended by the haughty shields of parasols, carriage after carriage went by.

"Uncle James has just passed, with his female folk," said young Jolyon.

His father looked black. "Did your uncle see us? Yes? Hmph! What's *he* want, coming down into these parts?"

An empty cab drove up at this moment, and old Jolyon stopped it.

"I shall see you again before long, my boy!" he said. "Don't you go paying any attention to what I've been saying about young Bosinney— I don't believe a word of it!"

Kissing the children, who tried to detain him, he stepped in and was borne away.

Young Jolyon, who had taken Holly up in his arms, stood motionless at the corner, looking after the cab.

Chapter VII

AFTERNOON AT TIMOTHY'S

I F old Jolyon, as he got into his cab, had said: 'I *won't* believe a
word of it!' he would more truthfully haxe expressed his senti-
ments.

The notion that James and his womankind had seen him in the company of his son had awakened in him not only the impatience he always
felt when crossed, but that secret hostility natural between brothers, the
roots of which—little nursery rivalries—someimes toughen and deepen
as life goes on, and, all hidden, support a plant capable of producing in
season the bitterest fruits.

Hitherto there had been between these six brothers no more un-
friendly feeling than that caused by the secret and natural doubt that the
others might be richer than themselves; a feeling increased to the pitch
of curiosity by the approach of death—that end of all handicaps—and
the great 'closeness' of their man of business, who, with some sagacity,
would profess to Nicholas ignorance of James's income, to James ignorance of old Jolyon's, to Jolyon ignorance of Roger's, to Roger ignorance of Swithin's, while to Swithin he would say most irritatingly that
Nicholas must be a rich man. Timothy alone was exempt, being in
gilt-edged securities.

But now, between two of them at least, had arisen a very different
sense of injury. From the moment when James had the impertinence to
pry into his affairs—as he put it—old Jolyon no longer chose to credit
this story about Bosinney. His grand-daughter slighted through a member of 'that fellow's' family! He made up his mind that Bosinney was
maligned. There must be some other reason for his defection.

June had flown out at him, or something; she was as touchy as she
could be!

He would, however, let Timothy have a bit of his mind, and see if he
would go on dropping hints! And he would not let the grass grow under

his feet either, he would go there at once, and take very good care that he didn't have to go again on the same errand.

He saw James's carriage blocking the pavement in front of 'The Bower.' So they had got there before him—cackling about having seen him, he dared say! And further on, Swithin's greys were turning their noses towards the noses of James's bays, as though in conclave over the family, while their coachmen were in conclave above.

Old Jolyon, depositing his hat on the chair in the narrow hall, where that hat of Bosinney's had so long ago been mistaken for a cat, passed his thin hand grimly over his face with its great drooping white moustaches, as though to remove all traces of expression, and made his way upstairs.

He found the front drawing-room full. It was full enough at the best of times—without visitors—without anyone in it—for Timothy and his sisters, following the tradition of their generation, considered that a room was not quite 'nice' unless it was 'properly' furnished. It held, therefore, eleven chairs, a sofa, three tables, two cabinets, innumerable knicknacks, and part of a large grand piano. And now, occupied by Mrs. Small, Aunt Hester, by Swithin, James, Rachel, Winifred, Euphemia, who had come in again to return 'Passion and Paregoric' which she had read at lunch and her chum Frances, Roger's daughter (the musical Forsyte, the one who composed songs), there was only one chair left unoccupied, except, of course, the two that nobody ever sat on—and the only standing room was occupied by the cat, on whom old Jolyon promptly stepped.

In these days it was by no means unusual for Timothy to have so many visitors. The family had always, one and all, had a real respect for Aunt Ann, and now that she was gone, they were coming far more frequently to The Bower, and staying longer.

Swithin had been the first to arrive, and seated torpid in a red satin chair with a gilt back, he gave every appearance of lasting the others out. And symbolizing Bosinney's name 'the big one,' with his great stature and bulk, his thick white hair, his puffy immovable shaven face, he looked more primeval than ever in the highly upholstered room.

His conversation, as usual of late, had turned at once upon Irene, and he had lost no time in giving Aunts Juley and Hester his opinion with regard to this rumour he heard was going about. No—as he said—she might want a bit of flirtation—a pretty woman must have her fling; but more than that he did not believe. Nothing open; she had too much good sense, too much proper appreciation of what was due to her position, and to the family! No sc—— he was going to say 'scandal' but the very idea was so preposterous that he waved his hand as though to say—'but let that pass!'

Granted that Swithin took a bachelor's view of the situation—still what indeed was not due to that family in which so many had done so well for themselves, had attained a certain position? If he *had* heard in dark, pessimistic moments the words 'yeoman' and 'very small beer' used in connection with his origin, did he believe them?

No! he cherished, hugging it pathetically to his bosom, the secret theory that there was something distinguished somewhere in his ancestry.

"Must be," he once said to young Jolyon, before the latter went to the bad. "Look at us, *we've* got on! There must be good blood in us somewhere."

He had been fond of young Jolyon: the boy had been in a good set at College, had known that old ruffian Sir Charles Fiste's sons—a pretty rascal one of them had turned out, too; and there was style about him— it was a thousand pities he had run off with that half-foreign governess! If he must go off like that why couldn't he have chosen someone who would have done them credit! And what was he now?—an underwriter at Lloyd's; they said he even painted pictures—pictures! Damme! he might have ended as Sir Jolyon Forsyte, Bart., with a seat in Parliament, and a place in the country.

It was Swithin who, following the impulse which sooner or later urges thereto some member of every great family, went to the Heralds' Office, where they assured him that he was undoubtedly of the same family as the well-known Forsites with an 'i,' whose arms were 'three dexter buckles on a sable ground gules,' hoping no doubt to get him to take them up.

Swithin, however, did not do this, but having ascertained that the crest was a 'pheasant proper,' and the motto 'For Forsite,' he had the pheasant proper placed upon his carriage and the buttons of his coach-man, and both crest and motto on his writing-paper. The arms he hugged to himself, partly because, not having paid for them, he thought it would look ostentatious to put them on his carriage, and he hated ostentation, and partly because he, like any practical man all over the country, had a secret dislike and contempt for things he could not understand—he found it hard, as anyone might, to swallow 'three dexter buckles on a sable ground gules.'

He never forgot, however, their having told him that if he paid for them he would be entitled to use them, and it strengthened his conviction that he was a gentleman. Imperceptibly the rest of the family absorbed the 'pheasant proper,' and some, more serious than others, adopted the motto; old Jolyon, however, refused to use the latter, saying that it was humbug—meaning nothing, so far as he could see.

Among the older generation it was perhaps known at bottom from what great historical event they derived their crest; and if pressed on the subject, sooner than tell a lie—they did not like telling lies, having an impression that only Frenchmen and Russians told them—they would confess hurriedly that Swithin had got hold of it somehow.

Among the younger generation the matter was wrapped in a discretion proper. They did not want to hurt the feelings of their elders, nor to feel ridiculous themselves; they simply used the crest. . . .

"No," said Swithin, "he had had an opportunity of seeing for himself, and what he should say was, that there was nothing in her manner to that young Buccaneer or Bosinney or whatever his name was, different from her manner to himself; in fact, he should rather say. . . ." But here the entrance of Frances and Euphemia put an unfortunate stop to the conversation, for this was not a subject which could be discussed before young people.

And though Swithin was somewhat upset at being stopped like this on the point of saying something important, he soon recovered his affability. He was rather fond of Frances—Francie, as she was called in the family. She was so smart, and they told him she made a pretty little pot of pin-money by her songs; he called it very clever of her.

He rather prided himself indeed on a liberal attitude towards women, not seeing any reason why they shouldn't paint pictures, or write tunes, or books even, for the matter of that, especially if they could turn a useful penny by it; not at all—kept them out of mischief. It was not as if they were men!

'Little Francie,' as she was usually called with good-natured contempt, was an important personage, if only as a standing illustration of the attitude of Forsytes towards the Arts. She was not really 'little,' but rather tall, with dark hair for a Forsyte, which, together with a grey eye, gave her what was called 'a Celtic appearance.' She wrote songs with titles like 'Breathing Sighs,' or 'Kiss me, Mother, ere I die,' with a refrain like an anthem:

> 'Kiss me, Mother, ere I die;
> Kiss me—kiss me, Mother, ah!
> Kiss, ah! kiss me e—ere I—
> Kiss me, Mother, ere I d—d—die!'

She wrote the words to them herself, and other poems. In lighter moments she wrote waltzes, one of which, the 'Kensington Coil,' was almost national to Kensington, having a sweet dip in it. Thus:

It was very original. Then there were her 'Songs for Little People,' at once educational and witty, especially 'Gran'ma's Porgie,' and that ditty, almost prophetically imbued with the coming Imperial spirit, entitled 'Black him in his little eye.'

Any publisher would take these, and reviews like 'High Living,' and the 'Ladies' Genteel Guide' went into raptures over: 'Another of Miss Francie Forsyte's spirited ditties, sparkling and pathetic. We ourselves were moved to tears and laughter. Miss Forsyte should go far.'

With the true instinct of her breed, Francie had made a point of knowing the right people—people who would write about her, and talk about her, and people in Society, too—keeping a mental register of just where to exert her fascinations, and an eye on that steady scale of rising prices, which in her mind's eye represented the future. In this way she caused herself to be universally respected.

Once, at a time when her emotions were whipped by an attachment—for the tenor of Roger's life, with its whole-hearted collection of house property, had induced in his only daughter a tendency towards passion—she turned to great and sincere work, choosing the sonata form, for the violin. This was the only one of her productions that troubled the Fro-sytes. They felt at once that it would not sell.

Roger, who liked having a clever daughter well enough, and often alluded to the amount of pocket-money she made for herself, was upset by this violin sonata.

"Rubbish like that!" he called it. Francie had borrowed young Flageoletti from Euphemia, to play it in the drawing-room at Prince's Gardens.

As a matter of fact Roger was right. It *was* rubbish, but—annoying! the sort of rubbish that wouldn't sell. As every Forsyte knows, rubbish that sells is not rubbish at all—far from it.

And yet, in spite of the sound common sense which fixed the worth of art at which it would fetch, some of the Forsytes—Aunt Hester, for instance, who had always been musical—could not help regretting that Francie's music was not 'classical'; the same with her poems. But then, as Aunt Hester said, they didn't see any poetry nowadays, all the poems were 'little light things.' There was nobody who could write a poem like 'Paradise Lost,' or 'Childe Harold'; either of which made you feel that you really had read something. Still, it was nice for Francie to have some-thing to occupy her; while other girls were spending money shopping she was making it! And both Aunt Hester and Aunt Juley were always ready to listen to the latest story of how Francie had got her price increased.

They listened now, together with Swithin, who sat pretending not to, for these young people talked so fast and mumbled so, he never could catch what they said!

"And I can't think," said Mrs. Septimus, "how you do it. I should never have the audacity!"

Francie smiled lightly. "I'd much rather deal with a man than a woman. Women are so sharp!"

"My dear," cried Mrs. Small, "I'm sure we're not."

Euphemia went off into her silent laugh, and, ending with the squeak, said, as though being strangled: "Oh, you'll kill me some day, auntie."

Swithin saw no necessity to laugh; he detested people laughing when he himself perceived no joke. Indeed, he detested Euphemia altogether, to whom he always alluded as 'Nick's daughter, what's she called—the pale one?' He had just missed being her godfather—indeed, would have been, had he not taken a firm stand against her outlandish name. He hated becoming a godfather. Swithin then said to Francie with dignity: "It's a fine day—er—for the time of year." But Euphemia, who knew perfectly well that he had refused to be her godfather, turned to Aunt Hester, and began telling her how she had seen Irene—Mrs. Soames—at the Church and Commercial Stores.

"And Soames was with her?" said Aunt Hester, to whom Mrs. Small had as yet had no opportunity of relating the incident.

"*Soames* with her? Of *course* not!"

"But was she all alone in London?"

"Oh, no; there was Mr. Bosinney with her. She was *perfectly* dressed."

But Swithin, hearing the name Irene, looked severely at Euphemia, who, it is true, never did look well in a dress, whatever she may have done on other occasions, and said:

"Dressed like a lady, I've no doubt. It's a pleasure to see her."

At this moment James and his daughters were announced. Dartie, feeling badly in want of a drink, had pleaded an appointment with his dentist, and, being put down at the Marble Arch, had got into a hansom, and was already seated in the window of his club in Piccadilly.

His wife, he told his cronies, had wanted to take him to pay some calls. It was not in his line—not exactly. Haw!

Hailing the waiter, he sent him out to the hall to see what had won the 4.30 race. He was dog-tired, he said, and that was a fact; had been drivin' about with his wife to 'shows' all the afternoon. Had put his foot down at last. A fellow must live his own life.

At this moment, glancing out of the bay window—for he loved this seat whence he could see everybody pass—his eye unfortunately, or perhaps fortunately, chanced to light on the figure of Soames, who was mousing across the road from the Green Park side, with the evident intention of coming in, for he, too, belonged to 'The Iseeum.'

Dartie sprang to his feet; grasping his glass, he muttered something about 'that 4.30 race,' and swiftly withdrew to the card-room, where Soames never came. Here, in complete isolation and a dim light, he lived his own life till half-past seven, by which hour he knew Soames must certainly have left the club.

It would not do, as he kept repeating to himself whenever he felt the impulse to join the gossips in the bay-window getting too strong for him—it absolutely would not do, with finances as low as his, and the 'old man' (James) rusty ever since that business over the oil shares, which was no fault of his, to risk a row with Winifred.

If Soames were to see him in the club it would be sure to come round to her that he wasn't at the dentist's at all. He never knew a family where things 'came round' so. Uneasily, amongst the green baize card-tables, a frown on his olive-coloured face, his check trousers crossed, and patent-leather boots shining through the gloom, he sat biting his fore-finger, and wondering where the deuce he was to get the money if Erotic failed to win the Lancashire Cup.

His thoughts turned gloomily to the Forsytes. What a set they were! There was no getting anything out of them—a least, it was a matter of extreme difficulty. They were so d——d particular about money matters; not a sportsman amongst the lot, unless it were George. That fellow Soames, for instance, would have a fit if you tried to borrow a tenner from him, or, if he didn't have a fit, he looked at you with his cursed supercilious smile, as if you were a lost soul because you were in want of money.

And that wife of his (Dartie's mouth watered involuntarily), he had tried to be on good terms with her, as one naturally would with any pretty sister-in-law, but he would be cursed if the—(he mentally used a coarse word)—would have anything to say to him—she looked at him, indeed, as if he were dirt—and yet she could go far enough, he wouldn't mind betting. He knew women; they weren't made with soft eyes and figures like that for nothing, as that fellow Soames would jolly soon find out, if there were anything in what he had heard about this Buccaneer Johnny.

Rising from his chair, Dartie took a turn across the room, ending in front of the looking-glass over the marble chimney-piece; and there he stood for a long time contemplating in the glass the reflection on his face. It had that look, peculiar to some men, of having been steeped in linseed oil, with its waxed dark moustaches and the little distinguished commencements of side whiskers; and concernedly he felt the promise of a pimple on the side of his slightly curved and fattish nose.

In the meantime old Jolyon had found the remaining chair in Timothy's commodious drawing-room. His advent had obviously put a stop to the conversation, decided awkwardness having set in. Aunt

Juley, with her well-known kindheartedness, hastened to set people at their ease again.

"Yes, Jolyon," she said, "we were just saying that you haven't been here for a long time; but we mustn't be surprised. You're busy, of course? James was just saying what a busy time of year——"

"Was he?" said old Jolyon, looking hard at James. "It wouldn't be half so busy if everybody minded their own business."

James, brooding in a small chair from which his knees ran uphill, shifted his feet uneasily, and put one of them down on the cat, which had unwisely taken refuge from old Jolyon beside him.

"Here, you've got a cat here," he said in an injured voice, withdrawing his foot nervously as he felt it squeezing into the soft, furry body.

"Several," said old Jolyon, looking at one face and another; "I trod on one just now."

A silence followed.

Then Mrs. Small, twisting her fingers and gazing round with pathetic calm, asked: "And how is dear June?"

A twinkle of humour shot through the sternness of old Jolyon's eyes. Extraordinary old woman, Juley! No one quite like her for saying the wrong thing!

"Bad!" he said; "London don't agree with her—too many people about, too much clatter and chatter by half." He laid emphasis on the words, and again looked James in the face.

Nobody spoke.

A feeling of its being too dangerous to take a step in any direction, or hazard any remark, had fallen on them all. Something of the sense of the impending, that comes over the spectator of a Greek tragedy, had entered that upholstered room, filled with those white-haired, frock-coated old men, and fashionably attired women, who were all of the same blood, between all of whom existed an unseizable resemblance.

Not that they were conscious of it—the visits of such fateful, bitter spirits are only felt.

Then Swithin rose. He would not sit there, feeling like that—*he* was not to be put down by anyone! And, manoeuvring round the room with added pomp, he shook hands with each separately.

"You tell Timothy from me," he said, "that he coddles himself too much!" Then, turning to Francie, whom he considered 'smart,' he added:

"You come with me for a drive one of these days." But this conjured up the vision of that other eventful drive which had been so much talked about, and he stood quite still for a second, with glassy eyes, as though waiting to catch up with the significance of what he himself had said; then, suddenly recollecting that he didn't care a damn, he turned to old Jolyon: "Well, good-bye, Jolyon! You shouldn't go about without an overcoat; you'll be getting sciatica or something!" And, kicking the cat slightly with the pointed tip of his his patent leather boot, he took his huge form away.

When he had gone everyone looked secretly at the others, to see how they had they had taken the mention of the word 'drive'—the word which had become famous, and acquired an overwhelming importance, as the only official—so to speak—news in connection with the vague and sinister rumour clinging to the family tongue.

Euphemia, yielding to an impulse, said with a short laugh: "I'm glad Uncle Swithin doesn't ask me to go for drives."

Mrs. Small, to reassure her and smooth over any little awkwardness the subject might have, replied: "My dear, he likes to take somebody well dressed, who will do him a little credit. I shall never forget the drive he took me. It was an experience!" And her chubby round old face was spread for a moment with a strange contentment; then broke into pouts, and tears came into her eyes. She was thinking of that long ago driving tour she had once taken with Septimus Small.

James, who had relapsed into his nervous brooding in the little chair, suddenly roused himself: "He's a funny fellow, Swithin," he said, but in a half-hearted way.

Old Jolyon's silence, his stern eyes, held them all in a kind of paralysis. He was disconcerted himself by the effect of his own words—an effect which seemed to deepen the importance of the very rumour he had come to scotch; but he was still angry.

He had not done with them yet— No, no—he would give them another rub or two!

He did not wish to rub his nieces, he had no quarrel with them—a young and presentable female always appealed to old Jolyon's clemency —but that fellow James, and, in a less degree perhaps, those others, deserved all they would get. And he, too, asked for Timothy.

As though feeling that some danger threatened her younger brother,

Aunt Juley suddenly offered him tea: "There it is," she said, "all cold and nasty, waiting for you in the back drawing-room, but Smither shall make you some fresh."

Old Jolyon rose: "Thank you," he said, looking straight at James, "but I've no time for tea, and—scandal, and the rest of it! It's time I was at home. Good-bye, Julia; good-bye, Hester; good-bye, Winifred."

Without more ceremonious adieux, he marched out.

Once again in his cab, his anger evaporated, for so it ever was with his wrath—when he had rapped out, it was gone. Sadness came over his spirit. He had stopped their mouths, maybe, but at what a cost! At the cost of certain knowledge that the rumour he had been resolved not to believe was true. June was abandoned, and for the wife of that fellow's son! He felt it was true, and hardened himself to treat it as if it were not; but the pain he hid beneath this resolution began slowly, surely, to vent itself in a blind resentment against James and his son.

The six women and one man left behind in the little drawing-room began talking as easily as might be after such an occurrence, for though each one of them knew for a fact that he or she never talked scandal, each one of them also knew that the other six did; all were therefore angry and at a loss. James only was silent, disturbed to the bottom of his soul.

Presently Francie said: "Do you know, I think Uncle Jolyon is terribly changed this last year. What do *you* think, Aunt Hester?"

Aunt Hester made a little movement of recoil: "Oh, ask your Aunt Julia!" she said; "I know nothing about it."

No one else was afraid of assenting, and James muttered gloomily at the floor: "He's not half the man he was."

"I've noticed it a long time," went on Francie; "he's aged tremendously."

Aunt Juley shook her head; her face seemed suddenly to have become one immense pout.

"Poor dear Jolyon," she said, "somebody ought to see to it for him!"

There was again silence; then, as though in terror of being left solitarily behind, all five visitors rose simultaneously, and took their departure.

Mrs. Small, Aunt Hester, and their cat were left once more alone, the

164

sound of a door closing in the distance announced the approach of Timothy.

That evening, when Aunt Hester had just got off to sleep in the back bedroom that used to be Aunt Juley's before Aunt Juley took Aunt Ann's, her door was opened, and Mrs. Small, in a pink nightcap, a candle in her hand, entered: "Hester!" she said. "Hester!"

Aunt Hester faintly rustled the sheet.

"Hester," repeated Aunt Juley, to make quite sure that she had awakened her, "I am quite troubled about poor dear Jolyon. *What,*" Aunt Juley dwelt on the word, "do you think ought to be done?"

Aunt Hester again rustled the sheet, her voice was heard faintly pleading: "Done? How should I know?"

Aunt Juley turned away satisfied, and closing the door with extra gentleness so as not to disturb dear Hester, let it slip through her fingers and fall to with a 'crack.'

Back in her own room, she stood at the window gazing at the moon over the trees in the Park, through a chink in the muslin curtains, close drawn lest anyone should see. And there, with her face all round and pouting in its pink cap, and her eyes wet, she thought of 'dear Jolyon,' so old and so lonely, and how she could be of some use to him; and how he would come to love her, as she had never been loved since—since poor Septimus went away.

Chapter VIII

DANCE AT ROGER'S

ROGER'S house in Prince's Gardens was brilliantly alight. Large numbers of wax candles had been collected and placed in cut-glass chandeliers, and the parquet floor of the long, double drawing-room reflected these constellations. An appearance of real spaciousness had been secured by moving out all the furniture on to the upper landings, and enclosing the room with those strange appendages of civilization known as 'rout' seats.

In a remote corner, embowered in palms, was a cottage piano, with a copy of the 'Kensington Coil' open on the music-stand.

Roger had objected to a band. He didn't see in the least what they wanted with a band; he wouldn't go to the expense, and there was an end of it. Francie (her mother, whom Roger had long since reduced to chronic dyspepsia, went to bed on such occasions), had been obliged to content herself with supplementing the piano by a young man who played the cornet, and she so arranged with palms that anyone who did not look into the heart of things might imagine there were several musicians secreted there. She made up her mind to tell them to play loud—there was a lot of music in a cornet, if the man would only put his soul into it.

In the more cultivated American tongue, she was 'through' at last—through that tortuous labyrinth of make-shifts, which must be traversed before fashionable display can be combined with the sound economy of a Forsyte. Thin but brilliant, in her maize-coloured frock with much tulle about the shoulders, she went from place to place, fitting on her gloves, and casting her eye over it all.

To the hired butler (for Roger only kept maids) she spoke about the wine. Did he quite understand that Mr. Forsyte wished a dozen bottles of the champagne from Whiteley's to be put out? But if that were finished (she did not suppose it would be, most of the ladies would drink water, no doubt), but if it were, there was the champagne cup, and he must do the best he could with that.

She hated having to say this sort of thing to a butler, it was so *infra dig.;* but what could you do with father? Roger, indeed, after making himself consistently disagreeable about the dance, would come down presently, with his fresh colour and bumpy forehead, as though he had been its promoter; and he would smile, and probably take the prettiest woman in to supper; and at two o'clock, just as they were getting into the swing, he would go up secretly to the musicians and tell them to play 'God Save the Queen,' and go away.

Francie devoutly hoped he might soon get tired, and slip off to bed.

The three or four devoted girl friends who were staying in the house for this dance, had partaken with her, in a small, abandoned room upstairs, of tea and cold chicken-legs, hurriedly served; the men had been sent out to dine at Eustace's Club, it being felt that they must be fed up.

Punctually on the stroke of nine arrived Mrs. Small alone. She made elaborate apologies for the absence of Timothy, omitting all mention of Aunt Hester, who, at the last minute, had said she could not be bothered. Francie received her effusively, and placed her on a rout seat, where she left her, pouting and solitary in lavender-coloured satin—the first time she had worn colour since Aunt Ann's death.

The devoted maiden friends came now from their rooms, each by magic arrangement in a differently coloured frock, but all with the same liberal allowance of tulle on the shoulders and at the bosom—for they were, by some fatality, lean to a girl. They were all taken up to Mrs. Small. None stayed with her more than a few seconds, but clustering together talked and twisted their programmes, looking secretly at the door for the first appearance of a man.

Then arrived in a group a number of Nicholases, always punctual—the fashion up Ladbroke Grove way; and close behind them Eustace and his men, gloomy and smelling rather of smoke.

Three or four of Francie's lovers now appeared, one after the other; she had made each promise to come early. They were all clean-shaven and sprightly, with that peculiar kind of young-man sprightliness which had recently invaded Kensington; they did not seem to mind each other's presence in the least, and wore their ties bunching out at the ends, white waistcoats, and socks with clocks. All had handkerchiefs concealed in their cuffs. They moved buoyantly, each armoured in professional gaiety, as though he had come to do great deeds. Their faces when they danced, far from wearing the traditional solemn look of the dancing Englishman, were irresponsible, charming, suave; they bounded, twirling their partners at great pace, without pedantic attention to the rhythm of the music.

At other dancers they looked with a kind of airy scorn—they, the light brigade, the heroes of a hundred Kensington 'hops'—from whom alone could the right manner and smile and step be hoped.

After this the stream came fast; chaperones silting up along the wall facing the entrance, the volatile element swelling the eddy in the larger room.

Men were scarce, and wallflowers wore their peculiar, pathetic expression, a patient, sourish smile which seemed to say: "Oh, no! don't mistake me, *I* know you are not coming up to me. I can hardly expect that!" And Francie would plead with one of her lovers, or with some callow youth: "Now, to please me, do let me introduce you to Miss Pink; such a nice girl, really!" and she would bring him up, and say: "Miss Pink— Mr. Gathercole. *Can* you spare him a dance?" Then Miss Pink, smiling her forced smile, colouring a little, answered: "Oh! I think so!" and screening her empty card, wrote on it the name of Gathercole, spelling it passionately in the district that he proposed, about the second extra.

But when the youth had murmured that it was hot, and passed, she relapsed into her attitude of hopeless expectation, into her patient, sourish smile.

Mothers, slowly fanning their faces, watched their daughters, and in their eyes could be read all the story of those daughters' fortunes. As for themselves, to sit hour after hour, dead tired, silent, or talking spasmodically—what did it matter, so long as the girls were having a good time! But to see them neglected and passed by! Ah! they smiled, but their eyes stabbed like the eyes of an offended swan; they longed to pluck young Gathercole by the slack of his dandified breeches, and drag him to their daughters—the jackanapes!

And all the cruelties and hardness of life, its pathos and unequal chances, its conceit, self-forgetfulness, and patience, were presented on the battle-field of this Kensington ball-room.

Here and there, too, lovers—not lovers like Francie's, a peculiar breed, but simply lovers—trembling, blushing, silent, sought each other by flying glances, sought to meet and touch in the mazes of the dance, and now and again dancing together, struck some beholder by the light in their eyes.

Not a second before ten o'clock came the Jameses—Emily, Rachel, Winifred (Dartie had been left behind, having on a former occasion drunk too much of Roger's champagne), and Cicely, the youngest, making her début; behind them, following in a hansom from the paternal mansion where they had dined, Soames and Irene.

All these ladies had shoulder-straps and no tulle—thus showing at once, by a bolder exposure of flesh, that they came from the more fashionable side of the Park.

Soames, sidling back from the contact of the dancers, took up a position against the wall. Guarding himself with his pale smile, he stood watching. Waltz after waltz began and ended, couple after couple brushed by with smiling lips, laughter, and snatches of talk; or with set lips, and eyes searching the throng; or again, with silent, parted lips, and eyes on each other. And the scent of festivity, the odour of flowers, and hair, of essences that women love, rose suffocatingly in the heat of the summer night.

Silent, with something of scorn in his smile, Soames seemed to notice nothing; but now and again his eyes, finding that which they sought, would fix themselves on a point in the shifting throng, and the smile die off his lips.

He danced with no one. Some fellows danced with their wives; his sense of 'form' had never permitted him to dance with Irene since their marriage, and the God of the Forsytes alone can tell whether this was a relief to him or not.

She passed, dancing with other men, her dress, iris-coloured, floating away from her feet. She danced well; he was tired of hearing women say with an acid smile: "How beautifully your wife dances, Mr. Forsyte —it's quite a pleasure to watch her!" Tired of answering them with his sidelong glance: "You think so?"

A young couple close by flirted a fan by turns, making an unpleasant draught. Francie and one of her lovers stood near. They were talking of love.

He heard Roger's voice behind, giving an order about supper to a servant. Everything was very second-class! He wished that he had not come! He had asked Irene whether she wanted him; she had answered with that maddening smile of hers: "Oh, no!"

Why *had* he come? For the last quarter of an hour he had not even seen her. Here was George advancing with his Quilpish face; it was too late to get out of his way.

"Have you seen 'The Buccaneer'?" said this licensed wag; "he's on the warpath—hair cut and everything!"

Soames said he had not, and crossing the room, half-empty in an interval of the dance, he went out on the balcony, and looked down into the street.

A carriage had driven up with late arrivals, and round the door hung some of those patient watchers of the London streets who spring up to the call of light or music; their faces, pale and upturned above their black and rusty figures, had an air of stolid watching that annoyed Soames. Why were they allowed to hang about; why didn't the bobby move them on?

But the policeman took no notice of them; his feet were planted apart on the strip of crimson carpet stretched across the pavement; his face, under the helmet, wore the same stolid, watching look as theirs.

Across the road, through the railings, Soames could see the branches of trees shining, faintly stirring in the breeze, by the gleam of the street lamps; beyond, again, the upper lights of the houses on the other side, so many eyes looking down on the quiet blackness of the garden; and over all, the sky, that wonderful London sky, dusted with the innumerable reflection of countless lamps; a dome woven over between its stars with the refraction of human needs and human fancies—immense mirror of pomp and misery that night after night stretches its kindly mocking over miles of houses and gardens, mansions and squalor, over Forsytes, policemen, and patient watchers in the streets.

Soames turned away, and, hidden in the recess, gazed into the lighted room. It was cooler out there. He saw the new arrivals, June and her grandfather, enter. What had made them so late? They stood by the doorway. They looked fagged. Fancy Uncle Jolyon turning out at this time of night! Why hadn't June come to Irene, as she usually did, and it occurred to him suddenly that he had seen nothing of June for a long time now.

Watching her face with idle malice, he saw it change, grow so pale that he thought she would drop, then flame out crimson. Turning to see at what she was looking, he saw his wife on Bosinney's arm, coming from the conservatory at the end of the room. Her eyes were raised to his, as though answering some question he had asked, and he was gazing at her intently.

Soames looked again at June. Her hand rested on old Jolyon's arm; she seemed to be making a request. He saw a surprised look on his uncle's face; they turned and passed through the door out of his sight.

The music began again—a waltz—and, still as a statue in the recess of the window, his face unmoved, but no smile on his lips, Soames waited. Presently, within a yard of the dark balcony, his wife and Bosinney passed. He caught the perfume of the gardenias that she wore, saw the rise and fall of her bosom, the languor in her eyes, her parted lips, and a look on her face that he did not know. To the slow, swinging measure they danced by, and it seemed to him that they clung to each other; he saw her raise her eyes, soft and dark, to Bosinney's and drop them again.

Very white, he turned back to the balcony, and leaning on it, gazed down on the Square; the figures were still there looking up at the light with dull persistency, the policeman's face, too, upturned, and staring, but he saw nothing of them. Below, a carriage drew up, two figures got in, and drove away. . . .

That evening June and old Jolyon sat down to dinner at the usual hour. The girl was in her customary high-necked frock, old Jolyon had not dressed.

At breakfast she had spoken of the dance at Uncle Roger's, she wanted to go; she had been stupid enough, she said, not to think of asking anyone to take her. It was too late now.

Old Jolyon lifted his keen eyes. June was used to going to dances with Irene as a matter of course! And deliberately fixing his gaze on her, he asked: "Why don't you get Irene?"

No! June did not want to ask Irene; she would only go if—if her grandfather wouldn't mind just for once—for a little time!

At her look, so eager and so worn, old Jolyon had grumblingly consented. He did not know what she wanted, he said, with going to a dance like this, a poor affair, he would wager; and she no more fit for it than a cat! What she wanted was sea air, and after his general meeting of the

171

Globular Gold Concessions he was ready to take her. She didn't want to go away? Ah! she would knock herself up! Stealing a mournful look at her, he went on with his breakfast.

June went out early, and wandered restlessly about in the heat. Her little light figure that lately had moved so languidly about its business, was all on fire. She bought herself some flowers. She wanted—she meant to look her best. *He* would be there! She knew well enough that he had a card. She would show him that she did not care. But deep down in her heart she resolved that evening to win him back. She came in flushed, and talked brightly all lunch; old Jolyon was there, and he was deceived.

In the afternoon she was overtaken by a desperate fit of sobbing. She strangled the noise against the pillows of her bed, but when at last it ceased she saw in the glass a swollen face with reddened eyes, and violet circles round them. She stayed in the darkened room till dinner time.

All through that silent meal the struggle went on within her. She looked so shadowy and exhausted that old Jolyon told 'Sankey' to countermand the carriage, he would not have her going out. She was to go to bed! She made no resistance. She went up to her room, and sat in the dark. At ten o'clock she rang for her maid.

"Bring some hot water, and go down and tell Mr. Forsyte that I feel perfectly rested. Say that if he's too tired I can go to the dance by myself."

The maid looked askance, and June turned on her imperiously. "Go," she said, "bring the hot water at once!"

Her ball-dress still lay on the sofa, and with a sort of fierce care she arrayed herself, took the flowers in her hand, and went down, her small face carried high under its burden of hair. She could hear old Jolyon in his room as she passed.

Bewildered and vexed, he was dressing. It was past ten, they would not get there till eleven; the girl was mad. But he dared not cross her—the expression of her face at dinner haunted him.

With great ebony brushes he smoothed his hair till it shone like silver under the light; then he, too, came out on the gloomy staircase.

June met him below, and, without a word, they went to the carriage.

When, after that drive which seemed to last for ever, she entered Roger's drawing-room, she disguised under a mask of resolution a very torment of nervousness and emotion. The feeling of shame at what might be called 'running after him' was smothered by the dread that he might not be there, that she might not see him after all, and by that dogged resolve—somehow, she did not know how—to win him back.

The sight of the ballroom, with its gleaming floor, gave her a feeling of joy, of triumph, for she loved dancing, and when dancing she floated, so light was she, like a strenuous, eager little spirit. He would surely ask her to dance, and if he danced with her it would all be as it was before. She looked about her eagerly.

The sight of Bosinney coming with Irene from the conservatory, with that strange look of utter absorption on his face, struck her too suddenly. The had not seen—no one should see—her distress, not even her grandfather.

She put her hand on Jolyon's arm, and said very low:

"I must go home, Gran; I feel ill."

He hurried her away, grumbling to himself that he had known how it would be.

To her he said nothing; only when they were once more in the carriage, which by some fortunate chance had lingered near the door, he asked her: "What is it, my darling?"

Feeling her whole slender body shaken by sobs, he was terribly alarmed. She must have Blank to-morrow. He would insist upon it. He could not have her like this. . . . There, there!

June mastered her sobs, and squeezing his hand feverishly, she lay back in her corner, her face muffled in a shawl.

He could only see her eyes, fixed and staring in the dark, but he did not cease to stroke her hand with his thin fingers.

Chapter IX

EVENING AT RICHMOND

OTHER eyes besides the eyes of June and of Soames had seen 'those two' (as Euphemia had already begun to call them) coming from the conservatory; other eyes had noticed the look on Bosinney's face.

There are moments when Nature reveals the passion hidden beneath the careless calm of her ordinary moods—violent spring flashing white on almond-blossom through the purple clouds; a snowy, moonlit peak, with its single star, soaring up to the passionate blue; or against the flames of sunset, an old yew-tree standing dark guardian of some fiery secret.

There are moments, too, when in a picture-gallery, a work, noted by the casual spectator as '. . . Titian—remarkably fine,' breaks through the defences of some Forsyte better lunched perhaps than his fellows, and holds him spellbound in a kind of ecstacy. There are things, he feels—there are things here which—well, which are things. Something unreasoning, unreasonable, is upon him; when he tries to define it with the precision of a practical man, it eludes him, slips away, as the glow of the wine he has drunk is slipping away, leaving him cross, and conscious of his liver. He feels that he has been extravagant, prodigal of something; virtue has gone out of him. He did not desire this glimpse of what lay under the three stars of his catalogue. God forbid that he should know anything about the forces of Nature! God forbid that he should admit for a moment that there are such things! Once admit that, and where was he? One paid a shilling for entrance, and another for the programme.

The look which June had seen, which other Forsytes had seen, was like the sudden flashing of a candle through a hole in some imaginary canvas, behind which it was being moved—the sudden flaming-out of a vague, erratic glow, shadowy and enticing. It brought home to onlookers

174

the consciousness that dangerous forces were at work. For a moment they noticed it with pleasure, with interest, then felt they must not notice it at all.

It supplied, however, the reason of June's coming so late and disappearing again without dancing, without even shaking hands with her lover. She was ill, it was said, and no wonder.

But here they looked at each other guiltily. They had no desire to spread scandal, no desire to be ill-natured. Who would have? And to outsiders no word was breathed, unwritten law keeping them silent.

Then came the news that June had gone to the seaside with old Jolyon.

He had carried her off to Broadstairs, for which place there was just then a feeling, Yarmouth having lost caste, in spite of Nicholas, and no Forsyte going to the sea without intending to have an air for his money such as would render him bilious in a week. That fatally aristocratic tendency of the first Forsyte to drink Madeira had left his descendants undoubtedly accessible.

So June went to the sea. The family awaited developments; there was nothing else to do.

But how far—how far had 'those two' gone? How far were they going to go? Could they really be going at all? Nothing could surely come of it, for neither of them had any money. At the most a flirtation, ending, as all such attachments should, at the proper time.

Soames's sister, Winifred Dartie, who had imbibed with the breezes of Mayfair—she lived in Green Street—more fashionable principles in regard to matrimonial behaviour than were current, for instance, in Ladbroke Grove, laughed at the idea of there being anything in it. The 'little thing'—Irene was taller than herself, and it was real testimony to the solid worth of a Forsyte that she should always thus be a 'little thing'—the little thing was bored. Why shouldn't she amuse herself? Soames was rather tiring; and as to Mr. Bosinney—only that buffoon George would have called him the Buccaneer—she maintained that he was very *chic*.

This dictum—that Bosinney was *chic*—caused quite a sensation. It failed to convince. That he was 'good-looking in a way' they were prepared to admit, but that anyone could call a man with his pronounced cheekbones, curious eyes, and soft felt hats *chic* was only another instance of Winifred's extravagant way of running after something new.

It was that famous summer when extravagance was fashionable, when the very earth was extravagant, chestnut-trees spread with blossom, and flowers drenched in perfume, as they had never been before; when roses blew in every garden; and for the swarming stars the nights had hardly space; when every day and all day long the sun, in full armour, swung his brazen shield above the Park, and people did strange things, lunching and dining in the open air. Unprecedented was the tale of cabs and carriages that streamed across the bridges of the shining river, bearing the upper-middle class in thousands to the green glories of Bushey, Richmond, Kew, and Hampton Court. Almost every family with any pretensions to be of the carriage-class paid one visit that year to the horse-chestnuts at Bushey, or took one drive amongst the Spanish chestnuts of Richmond Park. Bowling smoothly, if dustily, along, in a cloud of their own creation, they would stare fashionably at the antlered heads which the great slow deer raised out of a forest of bracken that promised to autumn lovers such cover as was never seen before. And now and again, as the amorous perfume of chestnut flowers and of fern was drifted too near, one would say to the other: "My dear! What a peculiar scent!"

And the lime-flowers that year were of rare prime, near honey-coloured. At the corners of London squares they gave out, as the sun went down, a perfume sweeter than the honey bees had taken—a perfume that stirred a yearning unnamable in the hearts of Forsytes and their peers, taking the cool after dinner in the precincts of those gardens to which they alone had keys.

And that yearning made them linger amidst the dim shapes of flower-beds in the failing daylight, made them turn, and turn, and turn again, as though lovers were waiting for them—waiting for the last light to die away under the shadow of the branches.

Some vague sympathy evoked by the scent of the limes, some sisterly desire to see for herself, some idea of demonstrating the soundness of her dictum that there was 'nothing in it'; or merely the craving to drive down to Richmond, irresistible that summer, moved the mother of the little Darties (of little Publius, of Imogen, Maud, and Benedict) to write the following note to her sister-in-law:

176

'June 30.

'DEAR IRENE,

'I hear that Soames is going to Henley to-morrow for the night. I thought it would be great fun if we made up a little party and drove down to Richmond. Will you ask Mr. Bosinney, and I will get young Flippard.

'Emily (they called their mother Emily—it was so *chic*) will lend us the carriage. I will call for you and your young man at seven o'clock.

'Your affectionate sister,

'WINIFRED DARTIE.

'Montague believes the dinner at the Crown and Sceptre to be quite eatable.'

Montague was Dartie's second and better-known name—his first being Moses; for he was nothing if not a man of the world.

Her plan met with more opposition from Providence than so benevolent a scheme deserved. In the first place young Flippard wrote:

'DEAR MRS. DARTIE,

'Awfully sorry. Engaged too deep.

'Yours,

'AUGUSTUS FLIPPARD.'

It was late to send into the bye-ways and hedges to remedy this misfortune. With the promptitude and conduct of a mother, Winifred fell back on her husband. She had, indeed, the decided but tolerant temperament that goes with a good deal of profile, fair hair, and greenish eyes. She was seldom or never at a loss; or if at a loss, was always able to convert it into a gain.

Dartie, too, was in good feather. Erotic had failed to win the Lancashire Cup. Indeed, that celebrated animal, owned as he was by a pillar of the turf, who had secretly laid many thousands against him, had not even started. The forty-eight hours that followed his scratching were among the darkest in Dartie's life.

Visions of James haunted him day and night. Black thoughts about Soames mingled with the faintest hopes. On the Friday night he got

177

drunk, so greatly was he affected. But on Saturday morning the true Stock Exchange instinct triumphed within him. Owing some hundreds, which by no possibility could he pay, he went into town and put them all on Concertina for the Saltown Borough Handicap.

As he said to Major Scrotton, with whom he lunched at the Iseeum: "That little Jew boy, Nathans, had given him the tip. He didn't care a cursh. He wash in—a mucker. If it didn't come up—well then, damme, the old man would have to pay!"

A bottle of Pol Roger to his own cheek had given him a new contempt for James.

It came up. Concertina was squeezed home by her neck—a terrible squeak! But, as Dartie said: There was nothing like pluck!

He was by no means averse to the expedition to Richmond. He would 'stand' it himself! He cherished an admiration for Irene, and wished to be on more playful terms with her.

At half-past five the Park Lane footman came round to say: Mrs. Forsyte was very sorry, but one of her horses was coughing!

Undaunted by this further blow, Winifred at once despatched little Publius (now aged seven) with the nursery governess to Montpellier Square.

They would go down in hansoms and meet at the Crown and Sceptre at 7.45.

Dartie, on being told, was pleased enough. It was better than going down with your back to the horses! He had no objection to driving down with Irene. He supposed they would pick up the others at Montpellier Square, and swop hansoms there?

Informed that the meet was at the Crown and Sceptre, and that he would have to drive with his wife, he turned sulky, and said it was d——d slow!

At seven o'clock they started, Dartie offering to bet the driver half-a-crown he didn't do it in the three-quarters of an hour.

Twice only did husband and wife exchange remarks on the way.

Dartie said: "It'll put Master Soames's nose out of joint to hear his wife's been drivin in a hansom with Master Bosinney!"

Winifred replied: "Don't talk such nonsense, Monty!"

"Nonsense!" repeated Dartie. "You don't know women, my fine lady!"

178

On the other occasion he merely asked: "How am I looking? A bit puffy about the gills? That fizz old George is so fond of is a windy wine!"

He had been lunching with George Forsyte at the Haversnake.

Bosinney and Irene had arrived before them. They were standing in one of the long French windows overlooking the river.

Windows that summer were open all day long, and all night too, and day and night the scents of flowers and trees came in, the hot scent of parching grass, and the cool scent of the heavy dews.

To the eye of the observant Dartie his two guests did not appear to be making much running, standing there close together, without a word. Bosinney was a hungry-looking creature—not much go about *him!*

He left them to Winifred, however, and busied himself to order the dinner.

A Forsyte will require good, if not delicate feeding, but a Dartie will tax the resources of a Crown and Sceptre. Living as he does, from hand to mouth, nothing is too good for him to eat; and he will eat it. His drink, too, will need to be carefully provided; there is much drink in this country 'not good enough' for a Dartie; he will have the best. Paying for things vicariously, there is no reason why he should stint himself. To stint yourself is the mark of a fool, not a Dartie.

The best of everything! No sounder principle on which a man can base his life, whose father-in-law has a very considerable income, and a partiality for his grandchildren.

With his not unable eye Dartie had spotted this weakness in James the very first year after little Publius's arrival (an error); he had profited by his perspicacity. Four little Darties were now a sort of perpetual insurance.

The feature of the feast was unquestionably the red mullet. This delectable fish, brought from a considerable distance in a state of almost perfect preservation, was first fried, then boned, then served in ice, with Madeira punch in place of sauce, according to a recipe known to a few men of the world.

Nothing else calls for remark except the payment of the bill by Dartie.

He had made himself extremely agreeable throughout the meal; his bold, admiring stare seldom abandoning Irene's face and figure. As he was obliged to confess to himself, he got no change out of her—she was cool enough, as cool as her shoulders looked under their veil of creamy lace. He expected to have caught her out in some little game with Bosinney; but not a bit of it, she kept up her end remarkably well. As for that architect chap, he was as glum as a bear with a sore head—Winifred could barely get a word out of him; he ate nothing, but he certainly took his liquor, and his face kept getting whiter, and his eyes looked queer.

It was all very amusing.

For Dartie himself was in capital form, and talked freely, with a certain poignancy, being no fool. He told two or three stories verging on the improper, a concession to the company, for his stories were not used to verging. He proposed Irene's health in a mock speech. Nobody drank it, and Winifred said: "Don't be such a clown, Monty!"

At her suggestion they went after dinner to the public terrace overlooking the river.

"I should like to see the common people making love," she said, "it's such fun!"

There were numbers of them walking in the cool, after the day's heat, and the air was alive with the sound of voices, coarse and loud, or soft as though murmuring secrets.

It was not long before Winifred's better sense—she was the only Forsyte present—secured them an empty bench. They sat down in a row. A heavy tree spread a thick canopy above their heads, and the haze darkened slowly over the river.

Dartie sat at the end, next to him Irene, then Bosinney, then Winifred. There was hardly room for four, and the man of the world could feel Irene's arm crushed against his own; he knew that she could not withdraw it without seeming rude, and this amused him; he devised every now and again a movement that would bring her closer still. He thought: 'That Buccaneer Johnny shan't have it all to himself! It's a pretty tight fit, certainly!'

From far down below on the dark river came drifting the tinkle of a mandoline, and voices singing the old round:

> 'A boat, a boat, unto the ferry,
> For we'll go over and be merry,
> And laugh, and quaff, and drink brown sherry!'

And suddenly the moon appeared, young and tender, floating up on her back from behind a tree; and as though she had breathed, the air was cooler, but down that cooler air came always the warm odour of the limes.

Over his cigar Dartie peered round at Bosinney, who was sitting with his arms crossed, staring straight in front of him, and on his face the look of a man being tortured.

And Dartie shot a glance at the face between, so veiled by the over-hanging shadow that it was but like a darker piece of the darkness shaped and breathed on; soft, mysterious, enticing.

A hush had fallen on the noisy terrace, as if all the strollers were thinking secrets too precious to be spoken.

And Dartie thought: 'Women!'

The glow died above the river, the singing ceased; the young moon hid behind a tree, and all was dark. He passed himself against Irene.

He was not alarmed at the shuddering that ran through the limbs he touched, or at the troubled, scornful look of her eyes. He felt her trying to draw herself away, and smiled.

It must be confessed that the man of the world had drunk quite as much as was good for him.

With thick lips parted under his well-curled moustaches, and his bold eyes aslant upon her, he had the malicious look of a satyr.

Along the pathway of sky between the hedges of the tree tops the stars clustered forth; like mortals beneath, they seemed to shift and swarm and whisper. Then on the terrace the buzz broke out once more, and Dartie thought: 'Ah! he's a poor, hungry-looking devil, that Bosinney!' and again he pressed himself against Irene.

The movement deserved a better success. She rose, and they all followed her.

The man of the world was more than ever determined to see what she was made of. Along the terrace he kept close at her elbow. He had within him much good wine. There was the long drive home, the long drive and the warm dark and the pleasant closeness of the hansom cab—with its insulation from the world devised by some great and good man. That hungry architect chap might drive with his wife—he wished him joy of her! And, conscious that his voice was not too steady, he was careful not to speak; but a smile had become fixed on his thick lips.

They strolled along toward the cabs awaiting them at the farther end. His plan had the merit of all great plans, an almost brutal simplicity— he would merely keep at her elbow till she got in, and get in quickly after her.

But when Irene reached the cab she did not get in; she slipped, instead, to the horse's head. Dartie was not at the moment sufficiently master of his legs to follow. She stood stroking the horse's nose, and, to his annoyance, Bosinney was at her side first. She turned and spoke to him rapidly, in a low voice; the words 'That man' reached Dartie. He stood stubbornly by the cab step, waiting for her to come back. He knew a trick worth two of that!

Here, in the lamp-light, his figure (no more than medium height), well squared in its white evening waistcoat, his light overcoat flung over his arm, a pink flower in his buttonhole, and on his dark face that look of confident, good-humoured insolence, he was at his best—a thorough man of the world.

Winifred was already in her cab. Dartie reflected that Bosinney would have a poorish time in that cab if he didn't look sharp! Suddenly he received a push which nearly overturned him in the road. Bosinney's voice hissed in his ear: "I am taking Irene back; do you understand?" He saw a face white with passion, and eyes that glared at him like a wild cat's.

"Eh?" he stammered. "What? Not a bit! You take my wife!"

"Get away!" hissed Bosinney—"or I'll throw you into the road!"

Dartie recoiled; he saw as plainly as possible that the fellow meant it. In the space he made Irene had slipped by, her dress brushed his legs. Bosinney stepped in after her.

"Go on!" he heard the Buccaneer cry. The cabman flicked his horse. It sprang forward.

Dartie stood for a moment dumbfounded; then, dashing at the cab where his wife sat, he scrambled in.

"Drive on!" he shouted to the driver, "and don't you lose sight of that fellow in front!"

Seated by his wife's side, he burst into imprecations. Calming himself at last with a supreme effort, he added: "A pretty mess you've made of it, to let the Buccaneer drive home with her; why on earth couldn't you keep hold of him? He's mad with love; any fool can see that!"

He drowned Winifred's rejoinder with fresh calls to the Almighty; nor was it until they reached Barnes that he ceased a Jeremiad, in the course of which he had abused her, her father, her brother, Irene, Bosinney, the name of Forsyte, his own children, and cursed the day when he had ever married.

Winifred, a woman of strong character, let him have his say, at the end of which he lapsed into sulky silence. His angry eyes never deserted the back of that cab, which, like a lost chance, haunted the darkness in front of him.

Fortunately he could not hear Bosinney's passionate pleading—that pleading which the man of the world's conduct had let loose like a flood; he could not see Irene shivering, as though some garment had been torn from her, nor her eyes, black and mournful, like the eyes of a beaten child. He could not hear Bosinney entreating, entreating, always entreating; could not hear her sudden, soft weeping, nor see that poor, hungry-looking devil, awed and trembling, humbly touching her hand.

In Montpellier Square their cabman, following his instructions to the letter, faithfully drew up behind the cab in front. The Darties saw Bosinney spring out, and Irene follow, and hasten up the steps with bent head. She evidently had her key in her hand, for she disappeared at once. It was impossible to tell whether she had turned to speak to Bosinney.

The latter came walking past their cab; both husband and wife had an admirable view of his face in the light of a street lamp. It was working with violent emotion.

"Good-night, Mr. Bosinney!" called Winifred.

Bosinney started, clawed off his hat, and hurried on. He had obviously forgotten their existence.

"There!" said Dartie, "did you see the beast's face? What did I say? Fine games!" He improved the occasion.

There had so clearly been a crisis in the cab that Winifred was unable to defend her theory.

She said: "I shall say nothing about it. I don't see any use in making a fuss!"

With that view Dartie at once concurred; looking upon James as a private preserve, he disapproved of his being disturbed by the troubles of others.

"Quite right," he said; "let Soames look after himself. He's jolly well able to!"

Thus speaking, the Darties entered their habitat in Green Street, the rent of which was paid by James, and sought a well-earned rest. The hour was midnight, and no Forsytes remained abroad in the streets to spy out Bosinney's wanderings; to see him return and stand against the rails of the Square garden, back from the glow of the street lamp; to see him stand there in the shadow of trees, watching the house where in the dark was hidden she whom he would have given the world to see for a single minute—she who was now to him the breath of the lime-trees, the meaning of the light and the darkness, the very beating of his own heart.

Chapter X

DIAGNOSIS OF A FORSYTE

IT is in the nature of a Forsyte to be ignorant that he is a Forsyte; but young Jolyon was well aware of being one. He had not known it till after the decisive step which had made him an outcast; since then the knowledge had been with him continually. He felt it throughout his alliance, throughout all his dealings with his second wife, who was emphatically not a Forsyte.

He knew that if he had not possessed in great measure the eye for what he wanted, the tenacity to hold on to it, the sense of the folly of wasting that for which he had given so big a price—in other words, the 'sense of property'—he could never have retained her (perhaps never would have desired to retain her) with him through all the financial troubles, slights, and misconstructions of those fifteen years; never have induced her to marry him on the death of his first wife; never have lived it all through, and come up, as it were, thin, but smiling.

He was one of those men who, seated cross-legged like miniature Chinese idols in the cages of their own hearts, are ever smiling at themselves a doubting smile. Not that this smile, so intimate and eternal, interfered with his actions, which, like his chin and his temperament, were quite a peculiar blend of softness and determination.

He was conscious, too, of being a Forsyte in his work, that painting of water-colours to which he devoted so much energy, always with an eye on himself, as though he could not make so unpractical a pursuit quite seriously, and always with a certain queer uneasiness that he did not make more money at it.

It was, then, this consciousness of what it meant to be a Forsyte, that made him receive the following letter from old Jolyon, with a mixture of sympathy and disgust:

185

'SHELDRAKE HOUSE,
'BROADSTAIRS,
'*July* 1.

'MY DEAR JO,'

(The Dad's handwriting had altered very little in the thirty odd years that he remembered it.)

'We have been here now a fortnight, and have had good weather on the whole. The air is bracing, but my liver is out of order, and I shall be glad enough to get back to town. I cannot say much for June, her health and spirits are very indifferent, and I don't see what is to come of it. She says nothing, but it is clear that she is harping on this engagement, which is an engagement and no engagement, and—goodness knows what. I have grave doubts whether she ought to be allowed to return to London in the present state of affairs, but she is so self-willed that she might take it into her head to come up at any moment. The fact is someone ought to speak to Bosinney and ascertain what he means. I'm afraid of this myself, for I should certainly rap him over the knuckles, but I thought that you, knowing him at the Club, might put in a word, and get to ascertain what the fellow is about. You will of course in no way commit June. I shall be glad to hear from you in the course of a few days whether you have succeeded in gaining any information. The situation is very distressing to me, I worry about it at night. With my love to Jolly and Holly.

'I am,

'Your affect. father,
'JOLYON FORSYTE.'

Young Jolyon pondered this letter so long and seriously that his wife noticed his preoccupation, and asked him what was the matter. He replied: "Nothing."

It was a fixed principle with him never to allude to June. She might take alarm, he did not know what she might think; he hastened, therefore, to banish from his manner all traces of absorption, but in this he was about as successful as his father would have been, for he had inherited all old Jolyon's transparency in matters of domestic finesse; and young Mrs. Jolyon, busying herself over the affairs of the house, went about with tightened lips, stealing at him unfathomable looks.

He started for the Club in the afternoon with the letter in his pocket, and without having made up his mind.

To sound a man as to 'his intentions' was peculiarly unpleasant to him; nor did his own anomalous position diminish this unpleasantness. It was so like his family, so like all the people they knew and mixed with, to enforce what they called their rights over a man, to bring him up to the mark; so like them to carry their business principles into their private relations!

And how that phrase in the letter—'You will, of course, in no way commit June'—gave the whole thing away.

Yet the letter, with the personal grievance, the concern for June, the 'rap over the knuckles,' was all so natural. No wonder his father wanted to know what Bosinney meant, no wonder he was angry.

It was difficult to refuse! But why give the thing to him to do? That was surely quite unbecoming; but so long as a Forsyte got what he was after, he was not too particular about the means, provided appearances were saved.

How should he set about it, or how refuse? Both seemed impossible. So, young Jolyon!

He arrived at the Club at three o'clock, and the first person he saw was Bosinney himself, seated in a corner, staring out of the window.

Young Jolyon sat down not far off, and began nervously to reconsider his position. He looked covertly at Bosinney sitting there unconscious. He did not know him very well, and studied him attentively for perhaps the first time; an unusual-looking man, unlike in dress, face, and manner to most of the other members of the Club—young Jolyon himself, however different he had become in mood and temper, had always retained the neat reticence of Forsyte appearance. He alone among Forsytes was ignorant of Bosinney's nickname. The man was unusual, not eccentric, but unusual; he looked worn, too, haggard, hollow in the cheeks beneath those broad, high cheekbones, though without any appearance of ill-health, for he was strongly built, with curly hair that seemed to show all the vitality of a fine constitution.

Something in his face and attitude touched young Jolyon. He knew what suffering was like, and this man looked as if he were suffering.

He got up and touched his arm.

Bosinney started, but exhibited no sign of embarrassment on seeing who it was.

Young Jolyon sat down.

"I haven't seen you for a long time," he said. "How are you getting on with my cousin's house?"

"It'll be finished in about a week."

"I congratulate you!"

"Thanks—I don't know that it's much of a subject for congratulation."

"No?" queried young Jolyon; "I should have thought you'd be glad to get a long job like that off your hands; but I suppose you feel it much as I do when I part with a picture—a sort of child?"

He looked kindly at Bosinney.

"Yes," said the latter more cordially, "it goes out from you and there's an end of it. I didn't know you painted."

"Only water-colours; I can't say I believe in my work."

"Don't believe in it? Then how can you do it? Work's no use unless you believe in it!"

"Good," said young Jolyon; "it's exactly what I've always said. By-the-bye, have you noticed that whenever one says, 'Good,' one always adds 'it's exactly what I've always said'! But if you ask me how I do it, I answer, because I'm a Forsyte."

"A Forsyte! I never thought of you as one!"

"A Forsyte," replied young Jolyon, "is not an uncommon animal. There are hundreds among the members of this Club. Hundreds out there in the streets; you meet them wherever you go!"

"And how do you tell them, may I ask?" said Bosinney.

"By their sense of property. A Forsyte takes a practical—one might say a commonsense—view of things, and a practical view of things is based fundamentally on a sense of property. A Forsyte, you will notice, never gives himself away."

"Joking?"

Young Jolyon's eye twinkled.

"Not much. As a Forsyte myself, I have no business to talk. But I'm a kind of thoroughbred mongrel; now, there's no mistaking you. You're as different from me as I am from my Uncle James, who is the perfect specimen of a Forsyte. His sense of property is extreme, while you have practically none. Without me in between, you would seem like a different species. I'm the missing link. We are, of course, all of us the slaves of property, and I admit that it's a question of degree, but what I call a

'Forsyte' is a man who is decidedly more than less a slave of property. He knows a good thing, he knows a safe thing, and his grip on property —it doesn't matter whether it be wives, houses, money, or reputation— is his hall-mark."

"Ah!" murmured Bosinney. "You should patent the word."

"I should like," said young Jolyon, "to lecture on it: 'Properties and quality of a Forsyte: This little animal, disturbed by the ridicule of his own sort, is unaffected in his motions by the laughter of strange creatures (you or I). Hereditarily disposed to myopia, he recognises only the persons and habitats of his own species, amongst which he passes an existence of competitive tranquillity."

"You talk of them," said Bosinney, "as if they were half England."

"They are," repeated young Jolyon, "half England, and the better half, too, the safe half, the three per cent. half, the half that counts. It's their wealth and security that makes everything possible; makes your art possible, makes literature, science, even religion, possible. Without Forsytes, who believe in none of these things, but turn them all to use, where should we be? My dear sir, the Forsytes are the middlemen, the commercials, the pillars of society, the cornerstones of convention; everything that is admirable!"

"I don't know whether I catch your drift," said Bosinney, "but I fancy there are plenty of Forsytes, as you call them, in my profession."

"Certainly," replied young Jolyon. "The great majority of architects, painters, or writers have no principles, like any other Forsytes. Art, literature, religion, survive by virtue of the few cranks who really believe in such things, and the many Forsytes who make a commercial use of them. At a low estimate, three-fourths of our Royal Academicians are Forsytes, seven-eighths of our novelists, a large proportion of the press. Of science I can't speak; they are magnificently represented in religion; in the House of Commons perhaps more numerous than anywhere; the aristocracy speaks for itself. But I'm not laughing. It is dangerous to go against the majority—and what a majority!" He fixed his eye on Bosinney: "It's dangerous to let anything carry you away—a house, a picture, a—woman!"

They looked at each other. And, as though he had done that which no Forsyte did—given himself away, young Jolyon drew into his shell. Bosinney broke the silence.

"Why do you take your own people as the type?" said he.

189

"My people," replied young Jolyon, "are not very extreme, and they have their own private peculiarities, like every other family, but they possess in a remarkable degree those two qualities which are the real tests of a Forsyte—the power of never being able to give yourself up to anything soul and body, and the 'sense of property.'"

Bosinney smiled: "How about the big one, for instance?"

"Do you mean Swithin?" asked young Jolyon. "Ah! in Swithin there's some primeval still. The town and middle-class life haven't digested him yet. All the old centuries of farmwork and brute force have settled in him, and there they've stuck, for all he's so distinguished."

Bosinney seemed to ponder. "Well, you've hit your cousin Soames off to the life," he said suddenly. *"He'll* never blow his brains out."

Young Jolyon shot at him a penetrating glance.

"No," he said; "he won't. That's why he's to be reckoned with. Look out for their grip! It's easy to laugh, but don't mistake me. It doesn't do to despise a Forsyte; it doesn't do to disregard them!"

"Yet you've done it yourself!"

Young Jolyon acknowledged the hit by losing his smile.

"You forget," he said with a queer pride, "I can hold on, too—I'm a Forsyte myself. We're all in the path of great forces. The man who leaves the shelter of the wall—well—you know what I mean. I don't," he ended very low, as though uttering a threat, "recommend every man to—go—my—way. It depends."

The colour rushed into Bosinney's face, but soon receded, leaving it sallow-brown as before. He gave a short laugh, that left his lips fixed in a queer, fierce smile; his eyes mocked young Jolyon.

"Thanks," he said. "It's deuced kind of you. But you're not the only chaps that can hold on." He rose.

Young Jolyon looked after him as he walked away, and, resting his head on his hand, sighed.

In the drowsy, almost empty room the only sounds were the rustle of newspapers, the scraping of matches being struck. He stayed a long time without moving, living over again those days when he, too, had sat long hours watching the clock, waiting for the minutes to pass—long hours full of the torments of uncertainty, and of a fierce, sweet aching; and the slow, delicious agony of that season came back to him with its old poignancy. The sight of Bosinney, with his haggard face, and his

190

restless eyes always wandering to the clock, had roused in him a pity, with which was mingled strange, irresistible envy.

He knew the signs so well. Whither was he going—to what sort of fate? What kind of woman was it who was drawing him to her by that magnetic force which no consideration of honour, no principle, no interest could withstand; from which the only escape was flight.

Flight! But why should Bosinney fly? A man fled when he was in danger of destroying hearth and home, when there were children, when he felt himself trampling down ideals, breaking something. But here, so he had heard, it was all broken to his hand.

He himself had not fled, nor would he fly if it were all to come over again. Yet he had gone further than Bosinney, had broken up his own unhappy home, not someone else's. And the old saying came back to him: 'A man's fate lies in his own heart.'

In his own heart! The proof of the pudding was in the eating—Bosinney had still to eat his pudding.

His thoughts passed to the woman, the woman whom he did not know, but the outline of whose story he had heard.

An unhappy marriage! No ill-treatment—only that indefinable malaise, that terrible blight which killed all sweetness under Heaven; and so from day to day, from night to night, from week to week, from year to year, till death should end it!

But young Jolyon, the bitterness of whose own feelings time had assuaged, saw Soames's side of the question too. Whence should a man like his cousin, saturated with all the prejudices and beliefs of his class, draw the insight or inspiration necessary to break up this life? It was a question of imagination, of projecting himself into the future beyond the unpleasant gossip, sneers, and tattle that followed on such separations, beyond the passing pangs that the lack of the sight of her would cause, beyond the grave disapproval of the worthy. But few men, and especially few men of Soames's class, had imagination enough for that. A deal of mortals in this world, and not enough imagination to go round! And sweet Heaven, what a difference between theory and practice; many a man, perhaps even Soames, held chivalrous views on such matters, who when the shoe pinched found a distinguishing factor that made of himself an exception.

Then, too, he distrusted his judgment. He had been through the experience himself, had tasted to the dregs the bitterness of an unhappy marriage, and how could he take the wide and dispassionate view of those who had never been within sound of the battle? His evidence was too first-hand—like the evidence on military matters of a soldier who had been through much active service, against that of civilians who have not suffered the disadvantage of seeing things too close. Most people would consider such a marriage as that of Soames and Irene quite fairly successful; he had money, she had beauty; it was a case for compromise. There was no reason why they should not jog along, even if they hated each other. It would not matter if they went their own ways a little so long as the decencies were observed—the sanctity of the marriage tie, of the common home, respected. Half the marriages of the upper classes were conducted on these lines: Do not offend the susceptibilities of Society; do not offend the susceptibilities of the Church. To avoid offending these is worth the sacrifice of any private feelings. The advantages of the stable home are visible, tangible, so many pieces of property; there is no risk in the *status quo*. To break up a home is at the best a dangerous experiment, and selfish into the bargain.

This was the case for the defence, and young Jolyon sighed.

'The core of it all,' he thought, 'is property, but there are many people who would not like it put that way. To them it is "the sanctity of the marriage tie"; but the sanctity of the marriage tie is dependent on the sanctity of the family, and the sanctity of the family is dependent on the sanctity of property. And yet I imagine all these people are followers of One who never owned anything. It is curious!'

And again young Jolyon sighed.

'Am I going on my way home to ask any poor devils I meet to share my dinner, which will then be too little for myself, or, at all events, for my wife, who is necessary to my health and happiness? It may be that after all Soames does well to exercise his rights and support by his practice the sacred principle of property which benefits us all, with the exception of those who—suffer by the process.'

And so he left his chair, threaded his way through the maze of seats, took his hat, and languidly up the hot streets crowded with carriages, reeking with dusty odours, wended his way home.

Before reaching Wistaria Avenue he removed old Jolyon's letter from his pocket, and tearing it carefully into tiny pieces, scattered them in the dust of the road.

He let himself in with his key, and called his wife's name. But she had gone out, taking Jolly and Holly, and the house was empty; alone in the garden the dog Balthasar lay in the shade snapping at flies.

Young Jolyon took his seat there, too, under the pear-tree that bore no fruit.

Chapter XI

BOSINNEY ON PAROLE

THE day after the evening at Richmond Soames returned from Henley by a morning train. Not constitutionally interested in amphibious sports, his visit had been one of business rather than pleasure, a client of some importance having asked him down.

He went straight to the City, but finding things slack, he left at three o'clock glad of this chance to get home quietly. Irene did not expect him. Not that he had any desire to spy on her actions, but there was no harm in thus unexpectedly surveying the scene.

After changing to Park clothes he went into the drawing-room. She was sitting idly in the corner of the sofa, her favourite seat; and there were circles under her eyes, as though she had not slept.

He asked: "How is it you're in? Are you expecting somebody?"

"Yes—that is, not particularly."

"Who?"

"Mr. Bosinney said he might come."

"Bosinney. He ought to be at work."

To this she made no answer.

"Well," said Soames, "I want you to come out to the Stores with me, and after that we'll go to the Park."

"I don't want to go out; I have a headache."

Soames replied: "If ever I want you to do anything, you've always got a headache. It'll do you good to come and sit under the trees."

She did not answer.

Soames was silent for some minutes; at last he said: "I don't know what your idea of a wife's duty is. I never have known!"

He hadn't expected her to reply, but she did.

"I have tried to do what you want; it's not my fault that I haven't been able to put my heart into it."

"Whose fault is it, then?" He watched her askance.

"Before we were married you promised to let me go if our marriage was not a success. Is it a success?"

Soames frowned.

"Success," he stammered—"it would be a success if you behaved yourself properly!"

"I have tried," said Irene. "Will you let me go?"

Soames turned away. Secretly alarmed, he took refuge in bluster.

"Let you go? You don't know what you're talking about. Let you go? How can I let you go? We're married, aren't we? Then, what are you talking about? For God's sake, don't let's have any of this sort of nonsense! Get your hat on, and come and sit in the Park."

"Then you won't let me go?"

He felt her eyes resting on him with a strange, touching look.

"Let you go!" he said; "and what on earth would you do with yourself if I did? You've got no money!"

"I could manage somehow."

He took a swift turn up and down the room; then came and stood before her.

"Understand," he said, "once and for all, I won't have you say this sort of thing. Go and get your hat on!"

She did not move.

"I suppose," said Soames, "you don't want to miss Bosinney if he comes!"

Irene got up slowly and left the room. She came down with her hat on.

They went out.

In the Park, the motley hour of mid-afternoon, when foreigners and other pathetic folk drive, thinking themselves to be in fashion, had passed; the right, the proper, hour had come, was nearly gone, before Soames and Irene seated themselves under the Achilles statue.

It was some time since he had enjoyed her company in the Park. That was one of the past delights of the first two seasons of his married life, when to feel himself the possessor of this gracious creature before all London had been his greatest, though secret, pride. How many afternoons had he not sat beside her, extremely neat, with light grey gloves and faint, supercilious smile nodding to acquaintances, and now and again removing his hat!

His light grey gloves were still on his hands, and on his lips his smile sardonic, but where the feeling in his heart?

The seats were emptying fast, but still he kept her there, silent and pale, as though to work out a secret punishment. Once or twice he made some comment, and she bent her head, or answered "Yes" with a tired smile.

Along the rails a man was walking so fast that people stared after him when he passed.

"Look at that ass!" said Soames; "he must be mad to walk like that in this heat!"

He turned; Irene had made a rapid movement.

"Hallo!" he said: "it's our friend the Buccaneer!"

And he sat still, with his sneering smile, conscious that Irene was sitting still, and smiling too.

"Will she bow to him?" he thought.

But she made no sign.

Bosinney reached the end of the rails, and came walking back amongst the chairs, quartering his ground like a pointer. When he saw them he stopped dead, and raised his hat.

The smile never left Soames's face; he also took off his hat.

Bosinney came up, looking exhausted, like a man after hard physical exercise; the sweat stood in drops on his brow, and Soames's smile seemed to say: "You've had a trying time, my friend!" ... "What are *you* doing in the Park?" he asked. "We thought you despised such frivolity!"

Bosinney did not seem to hear; he made his answer to Irene: "I've been round to your place; I hoped I should find you in."

Somebody tapped Soames on the back, and spoke to him; and in the exchange of those platitudes over his shoulder, he missed her answer, and took a resolution.

"We're just going in," he said to Bosinney; "you'd better come back to dinner with us." Into that invitation he put a strange bravado, a stranger pathos: "You can't deceive me," his look and voice seemed saying, "but see—I trust you—I'm not afraid of you!"

They started back to Montpellier Square together, Irene between them. In the crowded streets Soames went on in front. He did not listen to their conversation; the strange resolution of trustfulness he had taken seemed to animate even his secret conduct. Like a gambler, he said to himself: 'It's a card I dare not throw away—I must play it for what it's worth. I have not too many chances.'

He dressed slowly, heard her leave her room and go downstairs, and, for full five minutes after, dawdled about in his dressing-room. Then he went down, purposely shutting the door loudly to show that he was coming. He found them standing by the hearth, perhaps talking, perhaps not; he could not say.

He played his part out in the farce, the long evening through—his manner to his guest more friendly than it had ever been before; and when at last Bosinney went, he said: "You must come again soon; Irene likes to have you to talk about the house!" Again his voice had the strange bravado and the stranger pathos; but his hand was cold as ice.

Loyal to his resolution, he turned away from their parting, turned away from his wife as she stood under the hanging lamp to say goodnight—away from the sight of her golden head shining so under the light, of her smiling mournful lips; away from the sight of Bosinney's eyes looking at her, so like a dog's looking at its master.

And he went to bed with the certainty that Bosinney was in love with his wife.

The summer night was hot, so hot and still that through every opened window came in but hotter air. For long hours he lay listening to her breathing.

She could sleep, but he must lie awake. And, lying awake, he hardened himself to play the part of the serene and trusting husband.

In the small hours he slipped out of bed, and passing into his dressing-room, leaned by the open window.

He could hardly breathe.

A night four years ago came back to him—the night but one before his marriage; as hot and stifling as this.

He remembered how he had lain in a long cane chair in the window of his sitting-room off Victoria Street. Down below in a side street a man had banged at a door, a woman had cried out; he remembered, as though it were now, the sound of the scuffle, the slam of the door, the dead silence that followed. And then the early water-cart, cleansing the reek of the streets, had approached through the strange-seeming, useless lamp-light; he seemed to hear again its rumble, nearer and nearer, till it passed and slowly died away.

He leaned far out of the dressing-room window over the little court below, and saw the first light spread. The outlines of dark walls and roofs were blurred for a moment, then came out sharper than before.

He remembered how that other night he had watched the lamps paling all the length of Victoria Street; how he had hurried on his clothes and gone down into the street, down past houses and squares, to the street where she was staying, and there had stood and looked at the front of the little house, as still and grey as the face of a dead man.

And suddenly it shot through his mind, like a sick man's fancy: What's *he* doing?—that fellow who haunts me, who was here this evening, who's in love with my wife—prowling out there, perhaps, looking for her as I know he was looking for her this afternoon; watching my house now, for all I can tell!

He stole across the landing to the front of the house, stealthily drew aside a blind, and raised a window.

The grey light clung about the trees of the square, as though Night, like a great downy moth, had brushed them with her wings. The lamps were still alight, all pale, but not a soul stirred—no living thing in sight!

Yet suddenly, very faint, far off in the deathly stillness, he heard a cry writhing, like the voice of some wandering soul barred out of heaven, and crying for its happiness. There it was again—again! Soames shut the window, shuddering.

Then he thought: 'Ah! it's only the peacocks, across the water.'

Chapter XII

JUNE PAYS SOME CALLS

O LD JOLYON stood in the narrow hall at Broadstairs, inhaling that odour of oilcloth and herrings which permeates all respectable seaside lodging-houses. On a chair—a shiny leather chair, displaying its horsehair through a hole in the top left-hand corner—stood a black despatch case. This he was filling with papers, with the *Times,* and a bottle of Eau-de-Cologne. He had meetings that day of the 'Globular Gold Concessions' and the 'New Colliery Company, Limited,' to which he was going up, for he never missed a Board; to 'miss a Board' would be one more piece of evidence that he was growing old, and this his jealous Forsyte spirit could not bear.

His eyes, as he filled that black despatch case, looked as if at any moment they might blaze up with anger. So gleams the eye of a schoolboy, baited by a ring of his companions; but he controls himself, deterred by the fearful odds against him. And old Jolyon controlled himself, keeping down, with his masterful restraint now slowly wearing out, the irritation fostered in him by the conditions of his life.

He had received from his son an unpractical letter, in which by rambling generalities the boy seemed trying to get out of answering a plain question. 'I've seen Bosinney,' he said; 'he is not a criminal. The more I see of people the more I am convinced that they are never good or bad—merely comic, or pathetic. You probably don't agree with me!'

Old Jolyon did not; he considered it cynical to so express oneself; he had not yet reached that point of old age when even Forsytes—bereft of those illusions and principles which they have cherished carefully for practical purposes but never believed in, bereft of all corporeal enjoyment, stricken to the very heart by having nothing left to hope for —break through the barriers of reserve and say things they would never have believed themselves capable of saying.

Perhaps he did not believe in 'goodness' and 'badness' any more than

199

his son; but as he would have said: He didn't know—couldn't tell; there might be something in it; and why, by an unnecessary expression of disbelief, deprive yourself of possible advantage?

Accustomed to spending his holidays among the mountains, though (like a true Forsyte) he had never attempted anything too adventurous or too foolhardy, he had been passionately fond of them. And when the wonderful view (mentioned in Baedeker—'fatiguing but repaying') was disclosed to him after the effort of the climb, he had doubtless felt the existence of some great, dignified principle crowning the chaotic strivings, the petty precipices, and ironic little dark chasms of life. This was as near to religion, perhaps, as his practical spirit had ever gone.

But it was many years since he had been to the mountains. He had taken June there two seasons running, after his wife died, and had realized bitterly that his walking days were over.

To that old mountain-given confidence in a supreme order of things he had long been a stranger.

He knew himself to be old, yet he felt young; and this troubled him. It troubled and puzzled him, too, to think that he, who had always been so careful, should be father and grandfather to such as seemed born to disaster. He had nothing to say against Jo—who could say anything against the boy, an amiable chap?—but his position was deplorable, and this business of June's nearly as bad. It seemed like fatality, and a fatality was one of those things no man of his character could either understand or put up with.

In writing to his son he did not really hope that anything would come of it. Since the ball at Roger's he had seen too clearly how the land lay— he could put two and two together quicker than most men—and, with the example of his own son before his eyes, knew better than any Forsyte of them all that the pale flame singes men's wings whether they will or no.

In the days before June's engagement, when she and Mrs. Soames were always together, he had seen enough of Irene to feel the spell she cast over men. She was not a flirt, not even a coquette—words dear to the heart of his generation, which loved to define things by a good, broad, inadequate word—but she was dangerous. He could not say why. Tell him of a quality innate in some women—a seductive power beyond their own control! He would but answer: 'Humbug!' She was dangerous, and there was an end of it. He wanted to close his eyes to that affair. If it was, it was; *he* did not want to hear any more about it—he only wanted to save June's position and her peace of mind. He still hoped she might once more become a comfort to himself.

And so he had written. He got little enough out of the answer. As to what young Jolyon had made of the interview, there was practically only the queer sentence: 'I gather that he's in the stream.' The stream! What stream? What was this new-fangled way of talking?

He sighed, and folded the last of the papers under the flap of the bag; he knew well enough what was meant.

June came out of the dining-room, and helped him on with his summer coat. From her costume, and the expression of her little resolute face, he saw at once what was coming.

"I'm going with you," she said.

"Nonsense, my dear; I go straight into the city. I can't have you racketting about!"

"I must see old Mrs. Smeech."

"Oh, your precious 'lame ducks'!" grumbled out old Jolyon. He did not believe her excuse, but ceased his opposition. There was no doing anything with that pertinacity of hers.

At Victoria he put her into the carriage which had been ordered for himself—a characteristic action, for he had no petty selfishnesses.

"Now, don't you go tiring yourself, my darling," he said, and took a cab on into the city.

June went first to a back-street in Paddington, where Mrs. Smeech, her 'lame duck,' lived—an aged person, connected with the charring interest; but after half an hour spent in hearing her habitually lamentable recital, and dragooning her into temporary comfort, she went on to Stanhope Gate. The great house was closed and dark.

She had decided to learn something at all costs. It was better to face the worst, and have it over. And this was her plan: To go first to Phil's aunt, Mrs. Baynes, and, failing information there, to Irene herself. She had no clear notion of what she would gain by these visits.

At three o'clock she was in Lowndes Square. With a woman's instinct when trouble is to be faced, she had put on her best frock, and went to the battle with a glance as courageous as old Jolyon's itself. Her tremors had passed into eagerness.

Mrs. Baynes, Bosinney's aunt (Louisa was her name), was in her kitchen when June was announced, organizing the cook, for she was an excellent housewife, and, as Baynes always said, there was 'a lot in a good dinner.' He did his best work after dinner. It was Baynes who built that remarkably fine row of tall crimson houses in Kensington which compete with so many others for the title of 'the ugliest in London.'

On hearing June's name, she went hurriedly to her bedroom, and, taking two large bracelets from a red morocco case in a locked drawer, put them on her white wrists—for she possessed in a remarkable degree that 'sense of property,' which, as we know, is the touchstone of Forsyteism, and the foundation of good morality.

Her figure, of medium height and broad build, with a tendency to embonpoint, was reflected by the mirror of her whitewood wardrobe, in a gown made under her own organization, of one of those half-tints, reminiscent of the distempered walls of corridors in large hotels. She raised her hands to her hair, which she wore *à la* Princesse de Galles, and touched it here and there, settling it more firmly on her head, and her eyes were full of an unconscious realism, as though she were looking in the face one of life's sordid facts, and making the best of it. In youth her cheeks had been of cream and roses, but they were mottled now by middle-age, and again that hard, ugly directness came into her eyes as she dabbed a powder-puff across her forehead. Putting the puff down, she stood quite still before the glass, arranging a smile over her high, important nose, her chin, (never large, and now growing smaller with the increase of her neck), her thin-lipped, down-drooping mouth. Quickly, not to lose the effect, she grasped her skirts strongly in both hands, and went downstairs.

She had been hoping for this visit for some time past. Whispers had reached her that things were not all right between her nephew and his fiancée. Neither of them had been near her for weeks. She had asked Phil to dinner many times; his invariable answer had been 'Too busy.'

Her instinct was alarmed, and the instinct in such matters of this excellent woman was keen. She ought to have been a Forsyte; in young Jolyon's sense of the word, she certainly had that privilege, and merits description as such.

She had married off her three daughters in a way that people said was beyond their deserts, for they had the professional plainness only to be found, as a rule, among the female kind of the more legal callings. Her name was upon the committees of numberless charities connected with the Church—dances, theatricals, or bazaars—and she never lent her name unless sure beforehand that everything had been thoroughly organized.

She believed, as she often said, in putting things on a commercial basis; the proper function of the Church, of charity, indeed, of everything, was to strengthen the fabric of 'Society.' Individual action, therefore, she considered immoral. Organization was the only thing, for by organization alone could you feel sure that you were getting a return for your money. Organization—and again, organization! And there is no doubt that she was what old Jolyon called her—"a 'dab' at that"—he went further, he called her "a humbug."

The enterprises to which she lent her name were organized so admirably that by the time the takings were handed over, they were indeed skim milk divested of all cream of human kindness. But as she often justly remarked, sentiment was to be deprecated. She was, in fact, a little academic.

This great and good woman, so highly thought of in ecclesiastical circles, was one of the principal priestesses in the temple of Forsyteism, keeping alive day and night a sacred flame to the God of Property, whose altar is inscribed with those inspiring words: 'Nothing for nothing, and really remarkably little for sixpence.'

When she entered a room it was felt that something substantial had come in, which was probably the reason of her popularity as a patroness. People liked something substantial when they had paid money for it; and they would look at her—surrounded by her staff in charity ball-rooms, with her high nose and her broad, square figure, attired in an uniform covered with sequins—as though she were a general.

The only thing against her was that she had not a double name. She was a power in upper middle-class society, with its hundred sets and circles, all intersecting on the common battle-field of charity functions, and on that battle-field brushing skirts so pleasantly with the skirts of Society with the capital 'S.' She was a power in society with the smaller 's,' that larger, more significant, and more powerful body, where the commercially Christian institutions, maxims, and 'principle,' which Mrs. Baynes embodied, were real life-blood, circulating freely, real business

203

currency, not merely the sterilized imitation that flowed in the veins of smaller Society with the larger 'S.' People who knew her felt her to be sound—a sound woman, who never gave herself away, nor anything else, if she could possibly help it.

She had been on the worst sort of terms with Bosinney's father, who had not infrequently made her the object of an unpardonable ridicule. She alluded to him now that he was gone as her 'poor, dear, irreverend brother.'

She greeted June with the careful effusion of which she was a mistress, a little afraid of her as far as a woman of her eminence in the commercial and Christian world could be afraid—for so slight a girl June had a great dignity, the fearlessness of her eyes gave her that. And Mrs. Baynes, too, shrewdly recognized that behind the uncompromising frankness of June's manner there was much of the Forsyte. If the girl had been merely frank and courageous, Mrs. Baynes would have thought her 'cranky,' and despised her; if she had been merely a Forsyte, like Francie—let us say—she would have patronized her from sheer weight of metal; but June, small though she was—Mrs. Baynes habitually admired quantity—gave her an uneasy feeling; and she placed her in a chair opposite the light.

There was another reason for her respect—which Mrs. Baynes, too, good a churchwoman to be worldly, would have been the last to admit—she often heard her husband describe old Jolyon as extremely well off, and was biassed towards his granddaughter for the soundest of all reasons. To-day she felt the emotion with which we read a novel describing a hero and an inheritance, nervously anxious lest, by some frightful lapse of the novelist, the young man should be left without it at the end.

Her manner was warm; she had never seen so clearly before how distinguished and desirable a girl this was. She asked after old Jolyon's health. A wonderful man for his age; so upright, and young-looking, and how old was he? Eighty-one! She would never have thought it! They were at the sea! Very nice for them; she supposed June heard from Phil every day? Her light grey eyes became more prominent as she asked this question; but the girl met the glance without flinching.

"No," she said, "he never writes!"

Mrs. Baynes's eyes dropped; they had no intention of doing so, but they did. They recovered immediately.

"Of course not. That's Phil all over—he was always like that!"

"Was he?" said June.

The brevity of the answer caused Mrs. Baynes's bright smile a moment's hesitation; she disguised it by a quick movement, and spreading her skirts afresh, said: "Why, my dear—he's quite the most harum-scarum person; one never pays the slightest attention to what *he* does!"

The conviction came suddenly to June that she was wasting her time; even were she to put a question point-blank, she would never get anything out of this woman.

"Do you see him?" she asked, her face crimsoning.

The perspiration broke out on Mrs. Baynes's forehead beneath the powder.

"Oh, yes! I don't remember when he was here last—indeed, we haven't seen much of him lately. He's so busy with your cousin's house; I'm told it'll be finished directly. We must organize a little dinner to celebrate the event; do come and stay the night with us!"

"Thank you," said June. Again she thought: 'I'm only wasting my time. This woman will tell me nothing.'

She got up to go. A change came over Mrs. Baynes. She rose too; her lips twitched, she fidgeted her hands. Something was evidently very wrong, and she did not dare to ask this girl, who stood there, a slim, straight little figure, with her decided face, her set jaw, and resentful eyes. She was not accustomed to be afraid of asking questions—all organization was based on the asking of questions!

But the issue was so grave that her nerve, normally strong, was fairly shaken; only that morning her husband had said: "Old Mr. Forsyte must be worth well over a hundred thousand pounds!"

And this girl stood there, holding out her hand—holding out her hand!

The chance might be slipping away—she couldn't tell—the chance of keeping her in the family, and yet she dared not speak.

Her eyes followed June to the door.

It closed.

Then with an exclamation Mrs. Baynes ran forward, wobbling her bulky frame from side to side, and opened it again.

Too late! She heard the front door click, and stood still, an expression of real anger and mortification on her face.

June went along the Square with her bird-like quickness. She detested that woman now—whom in happier days she had been accustomed to think so kind. Was she always to be put off thus, and forced to undergo this torturing suspense?

She would go to Phil himself, and ask him what he meant. She had the right to know. She hurried on down Sloane Street till she came to Bosinney's number. Passing the swing-door at the bottom, she ran up the stairs, her heart thumping painfully.

At the top of the third flight she paused for breath, and holding on to the bannisters, stood listening. No sound came from above.

With a very white face she mounted the last flight. She saw the door, with his name on the plate. And the resolution that had brought her so far evaporated.

The full meaning of her conduct came to her. She felt hot all over; the palms of her hands were moist beneath the thin silk covering of her gloves.

She drew back to the stairs, but did not descend. Leaning against the rail she tried to get rid of a feeling of being choked; and she gazed at the door with a sort of dreadful courage. No! she refused to go down. Did it matter what people thought of her? They would never know! No one would help her if she did not help herself! She would go through with it.

Forcing herself, therefore, to leave the support of the wall, she rang the bell. The door did not open, and all her shame and fear suddenly abandoned her; she rang again and again, as though in spite of its emptiness she could drag some response out of that closed room, some recompense for the shame and fear that visit had cost her. It did not open; she left off ringing, and, sitting down at the top of the stairs, buried her face in her hands.

Presently she stole down, out into the air. She felt as though she had passed through a bad illness, and had no desire now but to get home as quickly as she could. The people she met seemed to know where she had been, what she had been doing; and suddenly—over on the opposite side, going towards his rooms from the direction of Montpellier Square—she saw Bosinney himself.

She made a movement to cross into the traffic. Their eyes met, and he raised his hat. An omnibus passed, obscuring her view; then, from the edge of the pavement, through a gap in the traffic, she saw him walking on.

And June stood motionless, looking after him.

Chapter XIII

PERFECTION OF THE HOUSE

O NE mockturtle, clear; one oxtail; two glasses of port.' In the upper room at French's, where a Forsyte could still get heavy English food, James and his son were sitting down to lunch.

Of all eating-places James liked best to come here; there was something unpretentious, well flavoured, and filling about it, and though he had been to a certain extent corrupted by the necessity for being fashionable, and the trend of habits keeping pace with an income that *would* increase, he still hankered in quiet City moments after the tasty fleshpots of his earlier days. Here you were served by hairy English waiters in aprons; there was sawdust on the floor, and three round gilt looking-glasses hung just above the line of sight. They had only recently done away with the cubicles, too, in which you could have your chop, prime chump, with a floury potato, without seeing your neighbours, like a gentleman.

He tucked the top corner of his napkin behind the third button of his waistcoat, a practice he had been obliged to abandon years ago in the West End. He felt that he should relish his soup—the entire morning had been given to winding up the estate of an old friend.

After filling his mouth with household bread, stale, he at once began: "How are you going down to Robin Hill? You going to take Irene? You'd better take her. I should think there'll be a lot that'll want seeing to."

Without looking up, Soames answered: "She won't go."

"Won't go? What's the meaning of that? She's going to live in the house, isn't she?"

Soames made no reply.

"I don't know what's coming to women nowadays," mumbled James; "I never used to have any trouble with them. She's had too much liberty. She's spoiled——"

Soames lifted his eyes: "I won't have anything said against her," he said unexpectedly.

The silence was only broken now by the supping of James's soup.

The waiter brought the two glasses of port, but Soames stopped him. "That's not the way to serve port," he said; "take them away, and bring the bottle."

Rousing himself from his reverie over the soup, James took one of his rapid shifting surveys of surrounding facts.

"Your mother's in bed," he said; "you can have the carriage to take you down. I should think Irene'd like the drive. This young Bosinney'll be there, I suppose, to show you over?"

Soames nodded.

"I should like to go and see for myself what sort of a job he's made finishing off," pursued James. "I'll just drive round and pick you both up."

"I am going down by train," replied Soames. "If you like to drive round and see, Irene might go with you, I can't tell."

He signed to the waiter to bring the bill, which James paid.

They parted at St. Paul's, Soames branching off to the station, James taking his omnibus westwards.

He had secured the corner seat next the conductor, where his long legs made it difficult for anyone to get in, and at all who passed him he looked resentfully, as if they had no business to be using up his air.

He intended to take an opportunity this afternoon of speaking to Irene. A word in time saved nine; and now that she was going to live in the country there was a chance for her to turn over a new leaf! He could see that Soames wouldn't stand very much more of her goings on!

It did not occur to him to define what he meant by her 'goings on'; the expression was wide, vague, and suited to a Forsyte. And James had more than his common share of courage after lunch.

On reaching home, he ordered out the barouche, with special instructions that the groom was to go too. He wished to be kind to her, and to give her every chance.

When the door of No. 62 was opened he could distinctly hear her singing, and said so at once, to prevent any chance of being denied entrance.

Yes, Mrs. Soames was in, but the maid did not know if she was seeing people.

James, moving with the rapidity that ever astonished the observers of

his long figure and absorbed expression, went forthwith into the drawing-room without permitting this to be ascertained. He found Irene
seated at the piano with her hands arrested on the keys, evidently listening to the voices in the hall. She greeted him without smiling.

"Your mother-in-law's in bed," he began, hoping at once to enlist her
sympathy. "I've got the carriage here. Now, be a good girl, and put on
your hat and come with me for a drive. It'll do you good!"

Irene looked at him as though about to refuse, but, seeming to change
her mind, went upstairs, and came down again with her hat on.

"Where are you going to take me?" she asked.

"We'll just go down to Robin Hill," said James, spluttering out his
words very quick; "the horses want exercise, and I should like to see
what they've been doing down there."

Irene hung back, but again changed her mind, and went out to the
carriage, James brooding over her closely, to make quite sure.

It was not before he had got her more than halfway that he began:
"Soames is very fond of you—he won't have anything said against you;
why don't you show him more affection?"

Irene flushed, and said in a low voice: "I can't show what I haven't
got."

James looked at her sharply; he felt that now he had her in his own
carriage, with his own horses and servants, he was really in command
of the situation. She could not put him off; nor would she make a scene
in public.

"I can't think what you're about," he said. "He's a very good husband!"

Irene's answer was so low as to be almost inaudible among the sounds
of traffic. He caught the words: "You are not married to him!"

"What's that got to do with it? He's given you everything you want.
He's always ready to take you anywhere, and now he's built you this
house in the country. It's not as if you had anything of your own."

"No."

Again James looked at her; he could not make out the expression on
her face. She looked almost as if she were going to cry, and yet——

"I'm sure," he muttered hastily, "we've all tried to be kind to you."

Irene's lips quivered; to his dismay James saw a tear steal down her
cheek. He felt a choke rise in his own throat.

"We're all fond of you," he said, "if you'd only"—he was going to say, "behave yourself," but changed it to—"if you'd only be more of a wife to him."

Irene did not answer, and James, too, ceased speaking. There was something in her silence which disconcerted him; it was not the silence of obstinacy, rather that of acquiescence in all that he could find to say. And yet he felt as if he had not had the last word. He could not understand this.

He was unable, however, to long keep silence.

"I suppose that young Bosinney," he said, "will be getting married to June now?"

Irene's face changed. "I don't know," she said; "you should ask *her*."

"Does she write to you?"

"No."

"How's that?" said James. "I thought you and she were such great friends."

Irene turned on him. "Again," she said, "you should ask *her!*"

"Well," flustered James, frightened by her look, "it's very odd that I can't get a plain answer to a plain question, but there it is."

He sat ruminating over his rebuff, and burst out at last:

"Well, I've warned you. You won't look ahead. Soames he doesn't say much, but I can see he won't stand a great deal more of this sort of thing. You'll have nobody but yourself to blame, and, what's more, you'll get no sympathy from anybody."

Irene bent her head with a little smiling bow. "I am very much obliged to you."

James did not what on earth to answer.

The bright hot morning had changed slowly to a grey, oppressive afternoon; a heavy bank of clouds, with the yellow tinge of coming thunder, had risen in the south, and was creeping up. The branches of the trees drooped motionless across the road without the smallest stir of foliage. A faint odour of glue from the heated horses clung in the thick air; the coachman and groom, rigid and unbending, exchanged stealthy murmurs on the box, without ever turning their heads.

To James's great relief they reached the house at last; the silence and impenetrability of this woman by his side, whom he had always thought so soft and mild, alarmed him.

The carriage put them down at the door, and they entered.

The hall was cool, and so still that it was like passing into a tomb; a

210

shudder ran down James's spine. He quickly lifted the heavy leather curtains between the columns into the inner court.

He could not restrain an exclamation of approval.

The decoration was really in excellent taste. The dull ruby tiles that extended from the foot of the walls to the verge of a circular clump of tall iris plants, surrounding in turn a sunken basin of white marble filled with water, were obviously of the best quality. He admired extremely the purple leather curtains drawn along one entire side, framing a huge white-tiled stove. The central partitions of the skylight had been slid back, and the warm air from outside penetrated into the very heart of the house.

He stood, his hands behind him, his head bent back on his high, narrow shoulders, spying the tracery on the columns and the pattern of the frieze which ran round the ivory-coloured walls under the gallery. Evidently, no pains had been spared. It was quite the house of a gentleman. He went up to the curtains, and, having discovered how they were worked, drew them asunder and disclosed the picture-gallery, ending in a great window taking up the whole end of the room. It had a black oak floor, and its walls, again, were of ivory white. He went on throwing open doors, and peeping in. Everything was in apple-pie order, ready for immediate occupation.

He turned round at last to speak to Irene, and saw her standing over in the garden entrance, with her husband and Bosinney.

Though not remarkable for sensibility, James felt at once that something was wrong. He went up to them, and, vaguely alarmed, ignorant of the nature of the trouble, made an attempt to smooth things over.

"How are you, Mr. Bosinney?" he said, holding out his hand. "You've been spending money pretty freely down here, I should say!"

Soames turned his back and walked away. James looked from Bosinney's frowning face to Irene, and, in his agitation, spoke his thoughts aloud: "Well, I can't tell what's the matter. Nobody tells me anything!" And, making off after his son, he heard Bosinney's short laugh, and his "Well, thank God! You look so——" Most unfortunately he lost the rest.

What had happened? He glanced back. Irene was very close to the architect, and her face not like the face he knew of her. He hastened up to his son.

Soames was pacing the picture-gallery.

"What's the matter?" said James. "What's all this?"

Soames looked at him with his supercilious calm unbroken, but James knew well enough that he was violently angry.

"Our friend," he said, "has exceeded his instructions again, that's all. So much the worse for him this time."

He turned round and walked back towards the door. James followed hurriedly, edging himself in front. He saw Irene take her finger from before her lips, heard her say something in her ordinary voice, and began to speak before he reached them.

"There's a storm coming on. We'd better get home. We can't take you, I suppose, Mr. Bosinney? No, I suppose not. Then, good-bye!" He held out his hand. Bosinney did not take it, but, turning with a laugh, said:

"Good-bye, Mr. Forsyte. Don't get caught in the storm!" and walked away.

"Well," began James, "I don't know——"

But the sight of Irene's face stopped him. Taking hold of his daughter-in-law by the elbow, he escorted her towards the carriage. He felt certain, quite certain, they had been making some appointment or other. . . .

Nothing in this world is more sure to upset a Forsyte than the discovery that something on which he has stipulated to spend a certain sum has cost more. And this is reasonable, for upon the accuracy of his estimates the whole policy of his life is ordered. If he cannot rely on definite values of property, his compass is amiss; he is adrift upon bitter waters without a helm.

After writing to Bosinney in the terms that have already been chronicled, Soames had dismissed the cost of the house from his mind. He believed that he had made the matter of the final cost so very plain that the possibility of its being again exceeded had really never entered his head. On hearing from Bosinney that his limit of twelve thousand pounds would be exceeded by something like four hundred, he had grown white with anger. His original estimate of the cost of the house completed had been ten thousand pounds, and he had often blamed himself severely for allowing himself to be led into repeated excesses. Over this last expenditure, however, Bosinney had put himself completely in the wrong. How on earth a fellow could make such an ass of himself Soames could not conceive; but he had done so, and all the ran-cour and hidden jealousy that had been burning against him for so long was now focussed in rage at this crowning piece of extravagance. The attitude of the confident and friendly husband was gone. To preserve property—his wife—he had assumed it, to preserve property of another kind he lost it now.

"Ah!" he had said to Bosinney when he could speak, "and I suppose you're perfectly contented with yourself. But I may as well tell you that you've altogether mistaken your man!"

What he meant by those words he did not quite know at the time, but after dinner he looked up the correspondence between himself and Bosinney to make quite sure. There could be no two opinions about it— the fellow had made himself liable for that extra four hundred, or, at all events, for three hundred and fifty of it, and he would have to make it good.

He was looking at his wife's face when he came to this conclusion. Seated in her usual seat on the sofa, she was altering the lace on a collar. She had not once spoken to him all the evening.

He went up to the mantelpiece, and contemplating his face in the mirror said: "Your friend the Buccaneer has made a fool of himself; he will have to pay for it!"

She looked at him scornfully, and answered: "I don't know what you are talking about!"

"You soon will. A mere trifle, quite beneath your contempt—four hundred pounds."

"Do you mean that you are going to make him pay that towards this hateful house?"

"I do."

"And you know he's got nothing?"

"Yes."

"Then you are meaner than I thought you."

Soames turned from the mirror, and unconsciously taking a china cup from the mantelpiece, clasped his hands around it as though pray-ing. He saw her bosom rise and fall, her eyes darkening with anger, and taking no notice of the taunt, he asked quietly:

"Are you carrying on a flirtation with Bosinney?"

"No, I am not!"

Her eyes met his, and he looked away. He neither believed nor disbelieved her, but he knew that he had made a mistake in asking; he never had known, never would know, what she was thinking. The sight of her inscrutable face, the thought of all the hundreds of evenings he had seen her sitting there like that soft and passive, but unreadable, unknown, enraged him beyond measure.

"I believe you are made of stone," he said, clenching his fingers so hard that he broke the fragile cup. The pieces fell into the grate. And Irene smiled.

"You seem to forget," she said, "that cup is not!"

Soames gripped her arm. "A good beating," he said, "is the only thing that would bring you to your senses," but turning on his heel, he left the room.

Chapter XIV

SOAMES SITS ON THE STAIRS

SOAMES went upstairs that night with the feeling that he had gone too far. He was prepared to offer excuses for his words.

He turned out the gas still burning in the passage outside their room. Pausing, with his hand on the knob of the door, he tried to shape his apology, for he had no intention of letting her see that he was nervous.

But the door did not open, nor when he pulled it and turned the handle firmly. She must have locked it for some reason, and forgotten.

Entering his dressing-room, where the gas was also light and burning low, he went quickly to the other door. That too was locked. Then he noticed that the camp bed which he occasionally used was prepared, and his sleeping-suit laid out upon it. He put his hand up to his forehead, and brought it away wet. It dawned on him that he was barred out.

He went back to the door, and rattling the handle stealthily, called: "Unlock the door, do you hear? Unlock the door!"

There was a faint rustling, but no answer.

"Do you hear? Let me in at once—I insist on being let in!"

He could catch the sound of her breathing close to the door, like the breathing of a creature threatened by danger.

There was something terrifying in this inexorable silence, in the impossibility of getting at her. He went back to the other door, and putting his whole weight against it, tried to burst it open. The door was a new one—he had had them renewed himself, in readiness for their coming in after the honeymoon. In a rage he lifted his foot to kick in the panel; the thought of the servants restrained him, and he felt suddenly that he was beaten.

Flinging himself down in the dressing-room, he took up a book.

But instead of the print he seemed to see his wife—with her yellow hair flowing over her bare shoulders, and her great dark eyes—standing like an animal at bay. And the whole meaning of her act of revolt came to him. She meant it to be for good.

He could not sit still, and went to the door again. He could still hear her, and he called: "Irene! Irene!"

He did not mean to make his voice pathetic. In ominous answer, the faint sounds ceased. He stood with clenched hands, thinking.

Presently he stole round on tiptoe, and running suddenly at the other door, made a supreme effort to break it open. It creaked, but did not yield. He sat down on the stairs and buried his face in his hands.

For a long time he sat there in the dark, the moon through the skylight above laying a pale smear which lengthened slowly towards him down the stairway. He tried to be philosophical.

Since she had locked her doors she had no further claim as a wife, and he would console himself with other women!

It was but a spectral journey he made among such delights—he had no appetite for these exploits. He had never had much, and he had lost the habit. He felt that he could never recover it. His hunger could only be appeased by his wife, inexorable and frightened, behind these shut doors. No other woman could help him.

This conviction came to him with terrible force out there in the dark.

His philosophy left him; and surly anger took its place. Her conduct was immoral, inexcusable, worthy of any punishment within his power. He desired no one but her, and she refused him!

She must really hate him, then! He had never believed it yet. He did not believe it now. It seemed to him incredible. He felt as though he had lost for ever his power of judgment. If she, so soft and yielding as he had always judged her, could take this decided step—what could not happen?

Then he asked himself again if she were carrying on an intrigue with Bosinney. He did not believe that she was; he could not afford to believe such a reason for her conduct—the thought was not to be faced.

It would be unbearable to contemplate the necessity of making his marital relations public property. Short of the most convincing proofs he must still refuse to believe, for he did not wish to punish himself. And all the time at heart—he *did* believe.

The moonlight cast a greyish tinge over his figure, hunched against the staircase wall.

Bosinney was in love with her! He hated the fellow, and would not spare him now. He could and would refuse to pay a penny piece over twelve thousand and fifty pounds—the extreme limit fixed in the correspondence; or rather he would pay, he would pay and sue him for damages. He would go to Jobling and Boulter and put the matter in their hands. He would ruin the impecunious beggar! And suddenly—though what connection between the thoughts?—he reflected that Irene had no money either. They were both beggars. This gave him a strange satisfaction.

The silence was broken by a faint creaking through the wall. She was going to bed at last. Ah! Joy and pleasant dreams! If she threw the door open wide he would not go in now!

But his lips, that were twisted in a bitter smile, twitched; he covered his eyes with his hands. . . .

It was late the following afternoon when Soames stood in the dining-room window gazing gloomily into the Square.

The sunlight still showered on the plane-trees, and in the breeze their gay broad leaves shone and swung in rhyme to a barrel organ at the corner. It was playing a waltz, an old waltz that was out of fashion, with a fateful rhythm in the notes; and it went on and on, though nothing indeed but leaves danced to the tune.

The woman did not look too gay, for she was tired; and from the tall houses no one threw her down coppers. She moved the organ on, and three doors off began again.

It was the waltz they had played at Roger's when Irene had danced with Bosinney; and the perfume of the gardenias she had worn came back to Soames, drifted by the malicious music, as it had been drifted to him then, when she passed, her hair glistening, her eyes so soft, drawing Bosinney on and on down an endless ballroom.

The organ woman plied her handle slowly; she had been grinding her tune all day—grinding it in Sloane Street hard by, grinding it perhaps to Bosinney himself.

Soames turned, took a cigarette from the carven box, and walked back to the window. The tune had mesmerized him, and there came into his view Irene, her sunshade furled, hastening homewards down the Square, in a soft, rose-coloured blouse with drooping sleeves, that he did not know. She stopped before the organ, took out her purse, and gave the woman money.

217

Soames shrank back and stood where he could see into the hall.

She came in with her latch-key, put down her sunshade, and stood looking at herself in the glass. Her cheeks were flushed as if the sun had burned them; her lips were parted in a smile. She stretched her arms out as though to embrace herself, with a laugh that for all the world was like a sob.

Soames stepped forward.

"Very—pretty!" he said.

But as though shot she spun round, and would have passed him up the stairs. He barred the way.

"Why such a hurry?" he said, and his eyes fastened on a curl of hair fallen loose across her ear.

He hardly recognised her. She seemed on fire, so deep and rich the colour of her cheeks, her eyes, her lips, and of the unusual blouse she wore.

She put up her hand and smoothed back the curl. She was breathing fast and deep, as though she had been running, and with every breath perfume seemed to come from her hair, and from her body, like perfume from an opening flower.

"I don't like that blouse," he said slowly, "it's a soft, shapeless thing!"

He lifted his finger towards her breast, but she dashed his hand aside.

"Don't touch me!" she cried.

He caught her wrist; she wrenched it away.

"And where may you have been?" he asked.

"In heaven—out of this house!" With those words she fled upstairs.

Outside—in thanksgiving—at the very door, the organ-grinder was playing the waltz.

And Soames stood motionless. What prevented him from following her?

Was it that, with the eyes of faith, he saw Bosinney looking down from that high window in Sloane Street, straining his eyes for yet another glimpse of Irene's vanished figure, cooling his flushed face, dreaming of the moment when she flung herself on his breast—the scent of her still in the air around, and the sound of her laugh that was like a sob?

MRS. MACANDER'S EVIDENCE

MANY people, no doubt, including the editor of the 'Ultra Vivisectionist,' then in the bloom of its first youth, would say that Soames was less than a man not to have removed the locks from his wife's doors, and, after beating her soundly, resumed wedded happiness.

Brutality is not so deplorably diluted by humaneness as it used to be, yet a sentimental segment of the population may still be relieved to learn that he did none of these things. For active brutality is not popular with Forsytes; they are too circumspect, and, on the whole, too soft-hearted. And in Soames there was some common pride, not sufficient to make him do a really generous action, but enough to prevent his indulging in an extremely mean one, except, perhaps, in very hot blood. Above all this true Forsyte refused to feel himself ridiculous. Short of actually beating his wife, he perceived nothing to be done; he therefore accepted the situation without another word.

Throughout the summer and autumn he continued to go to the office, to sort his pictures, and ask his friends to dinner.

He did not leave town; Irene refused to go away. The house at Robin Hill, finished though it was, remained empty and ownerless. Soames had brought a suit against the Buccaneer, in which he claimed from him the sum of three hundred and fifty pounds.

A firm of solicitors, Messrs. Freak and Able, had put in a defence on Bosinney's behalf. Admitting the facts, they raised a point on the correspondence which, divested of legal phraseology amounted to this: To speak of 'a *free* hand in the terms of this correspondence' is an Irish bull.

By a chance, fortuitous but not improbable in the close borough of legal circles, a good deal of information came to Soames's ear anent this line of policy, the working partner in his firm, Bustard, happening to sit next at dinner at Walmisley's, the Taxing Master, to young Chankery, of the Common Law Bar.

The necessity for talking what is known as 'shop,' which comes on all lawyers with the removal of the ladies, caused Chankery, a young and promising advocate, to propound an impersonal conundrum to his neighbour, whose name he did not know, for, seated as he permanently was in the background, Bustard had practically no name.

He had, said Chankery, a case coming on with a 'very nice point.' He then explained, preserving every professional discretion, the riddle in Soames's case. Everyone, he said, to whom he had spoken, thought it a nice point. The issue was small unfortunately, 'though d——d serious for his client he believed'—Walmisley's champagne was bad but plentiful. A judge would make short work of it, he was afraid. He intended to make a big effort—the point was a nice one. What did his neighbour say?

Bustard, a model of secrecy, said nothing. He related the incident to Soames however with some malice, for this quiet man was capable of human feeling, ending with his own opinion that the point *was* 'a very nice one.'

In accordance with his resolve, our Forsyte had put his interests into the hands of Jobling and Boulter. From the moment of doing so he regretted that he had not acted for himself. On receiving a copy of Bosinney's defence he went over to their offices.

Boulter, who had the matter in hand, Jobling having died some years before, told him that in his opinion it was rather a nice point; he would like counsel's opinion on it.

Soames told him to go to a good man, and they went to Waterbuck, Q.C., marking him ten and one, who kept the papers six weeks and then wrote as follows:

'In my opinion the true interpretation of this correspondence depends very much on the intention of the parties, and will turn upon the evidence given at the trial. I am of opinion that an attempt should be made to secure from the architect an admission the he understood he was not to spend at the outside more than twelve thousand and fifty pounds. With regard to the expression, "a free hand in the terms of this correspondence," to which my attention is directed, the point is a nice one; but

I am of opinion that upon the whole the ruling in "Boileau *v.* The Blasted Cement Co., Ltd.," will apply.'

Upon this opinion they acted, administering interrogatories, but to their annoyance Messrs. Freak and Able answered these in so masterly a fashion that nothing whatever was admitted and that without prejudice.

It was on October 1 that Soames read Waterbuck's opinion, in the dining-room before dinner. It made him nervous; not so much because of the case of 'Boileau *v.* The Blasted Cement Co., Ltd.,' as that the point had lately begun to seem to him, too, a nice one; there was about it just that pleasant flavour of subtlety so attractive to the best legal appetites. To have his own impression confirmed by Waterbuck, Q.C., would have disturbed any man.

He sat thinking it over, and staring at the empty grate, for though autumn had come, the weather kept as gloriously fine that jubilee year as if it were still high August. It was not pleasant to be disturbed; he desired too passionately to set his foot on Bosinney's neck.

Though he had not seen the architect since the last afternoon at Robin Hill, he was never free from the sense of his presence—never free from the memory of his worn face with its high cheekbones and enthusiastic eyes. It would not be too much to say that he had never got rid of the feeling of that night when he heard the peacock's cry at dawn—the feeling that Bosinney haunted the house. And every man's shape that he saw in the dark evenings walking past, seemed that of him whom George had so appropriately named the Buccaneer.

Irene still met him, he was certain; where, or how, he neither knew, nor asked, deterred by a vague and secret dread of too much knowledge. It all seemed subterranean nowadays.

Sometimes when he questioned his wife as to where she had been, which he still made a point of doing, as every Forsyte should, she looked very strange. Her self-possession was wonderful, but there were moments when, behind the mask of her face, inscrutable as it had always been to him, lurked an expression he had never been used to see there.

She had taken to lunching out too; when he asked Bilson if her mistress had been in to lunch, as often as not she would answer: "No, sir."

He strongly disapproved of her gadding about by herself, and told her so. But she took no notice. There was something that angered, amazed, yet almost amused, him about the calm way in which she disregarded his wishes. It was really as if she were hugging to herself the thought of a triumph over him.

He rose from the perusal of Waterbuck, Q.C.'s opinion, and, going upstairs, entered her room, for she did not lock her doors till bed-time—she had the decency, he found, to save the feelings of the servants. She was brushing her hair, and turned to him with strange fierceness.

"What do you want?" she said. "Please leave my room!"

He answered: "I want to know how long this state of things between us is to last? I have put up with it long enough."

"Will you please leave my room?"

"Will you treat me as your husband?"

"No."

"Then, I shall take steps to make you."

"Do!"

He stared, amazed at the calmness of her answer. Her lips were compressed in a thin line; her hair lay in fluffy masses on her bare shoulders, in all its strange golden contrast to her dark eyes—those eyes alive with the emotions of fear, hate, contempt, and odd, haunting triumph.

"Now, please, will you leave my room?"

He turned round, and went sulkily out.

He knew very well that he had no intention of taking steps, and he saw that she knew too—knew that he was afraid to.

It was a habit with him to tell her the doings of his day: how such and such clients had called; how he had arranged a mortgage for Parkes; how that long-standing suit of Fryer *v.* Forsyte was getting on, which, arising in the preternaturally careful disposition of his property by his great-uncle Nicholas, who had tied it up so that no one could get it at all, seemed likely to remain a source of income for several solicitors till the Day of Judgment.

And how he had called in at Jobson's, and seen a Boucher sold, which he had just missed buying of Talleyrand and Sons in Pall Mall.

He had an admiration for Boucher, Watteau, and all that school. It was a habit with him to tell her all these matters, and he continued to do it even now, talking for long spells at dinner, as though by the volubility of words he could conceal from himself the ache in his heart.

Often, if they were alone, he made an attempt to kiss her when she said good-night. He may have had some vague notion that some night she would let him; or perhaps only the feeling that a husband ought to kiss his wife. Even if she hated him, he at all events ought not to put himself in the wrong by neglecting this ancient rite.

And why did she hate him? Even now he could not altogether believe it. It was strange to be hated!—the emotion was too extreme; yet he hated Bosinney, that Buccaneer, that prowling vagabond, that night-wanderer. For in his thoughts Soames always saw him lying in wait—wandering. Ah, but he must be in very low water! Young Burkitt, the architect, had seen him coming out of a third-rate restaurant, looking terribly down in the mouth!

During all the hours he lay awake, thinking over the situation, which seemed to have no end—unless she should suddenly come to her senses —never once did the thought of separating from his wife seriously enter his head.

And the Forsytes! What part did they play in this stage of Soames's subterranean tragedy?

Truth to say, little or none, for they were at the sea.

From hotels, hydropathics, or lodging-houses, they were bathing daily; laying in a stock of ozone to last them through the winter.

Each section, in the vineyard of its own choosing, grew and culled and pressed and bottled the grapes of a pet sea-air.

The end of September began to witness their several returns.

In rude health and small omnibuses, with considerable colour in their cheeks, they arrived daily from the various termini. The following morning saw them back at their vocations.

On the next Sunday Timothy's was thronged from lunch till dinner.

Amongst other gossip, too numerous and interesting to relate, Mrs. Septimus Small mentioned that Soames and Irene had not been away.

It remained for a comparative outsider to supply the next evidence of interest.

It chanced that one afternoon late in September, Mrs. MacAnder, Winifred Dartie's greatest friend, taking a constitutional, with young Augustus Flippard, on her bicycle in Richmond Park, passed Irene and Bosinney walking from the bracken towards the Sheen Gate.

Perhaps the poor little woman was thirsty, for she had ridden long on a hard, dry road, and, as all London knows, to ride a bicycle and talk to

223

young Flippard will try the toughest constitution; or perhaps the sight of the cool bracken grove, whence 'those two' were coming down, excited her envy. The cool bracken grove on the top of the hill, with the oak boughs for roof, where the pigeons were raising an endless wedding hymn, and the autumn, humming, whispered to the ears of lovers in the fern, while the deer stole by. The bracken grove of irretrievable delights, of golden minutes in the long marriage of heaven and earth! The bracken grove, sacred to stags, to strange tree-stump fauns leaping around the silver whiteness of a birch-tree nymph at summer dusk!

This lady knew all the Forsytes, and having been at June's 'at home,' was not at a loss to see with whom she had to deal. Her own marriage, poor thing, had not been successful, but having had the good sense and ability to force her husband into pronounced error, she herself had passed through the necessary divorce proceedings without incurring censure.

She was therefore a judge of all that sort of thing, and lived in one of those large buildings, where in small sets of apartments, are gathered incredible quantities of Forsytes, whose chief recreation out of business hours is the discussion of each other's affairs.

Poor little woman, perhaps she was thirsty, certainly she was bored, for Flippard was a wit. To see 'those two' in so unlikely a spot was quite a merciful 'pick-me-up.'

At the MacAnder, like all London, Time pauses.

This small but remarkable woman merits attention; her all-seeing eye and shrewd tongue were inscrutably the means of furthering the ends of Providence.

With an air of being in at the death, she had an almost distressing power of taking care of herself. She had done more, perhaps, in her way than any woman about town to destroy the sense of chivalry which still clogs the wheel of civilization. So smart she was, and spoken of endearingly as 'the little MacAnder!'

Dressing tightly and well, she belonged to a Woman's Club, but was by no means the neurotic and dismal type of member who was always thinking of her rights. She took her rights unconsciously, they came natural to her, and she knew exactly how to make the most of them without exciting anything but admiration amongst that great class to whom she was affiliated, not precisely perhaps by manner, but by birth, breeding, and the true, the secret gauge, a sense of property.

The daughter of a Bedfordshire solicitor, by the daughter of a clergy-man, she had never, through all the painful experience of being married to a very mild painter with a cranky love of Nature, who had deserted her for an actress, lost touch with the requirements, beliefs, and inner feeling of Society; and, on attaining her liberty, she placed herself without effort in the very van of Forsyteism.

Always in good spirits, and 'full of information,' she was universally welcomed. She excited neither surprise nor disapprobation when encountered on the Rhine or at Zermatt, either alone, or travelling with a lady and two gentlemen; it was felt that she was perfectly capable of taking care of herself; and the hearts of all Forsytes warmed to that wonderful instinct, which enabled her to enjoy everything without giving anything away. It was generally felt that to such women as Mrs. MacAnder should we look for the perpetuation and increase of our best type of woman. She had never had any children.

If there was one thing more than another that she could not stand it was one of those soft women with what men called 'charm' about them, and for Mrs. Soames she always had an especial dislike.

Obscurely, no doubt, she felt that if charm were once admitted as the criterion, smartness and capability must go to the wall; and she hated—with a hatred the deeper that at times this so-called charm seemed to disturb all calculations—the subtle seductiveness which she could not altogether overlook in Irene.

She said, however, that she could see nothing in the woman—there was no 'go' about her—she would never be able to stand up for herself—anyone could take advantage of her, that was plain—she could not see in fact what men found to admire!

She was not really ill-natured, but, in maintaining her position after the trying circumstances of her married life, she had found it so necessary to be 'full of information,' that the idea of holding her tongue about 'those two' in the Park never occurred to her.

And it so happened that she was dining that very evening at Timothy's, where she went sometimes to 'cheer the old things up,' as she was wont to put it. The same people were always asked to meet her: Winifred Dartie and her husband; Francie, because she belonged to the artistic circles, for Mrs. MacAnder was known to contribute articles on dress to 'The Ladies Kingdom Come'; and for her to flirt with, provided they could be obtained, two of the Hayman boys, who though they never said anything, were believed to be fast and thoroughly intimate with all that was latest in smart Society.

At twenty-five minutes past seven she turned out the electric light in her little hall, and wrapped in her opera cloak with the chinchilla collar, came out into the corridor, pausing a moment to make sure she had her latch-key. These little self-contained flats were convenient; to be sure, she had no light and no air, but she could shut it up whenever she liked and go away. There was no bother with servants, and she never felt tired as she used to when poor, dear Fred was always about, in his mooney way. She retained no rancour against poor, dear Fred, he was such a fool; but the thought of that actress drew from her, even now, a little, bitter, derisive smile.

Firmly snapping the door to, she crossed the corridor, with its gloomy, yellow-ochre walls, and its infinite vista of brown, numbered doors. The lift was going down; and wrapped to the ears in the high cloak, with every one of her auburn hairs in its place, she waited motionless for it to stop at her floor. The iron gates clanked open; she entered. There were already three occupants, a man in a great white waistcoat, with a large, smooth face like a baby's and two old ladies in black with mittened hands.

Mrs. MacAnder smiled at them; she knew everybody; and all these three, who had been admirably silent before, began to talk at once. This was Mrs. MacAnder's successful secret. She provoked conversation.

Throughout a descent of five stories the conversation continued, the lift boy standing with his back turned, his cynical face protruding through the bars.

At the bottom they separated, the man in the white waistcoat sentimentally to the billiard-room, the old ladies to dine and say to each other: "A dear little woman!" "Such a rattle!" and Mrs. MacAnder to her cab.

When Mrs. MacAnder dined at Timothy's, the conversation (although Timothy himself could never be induced to be present) took that wider, man-of-the-world tone current among Forsytes at large, and this, no doubt, was what put her at a premium there.

Mrs. Small and Aunt Hester found it an exhilarating change. "If only," they said, "Timothy would meet her!" It was felt that she would do him good. She could tell you, for instance, the latest story of Sir

Charles Fiste's son at Monte Carlo; who was the real heroine of Tyne-mouth Eddy's fashionable novel that everyone was holding up their hands over, and what they were doing in Paris about wearing bloomers. She was so sensible, too, knowing all about that vexed question, whether to send young Nicholas's eldest into the navy as his mother wished, or make him an accountant as his father thought would be safer. She strongly deprecated the navy. If you were not exceptionally brilliant or exceptionally well connected, they passed you over so disgracefully, and what was it after all to look forward to, even if you became an admiral—a pittance! An acountant had many more chances, but let him be put with a good firm, where there was no risk at starting!

Sometimes she would give them a tip on the Stock Exchange; not that Mrs. Small or Aunt Hester ever took it. They had indeed no money to invest; but it seemed to bring them into such exciting touch with the realities of life. It was an event. They would ask Timothy, they said. But they never did, knowing in advance that it would upset him. Surreptitiously, however, for weeks after they would look in that paper, which they took with respect on account of its really fashionable proclivities, to see whether 'Bright's Rubies' or 'The Woollen Mackintosh Company' were up or down. Sometimes they could not find the name of the company at all; and they would wait until James or Roger or even Swithin came in, and ask them in voices trembling with curiosity how that 'Bolivia Lime and Speltrate' was doing—they could not find it in the paper.

And Roger would answer: "What do you want to know for? Some trash! You'll go burning your fingers—investing your money in lime, and things you know nothing about! Who told you?" and ascertaining what they had been told, he would go away, and, making inquiries in the City, would perhaps invest some of his own money in the concern.

It was about the middle of dinner, just in fact as the saddle of mutton had been brought in by Smither, that Mrs. MacAnder, looking airily round, said: "Oh! and whom do you think I passed to-day in Richmond Park? You'll never guess—Mrs. Soames and—Mr. Bosinney. They must have been down to look at the house!"

Winifred Dartie coughed, and no one said a word. It was the piece of evidence they had all unconsciously been waiting for.

To do Mrs. MacAnder justice, she had been to Switzerland and the

Italian lakes with a party of three, and had not heard of Soames's rupture with the architect. She could not tell, therefore, the profound impression her words would make.

Upright and a little flushed, she moved her small, shrewd eyes from face to face, trying to gauge the effect of her words. On either side of her a Hayman boy, his lean, taciturn, hungry face turned towards his plate, ate his mutton steadily.

These two, Giles and Jesse, were so alike and so inseparable that they were known as the Dromios. They never talked, and seemed always completely occupied in doing nothing. It was popularly supposed that they were cramming for an important examination. They walked without hats for long hours in the Gardens attached to their house, books in their hands, a fox-terrier at their heels, never saying a word, and smoking all the time. Every morning, about fifty yards apart, they trotted down Campden Hill on two lean hacks, with legs as long as their own, and every morning about an hour later, still fifty yards apart, they cantered up again. Every evening, wherever they had dined, they might be observed about half-past ten, leaning over the balustrade of the Alhambra promenade.

They were never seen otherwise than together; in this way passing their lives, apparently perfectly content.

Inspired by some dumb stirring within them of the feelings of gentlemen, they turned at this painful moment to Mrs. MacAnder, and said in precisely the same voice: "Have you seen the——?"

Such was her surprise at being thus addressed that she put down her fork; and Smither, who was passing, promptly removed her plate. Mrs. MacAnder, however, with presence of mind, said instantly: "I must have a little more of that nice mutton."

But afterwards in the drawing-room she sat down by Mrs. Small, determined to get to the bottom of the matter. And she began:

"What a charming woman, Mrs. Soames; such a sympathetic temperament! Soames is a really lucky man!"

Her anxiety for information had not made sufficient allowance for that inner Forsyte skin which refuses to share its troubles with outsiders; Mrs. Septimus Small, drawing herself up with a creak and rustle of her whole person, said, shivering in her dignity:

"My dear, it is a subject we do not talk about!"

Chapter II

NIGHT IN THE PARK

ALTHOUGH with her infallible instinct Mrs. Small had said the very thing to make her guest 'more intriguée than ever,' it is difficult to see how else she could truthfully have spoken.

It was not a subject which the Forsytes could talk about even among themselves—to use the word Soames had invented to characterize to himself the situation, it was 'subterranean.'

Yet, within a week of Mrs. MacAnder's encounter in Richmond Park, to all of them—save Timothy, from whom it was carefully kept—to James on his domestic beat from the Poultry to Park Lane, to George the wild one, on his daily adventure from the bow window at the Haversnake to the billiard room at the 'Red Pottle,' was it known that 'those two' had gone to extremes.

George (it was he who invented many of those striking expressions still current in fashionable circles) voiced the sentiment more accurately than any one when he said to his brother Eustace that 'the Buccaneer' was 'going it'; he expected Soames was about 'fed up.'

It was felt that he must be, and yet, what could be done? He ought perhaps to take steps; but to take steps would be deplorable.

Without an open scandal which they could not see their way to recommending, it was difficult to see what steps could be taken. In this impasse, the only thing was to say nothing to Soames, and nothing to each other; in fact, to pass it over.

By displaying towards Irene a dignified coldness, some impression might be made upon her; but she was seldom now to be seen, and there seemed a slight difficulty in seeking her out on purpose to show her coldness. Sometimes in the privacy of his bedroom James would reveal to Emily the real suffering that his son's misfortune caused him.

"I can't tell," he would say; "it worries me out of my life. There'll be a scandal, and that'll do him no good. I shan't say anything to him. There might be nothing in it. What do you think? She's very artistic, they

229

tell me. What? Oh, you're a 'regular Juley'! Well, I don't know; I expect the worst. This is what comes of having no children. I knew how it would be from the first. They never told me they didn't mean to have any children—nobody tells me anything!"

On his knees by the side of the bed, his eyes open and fixed with worry, he would breathe into the counterpane. Clad in his nightshirt, his neck poked forward, his back rounded, he resembled some long white bird.

"Our Father—" he repeated, turning over and over again the thought of this possible scandal.

Like old Jolyon, he, too, at the bottom of his heart set the blame of the tragedy down to family interference. What business had that lot—he began to think of the Stanhope Gate branch, including young Jolyon and his daughter, as 'that lot'—to introduce a person like this Bosinney into the family? (He had heard George's soubriquet, 'The Buccaneer,' but he could make nothing of that—the young man was an architect.)

He began to feel that his brother Jolyon, to whom he had always looked up and on whose opinion he had relied, was not quite what he had expected.

Not having his eldest brother's force of character, he was more sad than angry. His great comfort was to go to Winifred's, and take the little Darties in his carriage over to Kensington Gardens, and there, by the Round Pond, he could often be seen walking with his eyes fixed anxiously on little Publius Dartie's sailing-boat, which he had himself freighted with a penny, as though convinced that it would never again come to shore; while little Publius—who, James delighted to say, was not a bit like his father—skipping along under his lee, would try to get him to bet another that it never would, having found that it always did. And James would make the bet; he always paid—sometimes as many as three or four pennies in the afternoon, for the game seemed never to pall on little Publius—and always in paying he said: "Now, that's for your money-box. Why, you're getting quite a rich man!" The thought of his little grandson's growing wealth was a real pleasure to him. But little Publius knew a sweet-shop, and a trick worth two of that.

And they would walk home across the Park, James's figure, with high shoulders and absorbed and worried face, exercising its tall, lean protectorship, pathetically unregarded, over the robust child-figures of Imogen and little Publius.

But those Gardens and that Park were not sacred to James. Forsytes and tramps, children and lovers, rested and wandered day after day, night after night, seeking one and all some freedom from labour, from the reek and turmoil of the streets.

The leaves browned slowly, lingering with the sun and summer-like warmth of the nights.

On Saturday, October 5, the sky that had been blue all day deepened after sunset to the bloom of purple grapes. There was no moon, and a clear dark, like some velvety garment, was wrapped around the trees, whose thinned branches, resembling plumes, stirred not in the still, warm air. All London had poured into the Park, draining the cup of summer to its dregs.

Couple after couple, from every gate, they streamed along the paths and over the burnt grass, and one after another, silently out of the lighted spaces, stole into the shelter of the feathery trees, where, blotted against some trunk, or under the shadow of shrubs, they were lost to all but themselves in the heart of the soft darkness.

To fresh-comers along the paths, these forerunners formed but part of that passionate dusk, whence only a strange murmur, like the confused beating of hearts, came forth. But when that murmur reached each couple in the lamp-light their voices wavered, and ceased; their arms enlaced, their eyes began seeking, searching, probing the blackness. Suddenly, as though drawn by invisible hands, they, too, stepped over the railing, and, silent as shadows, were gone from the light.

The stillness, enclosed in the far, inexorable roar of the town, was alive with the myriad passions, hopes, and loves of multitudes of struggling human atoms; for in spite of the disapproval of that great body of Forsytes, the Municipal Council—to whom Love had long been considered, next to the Sewage Question, the gravest danger of the community—a process was going on that night in the Park, and in a hundred other parks, without which the thousand factories, churches, shops, taxes, and drains, of which they were custodians, were as arteries without blood, a man without a heart.

The instincts of self-forgetfulness, of passion, and of love, hiding under the trees, away from the trustees of their remorseless enemy, the 'sense of property,' were holding a stealthy revel, and Soames, returning from Bayswater—for he had been alone to dine at Timothy's—walking home along the water, with his mind upon that coming lawsuit, had the blood driven from his heart by a low laugh and the sound of kisses. He thought of writing to the *Times* the next morning, to draw the attention of the Editor to the condition of our parks. He did not, however, for he had a horror of seeing his name in print.

But starved as he was, the whispered sounds in the stillness, the half-seen forms in the dark, acted on him like some morbid stimulant. He left the path along the water and stole under the trees, along the deep shadow of little plantations, where the boughs of chestnut trees hung their great leaves low, and there was blacker refuge, shaping his course in circles which had for their object a stealthy inspection of chairs side by side against tree-trunks, of enlaced lovers, who stirred at his approach.

Now he stood still on the rise overlooking the Serpentine, where, in full lamp-light, black against the silver water, sat a couple who never moved, the woman's face buried on the man's neck—a single form, like a carved emblem of passion, silent and unashamed.

And, stung by the sight, Soames hurried on deeper into the shadow of the trees.

In this search, who knows what he thought and what he sought? Bread for hunger—light in darkness? Who knows what he expected to find—impersonal knowledge of the human heart—the end of his private subterranean tragedy—for, again, who knew, but that each dark couple, unnamed, unnameable, might not be he and she?

But it could not be such knowledge as this that he was seeking—the wife of Soames Forsyte sitting in the Park like a common wench! Such thoughts were inconceivable; and from tree to tree, with his noiseless step, he passed.

Once he was sworn at; once the whisper, "If only it could always be like this!" sent the blood flying again from his heart, and he waited there, patient and dogged, for the two to move. But it was only a poor thin slip of a shop-girl in her draggled blouse who passed him, clinging to her lover's arm.

A hundred other lovers too whispered that hope in the stillness of the trees, a hundred other lovers clung to each other.

But shaking himself with sudden disgust, Soames returned to the path, and left that seeking for he knew not what.

Chapter III

MEETING AT THE BOTANICAL

Y OUNG JOLYON, whose circumstances were not those of a
Forsyte, found at times a difficulty in sparing the money needful
for those country jaunts and researches into Nature, without having
prosecuted which no water-colour artist ever puts brush to paper.

He was frequently, in fact, obliged to take his colour-box into the
Botanical Gardens, and there, on his stool, in the shade of a monkey-
puzzler or in the lee of some india-rubber plant, he would spend long
hours sketching.

An Art critic who had recently been looking at his work had delivered himself as follows:

"In a way your drawings are very good; tone and colour, in some of
them certainly quite a feeling for Nature. But, you see, they're so scattered; you'll never get the public to look at them. Now, if you'd taken a
definite subject, such as 'London by Night,' or 'The Crystal Palace in the
Spring,' and made a regular series, the public would have known at
once what they were looking at. I can't lay too much stress upon that. All
the men who are making great names in Art, like Crum Stone or
Bleeder, are making them by avoiding the unexpected; by specializing
and putting their works all in the same pigeon-hole, so that the public
know at once where to go. And this stands to reason, for if a man's a
collector he doesn't want people to smell at the canvas to find out whom
his pictures are by; he wants them to be able to say at once, 'A capital
Forsyte!' It is all the more important for you to be careful to choose a
subject that they can lay hold of on the spot, since there's no very
marked originality in your style."

Young Jolyon, standing by the little piano, where a bowl of dried
rose leaves, the only produce of the garden, was deposited on a bit of
faded damask, listened with his dim smile.

Turning to his wife, who was looking at the speaker with an angry
expression on her thin face, he said:

233

"You see, dear?"

"I do *not*," she answered in her staccato voice, that still had a little foreign accent; "your style *has* originality."

The critic looked at her, smiled deferentially, and said no more. Like everyone else, he knew their history.

The words bore good fruit with young Jolyon; they were contrary to all that he believed in, to all that he theoretically held good in his Art, but some strange, deep instinct moved him against his will to turn them to profit.

He discovered therefore one morning that an idea had come to him for making a series of water colour drawings of London. How the idea had arisen he could not tell; and it was not till the following year, when he had completed and sold them at a very fair price, that in one of his impersonal moods, he found himself able to recollect the Art critic, and to discover in his own achievement another proof that he was a Forsyte.

He decided to commence with the Botanical Gardens, where he had already made so many studies, and chose the little artificial pond, sprinkled now with an autumn shower of red and yellow leaves, for though the gardeners longed to sweep them off, they could not reach them with their brooms. The rest of the gardens they swept bare enough, removing every morning Nature's rain of leaves; piling them in heaps, whence from slow fires rose the sweet, acrid smoke that, like the cuckoo's note for spring, the scent of lime trees for the summer, is the true emblem of the fall. The gardener's tidy souls could not abide the gold and green and russet pattern on the grass. The gravel paths must lie unstained, ordered, methodical, without knowledge of the realities of life, nor of that slow and beautiful decay which flings crowns underfoot to star the earth with fallen glories, whence, as the cycle rolls, will leap again wild spring.

Thus each leaf that fell was marked from the moment when it fluttered a good-bye and dropped, slow turning, from its twig.

But on that little pond the leaves floated in peace, and praised Heaven with their hues, the sunlight haunting over them.

And so young Jolyon found them.

Coming there one morning in the middle of October, he was disconcerted to find a bench about twenty paces from his stand occupied, for he had a proper horror of anyone seeing him at work.

A lady in a velvet jacket was sitting there, with her eyes fixed on the ground. A flowering laurel, however, stood between, and, taking shelter behind this, young Jolyon prepared his easel.

His preparations were leisurely; he caught, as every true artist should, at anything that might delay for a moment the effort of his work, and he found himself looking furtively at this unknown dame.

Like his father before him, he had an eye for a face. This face was charming!

He saw a rounded chin nestling in a cream ruffle, a delicate face with large dark eyes and soft lips. A black 'picture' hat concealed the hair; her figure was lightly poised against the back of the bench, her knees were crossed; the tip of a patent-leather shoe emerged beneath her skirt. There was something, indeed, inexpressibly dainty about the person of this lady, but young Jolyon's attention was chiefly riveted by the look on her face, which reminded him of his wife. It was as though its owner had come into contact with forces too strong for her. It troubled him, arousing vague feelings of attraction and chivalry. Who was she? And what doing there, alone?

Two young gentlemen of that peculiar breed, at once forward and shy, found in the Regent's Park, came by on their way to lawn tennis, and he noted with disapproval their furtive stares of admiration. A loitering gardener halted to do something unnecessary to a clump of pampas grass; he, too, wanted an excuse for peeping. A gentleman, old, and, by his hat, a professor of horticulture, passed three times to scrutinize her long and stealthily, a queer expression about his lips.

With all these men young Jolyon felt the same vague irritation. She looked at none of them, yet was he certain that every man who passed would look at her like that.

Her face was not the face of a sorceress, who in every look holds out to men the offer of pleasure; it had none of the 'devil's beauty' so highly prized among the first Forsytes of the land; neither was it of that type, no less adorable, associated with the box of chocolate; it was not of the spiritually passionate, or passionately spiritual order, peculiar to house-decoration and modern poetry; nor did it seem to promise to the play-wright material for the production of the interesting and neurasthenic figure, who commits suicide in the last act.

In shape and colouring, in its soft persuasive passivity, its sensuous purity, this woman's face reminded him of Titian's 'Heavenly Love,' a reproduction of which hung over the sideboard in his dining-room. And her attraction seemed to be in this soft passivity, in the feeling she gave that to pressure she must yield.

For what or whom was she waiting, in the silence, with the trees dropping here and there a leaf, and the thrushes strutting close on grass touched with the sparkle of the autumn rime?

Then her charming face grew eager, and, glancing round, with almost a lover's jealousy, young Jolyon saw Bosinney striding across the grass.

Curiously he watched the meeting, the look in their eyes, the long clasp of their hands. They sat down close together, linked for all their outward discretion. He heard the rapid murmur of their talk; but what they said he could not catch.

He had rowed in the galley himself! He knew the long hours of waiting and the lean minutes of a half-public meeting; the tortures of suspense that haunt the unhallowed lover.

It required, however, but a glance at their two faces to see that this was none of those affairs of a season that distract men and women about town; none of those sudden appetites that wake up ravening, and are surfeited and asleep again in six weeks. This was the real thing! This was what had happened to himself! Out of this anything might come!

Bosinney was pleading, and she so quiet, so soft, yet immovable in her passivity, sat looking over the grass.

Was he the man to carry her off, that tender, passive being, who would never stir a step for herself? Who had given him all herself, and would die for him, but perhaps would never run away with him!

It seemed to young Jolyon that he could hear her saying: "But, darling, it would ruin you!" For he himself had experienced to the full the gnawing fear at the bottom of each woman's heart that she is a drag on the man she loves.

And he peeped at them no more; but their soft, rapid talk came to his ears, with the stuttering song of some bird who seemed trying to remember the notes of spring: Joy—tragedy? Which—which?

And gradually their talk ceased; long silence followed.

'And where does Soames come in?' young Jolyon thought. 'People think she is concerned about the sin of deceiving her husband! Little they know of women! She's eating, after starvation—taking her revenge! And Heaven help her—for he'll take his.'

He heard the swish of silk, and, spying round the laurel, saw them walking away, their hands stealthily joined. . . .

At the end of July old Jolyon had taken his grand-daughter to the mountains; and on that visit (the last they ever paid) June recovered to a great extent her health and spirits. In the hotels, filled with British Forsytes—for old Jolyon could not bear a 'set of Germans,' as he called all foreigners—she was looked upon with respect—the only grand-daughter of that fine-looking, and evidently wealthy, old Mr. Forsyte. She did not mix freely with people—to mix freely with people was not June's habit—but she formed some friendships, and notably one in the Rhone Valley, with a French girl who was dying of consumption.

Determining at once that her friend should not die, she forgot, in the institution of a campaign against Death, much of her own trouble.

Old Jolyon watched the new intimacy with relief and disapproval; for this additional proof that her life was to be passed amongst 'lame ducks' worried him. Would she never make a friendship or take an interest in something that would be of real benefit to her?

'Taking up with a parcel of foreigners,' he called it. He often, however, brought home grapes or roses, and presented them to this 'Mam'-zelle' with an ingratiating twinkle.

Towards the end of September, in spite of June's disapproval, Mademoiselle Vigor breathed her last in the little hotel at St. Luc, to which they had moved her; and June took her defeat so deeply to heart that old Jolyon carried her away to Paris. Here, in contemplation of the 'Venus de Milo' and the 'Madeleine,' she took off her depression, and when, towards the middle of October, they returned to town, her grand-father believed that he had effected a cure.

No sooner, however, had they established themselves in Stanhope Gate than he perceived to his dismay a return of her old absorbed and brooding manner. She would sit, staring in front of her, her chin on her hand, like a little Norse spirit, grim and intent, while all around in the electric light, then just installed, shone the great drawing-room brocaded up to the frieze, full of furniture from Baple and Pullbred's. And in the huge gilt mirror were reflected those Dresden china groups of young men in tight knee breeches, at the feet of full-bosomed ladies nursing on their laps pet lambs, which old Jolyon had bought when he was a bachelor and thought so highly of in these days of degenerate taste. He was a man of most open mind, who, more than any Forsyte of them all, had moved with the times, but he could never forget that he had bought these groups at Jobson's, and given a lot of money for them. He often said to June, with a sort of disillusioned contempt:

"*You* don't care about them! They're not the gimcrack things you and your friends like, but they cost me seventy pounds!" He was not a man who allowed his taste to be warped when he knew for solid reasons that it was sound.

One of the first things that June did on getting home was to go round to Timothy's. She persuaded herself that it was her duty to call there, and cheer him with an account of all her travels; but in reality she went because she knew of no other place where, by some random speech, or roundabout question, she could glean news of Bosinney.

They received her most cordially: And how was her dear grandfather? He had not been to see them since May. Her Uncle Timothy was very poorly, he had had a lot of trouble with the chimney-sweep in his bedroom; the stupid man had let the soot down the chimney! It had quite upset her uncle.

June sat there a long time, dreading, yet passionately hoping, that they would speak of Bosinney.

But paralyzed by unaccountable discretion, Mrs. Septimus Small let fall no word, neither did she question June about him. In desperation the girl asked at last whether Soames and Irene were in town—she had not yet been to see anyone.

It was Aunt Hester who replied: "Oh, yes, they were in town, they had not been away at all. There was some little difficulty about the house," she believed. "June had heard, no doubt! She had better ask her Aunt Juley!"

June turned to Mrs. Small, who sat upright in her chair, her hands clasped, her face covered with innumerable pouts. In answer to the girl's look she maintained a strange silence, and when she spoke it was to ask June whether she had worn night-socks up in those high hotels where it must be so cold of a night.

June answered that she had not, she hated the stuffy things; and rose to leave.

Mrs. Small's infallibly chosen silence was far more ominous to her than anything that could have been said.

Before half an hour was over she had dragged the truth from Mrs.

Baynes in Lowndes Square, that Soames was bringing an action against Bosinney over the decoration of the house.

Instead of disturbing her, the news had a strangely calming effect; as though she saw in the prospect of this struggle new hope for herself. She learnt that the case was expected to come on in about a month, and there seemed little or no prospect of Bosinney's success.

"And whatever he'll do I can't think," said Mrs. Baynes; "it's very dreadful for him, you know—he's got no money—he's very hard up. And we can't help him, I'm sure. I'm told the money-lenders won't lend if you have no security, and he has none—none at all."

Her embonpoint had increased of late; she was in the full swing of autumn organization, her writing-table literally strewn with the menus of charity functions. She looked meaningly at June, with her round eyes of parrot-grey.

The sudden flush that rose on the girl's intent young face—she must have seen spring up before her a great hope—the sudden sweetness of her smile, often came back to Lady Baynes in after years (Baynes was knighted when he built that public Museum of Art which has given so much employment to officials, and so little pleasure to those working classes for whom it was designed).

The memory of that change, vivid and touching, like the breaking open of a flower, or the first sun after long winter, the memory, too, of all that came after, often intruded itself, unaccountably, inopportunely on Lady Baynes, when her mind was set upon the most important things.

This was the very afternoon of the day that young Jolyon witnessed the meeting in the Botanical Gardens, and on this day, too, old Jolyon paid a visit to his solicitors, Forsyte, Bustard, and Forsyte, in the Poultry. Soames was not in, he had gone down to Somerset House; Bustard was buried up to the hilt in papers and that inaccessible apartment, where he was judiciously placed, in order that he might do as much work as possible; but James was in the front office, biting a finger, and lugubriously turning over the pleadings in Forsyte *v.* Bosinney.

This sound lawyer had only a sort of luxurious dread of the 'nice point,' enough to set up a pleasurable feeling of fuss; for his good practical sense told him that if he himself were on the Bench he would not pay much attention to it. But he was afraid that this Bosinney would go bankrupt and Soames would have to find the money after all, and costs into the bargain. And behind this tangible dread there was always that intangible trouble, lurking in the background, intricate, dim, scandalous, like a bad dream, and of which this action was but an outward and visible sign.

He raised his head as old Jolyon came in, and muttered: "How are you, Jolyon? Haven't seen you for an age. You've been to Switzerland, they tell me. This young Bosinney, he's got himself into a mess. I knew how it would be!" He held out the papers, regarding his elder brother with nervous gloom.

Old Jolyon read them in silence, and while he read them James looked at the floor, biting his fingers the while.

Old Jolyon pitched them down at last, and they fell with a thump amongst a mass of affidavits in 're Buncombe, deceased,' one of the many branches of that parent and profitable tree, 'Fryer v. Forsyte.'

"I don't know what Soames is about," he said, "to make a fuss over a few hundred pounds. I thought he was a man of property."

James's long upper lip twitched angrily; he could not bear his son to be attacked in such a spot.

"It's not the money——" he began, but meeting his brother's glance, direct, shrewd, judicial, he stopped.

There was a silence.

"I've come in for my Will," said old Jolyon at last, tugging at his moustache.

James's curiosity was roused at once. Perhaps nothing in this life was more stimulating to him than a Will; it was the supreme deal with property, the final inventory of a man's belongings, the last word on what he was worth. He sounded the bell.

"Bring in Mr. Jolyon's Will," he said to an anxious, dark-haired clerk.

"You going to make some alterations?" And through his mind there flashed the thought: 'Now, am I worth as much as he?'

Old Jolyon put the Will in his breast pocket, and James twisted his long legs regretfully.

"You've made some nice purchases lately, they tell me," he said.

"I don't know where you get your information from," answered old Jolyon sharply. "When's this action coming on? Next month? I can't tell what you've got in your minds. You must manage your own affairs; but if you take my advice, you'll settle it out of Court. Good-bye!" With a cold handshake he was gone.

James, his fixed grey-blue eyes corkscrewing round some secret anxious image, began again to bite his finger.

Old Jolyon took his Will to the offices of the New Colliery Company, and sat down in the empty Board Room to read it through. He answered 'Down-by-the-starn' Hemmings so tartly when the latter, seeing his Chairman seated there, entered with the new Superintendent's first report, that the Secretary withdrew with regretful dignity; and sending for the transfer clerk, blew him up till the poor youth knew not where to look.

It was not—by George—as he (Down-by-the-starn) would have him know, for a whipper-snapper of a young fellow like him, to come down to that office, and think that he was God Almighty. He (Down-by-the-starn) had been head of that office for more years than a boy like him could count, and if he thought that when he had finished all his work, he could sit there doing nothing, he did not know him, Hemmings (Down-by-the-starn), and so forth.

On the other side of the green baize door old Jolyon sat at the long, mahogany-and-leather board table, his thick, loose-jointed, tortoise-shell eye-glasses perched on the bridge of his nose, his gold pencil moving down the clauses of his Will.

It was a simple affair, for there were none of those vexatious little legacies and donations to charities, which fritter away a man's possessions, and damage the majestic effect of that little paragraph in the morning papers accorded to Forsytes who die with a hundred thousand pounds.

A simple affair. Just a bequest to his son of twenty thousand, and 'as to the residue of my property of whatsoever kind whether realty or personalty, or partaking of the nature of either—upon trust to pay the proceeds rents annual produce dividends or interest thereof and thereon to my said grand-daughter June Forsyte or her assigns during her life to be for her sole use and benefit and without, etc. . . . and from and after her death or decease upon trust to convey assign transfer or make over the said last-mentioned lands hereditaments premises trust moneys stocks funds investments and securities or such as shall then stand for and represent the same unto such person or persons whether one or more for such intents purposes and uses and generally in such manner way and form in all respects as the said June Forsyte notwithstanding coverture shall by her last Will and Testament or any writing or writings in the nature of a Will testament or testamentary disposition to be by her duly made signed and published direct appoint or make over give and dispose of the same. And in default, etc. . . . . Provided always . . .' and so on, in seven folios of brief and simple phraseology.

The Will had been drawn by James in his palmy days. He had foreseen almost every contingency.

Old Jolyon sat a long time reading this Will; at last he took half a sheet of paper from the rack, and made a prolonged pencil note; then buttoning up the Will, he caused a cab to be called and drove to the offices of Paramor and Herring, in Lincoln's Inn Fields. Jack Herring was dead, but his nephew was still in the firm, and old Jolyon was closeted with him for half an hour.

He had kept the hansom, and on coming out, gave the driver the address—3, Wistaria Avenue.

He felt a strange, slow satisfaction, as though he had scored a victory over James and the man of property. They should not poke their noses into his affairs any more; he had just cancelled their trusteeships of his Will; he would take the whole of his business out of their hands, and put it into the hands of young Herring, and he would move the business of his Companies too. If that young Soames were such a man of property, he would never miss a thousand a year or so; and under his great white moustache old Jolyon grimly smiled. He felt that what he was doing was in the nature of retributive justice, richly deserved.

Slowly, surely, with the secret inner process that works the destruction of an old tree, the poison of the wounds to his happiness, his will, his pride, had corroded the comely edifice of his philosophy. Life had worn him down on one side, till, like that family of which he was the head, he had lost balance.

To him, borne northwards towards his son's house, the thought of the new disposition of property, which he had just set in motion, appeared vaguely in the light of a stroke of punishment, levelled at that family and that Society, of which James and his son seemed to him the representatives. He had made a restitution to young Jolyon, and restitution to young Jolyon satisfied his secret cravings for revenge—revenge against Time, sorrow, and interference, against all that incalculable sum of disapproval that had been bestowed by the world for fifteen years on his only son. It presented itself as the one possible way of asserting once more the domination of his will; of forcing James, and Soames, and the family, and all those hidden masses of Forsytes—a great stream rolling against the single dam of his obstinacy—to recognise once and for all that *he would be master.* It was sweet to think that at last he was going to make the boy a richer man by far than that son of James, that 'man of property.' And it was sweet to give to Jo, for he loved his son.

Neither young Jolyon nor his wife were in (young Jolyon indeed was not back from the Botanical), but the little maid told him that she expected the master at any moment:

"He's always at 'ome to tea, sir, to play with the children."

Old Jolyon said he would wait; and sat down patiently enough in the faded, shabby drawing-room, where, now that the summer chintzes were removed, the old chairs and sofas revealed all their threadbare deficiencies. He longed to send for the children; to have them there beside him, their supple bodies against his knees; to hear Jolly's: "Hallo, Gran!" and see his rush; and feel Holly's soft little hand stealing up against his cheek. But he would not. There was solemnity in what he had come to do, and until it was over he would not play. He amused himself by thinking how with two strokes of his pen he was going to restore the look of caste so conspicuously absent from everything in that little house; how he could fill these rooms, or others in some larger mansion, with triumphs of art from Baple and Pullbred's; how he could send little Jolly to Harrow and Oxford (he no longer had faith in Eton and Cambridge, for his son had been there); how he could procure little Holly the best musical instruction, the child had a remarkable aptitude.

As these visions crowded before him, causing emotion to swell his heart, he rose, and stood at the window, looking down into the little walled strip of garden, where the pear-tree, bare of leaves before its time, stood with gaunt branches in the slow-gathering mist of the autumn afternoon. The dog Balthasar, his tail curled tightly over a piebald, furry back, was walking at the farther end, sniffing at the plants, and at intervals placing his leg for support against the wall.

And old Jolyon mused.

What pleasure was there left but to give? It was pleasant to give, when you could find one who would be thankful for what you gave— one of your own flesh and blood! There was no such satisfaction to be had out of giving to those who did not belong to you, to those who had no claim on you! Such giving as that was a betrayal of the individualistic convictions and actions of his life, of all his enterprise, his labour, and his moderation, of the great and proud fact that, like tens of thousands of Forsytes before him, tens of thousands in the present, tens of thousands in the future, he had always made his own, and held his own, in the world.

And, while he stood there looking down on the smut-covered foliage of the laurels, the black-stained grass-plot, the progress of the dog Balthasar, all the suffering of the fifteen years during which he had been baulked of legitimate enjoyment mingled its gall with the sweetness of the approaching moment.

Young Jolyon came at last, pleased with his work, and fresh from long hours in the open air. On hearing that his father was in the drawing-room, he inquired hurriedly whether Mrs. Forsyte was at home, and being informed that she was not, heaved a sigh of relief. Then putting his painting materials carefully in the little coat-closet out of sight, he went in.

With characteristic decision old Jolyon came at once to the point. "I've been altering my arrangements, Jo," he said. "You can cut your coat a bit longer in the future—I'm settling a thousand a year on you at once. June will have fifty thousand at my death; and you the rest. That dog of yours is spoiling the garden. I shouldn't keep a dog, if I were you!"

The dog Balthasar, seated in the centre of the lawn, was examining his tail.

Young Jolyon looked at the animal, but saw him dimly, for his eyes were misty.

"Yours won't come short of a hundred thousand, my boy," said old Jolyon; "I thought you'd better know. I haven't much longer to live at my age. I shan't allude to it again. How's your wife? And—give her my love."

Young Jolyon put his hand on his father's shoulder, and, as neither spoke, the episode closed.

Having seen his father into a hansom, young Jolyon came back to the drawing-room and stood, where old Jolyon had stood, looking down on the little garden. He tried to realize all that this meant to him, and, Forsyte that he was, vistas of property were opened out in his brain; the years of half rations through which he had passed had not sapped his natural instincts. In extremely practical form, he thought of travel, of his wife's costume, the children's education, a pony for Jolly, a thousand things; but in the midst of all he thought, too, of Bosinney and his mistress, and the broken song of the thrush. Joy—tragedy! Which? Which?

The old past—the poignant, suffering, passionate, wonderful past, that no money could buy, that nothing could restore in all its burning sweetness—had come back before him.

When his wife came in he went straight up to her and took her in his arms; and for a long time he stood without speaking, his eyes closed, pressing her to him, while she looked at him with a wondering, adoring, doubting look in her eyes.

Chapter IV

VOYAGE INTO THE INFERNO

THE morning after a certain night on which Soames at last asserted his rights and acted like a man, he breakfasted alone.

He breakfasted by gaslight, the fog of late November wrapping the town as in some monstrous blanket till the trees of the Square even were barely visible from the dining-room window.

He ate steadily, but at times a sensation as though he could not swallow attacked him. Had he been right to yield to his overmastering hunger of the night before, and break down the resistance which he had suffered now too long from this woman who was his lawful and solemnly constituted helpmate?

He was strangely haunted by the recollection of her face, from before which, to soothe her, he had tried to pull her hands—of her terrible smothered sobbing, the like of which he had never heard, and still seemed to hear; and he was still haunted by the odd, intolerable feeling of remorse and shame he had felt, as he stood looking at her by the flame of the single candle, before silently slinking away.

And somehow, now that he had acted like this, he was surprised at himself.

Two nights before, at Winifred Dartie's, he had taken Mrs. MacAnder into dinner. She had said to him, looking in his face with her sharp, greenish eyes: "And so your wife is a great friend of that Mr. Bosinney's?"

Not deigning to ask what she meant, he had brooded over her words.

They had roused in him a fierce jealousy, which, with the peculiar perversion of this instinct, had turned to fiercer desire.

Without the incentive of Mrs. MacAnder's words he might never have done what he had done. Without their incentive and the accident of finding his wife's door for once unlocked, which had enabled him to steal upon her asleep.

Slumber had removed his doubts, but the morning brought them

246

again. One thought comforted him: No one would know—it was not the sort of thing that she would speak about.

And, indeed, when the vehicle of his daily business life, which needed so imperatively the grease of clean and practical thought, started rolling once more with the reading of his letters, those nightmare-like doubts began to assume less extravagant importance at the back of his mind. The incident was really not of great moment; women made a fuss about it in books; but in the cool judgment of right-thinking men, of men of the world, of such as he recollected often received praise in the Divorce Court, he had but done his best to sustain the sanctity of marriage, to prevent her from abandoning her duty, possibly, if she were still seeing Bosinney, from—— No, he did not regret it.

Now that the first step towards reconciliation had been taken, the rest would be comparatively—comparatively——

He rose and walked to the window. His nerve had been shaken. The sound of smothered sobbing was in his ears again. He could not get rid of it.

He put on his fur coat, and went out into the fog; having to go into the City, he took the underground railway from Sloane Square station.

In his corner of the first-class compartment filled with City men the smothered sobbing still haunted him, so he opened the *Times* with the rich crackle that drowns all lesser sounds, and, barricaded behind it, set himself steadily to con the news.

He read that a Recorder had charged a grand jury on the previous day with a more than usually long list of offences. He read of three murders, five manslaughters, seven arsons, and as many as eleven rapes—a surprisingly high number—in addition to many less conspicuous crimes, to be tried during a coming Sessions; and from one piece of news he went on to another, keeping the paper well before his face.

And still, inseparable from his reading, was the memory of Irene's tear-stained face, and the sounds from her broken heart.

The day was a busy one, including, in addition to the ordinary affairs of his practice, a visit to his brokers, Messrs. Grin and Grinning, to give them instructions to sell his shares in the New Colliery Co., Ltd., whose business he suspected, rather than knew, was stagnating (this enterprise afterwards slowly declined, and was ultimately sold for a song to an American syndicate); and a long conference at Waterbuck, Q.C.'s chambers, attended by Boulter, by Fiske, the junior counsel, and Waterbuck, Q.C., himself.

The case of Forsyte *v*. Bosinney was expected to be reached on the morrow, before Mr. Justice Bentham.

Mr. Justice Bentham, a man of common-sense rather than too great legal knowledge, was considered to be about the best man they could have to try the action. He was a 'strong' judge.

Waterbuck, Q.C., in pleasing conjunction with an almost rude neglect of Boulter and Fiske paid to Soames a good deal of attention, by instinct or the sounder evidence of rumour, feeling him to be a man of property.

He held with remarkable consistency to the opinion he had already expressed in writing, that the issue would depend to a great extent on the evidence given at the trial, and in a few well-directed remarks he advised Soames not to be too careful in giving that evidence. "A little bluffness, Mr. Forsyte," he said, "a little bluffness," and after he had spoken he laughed firmly, closed his lips tight, and scratched his head just below where he had pushed his wig back, for all the world like the gentleman-farmer for whom he loved to be taken. He was considered perhaps the leading man in breach of promise cases.

Soames used the underground again in going home.

The fog was worse than ever at Sloane Square station. Through the still, thick blur, men groped in and out; women, very few, grasped their reticules to their bosoms and handkerchiefs to their mouths; crowned with the weird excrescence of the driver, haloed by a vague glow of lamp-light that seemed to drown in vapour before it reached the pavement, cabs loomed dim-shaped ever and again, and discharged citizens bolting like rabbits to their burrows.

And these shadowy figures, wrapped each in his own little shroud of fog, took no notice of each other. In the great warren, each rabbit for himself, especially those clothed in the more expensive fur, who, afraid of carriages on foggy days, are driven underground.

One figure, however, not far from Soames, waited at the station door.

Some buccaneer or lover, of whom each Forsyte thought: 'Poor devil! looks as if he were having a bad time!' Their kind hearts beat a stroke faster for that poor, waiting, anxious lover in the fog; but they hurried by, well knowing that they had neither time nor money to spare for any suffering but their own.

Only a policeman, patrolling slowly and at intervals, took an interest in that waiting figure, the brim of whose slouch hat half-hid a face reddened by the cold, all thin, and haggard, over which a hand stole now and again to smooth away anxiety, or renew the resolution that kept him waiting there. But the waiting lover (if lover he were) was used to policemen's scrutiny, or too absorbed in his anxiety, for he never flinched. A hardened case, accustomed to long trysts, to anxiety, and fog, and cold, if only his mistress came at last. Foolish lover! Fogs last until the spring; there is also snow and rain, no comfort anywhere; gnawing fear if you bring her out, gnawing fear if you bid her stay at home!

"Serve him right; he should arrange his affairs better!"

So any respectable Forsyte. Yet, if that sounder citizen could have listened at the waiting lover's heart, out there in the fog and the cold, he would have said again: "Yes, poor devil! he's having a bad time!"

Soames got into his cab, and, with the glass down, crept along Sloane Street, and so along the Brompton Road, and home. He reached his house at five.

His wife was not in. She had gone out a quarter of an hour before. Out at such a time of night, into this terrible fog! What was the meaning of that?

He sat by the dining-room fire, with the door open, disturbed to the soul, trying to read the evening paper. A book was no good—in daily papers alone was any narcotic to such worry as his. From the customary events recorded in the journal he drew some comfort. 'Suicide of an actress'—'Grave indisposition of a Statesman' (that chronic sufferer)—'Divorce of an army officer'—'Fire in a colliery'—he read them all. They helped him a little—prescribed by the greatest of all doctors, our natural taste.

It was nearly seven when he heard her come in.

The incident of the night before had long lost its importance under stress of anxiety at her strange sortie into the fog. But now that Irene was home, the memory of her broken-hearted sobbing came back to him, and he felt nervous at the thought of facing her.

She was already on the stairs; her grey fur coat hung to her knees, its high collar almost hid her face, she wore a thick veil.

She neither turned to look at him nor spoke. No ghost or stranger could have passed more silently.

Bilson came to lay dinner, and told him that Mrs. Forsyte was not coming down; she was having the soup in her room.

For once Soames did not 'change'; it was, perhaps, the first time in his life that he had sat down to dinner with soiled cuffs, and, not even noticing them, he brooded long over his wine. He sent Bilson to light a fire in his picture-room, and presently went up there himself.

Turning on the gas, he heaved a deep sigh, as though amongst these treasures, the backs of which confronted him in stacks, around the little room, he had found at length his peace of mind. He went straight up to the greatest treasure of them all, an undoubted Turner, and, carrying it to the easel, turned its face to the light. There had been a movement in Turners, but he had not been able to make up his mind to part with it. He stood for a long time, his pale, clean-shaven face poked forward above his stand-up collar, looking at the picture as though he were adding it up; a wistful expression came into his eyes; he found, perhaps, that it came to too little. He took it down from the easel to put it back against the wall; but, in crossing the room, stopped, for he seemed to hear sobbing.

It was nothing—only the sort of thing that had been bothering him in the morning. And soon after, putting the high guard before the blazing fire, he stole downstairs.

Fresh for the morrow! was his thought. It was long before he went to sleep. . . .

It is now to George Forsyte that the mind must turn for light on the events of that fog-engulfed afternoon.

The wittiest and most sportsmanlike of the Forsytes had passed the day reading a novel in the paternal mansion at Princes' Gardens. Since a recent crisis in his financial affairs he had been kept on parole by Roger, and compelled to reside 'at home.'

Towards five o'clock he went out, and took train at South Kensington Station (for everyone to-day went Underground). His intention was to dine, and pass the evening playing billiards at the Red Pottle—that unique hostel, neither club, hotel, nor good gilt restaurant.

He got out at Charing Cross, choosing it in preference to his more usual St. James's Park, that he might reach Jermyn Street by better lighted ways.

On the platform his eyes—for in combination with a composed and fashionable appearance, George had sharp eyes, and was always on the look-out for fillips to his sardonic humour—his eyes were attracted by a man, who, leaping from a first-class compartment, staggered rather than walked towards the exit.

'So ho, my bird!' said George to himself; 'why, it's "the Buccaneer!" ' and he put his big figure on the trail. Nothing afforded him greater amusement than a drunken man.

Bosinney, who wore a slouch hat, stopped in front of him, spun around, and rushed back towards the carriage he had just left. He was too late. A porter caught him by the coat; the train was already moving on.

George's practised glance caught sight of the face of a lady clad in a grey fur coat at the carriage window. It was Mrs. Soames—and George felt that this was interesting!

And now he followed Bosinney more closely than ever—up the stairs, past the ticket collector into the street. In that progress, however, his feelings underwent a change; no longer merely curious and amused, he felt sorry for the poor fellow he was shadowing. 'The Buccaneer' was not drunk, but seemed to be acting under the stress of violent emotion; he was talking to himself, and all that George could catch were the words "Oh, God!" Nor did he appear to know what he was doing, or where going; but stared, hesitated, moved like a man out of his mind; and from being merely a joker in search of amusement, George felt that he must see the poor chap through.

He had 'taken the knock'—'taken the knock!' And he wondered what on earth Mrs. Soames had been saying, what on earth she had been telling him in the railway carriage. She had looked bad enough herself! It made George sorry to think of her travelling on with her trouble all alone.

He followed close behind Bosinney's elbow—a tall, burly figure, saying nothing, dodging warily—and shadowed him out into the fog. There was something here beyond a jest! He kept his head admirably, in spite of some excitement, for in addition to compassion, the instincts of the chase were roused within him.

Bosinney walked right out into the thoroughfare—a vast muffled blackness, where a man could not see six paces before him; where, all around, voices or whistles mocked the sense of direction; and sudden shapes came rolling slow upon them; and now and then a light showed like a dim island in an infinite dark sea.

And fast into this perilous gulf of night walked Bosinney, and fast after him walked George. If the fellow meant to put his 'two-penny' under a 'bus, he would stop it if he could! Across the street and back the hunted creature strode, not groping as other men were groping in that gloom, but driven forward as though the faithful George behind wielded a knout; and this chase after a haunted man began to have for George the strangest fascination.

But it was now that the affair developed in a way which ever afterwards caused it to remain green in his mind. Brought to a stand-still in the fog, he heard words which threw a sudden light on these proceedings. What Mrs. Soames had said to Bosinney in the train was now no longer dark. George understood from those mutterings that Soames had exercised his rights over an estranged and unwilling wife in the greatest —the supreme act of property.

His fancy wandered in the fields of this situation; it impressed him; he guessed something of the anguish, the sexual confusion and horror in Bosinney's heart. And he thought: 'Yes, it's a bit thick! I don't wonder the poor fellow is half-cracked!'

He had run his quarry to earth on a bench under one of the lions in Trafalgar Square, a monster sphynx astray like themselves in that gulf of darkness. Here, rigid and silent, sat Bosinney, and George, in whose patience was a touch of strange brotherliness, took his stand behind. He was not lacking in a certain delicacy—a sense of form—that did not permit him to intrude upon this tragedy, and he waited, quiet as the lion above, his fur collar hitched above his ears concealing the fleshy redness of his cheeks, concealing all but his eyes with their sardonic, compassionate stare. And men kept passing back from business on the way to their clubs—men whose figures shrouded in cocoons of fog came into view like spectres, and like spectres vanished. Then even in his compassion George's Quilpish humour broke forth in a sudden longing to pluck these spectres by the sleeve, and say:

"Hi, you Johnnies! You don't often see a show like this! Here's a poor devil whose mistress has just been telling him a pretty little story of her husband; walk up, walk up! He's taken the knock, you see."

In fancy he saw them gaping round the tortured lover; and grinned as he thought of some respectable, newly married spectre enabled by the state of his own affections to catch an inkling of what was going on within Bosinney; he fancied he could see his mouth getting wider and wider, and the fog going down and down. For in George was all that contempt of the middle-class—especially of the married middle-class—peculiar to the wild and sportsmanlike spirits in its ranks.

But he began to be bored. Waiting was not what he had bargained for.

'After all,' he thought, 'the poor chap will get over it; not the first time such a thing has happened in this little city!' But now his quarry again began muttering words of violent hate and anger. And following a sudden impulse George touched him on the shoulder.

Bosinney spun around.

"Who are you? What do you want?"

George could have stood it well enough in the light of the gas lamps, in the light of that everyday world of which he was so hardy a connoisseur; but in this fog, where all was gloomy and unreal, where nothing had that matter-of-fact value associated by Forsytes with earth, he was a victim to strange qualms, and as he tried to stare back into the eyes of this maniac, he thought:

'If I see a bobby, I'll hand him over; he's not fit to be at large.'

But waiting for no answer, Bosinney strode off into the fog, and George followed, keeping perhaps a little further off, yet more than ever set on tracking him down.

'He can't go on like this,' he thought. 'It's God's own miracle he's not been run over already.' He brooded no more on policemen, a sportsman's sacred fire alive again within him.

Into a denser gloom than ever Bosinney held on at a furious pace; but his pursuer perceived more method in his madness—he was clearly making his way westwards.

'He's really going for Soames!' thought George. The idea was attractive. It would be a sporting end to such a chase. He had always disliked his cousin.

The shaft of a passing cab brushed against his shoulder and made him leap aside. He did not intend to be killed for the Buccaneer, or anyone. Yet, with hereditary tenacity, he stuck to the trail through vapour that blotted out everything but the shadow of the hunted man and the dim moon of the nearest lamp.

Then suddenly, with the instinct of a town-stroller, George knew himself to be in Piccadilly. Here he could find his way blindfold; and freed from the strain of geographical uncertainty, his mind returned to Bosinney's trouble.

Down the long avenue of his man-about-town experience, bursting, as it were, through a smirch of doubtful amours, there stalked to him a memory of his youth. A memory, poignant still, that brought the scent of hay, the gleam of moonlight, a summer magic, into the reek and blackness of this London fog—the memory of a night when in the darkest shadow of a lawn he had overheard from a woman's lips that he was not her sole possessor. And for a moment George walked no longer in black Piccadilly, but lay again, with hell in his heart, and his face to the sweet-smelling, dewy grass, in the long shadow of poplars that hid the moon.

A longing seized him to throw his arm round the Buccaneer, and say, "Come, old boy. Time cures all. Let's go and drink it off!"

But a voice yelled at him, and he started back. A cab rolled out of blackness, and into blackness disappeared. And suddenly George perceived that he had lost Bosinney. He ran forward and back, felt his heart clutched by a sickening fear, the dark fear which lives in the wings of the fog. Perspiration started out on his brow. He stood quite still, listening with all his might.

"And then," as he confided to Dartie the same evening in the course of a game of billiards at the Red Pottle, "I lost him."

Dartie twirled complacently at his dark moustache. He had just put together a neat break of twenty-three, failing at a 'jenny.' "And who was *she?*" he asked.

George looked slowly at the 'man of the world's' fattish, sallow face, and a little grim smile lurked about the curves of his cheeks and his heavy-lidded eyes.

'No, no, my fine fellow,' he thought. 'I'm not going to tell *you.*' For though he mixed with Dartie a good deal, he thought him a bit of a cad.

"Oh, some little love-lady or other," he said, and chalked his cue.

"A love-lady!" exclaimed Dartie—he used a more figurative expression. "I made sure it was our friend Soa——"

"Did you?" said George curtly. "Then damme you've made an error."

He missed his shot. He was careful not to allude to the subject again till, towards eleven o'clock, having, in his poetic phraseology, 'looked

254

upon the drink when it was yellow,' he drew aside the blind, and gazed out into the street. The murky blackness of the fog was but faintly broken by the lamps of the 'Red Pottle,' and no shape of mortal man or thing was in sight.

"I can't help thinking of that poor Buccaneer," he said. "He may be wandering out there now in that fog. If he's not a corpse," he added with strange dejection.

"Corpse!" said Dartie, in whom the recollection of his defeat at Richmond flared up. *"He's* all right. Ten to one if he wasn't tight!"

George turned on him, looking really formidable, with a sort of savage gloom on his big face.

"Dry up!" he said. "Don't I tell you he's 'taken the knock!' "

Chapter V

THE TRIAL

O N the morning of his case, which was second in the list, Soames was again obliged to start without seeing Irene, and it was just as well, for he had not as yet made up his mind what attitude to adopt towards her.

He had been requested to be in court by half-past ten, to provide against the event of the first action (a breach of promise) collapsing, which however it did not, both sides showing a courage that afforded Waterbuck, Q.C., an opportunity for improving his already great reputation in this class of case. He was opposed by Ram, the other celebrated breach of promise man. It was a battle of giants.

The court delivered judgment just before the luncheon interval. The jury left the box for good, and Soames went out to get something to eat. He met James standing at the little luncheon-bar, like a pelican in the wilderness of the galleries, bent over a sandwich with a glass of sherry before him. The spacious emptiness of the great central hall, over which father and son brooded as they stood together, was marred now and then for a fleeting moment by barristers in wig and gown hurriedly bolting across, by an occasional old lady or rusty-coated man, looking up in a frightened way, and by two persons, bolder than their generation, seated in an embrasure arguing. The sound of their voices arose, together with a scent as of neglected wells, which, mingling with the odour of the galleries, combined to form the savour, like nothing but the emanation of a refined cheese, so indissolubly connected with the administration of British justice.

It was not long before James addressed his son.

"When's your case coming on? I suppose it'll be on directly. I shouldn't wonder if this Bosinney'd say anything; I should think he'd have to. He'll go bankrupt if it goes against him." He took a large bite at his sandwich and a mouthful of sherry. "Your mother," he said, "wants you and Irene to come and dine to-night."

A chill smile played round Soames's lips; he looked back at his father. Any one who had seen the look, cold and furtive, thus interchanged, might have been pardoned for not appreciating the real understanding between them. James finished his sherry at a draught.

"How much?" he asked.

On returning to the court Soames took at once his rightful seat on the front bench beside his solicitor. He ascertained where his father was seated with a glance so sidelong as to commit nobody.

James, sitting back with his hands clasped over the handle of his umbrella, was brooding on the end of the bench immediately behind counsel, whence he could get away at once when the case was over. He considered Bosinney's conduct in every way outrageous, but he did not wish to run up against him, feeling that the meeting would be awkward.

Next to the Divorce Court, this court was, perhaps, the favourite emporium of justice, libel, breach of promise, and other commercial actions being frequently decided there. Quite a sprinkling of persons unconnected with the law occupied the back benches, and the hat of a woman or two could be seen in the gallery.

The two rows of seats immediately in front of James were gradually filled by barristers in wigs, who sat down to make pencil notes, chat, and attend to their teeth; but his interest was soon diverted from these lesser lights of justice by the entrance of Waterbuck, Q.C., with the wings of his silk gown rustling, and his red, capable face supported by two short, brown whiskers. The famous Q.C. looked, as James freely admitted, the very picture of a man who could heckle a witness.

For all his experience, it so happened that he had never seen Waterbuck, Q.C., before, and, like many Forsytes in the lower branch of the profession, he had an extreme admiration for a good cross-examiner. The long, lugubrious folds in his cheeks relaxed somewhat after seeing him, especially as he now perceived that Soames alone was represented by silk.

Waterbuck, Q.C., had barely screwed round on his elbow to chat with his Junior before Mr. Justice Bentham himself appeared—a thin, rather hen-like man, with a little stoop, clean-shaven under his snowy wig. Like all the rest of the court, Waterbuck rose, and remained on his feet until the judge was seated. James rose but slightly; he was already comfortable, and had no opinion of Bentham, having sat next but one to him at dinner twice at the Bumley Tomms'. Bumley Tomm was rather a poor thing, though he had been so successful. James himself had given him his first brief. He was excited, too, for he had just found out that Bosinney was not in court.

'Now, what's he mean by that?' he kept on thinking.

The case having been called on, Waterbuck, Q.C., pushing back his papers, hitched his gown on his shoulder, and, with a semi-circular look around him, like a man who is going to bat, arose and addressed the court.

The facts, he said, were not in dispute, and all that his lordship would be asked was to interpret the correspondence which had taken place between his client and the defendant, an architect, with reference to the decoration of a house. He would, however, submit that this correspondence could only mean one very plain thing. After briefly reciting the history of the house at Robin Hill, which he described as a mansion, and the actual facts of expenditure, he went on as follows:

"My client, Mr. Soames Forsyte, is a gentleman, a man of property, who would be the last to dispute any legitimate claim that might be made against him, but he has met with such treatment from his architect in the matter of this house, over which he has, as your lordship has heard, already spent some twelve—some twelve thousand pounds, a sum considerably in advance of the amount he had originally contemplated, that as a matter of principle—and this I cannot too strongly emphasize —as a matter of principle, and in the interests of others, he has felt himself compelled to bring this action. The point put forward in defence by the architect I will suggest to your lordship is not worthy of a moment's serious consideration." He then read the correspondence.

His client, "a man of recognised position," was prepared to go into the box, and to swear that he never did authorize, that it was never in his mind to authorize, the expenditure of any money beyond the extreme limit of twelve thousand and fifty pounds, which he had clearly fixed; and not further to waste the time of the court, he would at once call Mr. Forsyte.

Soames then went into the box. His whole appearance was striking in its composure. His face, just supercilious enough, pale and clean-shaven, with a little line between the eyes, and compressed lips; his dress in unostentatious order, one hand neatly gloved, the other bare. He answered the questions put to him in a somewhat low, but distinct voice. His evidence under cross-examination savoured of taciturnity.

Had he not used the expression, "a free hand"?

"No."

"Come, come!"

The expression he had used was 'a free hand in the terms of this correspondence.'

"Would you tell the court that that was English?"

"Yes!"

"What do you say it means?"

"What it says!"

"Are you prepared to deny that it is a contradiction in terms?"

"Yes."

"You are not an Irishman?"

"No."

"Are you a well-educated man?"

"Yes."

"And yet you persist in that statement?"

"Yes."

Throughout this and much more cross-examination, which turned again and again around the 'nice point,' James sat with his hand behind his ear, his eyes fixed upon his son.

He was proud of him! He could not but feel that in similar circumstances he himself would have been tempted to enlarge his replies, but his instinct told him that this taciturnity was the very thing. He sighed with relief, however, when Soames, slowly turning, and without any change of expression, descended from the box.

When it came to the turn of Bosinney's Counsel to address the Judge, James redoubled his attention, and he searched the Court again and again to see if Bosinney were not somewhere concealed.

Young Chankery began nervously; he was placed by Bosinney's absence in an awkward position. He therefore did his best to turn that absence to account.

He could not but fear—he said—that his client had met with an accident. He had fully expected him there to give evidence; they had sent round that morning both to Mr. Bosinney's office and to his rooms (though he knew they were one and the same, he thought it was as well not to say so), but it was not known where he was, and this he considered to be ominous, knowing how anxious Mr. Bosinney had been to give his evidence. He had not, however, been instructed to apply for an adjournment, and in default of such instruction he conceived it his duty to go on. The plea on which he somewhat confidently relied, and which his client, had he not unfortunately been prevented in some way from attending, would have supported by his evidence, was that such an expression as a 'free hand' could not be limited, fettered, and rendered unmeaning, by any verbiage which might follow it. He would go further and say that the correspondence showed that whatever he might have said in his evidence, Mr. Forsyte had in fact never contemplated repudiating liability on any of the work ordered or executed by his architect. The defendant had certainly never contemplated such a contingency, or, as was demonstrated by his letters, he would never have proceeded with the work—a work of extreme delicacy, carried out with great care and efficiency, to meet and satisfy the fastidious taste of a connoisseur, a rich man, a man of property. He felt strongly on this point, and feeling strongly he used, perhaps, rather strong words when he said that this action was of a most unjustifiable, unexpected, indeed unprecedented character. If his Lordship had had the opportunity that he himself had made it his duty to take, to go over this very fine house and see the great delicacy and beauty of the decorations executed by his client—an artist in his most honourable profession—he felt convinced that not for one moment would his Lordship tolerate this, he would use no stronger word than, daring attempt to evade legitimate responsibility.

Taking the text of Soames's letters, he lightly touched on 'Boileau v. The Blasted Cement Company, Limited.' "It is doubtful," he said, "what that authority has decided; in any case I would submit it is just as much in my favour as in my friend's." He then argued the 'nice point' closely. With all due deference he submitted that Mr. Forsyte's expression nullified itself. His client not being a rich man, the matter was a serious one for him; he was a very talented architect, whose professional reputation was undoubtedly somewhat at stake. He concluded with a perhaps too personal appeal to the Judge, as a lover of the arts, to show himself the protector of artists, from what was occasionally—he said occasionally—the too iron hand of capital. "What," he said, "will be the position of the artistic professions, if men of property like this Mr. Forsyte refuse, and are allowed to refuse, to carry out the obligations of the commissions which they have given." . . . He would now call his client, in case he should at the last moment have found himself able to be present.

The name Philip Baynes Bosinney was called three times by the Ushers, and the sound of the calling echoed with strange melancholy through the Court and Galleries.

The crying of this name, to which no answer was returned, had upon James a curious effect: it was like calling for your lost dog about the streets. And the creepy feeling that it gave him, of a man missing, grated on his sense of comfort and security—on his cosiness. Though he could not have said why, it made him feel uneasy.

He looked now at the clock—a quarter to three! It would be all over in a quarter of an hour. Where could the young fellow be?

It was only when Mr. Justice Bentham delivered judgment that he got over the turn he had received.

Behind the wooden erection, by which he was fenced from more or-dinary mortals, the learned Judge leaned forward. The electric light, just turned on above his head, fell on his face, and mellowed it to an orange hue beneath the snowy crown of his wig; the amplitude of his robes grew before the eye; his whole figure, facing the comparative dusk of the court, radiated like some majestic and sacred body. He cleared his throat, took a sip of water, broke the nib of a quill against the desk, and, folding his bony hands before him, began.

To James he suddenly loomed much larger than he had ever thought Bentham would loom. It was the majesty of the law; and a person en-dowed with a nature far less matter-of-fact than that of James might have been excused for failing to pierce this halo, and disinter therefrom the somewhat ordinary Forsyte, who walked and talked in every-day life under the name of Sir Walter Bentham.

He delivered judgment in the following words:

"The facts in this case are not in dispute. On May 15 last the de-fendent wrote to the plaintiff, requesting to be allowed to withdraw from his professional position in regard to the decoration of the plain-tiff's house, unless he were given 'a free hand.' The plaintiff, on May 17, wrote back as follows: 'In giving you, in accordance with your request, this free hand, I wish you to clearly understand that the total cost of the house as handed over to me completely decorated, inclusive of your fee (as arranged between us) must not exceed twelve thousand pounds.' To this letter the defendant replied on May 18: 'If you think that in such a delicate matter as decoration I can bind myself to the exact pound, I am afraid you are mistaken.' On May 19 the plaintiff wrote as follows: 'I did not mean to say that if you should exceed the sum named in my letter to you by ten or twenty or even fifty pounds there would be any difficulty between us. You have a free hand in the terms of this correspondence, and I hope you will see your way to completing the decorations.' On May 20 the defendant replied thus shortly: 'Very well.'

"In completing these decorations, the defendant incurred liabilities and expenses which brought the total cost of this house up to the sum of twelve thousand four hundred pounds, all of which expenditure has been defrayed by the plaintiff. This action has been brought by the plaintiff to recover from the defendant the sum of three hundred and fifty pounds expended by him in excess of a sum of twelve thousand and fifty pounds, alleged by the plaintiff to have been fixed by this correspondence as the maximum sum that the defendant had authority to expend.

"The question for me to decide is whether or no the defendant is liable to refund to the plaintiff this sum. In my judgment he is so liable.

"What in effect the plaintiff has said is this: 'I give you a free hand to complete these decorations, provided that you keep within a total cost to me of twelve thousand pounds. If you exceed that sum by as much as fifty pounds, I will not hold you responsible; beyond that point you are no agent of mine, and I shall repudiate liability.' It is not quite clear to me whether, had the plaintiff in fact repudiated liability under his agent's contracts, he would, under all the circumstances, have been successful in so doing; but he has not adopted this course. He has accepted liability, and fallen back upon his rights against the defendant under the terms of the latter's engagement.

"In my judgment the plaintiff is entitled to recover this sum from the defendant.

"It has been sought, on behalf of the defendant, to show that no limit of expenditure was fixed or intended to be fixed by this correspondence. If this were so, I can find no reason for the plaintiff's importation into the correspondence of the figures of twelve thousand pounds and subsequently of fifty pounds. The defendant's contention would render these figures meaningless. It is manifest to me that by his letter of May 20 he assented to a very clear proposition, by the terms of which he must be held to be bound.

"For these reasons there will be judgment for the plaintiff for the amount claimed with costs."

James sighed, and stooping, picked up his umbrella which had fallen with a rattle at the words 'importation into this correspondence.'

Untangling his legs, he rapidly left the Court; without waiting for his son, he snapped up a hansom cab (it was a clear, grey afternoon) and drove straight to Timothy's where he found Swithin; and to him, Mrs. Septimus Small, and Aunt Hester, he recounted the whole proceedings, eating two muffins not altogether in the intervals of speech.

"Soames did very well," he ended; "he's got his head screwed on the right way. This won't please Jolyon. It's a bad business for that young Bosinney; he'll go bankrupt, I shouldn't wonder," and then after a long pause, during which he had stared disquietly into the fire, he added:

"He wasn't there—now why?"

There was a sound of footsteps. The figure of a thick-set man, with the ruddy brown face of robust health, was seen in the back drawing-room. The forefinger of his upraised hand was outlined against the black of his frock coat. He spoke in a grudging voice.

"Well, James," he said, "I can't—I can't stop," and turning round, he walked out.

It was Timothy.

James rose from his chair. "There!" he said, "there! I knew there was something wro——" He checked himself, and was silent, staring before him, as though he had seen a portent.

Chapter VI

SOAMES BREAKS THE NEWS

ON leaving the Court Soames did not go straight home. He felt disinclined for the City, and drawn by need for sympathy in his triumph, he, too, made his way, but slowly and on foot, to Timothy's in the Bayswater Road.

His father had just left; Mrs. Small and Aunt Hester, in possession of the whole story, greeted him warmly. They were sure he was hungry after all that evidence. Smither should toast him some more muffins, his dear father had eaten them all. He must put his legs up on the sofa; and he must have a glass of prune brandy, too. It was so strengthening.

Swithin was still present, having lingered later than his wont, for he felt in want of exercise. On hearing this suggestion, he 'pished.' A pretty pass young men were coming to! His own liver was out of order, and he could not bear the thought of anyone else drinking prune brandy.

He went away almost immediately, saying to Soames: "And how's your wife? You tell her from me that if she's dull, and likes to come and dine with me quietly, I'll give her such a bottle of champagne as she doesn't get every day." Staring down from his height on Soames he contracted his thick, puffy, yellow hand as though squeezing within it all this small fry, and throwing out his chest he waddled slowly away.

Mrs. Small and Aunt Hester were left horrified. Swithin was so droll!

They themselves were longing to ask Soames how Irene would take the result, yet knew that they must not; he would perhaps say something of his own accord, to throw some light on this, the present burning question in their lives, the question that from necessity of silence tortured them almost beyond bearing; for even Timothy had now been told, and the effect on his health was little short of alarming. And what, too, would June do? This, also, was a most exciting, if dangerous speculation!

They had never forgotten old Jolyon's visit, since when he had not once been to see them; they had never forgotten the feeling it gave all

264

who were present, that the family was no longer what it had been—that the family was breaking up.

But Soames gave them no help, sitting with his knees crossed, talking of the Barbizon school of painters, whom he had just discovered. These were the coming men, he said; he should not wonder if a lot of money were made over them; he had his eye on two pictures by a man called Corot, charming things; if he could get them at a reasonable price he was going to buy them—they would, he thought, fetch a big price some day.

Interested as they could not but be, neither Mrs. Septimus Small nor Aunt Hester could entirely acquiesce in being thus put off.

It was interesting—most interesting—and then Soames was so clever that they were sure he would do something with those pictures if anybody could; but what was his plan now that he had won his case; was he going to leave London at once, and live in the country, or what was he going to do?

Soames answered that he did not know, he thought they should be moving soon. He rose and kissed his aunts.

No sooner had Aunt Juley received this emblem of departure than a change came over her, as though she were being visited by dreadful courage; every little roll of flesh on her face seemed trying to escape from an invisible, confirming mask.

She rose to the full extent of her more than medium height, and said: "It has been on my mind a long time, dear, and if nobody else will tell you, I have made up my mind that——"

Aunt Hester interrupted her: "Mind, Julia, you do it—" she gasped—"on your own responsibility!"

Mrs. Small went on as though she had not heard: "I think you *ought* to know, dear, that Mrs. MacAnder saw Irene walking in Richmond Park with Mr. Bosinney."

Aunt Hester, who had also risen, sank back in her chair, and turned her face away. Really Juley was too—she should not do such things when she—Aunt Hester, was in the room; and, breathless with anticipation, she waited for what Soames would answer.

He had flushed the peculiar flush which always centred between his eyes; lifting his hand, and, as it were, selecting a finger, he bit a nail delicately; then, drawing it out between set lips, he said: "Mrs. Mac-Ander is a cat!"

Without waiting for any reply, he left the room.

When he went into Timothy's he had made up his mind what course to pursue on getting home. He would go up to Irene and say:

"Well, I've won my case, and there's an end of it! I don't want to be hard on Bosinney; I'll see if we can't come to some arrangement; he shan't be pressed. And now let's turn over a new leaf! We'll let the house, and get out of these fogs. We'll go down to Robin Hill at once. I—I never meant to be rough with you! Let's shake hands—and——" Perhaps she would let him kiss her, and forget!

When he came out of Timothy's his intentions were no longer so simple. The smouldering jealousy and suspicion of months blazed up within him. He would put an end to that sort of thing once and for all; he would not have her drag his name in the dirt! If she could not or would not love him, as was her duty and his right—she should not play him tricks with anyone else! He would tax her with it; threaten to divorce her! That would make her behave; she would never face that. But—but —what if she did? He was staggered; this had not occurred to him.

What if she did? What if she made him a confession? How would he stand then? He would have to bring a divorce!

A divorce! Thus close, the word was paralyzing, so utterly at variance with all the principles that had hitherto guided his life. Its lack of compromise appalled him; he felt like the captain of a ship, going to the side of his vessel, and, with his own hands throwing over the most precious of his bales. This jettisoning of his property with his own hand seemed uncanny to Soames. It would injure him in his profession. He would have to get rid of the house at Robin Hill, on which he had spent so much money, so much anticipation—and at a sacrifice. And she! She would no longer belong to him, not even in name! She would pass out of his life, and he—he should never see her again!

He traversed in the cab the length of a street without getting beyond the thought that he should never see her again!

But perhaps there was nothing to confess, even now very likely there was nothing to confess. Was it wise to push things so far? Was it wise to put himself into a position where he might have to eat his words? The result of this case would ruin Bosinney; a ruined man was desperate, but—what could he do? He might go abroad, ruined men always went abroad. What could *they* do—if indeed it *was* 'they'—without money? It would be better to wait and see how things turned out. If necessary, he could have her watched. The agony of his jealousy (for all the world like the crisis of an aching tooth) came on again; and he almost cried out. But he must decide, fix on some course of action before he got home. When the cab drew up at the door, he had decided nothing.

He entered, pale, his hands moist with perspiration, dreading to meet her, burning to meet her, ignorant of what he was to say or do.

The maid Bilson was in the hall, and in answer to his question: "Where is your mistress?" told him that Mrs. Forsyte had left the house about noon, taking with her a trunk and a bag.

Snatching the sleeve of his fur coat away from her grasp, he confronted her:

"What?" he exclaimed; "what's that you said?" Suddenly recollecting that he must not betray emotion, he added: "What message did she leave?" and noticed with secret terror the startled look of the maid's eyes.

"Mrs. Forsyte left no message, sir."

"No message; very well, thank you, that will do. I shall be dining out."

The maid went downstairs, leaving him still in his fur coat, idly turning over the visiting cards in the porcelain bowl that stood on the carved oak rug chest in the hall.

Mr. and Mrs. Bareham Culcher.	Lady Bellis.
Mrs. Septimus Small.	Miss Hermione Bellis.
Mrs. Baynes.	Miss Winifred Bellis.
Mr. Solomon Thornworthy.	Miss Ella Bellis.

Who the devil were all these people? He seemed to have forgotten all familiar things. The words 'no message—a trunk, and a bag,' played a hide-and-seek in his brain. It was incredible that she hed left no message, and, still in his fur coat, ran upstairs two steps at a time, as a young married man when he comes home will run up to his wife's room.

Everything was dainty, fresh, sweet-smelling; everything in perfect order. On the great bed with its lilac silk quilt, was the bag she had made and embroidered with her own hands to hold her sleeping things;

her slippers ready at the foot; the sheets even turned over at the head as though expecting her.

On the table stood the silver-mounted brushes and bottles from her dressing-bag, his own present. There must, then, be some mistake. What bag had she taken? He went to the bell to summon Bilson, but remembered in time that he must assume knowledge of where Irene had gone, take it all as a matter of course, and grope out the meaning for himself.

He locked the doors, and tried to think, but felt his brain going round; and suddenly tears forced themselves into his eyes.

Hurriedly pulling off his coat, he looked at himself in the mirror.

He was too pale, a greyish tinge all over his face; he poured out water, and began feverishly washing.

Her silver-mounted brushes smelt faintly of the perfumed lotion she used for her hair; and at this scent the burning sickness of his jealousy seized him again.

Struggling into his fur, he ran downstairs and out into the street.

He had not lost all command of himself, however, and as he went down Sloane Street he framed a story for use, in case he should not find her at Bosinney's. But if he should? His power of decision again failed; he reached the house without knowing what he should do if he did find her there.

It was after office hours, and the street door was closed; the woman who opened it could not say whether Mr. Bosinney were in or no; she had not seen him that day, not for two or three days; she did not attend to him now, nobody attended to him, he——

Soames interrupted her, he would go up and see for himself. He went up with a dogged, white face.

The top floor was unlighted, the door closed, no one answered his ringing, he could hear no sound. He was obliged to descend, shivering under his fur, a chill at his heart. Hailing a cab, he told the man to drive to Park Lane.

On the way he tried to recollect when he had last given her a cheque; she could not have more than three or four pounds, but there were her jewels; and with exquisite torture he remembered how much money she could raise on these; enough to take them abroad; enough for them to live on for months! He tried to calculate; the cab stopped, and he got out with the calculation unmade.

The butler asked whether Mrs. Soames was in the cab, the master had told him they were both expected to dinner.

Soames answered: "No, Mrs. Forsyte has a cold."

The butler was sorry.

Soames thought he was looking at him inquisitively, and remembering that he was not in dress clothes, asked: "Anybody here to dinner, Warmson?"

"Nobody but Mr. and Mrs. Dartie, sir."

Again it seemed to Soames that the butler was looking curiously at him. His composure gave way.

"What are you looking at?" he said. "What's the matter with me, eh?"

The butler blushed, hung up the fur coat, murmured something that sounded like: "Nothing, sir, I'm sure, sir," and stealthily withdrew.

Soames walked upstairs. Passing the drawing-room without a look, he went straight up to his mother's and father's bedroom.

James, standing sideways, the concave lines of his tall, lean figure displayed to advantage in shirt-sleeves and evening waistcoat, his head bent, the end of his white tie peeping askew from underneath one white Dundreary whisker, his eyes peering with intense concentration, his lips pouting, was hooking the top hooks of his wife's bodice. Soames stopped; he felt half-choked, whether because he had come upstairs too fast, or for some other reason. He—he himself had never—never been asked to——

He heard his father's voice, as though there were a pin in his mouth, saying: "Who's that? Who's there? What d'you want?" His mother's: "Here, Félice, come and hook this; your master'll never get done."

He put his hand up to his throat, and said hoarsely:

"It's I—Soames!"

He noticed gratefully the affectionate surprise in Emily's: "Well, my dear boy?" and James's, as he dropped the hook: "What, Soames! What's brought you up? Aren't you well?"

He answered mechanically: "I'm all right," and looked at them, and it seemed impossible to bring out his news.

James, quick to take alarm, began: "You don't look well. I expect you've taken a chill—it's liver, I shouldn't wonder. Your mother'll give you——"

But Emily broke in quietly: "Have you brought Irene?"

269

Soames shook his head.

"No," he stammered, "she—she's left me!"

Emily deserted the mirror before which she was standing. Her tall, full figure lost its majesty and became very human as she came running over to Soames.

"My dear boy! My *dear* boy!"

She put her lips to his forehead, and stroked his hand.

James, too, had turned full towards his son; his face looked older.

"Left you?" he said. "What d'you mean—left you? You never told me she was going to leave you."

Soames answered surlily: "How could I tell? What's to be done?"

James began walking up and down; he looked strange and stork-like without a coat. "What's to be done!" he muttered. "How should I know what's to be done? What's the good of asking me? Nobody tells me anything, and then they come and ask me what's to be done; and I should like to know how I'm to tell them! Here's your mother, there she stands; *she* doesn't say anything. What *I* should say you've got to do is to follow her."

Soames smiled; his peculiar, supercilious smile had never before looked pitiable.

"I don't know where she's gone," he said.

"Don't know where she's gone!" said James. "How d'you mean, don't know where she's gone? Where d'you suppose she's gone? She's gone after that young Bosinney, that's where she's gone. I knew how it would be."

Soames, in the long silence that followed, felt his mother pressing his hand. And all that passed seemed to pass as though his own power of thinking or doing had gone to sleep.

His father's face, dusky red, twitching as if he were going to cry, and words breaking out that seemed rent from him by some spasm in his soul.

"There'll be a scandal; I always said so." Then, no one saying anything: "And there you stand, you and your mother!"

And Emily's voice, calm, rather contemptuous: "Come, now, James! Soames will do all that he can."

And James, staring at the floor, a little brokenly: "Well, I can't help you; I'm getting old. Don't you be in too great a hurry, my boy."

And his mother's voice again: "Soames will do all he can to get her back. We won't talk of it. It'll all come right, I dare say."

And James: "Well, I can't see how it can come right. And if she hasn't gone off with that young Bosinney, my advice to you is not to listen to her, but to follow her and get her back."

Once more Soames felt his mother stroking his hand, in token of her approval, and as though repeating some form of sacred oath, he muttered between his teeth: "I will!"

All three went down to the drawing-room together. There, were gathered three girls and Dartie; had Irene been present, the family circle would have been complete.

James sank into his armchair, and except for a word of cold greeting to Dartie, whom he both despised and dreaded, as a man likely to be always in want of money, he said nothing till dinner was announced. Soames, too, was silent; Emily alone, a woman of cool courage, maintained a conversation with Winifred on trivial subjects. She was never more composed in her manner and conversation than that evening.

A decision having been come to not to speak of Irene's flight, no view was expressed by any other member of the family as to the right course to be pursued; there can be little doubt, from the general tone adopted in relation to the events as they afterwards turned out, that James's advice: "Don't you listen to her, follow her and get her back!" would, with here and there an exception, have been regarded as sound, not only in Park Lane, but amongst the Nicholases, the Rogers, and at Timothy's. Just as it would surely have been endorsed by that wider body of Forsytes all over London, who were merely excluded from judgment by ignorance of the story.

In spite then of Emily's efforts, the dinner was served by Warmson and the footman almost in silence. Dartie was sulky, and drank all he could get; the girls seldom talked to each other at any time. James asked once where June was, and what she was doing with herself in these days. No one could tell him. He sank back into gloom. Only when Winifred recounted how little Publius had given his bad penny to a beggar, did he brighten up.

"Ah!" he said, "that's a clever little chap. I don't know what'll become of him, if he goes on like this. An intelligent little chap, I call him!" But it was only a flash.

271

The courses succeeded one another solemnly, under the electric light, which glared down onto the table, but barely reached the principal ornament of the walls, a so-called 'Sea Piece by Turner,' almost entirely composed of cordage and drowning men. Champagne was handed, and then a bottle of James's prehistoric port, but as by the chill hand of some skeleton.

At ten o'clock Soames left; twice in reply to questions, he had said that Irene was not well; he felt he could no longer trust himself. His mother kissed him with her large soft kiss, and he pressed her hand, a flush of warmth in his cheeks. He walked away in the cold wind, which whistled desolately round the corners of the streets, under a sky of clear steel-blue, alive with stars; he noticed neither their frosty greeting, nor the crackle of the curled-up plane-leaves, nor the night-women hurrying in their shabby furs, nor the pinched faces of vagabonds at street corners. Winter was come! But Soames hastened home, oblivious; his hands trembled as he took the late letters from the gilt wire cage into which they had been thrust through the slit in the door.

None from Irene!

He went into the dining-room; the fire was bright there, his chair drawn up to it, slippers ready, spirit case, and carven cigarette box on the table; but after staring at it all for a minute or two, he turned out the light and went upstairs. There was a fire, too, in his dressing-room, but her room was dark and cold. It was into this room that Soames went.

He made a great illumination with candles, and for a long time continued pacing up and down between the bed and the door. He could not get used to the thought that she had really left him, and as though still searching for some message, some reason, some reading of all the mystery of his married life, he began opening every recess and drawer.

There were her dresses; he had always liked, indeed insisted, that she should be well-dressed—she had taken very few; two or three at most, and drawer after drawer, full of linen and silk things, was untouched.

Perhaps after all it was only a freak, and she had gone to the seaside for a few days' change. If only that were so, and she were really coming back, he would never again do as he had done that fatal night before last, never again run that risk—though it was her duty, her duty as a wife; though she did belong to him—he would never again run that risk; she was evidently not quite right in her head!

He stooped over the drawer where she kept her jewels; it was not locked, and came open as he pulled; the jewel box had the key in it. This surprised him until he remembered that it was sure to be empty. He opened it.

It was far from empty. Divided, in little green velvet compartments, were all the things he had given her, even her watch, and stuck into the recess that contained the watch was a three-cornered note addressed 'Soames Forsyte,' in Irene's handwriting.

'I think I have taken nothing that you or your people have given me.' And that was all.

He looked at the clasps and bracelets of diamonds and pearls, at the little flat gold watch with a great diamond set in sapphires, at the chains and rings, each in its nest, and the tears rushed up in his eyes and dropped upon them.

Nothing that she could have done, nothing that she *had* done, brought home to him like this the inner significance of her act. For the moment, perhaps, he understood nearly all there was to understand—understood that she loathed him, that she loathed him for years, that for all intents and purposes they were like people living in different worlds, that there was no hope for him, never had been; even, that she had suffered—that she was to be pitied.

In that moment of emotion he betrayed the Forsyte in him—forgot himself, his interests, his property—was capable of almost anything; was lifted into the pure ether of the selfless and unpractical.

Such moments pass quickly.

And as though with the tears he had purged himself of weakness, he got up, locked the box, and slowly, almost trembling, carried it with him into the other room.

Chapter VII

JUNE'S VICTORY

JUNE had waited for her chance, scanning the duller columns of the journals, morning and evening with an assiduity which at first puzzled old Jolyon; and when her chance came, she took it with all the promptitude and resolute tenacity of her character.

She will always remember best in her life that morning when at last she saw amongst the reliable Cause List of the *Times* newspaper, under the heading of Court XIII., Mr. Justice Bentham, the case of Forsyte *v.* Bosinney.

Like a gambler who stakes his last piece of money, she had prepared to hazard her all upon this throw; it was not her nature to contemplate defeat. How, unless with the instinct of a woman in love, she knew that Bosinney's discomfiture in this action was assured, cannot be told—on this assumption, however, she laid her plans, as upon a certainty.

Half-past eleven found her at watch in the gallery of Court XIII., and there she remained till the case of Forsyte *v.* Bosinney was over. Bosinney's absence did not disquiet her; she had felt instinctively that he would not defend himself. At the end of the judgment she hastened down, and took a cab to his rooms.

She passed the open street-door and the offices on the three lower floors without attracting notice; not till she reached the top did her difficulties begin.

Her ring was not answered; she had now to make up her mind whether she would go down and ask the caretaker in the basement to let her in to await Mr. Bosinney's return, or remain patiently outside the door, trusting that no one would come up. She decided on the latter course.

A quarter of an hour had passed in freezing vigil on the landing, before it occurred to her that Bosinney had been used to leave the key of his rooms under the door-mat. She looked and found it there. For some minutes she could not decide to make use of it; at last she let herself in and left the door open that anyone who came might see she was there on business.

This was not the same June who had paid the trembling visit five months ago; those months of suffering and restraint had made her less sensitive; she had dwelt on this visit so long, with such minuteness, that its terrors were discontinued beforehand. She was not there to fail this time, for if she failed no one could help her.

Like some mother beast on the watch over her young, her little quick figure never stood still in that room, but wandered from wall to wall, from window to door, fingering now one thing, now another. There was dust everywhere, the room could not have been cleaned for weeks, and June, quick to catch at anything that should buoy up her hope, saw in it a sign that he had been obliged, for economy's sake, to give up his servant.

She looked into the bedroom; the bed was roughly made, as though by the hand of man. Listening intently, she darted in, and peered into his cupboards. A few shirts and collars, a pair of muddy boots—the room was bare even of garments.

She stole back to the sitting-room, and now she noticed the absence of all the little things he had set store by. The clock that had been his mother's, the field-glasses that had hung over the sofa; two really valuable old prints of Harrow, where his father had been at school, and last, not least, the piece of Japanese pottery she herself had given him. All were gone; and in spite of the rage roused within her championing soul at the thought that the world should treat him thus, their disappearance augured happily for the success of her plan.

It was while looking at the spot where the piece of Japanese pottery had stood that she felt a strange certainty of being watched, and, turning, saw Irene in the open doorway.

The two stood gazing at each other for a minute in silence; then June walked forward and held out her hand. Irene did not take it.

When her hand was refused, June put it behind her. Her eyes grew steady with anger; she waited for Irene to speak; and thus waiting, took in, with who-knows-what rage of jealousy, suspicion, and curiosity, every detail of her friend's face and dress and figure.

Irene was clothed in her long grey fur; the travelling cap on her head left a wave of gold hair visible above her forehead. The soft fullness of the coat made her face as small as a child's.

Unlike June's cheeks, her cheeks had no colour in them, but were ivory white and pinched as if with cold. Dark circles lay round her eyes. In one hand she held a bunch of violets.

She looked back at June, no smile on her lips; and with those great dark eyes fastened on her, the girl, for all her startled anger, felt something of the old spell.

She spoke first, after all.

"What have you come for?" But the feeling that she herself was being asked the same question, made her add: "This horrible case. I came to tell him—he has lost it."

Irene did not speak, her eyes never moved from June's face, and the girl cried:

"Don't stand there as if you were made of stone!"

Irene laughed: "I wish to God I were!"

But June turned away: "Stop!" she cried, "don't tell me! I don't want to hear! I don't want to hear what you've come for. I don't want to hear!" And like some uneasy spirit, she began swiftly walking to and fro. Suddenly she broke out:

"I was here first. We can't both stay here together!"

On Irene's face a smile wandered up, and died out like a flicker of firelight. She did not move. And then it was that June perceived under the softness and immobility of this figure something desperate and resolved; something not to be turned away, something dangerous. She tore off her hat, and, putting both hands to her brow, pressed back the bronze mass of her hair.

"You have no right here!" she cried defiantly.

Irene answered: "I have no right anywhere——"

"What do you mean?"

"I have left Soames. You always wanted me to!"

June put her hands over her ears.

"Don't! I don't want to hear anything—I don't want to know anything. It's impossible to fight with you! What makes you stand like that? Why don't you go?"

Irene's lips moved; she seemed to be saying: "Where should I go?"

June turned to the window. She could see the face of a clock down in the street. It was nearly four. At any moment he might come! She looked back across her shoulder, and her face was distorted with anger.

But Irene had not moved; in her gloved hands she ceaselessly turned and twisted the little bunch of violets.

The tears of rage and disappointment rolled down June's cheeks.

"How *could* you come?" she said. "You have been a false friend to me!"

Again Irene laughed. June saw that she had played a wrong card, and broke down.

"Why have you come?" she sobbed. "You've ruined my life, and now you want to ruin his!"

Irene's mouth quivered; her eyes met June's with a look so mournful that the girl cried out in the midst of her sobbing, "No, no!"

But Irene's head bent till it touched her breast. She turned, and went quickly out, hiding her lips with the little bunch of violets.

June ran to the door. She heard the footsteps going down and down. She called out: "Come back, Irene! Come back!"

The footsteps died away. . . .

Bewildered and torn, the girl stood at the top of the stairs. Why had Irene gone, leaving her mistress of the field? What did it mean? Had she really given him up to her? Or had she———? And she was the prey of a gnawing uncertainty. . . . Bosinney did not come. . . .

About six o'clock that afternoon old Jolyon returned from Wistaria Avenue, where now almost every day he spent some hours, and asked if his grand-daughter were upstairs. On being told that she had just come in, he sent up to her room to request her to come down and speak to him.

He had made up his mind to tell her that he was reconciled with her father. In future bygones must be bygones. He would no longer live alone, or practically alone, in this great house; he was going to give it up, and take one in the country for his son, where they could all go and live together. If June did not like this, she could have an allowance and live by herself. It wouldn't make much difference to her, for it was a long time since she had shown him any affection.

But when June came down, her face was pinched and piteous; there was a strained, pathetic look in her eyes. She snuggled up in her old attitude on the arm of his chair, and what he said compared but poorly with the clear, authoritative, injured statement he had thought out with much care. His heart felt sore, as the great heart of a mother-bird feels sore when its youngling flies and bruises its wing. His words halted, as though he were apologizing for having at last deviated from the path of virtue, and succumbed, in defiance of sounder principles, to his more natural instincts.

He seemed nervous lest, in thus announcing his intentions, he should be setting his grand-daughter a bad example; and now that he came to the point, his way of putting the suggestion that, if she didn't like it, she could live by herself and lump it, was delicate in the extreme.

"And if, by any chance, my darling," he said, "you found you didn't get on with them, why, I could make that all right. You could have what you liked. We could find a little flat in London where you could set up, and I could be running to continually. But the children," he added, "are dear little things!"

Then, in the midst of this grave, rather transparent, explanation of changed policy, his eyes twinkled. "This'll astonish Timothy's weak nerves. That precious young thing will have something to say about this, or I'm a Dutchman!"

June had not yet spoken. Perched thus on the arm of his chair, with her head above him, her face was invisible. But presently he felt her warm cheek against his own, and knew that, at all events, there was nothing very alarming in her attitude towards his news. He began to take courage.

"You'll like your father," he said—"an amiable chap .Never was much push about him, but easy to get on with. You'll find him artistic and all that."

And old Jolyon bethought him of the dozen or so water-colour drawings all carefully locked up his bedroom; for now that this son was going to become a man of property he did not think them quite such poor things as heretofore.

"As to your—your stepmother," he said, using the word with some little difficulty, "I call her a refined woman—a bit of a Mrs. Gummidge, I shouldn't wonder—but very fond of Jo. And the children," he repeated —indeed, this sentence ran like music through all his solemn self-justification—"are sweet little things!"

If June had known, those words but reincarnated that tender love for little children, for the young and weak, which in the past had made him desert his son for her tiny self, and now, as the cycle rolled, was taking him for her.

But he began to get alarmed at her silence, and asked impatiently: "Well, what do you say?"

June slid down to his knee, and she in her turn began her tale. She thought it would all go splendidly; she did not see any difficulty, and she did not care a bit what people thought.

Old Jolyon wriggled. H'm! then people *would* think! He had thought that after all these years perhaps they wouldn't! Well, he couldn't help it! Nevertheless, he could not approve of his grand-daughter's way of putting it—she ought to mind what people thought!

Yet he said nothing. His feelings were too mixed, too inconsistent for expression.

No—went on June—she did not care; what business was it of theirs? There was only one thing—and with her cheek pressing against his knee, old Jolyon knew at once that this something was no trifle: As he was going to buy a house in the country, would he not—to please her— buy that splendid house of Soames' at Robin Hill? It was finished, it was perfectly beautiful, and no one would live in it now. They would all be so happy there.

Old Jolyon was on the alert at once. Wasn't the 'man of property' going to live in his new house, then? He never alluded to Soames now but under this title.

"No"—June said—"he was not; she knew that he was not!"

How did she know?

She could not tell him, but she knew. She knew nearly for certain! It was most unlikely; circumstances had changed! Irene's words still rang in her head: "I have left Soames. Where should I go?"

But she kept silence about that.

If her grandfather would only buy it and settle that wretched claim that ought never to have been made on Phil! It would be the very best thing for everybody, and everything—everything might come straight!

And June put her lips to his forehead, and pressed them close.

But old Jolyon freed himself from her caress, his face wore the judicial look which came upon it when he dealt with affairs. He asked: What did she mean? There was something behind all this—had she been seeing Bosinney?

June answered: "No; but I have been to his rooms."

"Been to his rooms? Who took you there?"

June faced him steadily. "I went alone. He has lost that case. I don't care whether it was right or wrong. I want to help him; and *I will!*"

Old Jolyon asked again: "Have you seen him?" His glance seemed to pierce right through the girl's eyes into her soul.

Again June answered: "No; he was not there. I waited, but he did not come."

Old Jolyon made a movement of relief. She had risen and looked down at him; so slight, and light, and young, but so fixed, and so determined; and disturbed, vexed, as he was, he could not frown away that fixed look. The feeling of being beaten, of the reins having slipped, of being old and tired, mastered him.

"Ah!" he said at last, "you'll get yourself into a mess one of these days, I can see. You want your own way in everything."

Visited by one of his strange bursts of philosophy, he added: "Like that you were born; and like that you'll stay until you die!"

And he, who in his dealings with men of business, with Boards, with Forsytes of all descriptions, with such as were not Forsytes, had always had his own way, looked at his indomitable grandchild sadly—for he felt in her that quality which above all others he unconsciously admired.

"Do you know what they say is going on?" he said slowly.

June crimsoned.

"Yes—no! I know—and I don't know—I don't care!" and she stamped her foot.

"I believe," said old Jolyon, dropping his eyes, "that you'd have him if he were dead!"

There was a long silence before he spoke again.

"But as to buying this house—you don't know what you're talking about!"

June said that she did. She knew that he could get it if he wanted. He would only have to give what it cost.

"What it cost! You know nothing about it. I won't go to Soames—I'll have nothing more to do with that young man."

"But you needn't; you can go to Uncle James. If you can't buy the house, will you pay his lawsuit claim? I know he is terribly hard up—I've seen it. You can stop it out of my money!"

A twinkle came into old Jolyon's eyes.

"Stop it out of your money! A pretty way! And what will you do, pray, without your money?"

But secretly, the idea of wrestling the house from James and his son had begun to take hold of him. He had heard on Forsyte 'Change much comment, much rather doubtful praise of this house. It was 'too artistic,' but a fine place. To take from the 'man of property' that on which he had set his heart, would be a crowning triumph over James, practical proof that he was going to make a man of property of Jo, to put him back in his proper position, and there to keep him secure. Justice once for all on those who had chosen to regard his son as a poor, penniless outcast!

He would see, he would see! It might be out of the question; he was not going to pay a fancy price, but if it could be done, why, perhaps he would do it!

And still more secretly he knew that he could not refuse her.

But he did not commit himself. He would think it over—he said to June.

Chapter VIII

BOSINNEY'S DEPARTURE

OLD JOLYON was not given to hasty decisions; it is probable that he would have continued to think over the purchase of the house at Robin Hill, had not June's face told him that he would have no peace until he acted.

At breakfast next morning she asked him what time she should order the carriage.

"Carriage!" he said, with some appearance of innocence; "what for? *I'm* not going out!"

She answered: "If you don't go early, you won't catch Uncle James before he goes into the City."

"James! what about your Uncle James?"

"The house," she replied, in such a voice that he no longer pretended ignorance.

"I've not made up my mind," he said.

"You must! You must! Oh! Gran—think of me!"

Old Jolyon grumbled out: "Think of you—I'm always thinking of you, but you don't think of yourself; you don't think what you're letting yourself in for. Well, order the carriage at ten"

At a quarter past he was placing his umbrella in the stand at Park Lane—he did not choose to relinquish his hat and coat; telling Warmson that he wanted to see his master, he went, without being announced, into the study, and sat down.

James was still in the dining-room talking to Soames, who had come round again before breakfast. On hearing who his visitor was, he muttered nervously: "Now, what's *he* want, I wonder?"

He then got up.

"Well," he said to Soames, "don't you go doing anything in a hurry. The first thing is to find out where she is—I should go to Stainer's about it; they're the best men, if they can't find her, nobody can." And suddenly moved to strange softness, he muttered to himself: "Poor little thing, *I* can't tell what she was thinking about!" and went out blowing his nose.

Old Jolyon did not rise on seeing his brother, but held out his hand, and exchanged with him the clasp of a Forsyte.

James took another chair by the table, and leaned his head on his hand.

"Well," he said, "how are you? We don't see much of *you* nowadays!"

Old Jolyon paid no attention to the remark.

"How's Emily?" he asked; and waiting for no reply, went on:

"I've come to see you about this affair of young Bosinney's. I'm told that new house of his is a white elephant."

"I don't know anything about a white elephant," said James, "I know he's lost his case, and I should say he'll go bankrupt."

Old Jolyon was not slow to seize the opportunity this gave him.

"I shouldn't wonder a bit!" he agreed; "and if he goes bankrupt, the 'man of property'—that is, Soames'll be out of pocket. Now, what I was thinking was this: If he's not going to live there——"

Seeing both surprise and suspicion in James's eye, he quickly went on: "I don't want to know anything; I suppose Irene's put her foot down—it's not material to me. But I'm thinking of a house in the country myself, not far from London, and if it suited me I don't say that I mightn't look at it, at a price."

James listened to this statement with a strange mixture of doubt, suspicion, and relief, merging into a dread of something behind, and tinged with the remains of his old undoubted reliance upon his elder brother's good faith and judgment. There was anxiety, too, as to what old Jolyon could have heard and how he had heard it; and a sort of hopefulness arising from the thought that if June's connection with Bosinney were completely at an end, her grandfather would hardly seem anxious to help the young fellow. Altogether he was puzzled; as he did not like either to show this, or to commit himself in any way, he said:

"They tell me you're altering your Will in favour of your son."

He had not been told this; he had merely added the fact of having seen old Jolyon with his son and grandchildren to the fact that he had taken his Will away from Forsyte, Bustard and Forsyte. The shot went home.

283

"Who told you that?" asked old Jolyon.

"I'm sure I don't know," said James; "I can't remember names—I know somebody told me Soames spent a lot of money on this house; he's not likely to part with it except at a good price."

"Well," said old Jolyon, "if he thinks I'm going to pay a fancy price, he's mistaken. I've not got the money to throw away that he seems to have. Let him try and sell it at a forced sale, and see what he'll get. It's not every man's house, I hear!"

James, who was secretly also of this opinion, answered: "It's a gentleman's house. Soames is here now if you'd like to see him."

"No," said old Jolyon, "I haven't got as far as that; and I'm not likely to, I can see that very well if I'm met in this manner!"

James was a little cowed; when it came to the actual figures of a commercial transaction he was sure of himself, for then he was dealing with facts, not with men; but preliminary negotiations such as these made him nervous—he never knew quite how far he could go.

"Well," he said, "I know nothing about it. Soames, he tells me nothing; I should think he'd entertain it—it's a question of price."

"Oh!" said old Jolyon, "don't let him make a favour of it!" He placed his hat on his head in dudgeon.

The door was opened and Soames came in.

"There's a policeman out here," he said with his half-smile, "for Uncle Jolyon."

Old Jolyon looked at him angrily, and James said: "A policeman? I don't know anything about a policeman. But I suppose *you* know something about him," he added to old Jolyon with a look of suspicion: "I suppose you'd better see him!"

In the hall an Inspector of Police stood stolidly regarding with heavy lidded pale-blue eyes the fine old English furniture picked up by James at the famous Mavrojano sale in Portman Square. "You'll find my brother in there," said James.

The Inspector raised his fingers respectfully to his peaked cap, and entered the study.

James saw him go in with a strange sensation.

"Well," he said to Soames, "I suppose we must wait and see what he wants. Your uncle's been here about the house!"

He returned with Soames into the dining-room, but could not rest.

"Now what *does* he want?" he murmured again.

"Who?" replied Soames: "the Inspector? They sent him round from Stanhope Gate, that's all I know. That 'nonconformist' of Uncle Jolyon's has been pilfering, I shouldn't wonder!"

But in spite of his calmness, he too was ill at ease.

At the end of ten minutes old Jolyon came in.

He walked up to the table, and stood there perfectly silent pulling at his long white moustaches. James gazed up at him with opening mouth; he had never seen his brother look like this.

Old Jolyon raised his hand, and said slowly:

"Young Bosinney has been run over in the fog and killed."

Then standing above his brother and his nephew, and looking down at him with his deep eyes: "There's—some—talk—of—suicide," he said.

James's jaw dropped. "*Suicide!* What should he do that for?"

Old Jolyon answered sternly: "God knows, if you and your son don't!"

But James did not reply.

For all men of great age, even for all Forsytes, life has had bitter experiences. The passer-by, who sees them wrapped in cloaks of custom, wealth, and comfort, would never suspect that such black shadows had fallen on their roads. To every man of great age—to Sir Walter Bentham himself—the idea of suicide has once at least been present in the ante-room of his soul; on the threshold, waiting to enter, held out from the inmost chamber by some chance reality, some vague fear, some painful hope. To Forsytes that final renunciation of property is hard. Oh! it is hard! Seldom—perhaps never—can they achieve it; and yet, how near have they not sometimes been!

So even with James! Then in the medley of his thoughts, he broke out: "Why I saw it in the paper yesterday: 'Run over in the fog!' They didn't know his name!" He turned from one face to the other in his confusion of soul; but instinctively all the time he was rejecting that rumor of suicide. He dared not entertain this thought, so against his interest, against the interest of his son, of every Forsyte. He strove against it; and as his nature ever unconsciously rejected that which it could not with safety accept, so gradually he overcame this fear. It was an accident! It must have been!

Old Jolyon broke in on his reverie.

"Death was instantaneous. He lay all day yesterday at the hospital. There was nothing to tell them who he was. I am going there now; you and your son had better come too."

No one opposing this command he led the way from the room.

The day was still and clear and bright, and driving over to Park Lane from Stanhope Gate, old Jolyon had had the carriage open. Sitting back on the padded cushions, finishing his cigar, he had noticed with pleasure the keen crispness of the air, the bustle of the cabs and people; the strange, almost Parisian, alacrity that the first fine day will bring into London streets after a spell of fog or rain. And he had felt so happy; he had not felt like it for months. His confession to June was off his mind; he had the prospect of his son's, above all, of his grandchildren's company in the future—(he had appointed to meet young Jolyon at the Hotch Potch that very morning to discuss it again); and there was the pleasurable excitement of a coming encounter, a coming victory, over James and the 'man of property' in the matter of the house.

He had the carriage closed now; he had no heart to look on gaiety; nor was it right that Forsytes should be seen driving with an Inspector of Police.

In that carriage the Inspector spoke again of the death:

"It was not so very thick just there. The driver says the gentleman must have had time to see what he was about, he seemed to walk right into it. It appears that he was very hard up, we found several pawn tickets at his rooms, his account at the bank is overdrawn, and there's this case in to-day's papers;" his cold blue eyes travelled from one to another of the three Forsytes in the carriage.

Old Jolyon watching from his corner saw his brother's face change, and the brooding, worried look deepen on it. At the Inspector's words, indeed, all James's doubts and fears revived. Hard up—pawn-tickets— an overdrawn account! These words that had all his life been a far-off nightmare to him, seemed to make uncannily real that suspicion of suicide which must on no account be entertained. He sought his son's eye; but lynx-eyed, taciturn, immovable, Soames gave no answering look. And to old Jolyon watching, divining the league of mutual defence between them, there came an overmastering desire to have his own son at his side, as though this visit to the dead man's body was a battle in which otherwise he must single-handed meet those two. And the thought of how to keep June's name out of the business kept whirring in his brain. James had his son to support him! Why should he not send for Jo?

Taking out his card-case, he pencilled the following message:

'Come round at once. I've sent the carriage for you.'

On getting out he gave this card to his coachman, telling him to drive as fast as possible to the Hotch Potch Club, and if Mr. Jolyon Forsyte were there to give him the card and bring him at once. If not there yet, he was to wait till he came.

He followed the others slowly up the steps, leaning on his umbrella, and stood a moment to get his breath. The Inspector said: "This is the mortuary, sir. But take your time."

In the bare, white-walled room, empty of all but a streak of sunshine smeared along the dustless floor, lay a form covered by a sheet. With a huge steady hand the Inspector took the hem and turned it back. A sightless face gazed up at them, and on either side of that sightless defiant face the three Forsytes gazed down; in each one of them the secret emotions, fears, and pity of his own nature rose and fell like the rising, falling waves of life, whose wash those white walls barred out now for ever from Bosinney. And in each one of them the trend of his nature, the odd essential spring, which moved him in fashions minutely, unalterably different from those of every other human being, forced him to a different attitude of thought. Far from the others, yet inscrutably close, each stood thus, alone with death, silent, his eyes lowered.

The Inspector asked softly:

"You identify the gentleman, sir?"

Old Jolyon raised his head and nodded. He looked at his brother opposite, at that long lean figure brooding over the dead man, with face dusky red, and strained grey eyes; and at the figure of Soames white and still by his father's side. And all that he had felt against those two was gone like smoke in the long white presence of Death. Whence comes it, how comes it—Death? Sudden reverse of all that goes before; blind setting forth on a path that leads to—where? Dark quenching of the fire! The heavy, brutal crushing-out that all men

287

must go through, keeping their eyes clear and brave unto the end! Small and of no import, insects though they are! And across old Jolyon's face there flitted a gleam, for Soames, murmuring to the Inspector, crept noiselessly away.

Then suddenly James raised his eyes. There was a queer appeal in that suspicious troubled look: "I know I'm no match for you," it seemed to say. And, hunting for handkerchief, he wiped his brow; then, bending sorrowful and lank over the dead man, he too turned and hurried out.

Old Jolyon stood, still as death, his eyes fixed on the body. Who shall tell of what he was thinking? Of himself, when his hair was brown like the hair of that young fellow dead before him? Of himself, with his battle just beginning, the long, long battle he had loved; the battle that was over for this young man almost before it had begun? Of his grand-daughter, with her broken hopes? Of that other woman? Of the strangeness, and the pity of it? And the irony, inscrutable, and bitter of that end? Justice! There was no justice for men, for they were ever in the dark!

Or perhaps in his philosophy he thought: Better to be out of it all! Better to have done with it, like this poor youth. . . .

Some one touched him on the arm.

A tear started up and wetted his eyelash. "Well," he said, "I'm no good here. I'd better be going. You'll come to me as soon as you can, Jo," and with his head bowed he went away.

It was young Jolyon's turn to take his stand beside the dead man, round whose fallen body he seemed to see all the Forsytes breathless, and prostrated. The stroke had fallen too swiftly.

The forces underlying every tragedy—forces that take no denial, working through cross currents to their ironical end, had met and fused with a thunder-clap, flung out the victim, and flattened to the ground all those that stood around.

Or so at all events young Jolyon seemed to see him, lying around Bosinney's body.

He asked the Inspector to tell him what had happened, and the latter, like a man who does not every day get such a chance, again detailed such facts as were known.

"There's more here, sir, however," he said, "than meets the eye. I don't believe in suicide, nor in pure accident, myself. It's more likely I think that he was suffering under great stress of mind, and took no notice of things about him. Perhaps you can throw some light on these."

He took from his pocket a little packet and laid it on the table. Carefully undoing it, he revealed a lady's handkerchief, pinned through the folds with a pin of discoloured Venetian gold, the stone of which had fallen from the socket. A scent of dried violets rose to young Jolyon's nostrils.

"Found in his breast pocket," said the Inspector; "the name has been cut away!"

Young Jolyon with difficulty answered: "I'm afraid I cannot help you!" But vividly there rose before him the face he had seen light up, so tremulous and glad, at Bosinney's coming! Of her he thought more than of his own daughter, more than of them all—of her with the dark, soft glance, the delicate passive face, waiting for the dead man, waiting even at that moment, perhaps, still and patient in the sunlight.

He walked sorrowfully away from the hospital toward his father's house, reflecting that this death would break up the Forsyte family. The stroke had indeed slipped past their defences into the very wood of their tree. They might flourish to all appearance as before, preserving a brave show before the eyes of London, but the trunk was dead, withered by the same flash that had stricken down Bosinney. And now the saplings would take its place, each one a new custodian of the sense of property.

Good forest of Forsytes! thought young Jolyon—soundest timber of our land!

Concerning the cause of his death—his family would doubtless reject with vigour the suspicion of suicide, which was so compromising! They would take it as an accident, a stroke of fate. In their hearts they would even feel it an intervention of Providence, a retribution—had not Bosinney endangered their two most priceless possessions, the pocket and the hearth? And they would talk of 'that unfortunate accident of young Bosinney's,' but perhaps they would not talk—silence might be better!

As for himself, he regarded the bus-driver's account of the accident as of very little value. For no one so madly in love committed suicide for want of money; nor was Bosinney the sort of fellow to set much store by a financial crisis. And so he too rejected this theory of suicide, the dead man's face rose too clearly before him. Gone in the heyday of his summer—and to believe thus that an accident had cut Bosinney off in the full sweep of his passion was more than ever pitiful to young Jolyon.

Then came a vision of Soames's home as it now was, and must be hereafter. The streak of lightning had flashed its clear uncanny gleam on bare bones with grinning spaces between, the disguising flesh was gone....

In the dining-room at Stanhope Gate old Jolyon was sitting alone when his son came in. He looked very wan in his great armchair. And his eyes travelling round the walls with their pictures of still life, and the masterpiece 'Dutch Fishing-Boats at Sunset' seemed as though passing their gaze over his life with its hopes, its gains, its achievements.

"Ah! Jo!" he said, "is that you? I've told poor little June. But that's not all of it. Are you going to Soames's? *She's* brought it on herself, I suppose; but somehow I can't bear to think of her, shut up there—and all alone." And holding up his thin, veiled hand, he clenched it.

Chapter IX

IRENE'S RETURN

AFTER leaving James and old Jolyon in the mortuary of the hospital, Soames hurried aimlessly along the streets. The tragic event of Bosinney's death altered the complexion of everything. There was no longer the same feeling that to lose a minute would be fatal, nor would he now risk communicating the fact of his wife's flight to anyone till the inquest was over.

That morning he had risen early, before the postman came, had taken the first-post letters from the box himself, and, though there had been none from Irene, he had made an opportunity of telling Bilson that her mistress was at the sea; he would probably, he said, be going down himself from Saturday to Monday. This had given him time to breathe, time to leave no stone unturned to find her.

But now, cut off from taking steps by Bosinney's death—that strange death, to think of which was like putting a hot iron to his heart, like lifting a great weight from it—he did not know how to pass his day; and he wandered here and there through the streets, looking at every face he met, devoured by a hundred anxieties.

And as he wandered, he thought of him who had finished his wandering, his prowling, and would never haunt his house again.

Already in the afternoon he passed posters announcing the identity of the dead man, and bought the papers to see what they said. He would stop their mouths if he could, and he went into the City, and was closeted with Boulter for a long time.

On his way home, passing the steps of Jobson's about half-past four, he met George Forsyte, who held out an evening paper to Soames, saying:

"Here! Have you seen this about the poor Buccaneer?"

Soames answered stonily: "Yes."

George stared at him. He had never liked Soames; he now held him responsible for Bosinney's death. Soames had done for him—done

291

for him by that act of property that had sent the Buccaneer to run amok that fatal afternoon.

'The poor fellow,' he was thinking, 'was so cracked with jealousy, so cracked for his vengeance, that he heard nothing of the omnibus in that infernal fog.'

Soames had done for him! And this judgment was in George's eyes.

"They talk of suicide here," he said at last. *"That* cat won't jump."

Soames shook his head. "An accident," he muttered.

Clenching his fist on the paper, George crammed it into his pocket. He could not resist a parting shot.

"H'mm! All flourishing at home? Any little Soameses yet?"

With a face as white as the steps of Jobson's, and a lip raised as if snarling, Soames brushed past him and was gone.

On reaching home, and entering the little lighted hall with his latchkey, the first thing that caught his eye was his wife's gold-mounted umbrella lying on the rug chest. Flinging off his fur coat, he hurried to the drawing-room.

The curtains were drawn for the night, a bright fire of cedarlogs burned in the grate, and by its light he saw Irene sitting in her usual corner on the sofa. He shut the door softly, and went towards her. She did not move, and did not seem to see him.

"So you've come back?" he said. "Why are you sitting here in the dark?"

Then he caught sight of her face, so white and motionless that it seemed as though the blood must have stopped flowing in her veins; and her eyes, that looked enormous, like the great, wide, startled brown eyes of an owl.

Huddled in her grey fur against the sofa cushions, she had a strange resemblance to a captive owl, bunched in its soft feathers against the wires of a cage. The supple erectness of her figure was gone, as though she had been broken by cruel exercise; as though there were no longer any reason for being beautiful, and supple, and erect.

"So you've come back," he repeated.

She never looked up, and never spoke, the firelight playing over her motionless figure.

Suddenly she tried to rise, but he prevented her; it was then that he understood.

She had come back like an animal wounded to death, not knowing where to turn, not knowing what she was doing. The sight of her figure, huddled in the fur, was enough.

He knew then for certain that Bosinney had been her lover; knew that she had seen the report of his death—perhaps, like himself, had bought a paper at the draughty corner of a street, and read it.

She had come back then of her own accord, to the cage she had pined to be free of—and taking in all the tremendous significance of this, he longed to cry: "Take your hated body, that I love, out of my house! Take away that pitiful white face, so cruel and soft—before I crush it. Get out of my sight; never let me see you again!"

And, at those unspoken words, he seemed to see her rise and move away, like a woman in a terrible dream, from which she was fighting to awake—rise and go out into the dark and cold, without a thought of him, without so much as the knowledge of his presence.

Then he cried, contradicting what he had not yet spoken, "No; stay there!" And turning away from her, he sat down in his accustomed chair on the other side of the hearth.

They sat in silence.

And Soames thought: "Why is all this? Why should I suffer so? What have I done? It is not my fault!'

Again he looked at her, huddled like a bird that is shot and dying, whose poor breast you see panting as the air is taken from it, whose poor eyes look at you who have shot it, with a slow, soft, unseeing look, taking farewell of all that is good—of the sun, and the air, and its mate.

So they sat, by the firelight, in the silence, one on each side of the hearth.

And the fume of the burning cedar logs, that he loved so well, seemed to grip Soames by the throat till he could bear it no longer. And going out into the hall he flung the door wide, to gulp down the cold air that came in; then without hat or overcoat went out into the Square.

Along the garden rails a half-starved cat came rubbing her way towards him, and Soames thought: 'Suffering! when will it cease, my suffering?'

At a front door across the way was a man of his acquaintance named

Rutter, scraping his boots, with an air of 'I am master here.' And Soames walked on.

From far in the clear air the bells of the church where he and Irene had been married were pealing in 'practice' for the advent of Christ, the chimes ringing out above the sound of traffic. He felt a craving for strong drink, to lull him to indifference, or rouse him to fury. If only he could burst out of himself, out of this web that for the first time in his life he felt around him. If only he could surrender to the thought: 'Divorce her—turn her out! She has forgotten you. Forget her!'

If only he could surrender to the thought: 'Let her go—she has suffered enough!'

If only he could surrender to the desire: 'Make a slave of her—she is in your power!'

If only he could surrender to the sudden vision: 'What does it all matter?' Forget himself for a minute, forget that it mattered what he did, forget that whatever he did he must sacrifice something.

If only he could act on an impulse!

He could forget nothing; surrender to no thought, vision, or desire; it was all too serious; too close around him, an unbreakable cage.

On the far side of the Square newspaper boys were calling their evening wares, and the ghoulish cries mingled and jangled with the sound of those church bells.

Soames covered his ears. The thought flashed across him that but for a chance, he himself, and not Bosinney, might be lying dead, and she, instead of crouching there like a shot bird with those dying eyes——

Something soft touched his legs, the cat was rubbing herself against them. And a sob that shook him from head to foot burst from Soames's chest. Then all was still again in the dark, where the houses seemed to stare at him, each with a master and mistress of its own, and a secret story of happiness or sorrow.

And suddenly he saw that his own door was open, and black against the light from the hall a man standing with his back turned. Something slid too in his breast, and he stole up close behind.

He could see his own fur coat flung across the carved oak chair; the

Persian rugs, the silver bowls, the rows of poreclain plates arranged along the walls, and this unknown man who was standing there.

And sharply he asked: "What is it you want, sir?"

The visitor turned. It was young Jolyon.

"The door was open," he said. "Might I see your wife for a minute, I have a message for her?"

Soames gave him a strange, sidelong stare.

"My wife can see no one," he muttered doggedly.

Young Jolyon answered gently: "I shouldn't keep her a minute." Soames brushed by him and barred the way.

"She can see no one," he said again.

Young Jolyon's glance shot past him into the hall, and Soames turned. There in the drawing-room doorway stood Irene, her eyes were wild and eager, her lips were parted, her hands outstretched. In the sight of both men that light vanished from her face; her hands dropped to her sides; she stood like stone.

Soames spun round, and met his visitor's eyes, and at the look he saw in them, a sound like a snarl escaped him. He drew his lips back in the ghost of a smile.

"This is my house," he said; "I manage my own affairs. I've told you once—I tell you again; we are not at home."

And in young Jolyon's face he slammed the door.

1902-5.

INTERLUDE

INDIAN SUMMER OF A FORSYTE

"And Summer's lease hath all too short a date."
—*Shakespeare.*

TO

ANDRÉ CHEVRILLON

Indian Summer of a Forsyte

I

ON the last day of May in the early 'nineties, about six o'clock of the evening, old Jolyon Forsyte sat under the oak tree below the terrace of his house at Robin Hill. He was waiting for the midges to bite him, before abandoning the glory of the afternoon. His thin brown hand, where blue veins stood out, held the end of a cigar in its tapering, long-nailed fingers—a pointed polished nail had survived with him from those earlier Victorian days when to touch nothing, even with the tips of the fingers, had been so distinguished. His domed forehead, great white moustache, lean cheeks, and long lean jaw were covered from the westering sunshine by an old brown Panama hat. His legs were crossed; in all his attitude was serenity and a kind of elegance, as of an old man who every morning put eau de Cologne upon his silk handkerchief. At his feet lay a woolly brown-and-white dog trying to be a Pomeranian— the dog Balthasar between whom and old Jolyon primal aversion had changed into attachment with the years. Close to his chair was a swing, and on the swing was seated one of Holly's dolls—called 'Duffer Alice' —with her body fallen over her legs and her doleful nose buried in a black petticoat. She was never out of disgrace, so it did not matter to her how she sat. Below the oak tree the lawn dipped down a bank, stretched to the fernery, and, beyond that refinement, became fields, dropping to the pond, the coppice, and the prospect—'Fine, remarkable'—at which Swithin Forsyte, from under this very tree, had stared five years ago when he drove down with Irene to look at the house. Old Jolyon had heard of his brother's exploit—that drive which had become quite celebrated on Forsyte 'Change. Swithin! And the fellow had gone and died, last November, at the age of only seventy-nine, renewing the doubt whether Forsytes could live for ever, which had first arisen when Aunt Ann passed away. Died! and left only Jolyon and James, Roger and Nicholas and Timothy, Julia, Hester, Susan! And old Jolyon thought: 'Eighty-five! I don't feel it—except when I get that pain.'

His memory went searching. He had not felt his age since he had
bought his nephew Soames's ill-starred house and settled into it here at
Robin Hill over three years ago. It was as if he had been getting younger
every spring, living in the country with his son and his grandchildren—
June, and the little ones of the second marriage, Jolly and Holly; living
down here out of the racket of London and the cackle of Forsyte
'Change,' free of his boards, in a delicious atmosphere of no work and
all play, with plenty of occupation in the perfecting and mellowing of
the house and its twenty acres, and in ministering to the whims of Holly
and Jolly. All the knots and crankiness, which had gathered in his heart
during that long and tragic business of June, Soames, Irene his wife, and
poor young Bosinney, had been smoothed out. Even June had thrown off
her melancholy at last—witness this travel in Spain she was taking now
with her father and her stepmother. Curiously perfect peace was left by
their departure; blissful, yet blank, because his son was not there. Jo was
never anything but a comfort and a pleasure to him nowadays—an amiable chap; but women, somehow—even the best—got a little on one's
nerves, unless of course one admired them.

Far-off a cuckoo called; a wood-pigeon was cooing from the first elm-
tree in the field, and how the daisies and buttercups had sprung up after
the last mowing! The wind had got into the sou'west, too—a delicious
air, sappy! He pushed his hat back and let the sun fall on his chin and
cheek. Somehow, to-day, he wanted company—wanted a pretty face to
look at. People treated the old as if they wanted nothing. And with the
un-Forsytean philosophy which ever intruded on his soul, he thought:
'One's never had enough! With a foot in the grave one'll want something, I shouldn't be surprised!' Down here—away from the exigencies
of affairs—his grandchildren, and the flowers, trees, birds of his little
domain, to say nothing of sun and moon and stars above them, said,
'Open, sesame,' to him day and night. And sesame had opened—how
much, perhaps, he did not know. He had always been responsive to what
they had begun to call 'Nature,' genuinely, almost religiously responsive,
though he had never lost his habit of calling a sunset a sunset and a
view a view, however deeply they might move him. But nowadays Nature actually made him ache, he appreciated it so. Every one of these
calm, bright, lengthening days, with Holly's hand in his, and the dog
Balthasar in front looking studiously for what he never found, he would

stroll, watching the roses open, fruit budding on the walls, sunlight brightening the oak leaves and saplings in the coppice, watching the water-lily leaves unfold and glisten, and the silvery young corn of the one wheatfield; listening to the starlings and skylarks, and the Alderney cows chewing the cud, flicking slow their tufted tails; and every one of these fine days he ached a little from sheer love of it all, feeling perhaps, deep down, that he had not very much longer to enjoy it. The thought that some day—perhaps not ten years hence, perhaps not five—all this world would be taken away from him, before he had exhausted his powers of loving it, seemed to him in the nature of an injustice brooding over his horizon. If anything came after this life, it wouldn't be what he wanted; not Robin Hill, and flowers and birds and pretty faces —too few, even now, of those about him! With the years his dislike of humbug had increased; the orthodoxy he had worn in the 'sixties, as he had worn side-whiskers out of sheer exuberance, had long dropped off, leaving him reverent before three things alone—beauty, upright conduct, and the sense of property; and the greatest of these now was beauty. He had always had wide interests, and, indeed could still read *The Times,* but he was liable at any moment to put it down if he heard a blackbird sing. Upright conduct, property—somehow, they were tiring; the blackbirds and the sunsets never tired him, only gave him an uneasy feeling that he could not get enough of them. Staring into the stilly radiance of the early evening and at the little gold and white flowers on the lawn, a thought came to him: This weather was like the music of 'Orfeo,' which he had recently heard at Covent Garden. A beautiful opera, not like Meyerbeer, nor even quite Mozart, but, in its way, perhaps even more lovely; something classical and of the Golden Age about it, chaste and mellow, and the Ravogli 'almost worthy of the old days'—highest praise he could bestow. The yearning of Orpheus for the beauty he was losing, for his love going down to Hades, as in life love and beauty did go—the yearning which sang and throbbed through the golden music, stirred also in the lingering beauty of the world that evening. And with the tip of his cork-soled, elastic-sided boot he involuntarily stirred the ribs of the dog Balthasar, causing the animal to wake and attack his fleas; for though he was supposed to have none, nothing could persuade him of the fact. When he had finished, he rubbed the place he had been scratching against his master's calf, and settled down again with his chin over the instep of the disturbing boot. And into old Jolyon's mind came a sudden recollection—a face he had seen at that opera three weeks ago—Irene, the wife of his precious nephew Soames, that man of property! Though he had not met her since the day of the 'at home' in his old house at Stanhope Gate, which celebrated his granddaughter June's ill-starred engagement to young Bosinney, he had remembered her at once, for he had always admired her—a very pretty creature. After the death of young Bosinney, whose mistress she had so reprehensibly become, he had heard that she had left Soames at once. Goodness only knew what she had been doing since. That sight of her face—a side view—in the row in front, had been literally the only reminder these three years that she was still alive. No one ever spoke of her. And yet Jo had told him something once—something which had upset him completely. The boy had got it from George Forsyte, he believed, who had seen Bosinney in the fog the day he was run over—something which explained the young fellow's distress—an act of Soames towards his wife—a shocking act. Jo had seen her, too, that afternoon, after the news was out, seen her for a moment, and his description had always lingered in old Jolyon's mind—'wild and lost' he had called her. And next day June had gone there—bottled up her feelings and gone there, and the maid had cried and told her how her mistress had slipped out in the night and vanished. A tragic business altogether! One thing was certain—Soames had never been able to lay hands on her again. And he was living at Brighton, and journeying up and down—a fitting fate, the man of property! For when he once took a dislike to anyone—as he had to his nephew—old Jolyon never got over it. He remembered still the sense of relief with which he had heard the news of Irene's disappearance. It had been shocking to think of her a prisoner in that house to which she must have wandered back, when Jo saw her, wandered back for a moment—like a wounded animal to its hole after seeing that news, 'Tragic death of an Architect,' in the street. Her face had struck him very much the other night—more beautiful than he had remembered, but like a mask, with something going on beneath it. A young woman still—twenty-eight perhaps. Ah, well! Very likely she had another lover by now. But at this subversive thought —for married women should never love: once, even, had been too much —his instep rose, and with it the dog Balthasar's head. The sagacious animal stood up and looked into old Jolyon's face. 'Walk?' he seemed to say; and old Jolyon answered: "Come on, old chap!"

Slowly, as was their wont, they crossed among the constellations of buttercups and daisies, and entered the fernery. This feature, where very little grew as yet, had been judiciously dropped below the level of the lawn so that it might come up again on the level of the other lawn and give the impression of irregularity, so important in horticulture. Its rocks and earth were beloved of the dog Balthasar, who sometimes found a mole there. Old Jolyon made a point of passing through it because, though it was not beautiful, he intended that it should be, some day, and he would think: 'I must get Varr to come down and look at it; he's better than Beech.' For plants, like houses and human complaints, required the best expert consideration. It was inhabited by snails, and if accompanied by his grandchildren, he would point to one and tell them the story of the little boy who said: 'Have plummers got leggers, Mother?' 'No, sonny.' 'Then darned if I haven't been and swallowed a snileybob.' And when they skipped and clutched his hand, thinking of the snileybob going down the little boy's 'red lane,' his eyes would twinkle. Emerging from the fernery, he opened the wicket gate, which just there led into the first field, a large and park-like area, out of which, within brick walls, the vegetable garden had been carved. Old Jolyon avoided this, which did not suit his mood, and made down the hill towards the pond. Balthasar, who knew a water-rat or two, gambolled in front, at the gait which marks an oldish dog who takes the same walk every day. Arrived at the edge, old Jolyon stood, noting another water-lily opened since yesterday; he would show it to Holly to-morrow, when 'his little sweet' had got over the upset which had followed on her eating a tomato at lunch—her little arrangements were very delicate. Now that Jolly had gone to school—his first term—Holly was with him nearly all day long, and he missed her badly. He felt that pain too, which often bothered him now, a little dragging at his left side. He looked back up the hill. Really, poor young Bosinney had made an uncommonly good job of the house; he would have done very well for himself if he had lived! And where was he now? Perhaps, still haunting this, the site of his last work, of his tragic love affair. Or was Philip Bosinney's spirit diffused in the general? Who could say? That dog was getting his legs muddy! And he moved towards the coppice. There had been the most delightful lot of bluebells, and he knew where some still lingered like little patches of sky fallen in between the trees, away out of the sun. He passed the cow-houses and the hen-houses there installed, and pursued a path into the thick of the saplings, making for one of the bluebell plots. Balthasar, preceding him once more, uttered a low growl. Old Jolyon stirred him with his foot, but the dog remained motionless, just where there was no room to pass, and the hair rose slowly along the centre of his woolly back. Whether from the growl and the look of the dog's stivered hair, or from the sensation which a man feels in a wood, old Jolyon also felt something move along his spine. And then the path turned, and there was an old mossy log, and on it a woman sitting. Her face was turned away, and he had just time to think: 'She's trespassing—I must have a board put up!' before she turned. Powers above! The face he had seen at the opera—the very woman he had just been thinking of! In that confused moment he saw things blurred, as if a spirit—queer effect—the slant of sunlight perhaps on her violet-grey frock! And then she rose and stood smiling, her head a little to one side. Old Jolyon thought: 'How pretty she is!' She did not speak, neither did he; and he realized why with a certain admiration. She was here no doubt because of some memory, and did not mean to try and get out of it by vulgar explanation.

"Don't let that dog touch your frock," he said; "he's got wet feet. Come here, you!"

But the dog Balthasar went on towards the visitor, who put her hand down and stroked his head. Old Jolyon said quickly:

"I saw you at the opera the other night; you didn't notice me."

"Oh, yes! I did."

He felt a subtle flattery in that, as though she had added: 'Do you think one could miss seeing you?'

"They're all in Spain," he remarked abruptly. "I'm alone; I drove up for the opera. The Ravogli's good. Have you seen the cow-houses?"

In a situation so charged with mystery and something very like emotion he moved instinctively towards that bit of property, and she moved beside him. Her figure swayed faintly, like the best kind of French figures; her dress, too, was a sort of French grey. He noticed two or three silver threads in her amber-coloured hair, strange hair with those dark eyes of hers, and that creamy-pale face. A sudden sidelong look from the velvety brown eyes disturbed him. It seemed to come from deep and far, from another world almost, or at all events from someone not living very much in this. And he said mechanically:

"Where are you living now?"

"I have a little flat in Chelsea."

He did not want to hear what she was doing, did not want to hear anything; but the perverse word came out:

"Alone?"

She nodded. It was a relief to know that. And it came into his mind that, but for a twist of fate, she would have been mistress of this coppice, showing these cow-houses to him, a visitor.

"All Alderneys," he muttered; "they give the best milk. This one's a pretty creature. Woa, Myrtle!"

The fawn-coloured cow, with eyes as soft and brown as Irene's own, was standing absolutely still, not having long been milked. She looked round at them out of the corner of those lustrous, mild, cynical eyes, and from her grey lips a little dribble of saliva threaded its way towards the straw. The scent of hay and vanilla and ammonia rose in the dim light of the cool cow-house; and old Jolyon said:

"You must come up and have some dinner with me. I'll send you home in the carriage."

He perceived a struggle going on within her; natural, no doubt, with her memories. But he wanted her company; a pretty face, a charming figure, beauty! He had been alone all the afternoon. Perhaps his eyes were wistful, for she answered: "Thank you, Uncle Jolyon. I should like to."

He rubbed his hands, and said:

"Capital! Let's go up, then!" And, preceded by the dog Balthasar, they ascended through the field. The sun was almost level in their faces now, and he could see, not only those silver threads, but little lines, just deep enough to stamp her beauty with a coin-like fineness—the special look of life unshared with others. 'I'll take her in by the terrace,' he thought: 'I won't make a common visitor of her.'

"What do you do all day?" he said.

"Teach music; I have another interest, too."

"Work!" said old Jolyon, picking up the doll from off the swing, and smoothing its black petticoat. "Nothing like it, is there? I don't do any now. I'm getting on. What interest is that?"

"Trying to help women who've come to grief." Old Jolyon did not quite understand. "To grief?" he repeated; then realised with a shock that she meant exactly what he would have meant himself if he had used that expression. Assisting the Magdalenes of London! What a weird and terrifying interest! And, curiosity overcoming his natural shrinking, he asked:

"Why? What do you do for them?"

"Not much. I've no money to spare. I can only give sympathy and food sometimes."

Involuntarily old Jolyon's hand sought his purse. He said hastily: "How d'you get hold of them?"

"I go to a hospital."

"A hospital! Phew!"

"What hurts me most is that once they nearly all had some sort of beauty."

Old Jolyon straigthened the doll. "Beauty!" he ejaculated: "Ha! Yes! A sad business!" and he moved towards the house. Through a French window, under sun-blinds not yet drawn up, he preceded her into the room where he was wont to study *The Times* and the sheets of an agricultural magazine, with huge illustrations of mangold wurzels, and the like, which provided Holly with material for her paint brush.

"Dinner's in half an hour. "You'd like to wash your hands! I'll take you to June's room."

He saw her looking round eagerly; what changes since she had last visited this house with her husband, or her lover, or both perhaps—he did not know, could not say! All that was dark, and he wished to leave it so. But what changes! And in the hall he said:

"My boy Jo's a painter, you know. He's got a lot of taste. It isn't mine, of course, but I've let him have his way."

She was standing very still, her eyes roaming through the hall and music room, as it now was—all thrown into one, under the great skylight. Old Jolyon had an odd impression of her. Was she trying to conjure somebody from the shades of that space where the colouring was all pearl-grey and silver? He would have had gold himself; more lively and solid. But Jo had French tastes, and it had come out shadowy like that, with an effect as of the fume of cigarettes the chap was always smoking, broken here and there by a little blaze of blue or crimson colour. It was not *his* dream! Mentally he had hung this space with those gold-framed masterpieces of still and stiller life which he had bought in days when quantity was precious. And now where were they? Sold for a song! That something which made him, alone among Forsytes, move with the times had warned him against the struggle to retain them. But in his study he still had 'Dutch Fishing Boats at Sunset.'

He began to mount the stairs with her, slowly, for he felt his side.

"These are the bathrooms," he said, "and other arrangements. I've had them tiled. The nurseries are along there. And this is Jo's and his wife's. They all communicate. But you remember, I expect."

Irene nodded. They passed on, up the gallery and entered a large room with a small bed, and several windows.

"This is mine," he said. The walls were covered with the photographs of children and water-colour sketches, and he added doubtfully:

"These are Jo's. The view's first-rate. You can see the Grand Stand at Epsom in clear weather."

The sun was down now, behind the house, and over the 'prospect' a luminous haze had settled, emanation of the long and prosperous day. Few houses showed, but fields and trees faintly glistened, away to a loom of downs.

"The country's changing," he said abruptly, "but there it'll be when we're all gone. Look at those thrushes—the birds are sweet here in the mornings. I'm glad to have washed my hands of London."

Her face was close to the window pane, and he was struck by its mournful look. 'Wish I could make her look happy!' he thought. 'A pretty face, but sad!' And taking up his can of hot water he went out into the gallery.

"This is June's room," he said, opening the next door and putting the can down; "I think you'll find everything." And closing the door behind her he went back to his own room. Brushing his hair with his great ebony brushes, and dabbing his forehead with eau de Cologne, he mused. She had come so strangely—a sort of visitation, mysterious, even romantic, as if his desire for company, for beauty, had been fulfilled by—whatever it was which fulfilled that sort of thing. And before the mirror he straightened his still upright figure, passed the brushes over his great white moustache, touched up his eyebrows with eau de Cologne, and rang the bell.

"I forgot to let them know that I have a lady to dinner with me. Let cook do something extra, and tell Beacon to have the landau and pair at half-past ten to drive her back to Town to-night. Is Miss Holly asleep?"

The maid thought not. And Old Jolyon, passing down the gallery, stole on tiptoe towards the nursery, and opened the door whose hinges he kept specially oiled that he might slip in and out in the evenings without being heard.

But Holly *was* asleep, and lay like a miniature Madonna, of that type which the old painters could not tell from Venus, when they had completed her. Her long dark lashes clung to her cheeks; on her face was perfect peace—her little arrangements were evidently all right again. And old Jolyon, in the twilight of the room, stood adoring her! It was so charming, solemn, and loving—that little face. He had more than his share of the blessed capacity of living again in the young. They were to him his future life—all of a future life—that his fundamental pagan sanity perhaps admitted. There she was with everything before her, and his blood—some of it—in her tiny veins. There she was, his little companion, to be made as happy as ever he could make her, so that she knew nothing but love. His heart swelled, and he went out, stifling the sound of his patent-leather boots. In the corridor an eccentric notion attacked him: To think that children should come to that which Irene had told him she was helping! Women who were all, once, little things like this one sleeping there! 'I must give her a cheque!' he mused; 'Can't bear to think of them!' They had never borne reflecting on, those poor outcasts; wounding too deeply the core of true refinement hidden under layers of conformity to the sense of property—wounding too grievously the deepest thing in him—a love of beauty which could give him, even now, a flutter of the heart, thinking of his evening in the society of a pretty woman. And he went downstairs, through the swinging doors, to the back regions. There, in the wine-cellar, was a hock worth at least two pounds a bottle, a Steinberg Cabinet, better than any Johannisberg that ever went down throat; a wine of perfect bouquet, sweet as a nectarine —nectar indeed! He got a bottle out, handling it like a baby, and holding it level to the light, to look. Enshrined in its coat of dust, that mellow-coloured, slender-necked bottle gave him deep pleasure. Three years to settle down again since the move from Town—ought to be in prime condition! Thirty-five years ago he had bought it—thank God he had kept his palate, and earned the right to drink it. She would appreciate this; not a spice of acidity in a dozen. He wiped the bottle, drew the cork with his own hands, put his nose down, inhaled its perfume, and went back to the music room.

Irene was standing by the piano; she had taken off her hat and a lace scarf she had been wearing, so that her gold-coloured hair was visible, and the pallor of her neck. In her grey frock she made a pretty picture for old Jolyon, against the rosewood of the piano.

He gave her his arm, and solemnly they went. The room, which had been designed to enable twenty-four people to dine in comfort, held now but a little round table. In his present solitude the big dining-table oppressed old Jolyon; he had caused it to be removed till his son came back. Here in the company of two really good copies of Raphael Madonnas he was wont to dine alone. It was the only disconsolate hour of his day, this summer weather. He had never been a large eater, like that great chap Swithin, or Sylvanus Heythorp, or Anthony Thornworthy, those cronies of past times; and to dine alone, overlooked by the Madonnas, was to him but a sorrowful occupation, which he got through quickly, that he might come to the more spiritual enjoyment of his coffee and cigar. But this evening was a different matter! His eyes twinkled at her across the little table and he spoke of Italy and Switzerland, telling her stories of his travels there, and other experiences which he could no longer recount to his son and grand-daughter because they knew them. This fresh audience was precious to him; he had never become one of those old men who ramble round and round the fields of reminiscence. Himself quickly fatigued by the insensitive, he instinctively avoided fatiguing others, and his natural flirtatiousness towards beauty guarded him specially in his relations with a woman. He would have liked to draw her out, but though she murmured and smiled and seemed to be enjoying what he told her, he remained conscious of that mysterious remoteness which constituted half her fascination. He could not bear women who threw their shoulders and eyes at you, and chattered away; or hard-mouthed women who laid down the law and knew more than you did. There was only one quality in a woman that appealed to him—charm; and the quieter it was, the more he liked it. And this one had charm, shadowy as afternoon sunlight on those Italian hills and valleys he had loved. The feeling, too, that she was, as it were, apart, cloistered, made her seem nearer to himself, a strangely desirable companion. When a man is very old and quite out of the running he loves to feel secure from the rivalries of youth, for he would still be first in the heart of beauty. And he drank his hock, and watched her lips, and felt nearly young. But the dog Balthasar lay watching her lips too, and despising in his heart the interruptions of their talk, and the tilting of those green-ish glasses full of a golden fluid which was distasteful to him.

The light was just failing when they went back into the music-room. And, cigar in mouth, old Jolyon said:

"Play me some Chopin."

By the cigars they smoke, and the composers they love, ye shall know the texture of men's souls. Old Jolyon could not bear a strong cigar or Wagner's music. He loved Beethoven and Mozart, Handel and Gluck, and Schumann, and, for some occult reason, the operas of Meyerbeer; but of late years he had been seduced by Chopin, just as in painting he had succumbed to Boticelli. In yielding to these tastes he had been con-scious of divergence from the standard of the Golden Age. Their poetry was not that of Milton and Byron and Tennyson; of Raphael and Titian; Mozart and Beethoven. It was, as it were, behind a veil; their poetry hit no one in the face, but slipped its fingers under the ribs and turned and twisted, and melted up the heart. And, never certain that this was healthy, he did not care a rap so long as he could see the pictures of the one or hear the music of the other.

Irene sat down at the piano under the electric lamp festooned with pearl-grey, and old Jolyon, in an armchair, whence he could see her, crossed his legs and drew slowly at his cigar. She sat a few moments with her hands on the keys, evidently searching her mind for what to give him. Then she began and within old Jolyon there arose a sorrowful pleasure, not quite like anything else in the world. He fell slowly into a trance, interrupted only by the movements of taking the cigar out of his mouth at long intervals, and replacing it. She was there, and the hock within him, and the scent of tobacco; but there, too, was a world of sun-shine lingering into moonlight, and pools with storks upon them, and bluish trees above, glowing with blurs of wine-red roses, and fields of lavender where milk-white cows were grazing, and a woman all sha-dowy, with dark eyes and a white neck, smiled, holding out her arms; and through air which was like music a star dropped and was caught on a cow's horn. He opened his eyes. Beautiful piece; she played well—the touch of an angel! And he closed them again. He felt miraculously sad and happy, as one does, standing under a lime-tree in full honey flower. Not live one's own life again, but just stand there and bask in the smile of a woman's eyes, and enjoy the bouquet! And he jerked his hand; the dog Balthasar had reached up and licked it.

"Beautiful!" He said: "Go on—more Chopin!"

She began to play again. This time the resemblance between her and 'Chopin' struck him. The swaying he had noticed in her walk was in her playing too, and the Nocturne she had chosen and the soft darkness of her eyes, the light on her hair, as of moonlight from a golden moon. Seductive, yes; but nothing of Delilah in her or in that music. A long blue spiral from his cigar ascended and dispersed. 'So we go out!' he thought. 'No more beauty! Nothing?'

Again Irene stopped.

"Would you like some Gluck? He used to write his music in a sun-lit garden, with a bottle of Rhine wine beside him."

"Ah! yes. Let's have 'Orfeo.'" Round about him now were fields of gold and silver flowers, white forms swaying in the sunlight, bright birds flying to and fro. All was summer. Lingering waves of sweetness and regret flooded his soul. Some cigar ash dropped, and taking out a silk handkerchief to brush it off, he inhaled a mingled scent as of snuff and eau de Cologne. 'Ah! he thought, 'Indian summer—that's all!' and he said: "You haven't played me 'Che faro.'"

She did not answer; did not move. He was conscious of something—some strange upset. Suddenly he saw her rise and turn away, and a pang of remorse shot through him. What a clumsy chap! Like Orpheus, she of course—she too was looking for her lost one in the hall of memory! And disturbed to the heart, he got up from his chair. She had gone to the great window at the far end. Gingerly he followed. Her hands were folded over her breast; he could just see her cheek, very white. And, quite emotionalized, he said: "There, there, my love!" The words had escaped him mechanically, for they were those he used to Holly when she had a pain, but their effect was instantaneously distressing. She raised her arms, covered her face with them, and wept.

Old Jolyon stood gazing at her with eyes very deep from age. The passionate shame she seemed feeling at her abandonment, so unlike the control and quietude of her whole presence was as if she had never before broken down in the presence of another being.

"There, there—there, there!" he murmured, and putting his hand out reverently, touched her. She turned, and leaned the arms which covered her face against him. Old Jolyon stood very still, keeping one thin hand on her shoulder. Let her cry her heart out—it would do her good! And the dog Balthasar, puzzled, sat down on his stern to examine them.

The window was still open, the curtains had not been drawn, the last of daylight from without mingled with faint intrusion from the lamp within; there was a scent of new-mown grass. With the wisdom of a long life old Jolyon did not speak. Even grief sobbed itself out in time; only Time was good for sorrow—Time who saw the passing of each mood, each emotion in turn; Time the layer-to-rest. There came into his mind the words: 'As panteth the hart after cooling streams'—but they were of no use to him. Then, conscious of a scent of violets, he knew she was drying her eyes. He put his chin forward, pressed his moustache against her forehead, and felt her shake with a quivering of her whole body, as of a tree which shakes itself free of raindrops. She put his hand to her lips, as if saying: "All over now! Forgive me!"

The kiss filled him with a strange comfort; he led her back to where she had been so upset. And the dog Balthasar, following, laid the bone of one of the cutlets they eaten at their feet.

Anxious to obliterate the memory of that emotion, he could think of nothing better than china; and moving with her slowly from cabinet to cabinet, he kept taking up bits of Dresden and Lowestoft and Chelsea, turning them round and round with his thin, veined hands, whose skin, faintly freckled, had such an aged look.

"I bought this at Jobson's," he would say; "cost me thirty pounds. It's very old. That dog leaves his bones all over the place. This old 'ship-bowl' I picked up at the sale when that precious rip, the Marquis, came to grief. But you don't remember. Here's a nice piece of Chelsea. Now, what would you say *this* was?" And he was comforted, feeling that, with her taste, she was taking a real interest in these things; for, after all, nothing better composes the nerves than a doubtful piece of china.

When the crunch of the carriage wheels was heard at last, he said:

"You must come again; you must come to lunch, then I can show you these by daylight, and my little sweet—she's a dear little thing. This dog seems to have taken a fancy to you."

For Balthasar, feeling that she was about to leave, was rubbing his side against her leg. Going out under the porch with her, he said:

'He'll get you up in an hour and a quarter. Take this for your *protégées,"* and he slipped a cheque for fifty pounds into her hand. He saw her brightened eyes, and heard her murmur: "Oh! Uncle Jolyon!" and a real throb of pleasure went through him. That meant one or two poor creatures helped a little, and it meant that she would come again. He put his hand in at the window and grasped hers once more. The carriage rolled away. He stood looking at the moon and the shadows of the trees, and thought: 'A sweet night! She——!'

II

Two days of rain, and summer set in bland and sunny. Old Jolyon walked and talked with Holly. At first he felt taller and full of a new vigour; then he felt restless. Almost every afternoon they would enter the coppice, and walk as far as the log. 'Well, she's not there!' he would think, 'of course not!' And he would feel a little shorter, and drag his feet walking up the hill home, with his hand clapped to his left side. Now and then the thought would move in him: 'Did she come—or did I dream it?' and he would stare at space, while the dog Balthasar stared at him. Of course she would not come again! He opened the letters from Spain with less excitement. They were not returning till July; he felt, oddly, that he could bear it. Every day at dinner he screwed up his eyes and looked at where she had sat. She was not there, so he unscrewed his eyes again.

On the seventh afternoon he thought: 'I must go up and get some boots.' He ordered Beacon, and set out. Passing from Putney towards Hyde Park he reflected: 'I might as well go to Chelsea and see her.' And he called out: "Just drive me to where you took that lady the other night." The coachman turned his broad red face, and his juicy lips answered: "The lady in grey, sir?"

"Yes, the lady in grey." What other ladies were there! Stodgy chap! The carriage stopped before a small three-storied block of flats, stand-

313

ing a little back from the river. With a practised eye old Jolyon saw that they were cheap. 'I should think about sixty pound a year,' he mused; and entering, he looked at the name-board. The name 'Forsyte, was not on it, but against 'First Floor, Flat C' were the words: 'Mrs. Irene Heron.' Ah! She had taken her maiden name again! And somehow this pleased him. He went upstairs slowly, feeling his side a little. He stood a moment, before ringing, to lose the feeling of drag and fluttering there. She would not be in! And then—Boots! The thought was black. What did he want with boots at his age? He could not wear out all those he had.

"Your mistress at home?"

"Yes, sir."

"Say Mr. Jolyon Forsyte."

"Yes, sir, will you come this way?"

Old Jolyon followed a very little maid—not more than sixteen one would say—into a very small dining-room where the sunblinds were drawn. It held a cottage piano and little else save a vague fragrance and good taste. He stood in the middle, with his top hat in his hand, and thought: 'I expect she's very badly off!' There was a mirror above the fireplace, and he saw himself reflected. An old-looking chap! He heard a rustle, and turned round. She was so close that his moustache almost brushed her forehead, just under her hair.

"I was driving up," he said. "Thought I'd look in on you, and ask you how you got up the other night."

And, seeing her smile, he felt suddenly relieved. She was really glad to see him, perhaps.

"Would you like to put on your hat and come for a drive in the Park?"

But while she was gone to put her hat on, he frowned. The Park! James and Emily! Mrs. Nicholas, or some other member of his precious family would be there very likely, prancing up and down. And they would go and wag their tongues about having seen him with her, afterwards. Better not! He did not wish to revive the echoes of the past on Forsyte 'Change. He removed a white hair from the lapel of his closely buttoned-up frock coat, and passed his hand over his cheeks, moustache, and square chin. It felt very hollow there under the cheekbones. He had not been eating much lately—he had better get that little whippersnapper who attended Holly to give him a tonic. But she had come back and when they were in the carriage, he said:

"Suppose we go and sit in Kensington Gardens instead?" and added with a twinkle: "No prancing up and down there," as if she had been in the secret of his thoughts.

Leaving the carriage, they entered those select precincts, and strolled towards the water.

"You've gone back to your maiden name, I see," he said: "I'm not sorry."

She slipped her hand under his arm: "Has June forgiven me, Uncle Jolyon?"

He answered gently: "Yes—yes; of course, why not?"

"And have you?"

"I? I forgave you as soon as I saw how the land really lay." And perhaps he had; his instinct had always been to forgive the beautiful.

She drew a deep breath. "I never regretted—I couldn't. Did you ever love very deeply, Uncle Jolyon?"

At that strange question old Jolyon stared before him. Had he? He did not seem to remember that he ever had. But he did not like to say this to the young woman whose hand was touching his arm, whose life was suspended, as it were, by memory of a tragic love. And he thought: 'If I had met *you* when I was young I—I might have made a fool of myself, perhaps.' And a longing to escape in generalities beset him.

"Love's a queer thing," he said, "fatal thing often. It was the Greeks—wasn't it?—made love into a goddess; they were right, I dare say, but then they lived in the Golden Age."

"Phil adored them."

Phil! The word jarred him, for suddenly—with his power to see all round a thing, he perceived why she was putting up with him like this. She wanted to talk about her lover! Well! If it was any pleasure to her! And he said: "Ah! There was a bit of the sculptor in him, I fancy."

"Yes. He loved balance and symmetry; he loved the wholehearted way the Greeks gave themselves to art."

Balance! The chap had no balance at all, if he remembered; as for symmetry—clean-built enough he was, no doubt; but those queer eyes of his, and high cheek-bones—Symmetry?

"You're of the Golden Age, too, Uncle Jolyon."

Old Jolyon looked round at her. Was she chaffing him? No, her eyes were soft as velvet. Was she flattering him? But if so, why? There was nothing to be had out of an old chap like him.

"Phil thought so. He used to say: 'But I can never tell him that I admire him.' "

Ah! There it was again. Her dead lover; her desire to talk of him! And he pressed her arm, half resentful of those memories, half grateful, as if he recognised what a link they were between herself and him.

"He was a very talented young fellow," he murmured. "It's hot; I feel the heat nowadays. Let's sit down."

They took two chairs beneath a chestnut tree whose broad leaves covered them from the peaceful glory of the afternoon. A pleasure to sit there and watch her, and feel that she liked to be with him. And the wish to increase that liking, if he could, made him go on:

"I expect he showed you a side of him I never saw. He'd be at his best with you. His ideas of art were a little new—to me"—he had stifled the word 'fangled.'

"Yes: but he used to say you had a real sense of beauty." Old Jolyon thought: 'The devil he did!' but answered with a twinkle: "Well, I have, or I shouldn't be sitting here with you." She was fascinating when she smiled with her eyes, like that!

"He thought you had one of those hearts that never grow old. Phil had real insight."

He was not taken in by this flattery spoken out of the past, out of a longing to talk of her dead lover—not a bit; and yet it was precious to hear, because she pleased his eyes and heart which—quite true!—had never grown old. Was that because—unlike her and her dead lover, he had never loved to desperation, had always kept his balance, his sense of symmetry. Well! It had left him power, at eighty-four, to admire beauty. And he thought, 'If I were a painter or a sculptor! But I'm an old chap. Make hay while the sun shines.'

A couple with arms entwined crossed on the grass before them, at the edge of the shadow from their tree. The sunlight fell cruelly on their pale, squashed, unkempt young faces. "We're an ugly lot!" said old Jolyon suddenly. "It amazes me to see how—love triumphs over that."

"Love triumphs over everything!"

316

"The young think so," he muttered.

"Love has no age, no limit, and no death."

With that glow in her pale face, her breast heaving, her eyes so large and dark and soft, she looked like Venus come to life! But this extravagance brought instant reaction, and, twinkling, he said: "Well, if it had limits, we shouldn't be born; for by George! it's got a lot to put up with."

Then, removing his top hat, he brushed it round with a cuff. The great clumsy thing heated his forehead; in these days he often got a rush of blood to the head—his circulation was not what it had been.

She still sat gazing straight before her, and suddenly she murmured: "It's strange enough that I'm alive."

Those words of Jo's 'Wild and lost' came back to him.

"Ah!" he said: "my son saw you for a moment—that day."

"Was it your son? I heard a voice in the hall; I thought for a second it was—Phil."

Old Jolyon saw her lips tremble. She put her hand over them, took it away again, and went on calmly: "That night I went to the Embankment; a woman caught me by the dress. She told me about herself. When one knows that others suffer, one's ashamed."

"One of *those?*"

She nodded, and horror stirred within old Jolyon, the horror of one who has never known a struggle with desperation. Almost against his will he muttered: "Tell me, won't you?"

"I didn't care whether I lived or died. When you're like that, Fate ceases to want to kill you. She took care of me three days—she never left me. I had no money. That's why I do what I can for them, now."

But old Jolyon was thinking: 'No money!' What fate could compare with that? Every other was involved in it.

"I wish you had come to me," he said. "Why didn't you?" But Irene did not answer.

"Because my name was Forsyte, I suppose? Or was it June who kept you away? How are you getting on now?" His eyes involuntarily swept her body. Perhaps even now she was—! And yet she wasn't thin—not really!

"Oh! with my fifty pounds a year, I make just enough." The answer did not reassure him; he had lost confidence. And that fellow Soames!

But his sense of justice stifled condemnation. No, she would certainly have died rather than take another penny from *him*. Soft as she looked, there must be strength in her somewhere—strength and fidelity. But what business had young Bosinney to have got run over and left her stranded like this!

"Well, you must come to me now," he said, "for anything you want, or I shall be quite cut up." And putting on his hat, he rose. "Let's go and get some tea. I told that lazy chap to put the horses up for an hour, and come for me at your place. We'll take a cab presently; I can't walk as I used to."

He enjoyed that stroll to the Kensington end of the gardens—the sound of her voice, the glancing of her eyes, the subtle beauty of a charming form moving beside him. He enjoyed their tea at Ruffel's in the High Street, and came out thence with a great box of chocolates swung on his little finger. He enjoyed the drive back to Chelsea in a hansom, smoking his cigar. She had promised to come down next Sunday and play to him again, and already in thought he was plucking carnations and early roses for her to carry back to town. It was a pleasure to give her a little pleasure, if it *were* pleasure from an old chap like him! The carriage was already there when they arrived. Just like that fellow, who was always late when he was wanted! Old Jolyon went in for a minute to say good-bye. The little dark hall of the flat was impregnated with a disagreeable odour of patchouli, and on a bench against the wall—its only furniture—he saw a figure sitting. He heard Irene say softly: "Just one minute." In the little drawing-room when the door was shut, he asked gravely: "One of your *protégées?*"

"Yes. Now thanks to you, I can do something for her."

He stood, staring and stroking that chin whose strength had frightened so many in its time. The idea of her thus actually in contact with this outcast, grieved and frightened him. What could she do for them? Nothing. Only soil and make trouble for herself, perhaps. And he said: "Take care, my dear! The world puts the worst construction on everything."

"I know that."

He was abashed by her quiet smile. "Well then—Sunday," he murmured: "Good-bye."

She put her cheek forward for him to kiss.

"Good-bye," he said again; "take care of yourself." And he went out, not looking towards the figure on the bench. He drove home by way of Hammersmith, that he might stop at a place he knew of and tell them to send her in two dozen of their best Burgundy. She must want picking-up sometimes! Only in Richmond Park did he remember that he had gone up to order himself some boots, and was surprised that he could have had so paltry an idea.

III

THE little spirits of the past which throng an old man's days had never pushed their faces up to his so seldom as in the seventy hours elapsing before Sunday came. The spirit of the future, with the charm of the unknown, put up her lips instead. Old Jolyon was not restless now, and paid no visits to the log, because she was *coming to lunch*. There is wonderful finality about a meal; it removes a world of doubts, for no one misses meals except for reasons beyond control. He played many games with Holly on the lawn, pitching them up to her who was batting so as to be ready to bowl to Jolly in the holidays. For she was not a Forsyte, but Jolly was—and Forsytes always bat, until they have re-signed and reached the age of eighty-five. The dog Balthasar, in attend-ance, lay on the ball as often as he could, and the page-boy fielded, till his face was like the harvest moon. And because the time was getting shorter, each day was longer and more golden than the last. On Friday night he took a liver pill, his side hurt him rather, and though it was not the liver side, there is no remedy like that. Anyone telling him that he had found a new excitement in life and that excitement was not good for him, would have been met by one of those steady and rather defiant looks of his deep-set iron-grey eyes, which seemed to say: 'I know my own business best.' He always had and always would.

On Sunday morning, when Holly had gone with her governess to church, he visited the strawberry beds. There, accompanied by the dog Balthasar, he examined the plants narrowly and succeeded in finding at least two dozen berries which were really ripe. Stooping was not good for him, and he became very dizzy and red in the forehead. Having placed the strawberries in a dish on the dining-table, he washed his hands and bathed his forehead with eau de Cologne. There, before the mirror, it occurred to him that he was thinner. What a 'threadpaper' he had been when he was young! It was nice to be slim—he could not bear a fat chap; and yet perhaps his cheeks were *too* thin! She was to arrive by train at half-past twelve and walk up, entering from the road past Drage's farm at the far end of the coppice. And, having looked into June's room to see that there was hot water ready, he set forth to meet her, leisurely, for his heart was beating. The air smelled sweet, larks sang, and the Grand Stand at Epsom was visible. A perfect day! On just such a one, no doubt, six years ago, Soames had brought young Bosinney down with him to look at the site before they began to build. It was Bosinney who had pitched on the exact spot for the house—as June had often told him. In these days he was thinking much about that young fellow, as if his spirit were really haunting the field of his last work, on the chance of seeing—her. Bosinney—the one man who had possessed her heart, to whom she had given her whole self with rapture! At his age one could not, of course, imagine such things, but there stirred in him a queer vague aching—as it were the ghost of an impersonal jealousy; and a feeling, too, more generous, of pity for that love so early lost. All over in a few poor months! Well, well! He looked at his watch before entering the coppice—only a quarter past, twenty-five minutes to wait! And then, turning the corner of the path, he saw her exactly where he had seen her the first time, on the log; and realised that she must have come by the earlier train to sit there alone for a couple of hours at least. Two hours of her society—missed! What memory could make that log so dear to her? His face showed what he was thinking, for she said at once:

"Forgive me, Uncle Jolyon; it was here that I first knew."

"Yes, yes; there it is for you whenever you like. You're looking a little Londony; you're giving too many lessons."

That she should have to give lessons worried him. Lessons to a parcel of young girls thumping out scales with their thick fingers!

"Where do you go to give them?" he asked.

"They're mostly Jewish families, luckily."

Old Jolyon stared; to all Forsytes Jews seem strange and doubtful.

"They love music, and they're very kind."

"They had better be, by George!" He took her arm—his side always hurt him a little going uphill—and said:

"Did you ever see anything like those buttercups? They came like that in a night."

Her eyes seemed really to fly over the field, like bees after the flowers and the honey. "I wanted you to see them—wouldn't let them turn the cows in yet." Then, remembering that she had come to talk about Bosinney, he pointed to the clock-tower over the stables:

"I expect *he* wouldn't have let me put that there—had no notion of time, if I remember."

But, pressing his arm to her, she talked of flowers instead, and he knew it was done that he might not feel she came because of her dead lover.

"The best flower I can show you," he said, with a sort of triumph, "is my little sweet. She'll be back from Church directly. There's something about her which reminds me a little of you," and it did not seem to him peculiar that he had put it thus, instead of saying: "There's something about you which reminds me a little of her." Ah! And here she was!

Holly, followed closely by her elderly French governess, whose digestion had been ruined twenty-two years ago in the siege of Strasbourg, came rushing towards them from under the oak tree. She stopped about a dozen yards away, to pat Balthasar and pretend that this was all she had in her mind. Old Jolyon who knew better, said:

"Well, my darling, here's the lady in grey I promised you."

Holly raised herself and looked up. He watched the two of them with a twinkle, Irene smiling, Holly beginning with grave inquiry, passing into a shy smile too, and then to something deeper. She had a sense of beauty, that child—knew what was what! He enjoyed the sight of the kiss between them.

"Mrs. Heron, Mam'zelle Beauce. Well, Mam'zelle—good sermon?"

For, now that he had not much more time before him, the only part of the service connected with this world absorbed what interest in church remained to him. Mam'zelle Beauce stretched out a spidery hand clad in a black kid glove—she had been in the best families—and the rather sad eyes of her lean yellowish face seemed to ask: "Are you well-brrred?" Whenever Holly or Jolly did anything unpleasing to her —a not uncommon occurrence—she would say to them: "The little Tayleurs never did that—they were such well-brred little children." Jolly hated the little Tayleurs; Holly wondered dreadfully how it was she fell so short of them. 'A thin rum little soul,' old Jolyon thought her —Mam'zelle Beauce.

Luncheon was a successful meal, the mushrooms which he himself had picked in the mushroom house, his chosen strawberries, and another bottle of the Steinberg cabinet filled him with a certain aromatic spirituality, and a conviction that he would have a touch of eczema tomorrow. After lunch they sat under the oak tree drinking Turkish coffee. It was no matter of grief to him when Mademoiselle Beauce withdrew to write her Sunday letter to her sister, whose future had been endangered in the past by swallowing a pin—an event held up daily in warning to the children to eat slowly and digest what they had eaten. At the foot of the bank, on a carriage rug, Holly and the dog Balthasar teased and loved each other, and in the shade old Jolyon with his legs crossed and his cigar luxuriously savoured, gazed at Irene sitting in the swing. A light, vaguely swaying, grey figure with a fleck of sunlight here and there upon it, lips just opened, eyes dark and soft under lids a little drooped. She looked content; surely it did her good to come and see him! The selfishness of age had not set its proper grip on him, for he could still feel pleasure in the pleasure of others, realising that what he wanted, though much, was not quite all that mattered.

"It's quiet here," he said; "you mustn't come down if you find it dull. But it's a pleasure to see you. My little sweet's is the only face which gives me any pleasure, except yours."

From her smile he knew that she was not beyond liking to be appreciated, and this reassured him. "That's not humbug," he said. "I never told a woman I admired her when I didn't. In fact I don't know when I've told a woman I admired her, except my wife in the old days; and wives are funny." He was silent, but resumed abruptly:

"She used to expect me to say it more often than I felt it, and there we were." Her face looked mysteriously troubled, and, afraid that he had said something painful, he hurried on:

"When my little sweet marries, I hope she'll find someone who knows what women feel. I shan't be here to see it, but there's too much topsy-turvydom in marriage; I don't want her to pitch up against that." And, aware that he had made bad worse, he added: "That dog *will* scratch."

A silence followed. Of what was she thinking, this pretty creature whose life was spoiled; who had done with love, and yet was made for love? Some day when he was gone, perhaps, she would find another mate—not so disorderly as that young fellow who had got himself run over. Ah! but her husband?

"Does Soames never trouble you?" he asked.

She shook her head. Her face had closed up suddenly. For all her softness there was something irreconcilable about her. And a glimpse of light on the inexorable nature of sex antipathies strayed into a brain which, belonging to early Victorian civilisation—so much older than this of his old age—had never thought about such primitive things.

"That's a comfort," he said. "You can see the Grand Stand to-day. Shall we take a turn round?"

Through the flower and fruit garden, against whose high outer walls peach trees and nectarines were trained to the sun, through the stables, the vinery, the mushroom house, the asparagus beds, the rosery, the summer house, he conducted her—even into the kitchen garden to see the tiny green peas which Holly loved to scoop out of their pods with her finger, and lick up from the palm of her little brown hand. Many delightful things he showed her, while Holly and the dog Balthasar danced ahead, or came to them at intervals for attention. It was one of the happiest afternoons he had ever spent, but it tired him and he was glad to sit down in the music room and let her give him tea. A special little friend of Holly's had come in—a fair child with short hair like a boy's. And the two sported in the distance, under the stairs, on the stairs, and up in the gallery. Old Jolyon begged for Chopin. She played studies, mazurkas, waltzes, till the two children, creeping near, stood at the foot of the piano—their dark and golden heads bent forward, listening. Old Jolyon watched.

"Let's see you dance, you two!"

Shyly, with a false start, they began. Bobbing and circling, earnest, not very adroit, they went past and past his chair to the strains of that waltz. He watched them and the face of her who was was playing turned smiling towards those little dancers thinking: 'Sweetest picture I've seen for ages.' A voice said:

"Hollee! *Mais enfin—qu'est-ce que tu fais là—danser, le dimanche! Viens, donc!*"

But the children came close to old Jolyon, knowing that he would save them, and gazed into a face which was decidedly 'caught out.'

"Better the day, better the deed, Mam'zelle. It's all my doing. Trot along, chicks, and have your tea."

And, when they were gone, followed by the dog Balthasar, who took every meal, he looked at Irene with a twinkle and said:

"Well, there we are! Aren't they sweet? Have you any little ones among your pupils?"

"Yes, three—two of them darlings."

Pretty?"

"Lovely!"

Old Jolyon sighed; he had an insatiable appetite for the very young. "My little sweet," he said, "is devoted to music; she'll be a musician some day. You wouldn't give me your opinion of her playing, I suppose?"

"Of course I will."

"You wouldn't like——" but he stifled the words "to give her lessons." The idea that she gave lessons was unpleasant to him; yet it would mean that he would see her reguluarly. She left the piano and came over to his chair.

"I would like, very much; but there is—June. When are they coming back?"

Old Jolyon frowned. "Not till the middle of next month. What does that matter?"

"You said June had forgiven me; but she could never forget, Uncle Jolyon."

Forget! She *must* forget, if he wanted her to.

But as if answering, Irene shook her head. "You know she couldn't; one doesn't forget."

Always that wretched past! And he said with a sort of vexed finality: "Well, we shall see."

He talked to her an hour or more, of the children, and a hundred little things, till the carriage came round to take her home. And when she had gone he went back to his chair, and sat there smoothing his face and chin, dreaming over the day.

That evening after dinner he went to his study and took a sheet of paper. He stayed for some minutes without writing, then rose and stood under the masterpiece 'Dutch Fishing Boats at Sunset.' He was not thinking of that picture, but of his life. He was going to leave her something in his Will; nothing could so have stirred the stilly deeps of thought and memory. He was going to leave her a portion of his wealth, of his aspirations, deeds, qualities, work—all that had made that wealth; going to leave her, too, a part of all he had missed in life, by his sane and steady pursuit of wealth. Ah! What had he missed? 'Dutch Fishing Boats' responded blankly; he crossed to the French window, and drawing the curtain aside, opened it. A wind had got up, and one of last year's oak leaves which had somehow survived the gardener's brooms, was dragging itself with a tiny clicking rustle along the stone terrace in the twilight. Except for that it was very quiet out there, and he could smell the heliotrope watered not long since. A bat went by. A bird uttered its last 'cheep.' And right above the oak tree the first star shone. Faust in the opera had bartered his soul for some fresh years of youth. Morbid notion! No such bargain was possible, that was *real* tragedy! No making oneself new again for love or life or anything. Nothing left to do but enjoy beauty afar off while you could, and leave it something in your Will. But how much? And, as if he could not make that calculation looking out into the mild freedom of the country night, he turned back and went up to the chimney-piece. There were his pet bronzes—a Cleopatra with the asp at her breast; a Socrates; a greyhound playing with her puppy; a strong man reining in some horses. 'They last!' he thought, and a pang went through his heart. They had a thousand years of life before them!

'How much?' Well! enough at all events to save her getting old before her time, to keep the lines out of her face as long as possible, and grey from soiling that bright hair. He might live another five years. She would be well over thirty by then. 'How much?' She had none of his blood in her! In loyalty to the tenor of his life for forty years and more, ever since he married and founded that mysterious thing, a family, came this warning thought—None of his blood, no right to anything! It was a luxury then, this notion. An extravagance, a petting of an old man's whim, one of those things done in dotage. His real future was vested in those who had his blood, in whom he would live on when he was gone. He turned away from the bronzes and stood looking at the old leather chair in which he had sat and smoked so many hundreds of cigars. And suddenly he seemed to see her sitting there in her grey dress, fragrant, soft, dark-eyed, graceful, looking up at him. Why! She cared nothing for him, really; all she cared for was that lost lover of hers. But she was there, whether she would or no, giving him pleasure with her beauty and grace. One had no right to inflict an old man's company, no right to ask her down to play to him and let him look at her—for no reward! Pleasure must be paid for in this world. 'How much?' After all, there was plenty; his son and his three grandchildren would never miss that little lump. He had made it himself, nearly every penny; he could leave it where he liked, allow himself this little pleasure. He went back to the bureau. 'Well, I'm going to,' he thought, 'let them think what they like. I'm going to!' And he sat down.

'How much?' Ten thousand, twenty thousand—how much? If only with his money he could buy one year, one month of youth. And startled by that thought, he wrote quickly:

'DEAR HERRING,—Draw me a codicil to this effect: "I leave to my niece Irene Forsyte, born Irene Heron, by which name she now goes, fifteen thousand pounds free of legacy duty."

'Yours faithfully,
'JOLYON FORSYTE.'

When he had sealed and stamped the envelope, he went back to the window and drew in a long breath. It was dark, but many stars shone now.

IV

HE woke at half-past two, an hour which long experience had taught him brings panic intensity to all awkward thoughts. Experience had also taught him that a further waking at the proper hour of eight showed the folly of such panic. On this particular morning the thought which gathered rapid momentum was that if he became ill, at his age not improbable, he would not see her. From this it was but a step to realisation that he would be cut off, too, when his son and June returned from Spain. How could he justify desire for the company of one who had stolen—early morning does not mince words—June's lover? That lover was dead; but June was a stubborn little thing; warm-hearted, but stubborn as wood, and—quite true—not one who forgot! By the middle

of next month they would be back. He had barely five weeks left to enjoy the new interest which had come into what remained of his life.
Darkness showed up to him absurdly clear the nature of his feeling.
Admiration for beauty—a craving to see that which delighted his eyes.
Preposterous, at his age! And yet—what other reason was there for asking June to undergo such painful reminder, and how prevent his son
and his son's wife from thinking him very queer? He would be reduced
to sneaking up to London, which tired him; and the least indisposition
would cut him off even from that. He lay with eyes open, setting his jaw
against the prospect, and calling himself an old fool, while his heart
beat loudly, and then seemed to stop beating altogether. He had seen the
dawn lighting the window chinks, heard the birds chirp and twitter, and
the cocks crow, before he fell asleep again, and awoke tired but sane.
Five weeks before he need bother, at his age an eternity! But that early
morning panic had left its mark, had slightly fevered the will of one
who had always had his own way. He would see her as often as he
wished! Why not go up to town and make that codicil at his solicitor's
instead of writing about it; she might like to go to the opera! But, by
train, for he would not have that fat chap Beacon grinning behind his
back. Servants were such fools; and, as likely as not, they had known all
the past history of Irene and young Bosinney—servants knew everything, and suspected the rest. He wrote to her that morning:

"MY DEAR IRENE,—I have to be up in town to-morrow. If you would
like to have a look in at the opera, come and dine with me quietly . . ."

But where? It was decades since he had dined anywhere in London
save at his Club or at a private house. Ah! that new-fangled place close
to Covent Garden . . .

"Let me have a line to-morrow morning to the Piedmont Hotel
whether to expect you there at 7 o'clock.
                    "Yours affectionately,
                              "JOLYON FORSYTE."

She would understand that he just wanted to give her a little pleasure;
for the idea that she should guess he had this itch to see her was instinc-

327

tively unpleasant to him; it was not seemly that one so old should go out of his way to see beauty, especially in a woman.

The journey next day, short though it was, and the visit to his lawyer's, tired him. It was hot too, and after dressing for dinner he lay down on the sofa in his bedroom to rest a little. He must have had a sort of fainting fit, for he came to himself feeling very queer; and with some difficulty rose and rang the bell. Why! it was past seven! And there he was and she would be waiting. But suddenly the dizziness came on again, and he was obliged to relapse on the sofa. He heard the maid's voice say:

"Did you ring, sir?"

"Yes, come here"; he could not see her clearly, for the cloud in front of his eyes. "I'm not well, I want some sal volatile."

"Yes, sir." Her voice sounded frightened.

Old Jolyon made an effort.

"Don't go. Take this message to my niece—a lady waiting in the hall —a lady in grey. Say Mr. Forsyte is not well—the heat. He is very sorry; if he is not down directly, she is not to wait dinner."

When she was gone, he thought feebly: 'Why did I say a lady in grey—she may be in anything. Sal volatile!' He did not go off again, yet was not conscious of how Irene came to be standing beside him, holding smelling salts to his nose, and pushing a pillow up behind his head. He heard her say anxiously: "Dear Uncle Jolyon, what is it?" was dimly conscious of the soft pressure of her lips on his hand; then drew a long breath of smelling salts, suddenly discovered strength in them, and sneezed.

"Ha!" he said, "it's nothing. How did you get here? Go down and dine—the tickets are on the dressing-table. I shall be all right in a minute."

He felt her cool hand on his forehead, smelled violets, and sat divided between a sort of pleasure and a determination to be all right.

"Why! You *are* in grey!" he said. "Help me up." Once on his feet he gave himself a shake.

"What business had I to go off like that!" And he moved very slowly to the glass. What a cadaverous chap! Her voice, behind him, murmured:

"You mustn't come down, Uncle; you must rest."

"Fiddlesticks! A glass of champagne'll soon set me to rights. I can't have you missing the opera."

But the journey down the corridor was troublesome. What carpets they had in these new-fangled places, so thick that you tripped up in them at every step! In the lift he noticed how concerned she looked, and said with the ghost of a twinkle:

"I'm a pretty host."

When the lift stopped he had to hold firmly to the seat to prevent its slipping under him; but after soup and a glass of champagne he felt much better, and began to enjoy an infirmity which had brought such solicitude into her manner towards him.

"I should have liked you for a daughter," he said suddenly; and watching the smile in her eyes, went on:

"You mustn't get wrapped up in the past at your time of life; plenty of that when you get to my age. That's a nice dress—I like the style."

"I made it myself."

Ah! A woman who could make herself a pretty frock had not lost her interest in life.

"Make hay while the sun shines," he said; "and drink that up. I want to see some colour in your cheeks. We mustn't waste life; it doesn't do. There's a new Marguerite to-night; let's hope she won't be fat. And Mephisto—anything more dreadful than a fat chap playing the Devil I can't imagine."

But they did not go to the opera after all, for in getting up from dinner the dizziness came over him again, and she insisted on his staying quiet and going to bed early. When he parted from her at the door of the hotel, having paid the cabman to drive her to Chelsea, he sat down again for a moment to enjoy the memory of her words: "You *are* such a darling to me, Uncle Jolyon!" Why! Who wouldn't be! He would have liked to stay up another day and take her to the Zoo, but two days running of him would bore her to death. No, he must wait till next Sunday; she had promised to come then. They would settle those lessons for Holly, if only for a month. It would be something. That little Mam'zelle Beauce wouldn't like it, but she would have to lump it. And crushing his old opera hat against his chest he sought the lift.

He drove to Waterloo next morning, struggling with a desire to say: 'Drive me to Chelsea.' But his sense of proportion was too strong.

Besides, he still felt shaky, and did not want to risk another aberration like that of last night, away from home. Holly, too, was expecting him, and what he had in his bag for her. Not that there was any cupboard love in his little sweet—she was a bundle of affection. Then, with the rather bitter cynicism of the old, he wondered for a second whether it was not cupboard love which made Irene put up with him. No, she was not that sort either. She had, if anything, too little notion of how to butter her bread, no sense of property, poor thing! Besides, he had not breathed a word about that codicil, nor should he—sufficient unto the day was the good thereof.

In the victoria which met him at the station Holly was restraining the dog Balthasar, and their caresses made 'jubey' his drive home. All the rest of that fine hot day and most of the next he was content and peaceful, reposing in the shade, while the long lingering sunshine showered gold on the lawns and the flowers. But on Thursday evening at his lonely dinner he began to count the hours; sixty-five till he would go down to meet her again in the little coppice, and walk up through the fields at her side. He had intended to consult the doctor about his fainting fit, but the fellow would be sure to insist on quiet, no excitement and all that; and he did not mean to be tied by the leg, did not want to be told of an infirmity—if there were one, could not afford to hear of it at his time of life, now that this new interest had come. And he carefully avoided making any mention of it in a letter to his son. It would only bring them back with a run! How far this silence was due to consideration for their pleasure, how far to regard for his own, he did not pause to consider.

That night in his study he had just finished his cigar and was dozing off, when he heard the rustle of a gown, and was conscious of a scent of violets. Opening his eyes he saw her, dressed in grey, standing by the fireplace, holding out her arms. The odd thing was that, though those arms seemed to hold nothing, they were curved as if round someone's neck, and her own neck was bent back, her lips open, her eyes closed. She vanished at once, and there were the mantelpiece and his bronzes. But those bronzes and the mantelpiece had not been there when she was, only the fireplace and the wall! Shaken and troubled, he got up. 'I must take medicine,' he thought; 'I can't be well.' His heart beat too fast, he had an asthmatic feeling in the chest; and going to the window, he opened it to get some air. A dog was barking far away, one of the dogs at Gage's farm no doubt, beyond the coppice. A beautiful still night, but dark. 'I dropped off,' he mused, 'that's it! And yet I'll swear my eyes were open!' A sound like a sigh seemed to answer.

"What's that?" he said sharply, "who's there?"

Putting his hand to his side to still the beating of his heart, he stepped out on the terrace. Something soft scurried by in the dark. "Shoo!" It was that great grey cat. 'Young Bosinney was like a great cat!' he thought. 'It was him in there, that she—that she was— He's got her still!' He walked to the edge of the terrace, and looked down into the darkness; he could just see the powdering of the daisies on the unmown lawn. Here to-day and gone to-morrow! And there came the moon, who saw all, young and old, alive and dead, and didn't care a dump! His own turn soon. For a single day of youth he would give what was left! And he turned again towards the house. He could see the windows of the night nursery up there. His little sweet would be asleep. 'Hope that dog won't wake her!' he thought. 'What is it makes us love, and makes us die! I must go to bed.'

And across the terrace stones, growing grey in the moonlight, he passed back within.

V

How should an old man live his days if not in dreaming of his well-spent past? In that, at all events, there is no agitating warmth, only pale winter sunshine. The shell can withstand the gentle beating of the dynamos of memory. The present he should distrust; the future shun. From beneath thick shade he should watch the sunlight creeping at his toes. If there be sun of summer, let him not go out into it, mistaking it for the Indian-summer sun! Thus peradventure he shall decline softly, slowly, imperceptibly, until impatient Nature clutches his wind-pipe and he gasps away to death some early morning before the world is aired, and they put on his tombstone: 'In the fulness of years!' yea! If he preserve his principles in perfect order, a Forsyte may live long after he is dead.

Old Jolyon was conscious of all this, and yet there was in him that which transcended Forsyteism. For it is written that a Forsyte shall not love beauty more than reason; nor his own way more than his own health. And something beat within him in these days that with each throb fretted at the thinning shell. His sagacity knew this, but it knew too that he could not stop that beating, nor would if he could. And yet, if you had told him he was living on his capital, he would have stared you down. No, no; a man did not live on his capital; it was not done! The shibboleths of the past are ever more real than the actualities of the present. And he, to whom living on one's capital had always been anathema, could not have borne to have applied so gross a phrase to his own case. Pleasure is healthful; beauty good to see; to live again in the youth of the young—and what else on earth was he doing!

Methodically, as had been the way of his whole life, he now arranged his time. On Tuesdays he journeyed up to town by train; Irene came and dined with him. And they went to the opera. On Thursdays he drove to town, and, putting that fat chap and his horses up, met her in Kensington Gardens, picking up the carriage after he had left her, and driving home again in time for dinner. He threw out the casual formula that he had business in London on those two days. On Wednesdays and Saturdays she came down to give Holly music lessons. The greater the pleasure he took in her society, the more scrupulously fastidious he became, just a matter-of-fact and friendly uncle. Not even in feeling, really, was he more—for, after all, there was his age. And yet, if she were late he fidgeted himself to death. If she missed coming, which happened twice, his eyes grew sad as an old dog's, and he failed to sleep.

And so a month went by—a month of summer in the fields, and in his heart, with summer's heat and the fatigue thereof. Who could have believed a few weeks back that he would have looked forward to his son's and his grand-daughter's return with something like dread! There was such a delicious freedom, such recovery of that independence a man enjoys before he founds a family, about these weeks of lovely weather, and this new companionship with one who demanded nothing, and remained always a little unknown, retaining the fascination of mystery. It was like a draught of wine to him who has been drinking water for so long that he has almost forgotten the stir wine brings to his blood, the narcotic to his brain. The flowers were coloured brighter, scents and music and the sunlight had a living value—were no longer mere reminders of past enjoyment. There was something now to live for which stirred him continually to anticipation. He lived in that, not in retrospection; the difference is considerable to any so old as he. The pleasures of the table, never of much consequence to one naturally abstemious, had lost all value. He ate little, without knowing what he ate; and every day grew thinner and more worn to look at. He was again a 'threadpaper'; and to this thinned form his massive forehead, with hollows at the temples, gave more dignity than ever. He was very well aware that he ought to see the doctor, but liberty was too sweet. He could not afford to pet his frequent shortness of breath and the pain in his side at the expense of liberty. Return to the vegetable existence he had led among the agricultural journals with the life-size mangold wurzels, before this new attraction came into his life—no! He exceeded his allowance of cigars. Two a day had always been his rule. Now he smoked three and sometimes four—a man will when he is filled with the creative spirit. But very often he thought: 'I must give up smoking, and coffee; I must give up rattling up to town.' But he did not; there was no one in any sort of authority to notice him, and this was a priceless boon. The servants perhaps wondered, but they were, naturally, dumb. Mam'zelle Beauce was too concerned with her own digestion, and too 'well-brrred' to make personal allusions. Holly had not as yet an eye for the relative appearance of him who was her plaything and her god. It was left for Irene herself to beg him to eat more, to rest in the hot part of the day, to take a tonic, and so forth. But she did not tell him that she was the cause of his thinness—for one cannot see the havoc oneself is working. A man of eighty-five has no passions, but the Beauty which produces passion works on in the old way, till death closes the eyes which crave the sight of Her.

On the first day of the second week in July he received a letter from his son in Paris to say that they would all be back on Friday. This had always been more sure than Fate; but, with the pathetic improvidence given to the old, that they may endure to the end, he had never quite admitted it. Now he did, and something would have to be done. He had ceased to be able to imagine life without this new interest, but that which is not imagined sometimes exists, as Forsytes are perpetually finding to their cost. He sat in his old leather chair, doubling up the letter, and mumbling with his lips the end of an unlighted cigar. After to-morrow his Tuesday expeditions to town would have to be abandoned. He could still drive up, perhaps, once a week, on the pretext of seeing his man of business. But even that would be dependent on his health, for now they would begin to fuss about him. The lessons! The lessons must go on! She must swallow down her scruples, and June must put her feelings in her pocket. She had done so once, on the day after the news of Bosinney's death; what she had done then, she could surely do again now. Four years since that injury was inflicted on her—not Christian to keep the memory of old sores alive. June's will was strong, but his was stronger, for his sands were running out. Irene was soft, surely she would do this for him, subdue her natural shrinking, sooner than give him pain! The lessons must continue; for if they did, he was secure. And lighting his cigar at last, he began trying to shape out how to put it to them all, and explain this strange intimacy; how to veil and wrap it away from the naked truth—that he could not bear to be deprived of the sight of beauty. Ah! Holly! Holly was fond of her, Holly liked her lessons. She would save him—his little sweet! And with that happy thought he became serene, and wondered what he had been worrying about so fearfully. He must not worry, it left him always curiously weak, and as if but half present in his own body.

That evening after dinner he had a return of the dizziness, though he did not faint. He would not ring the bell, because he knew it would mean a fuss, and make his going-up on the morrow more conspicuous. When one grew old, the whole world was in conspiracy to limit freedom, and for what reason?—just to keep the breath in him a little longer. He did not want it at such cost. Only the dog Balthasar saw his lonely recovery from that weakness; anxiously watched his master go to the sideboard and drink some brandy, instead of giving him a biscuit. When at last old Jolyon felt able to tackle the stairs he went up to bed. And, though still shaky next morning, the thought of the evening sustained and strengthened him. It was always such a pleasure to give her a good dinner—he suspected her of undereating when she was alone; and, at the opera to watch her eyes glow and brighten, the unconscious smiling of her lips. She hadn't much pleasure, and this was the last time he would be able to give her that treat. But when he was packing his bag he caught himself wishing that he had not the fatigue of dressing for dinner before him, and the exertion, too, of telling her about June's return.

The opera that evening was 'Carmen,' and he chose the last *entr'acte* to break the news, instinctively putting it off till the latest moment. She took it quietly, queerly; in fact, he did not know how she had taken it before the wayward music lifted up again and silence became necessary. The mask was down over her face, that mask behind which so much went on that he could not see. She wanted time to think it over, no doubt! He would not press her, for she would be coming to give her lesson to-morrow afternoon, and he should see her then when she had got used to the idea. In the cab he talked only of the Carmen; he had seen better in the old days, but this one was not bad at all. When he took her hand to say good-night, she bent quickly forward and kissed his forehead.

"Good-bye, dear Uncle Jolyon, you have been so sweet to me."

"To-morrow then," he said. "Good-night. Sleep well." She echoed softly: "Sleep well!" and from the cab window, already moving away, he saw her face screwed round towards him, and her hand put out in a gesture which seemed to linger.

He sought his room slowly. They never gave him the same, and he could not get used to these 'spick-and-spandy' bedrooms with new furniture and grey-green carpets sprinkled all over with pink roses. He was wakeful and that wretched Habanera kept throbbing in his head. His French had never been equal to its words, but its sense he knew, if it had any sense, a gipsy thing—wild and unaccountable. Well, there *was* in life something which upset all your care and plans—something which made men and women dance to its pipes. And he lay staring from deep-sunk eyes into the darkness where the unaccountable held sway. You thought you had hold of life, but it slipped away behind you, took you by the scruff of the neck, forced you here and forced you there, and then, likely as not, squeezed life out of you! It took the very stars like that, he shouldn't wonder, rubbed their noses together and flung them apart; it had never done playing its pranks. Five million people in this great blunderbuss of a town, and all of them at the mercy of that Life-Force, like a lot of little dried peas hopping about on a board when you struck your fist on it. Ah, well! Himself would not hop much longer—a good long sleep would do him good!

How hot it was up here!—how noisy! His forehead burned; she had kissed it just where he always worried! just there—as if she had known the very place and wanted to kiss it all away for him. But, instead, her lips left a patch of grievous uneasiness. She had never spoken in quite

335

that voice, had never before made that lingering gesture or looked back at him as she drove away. He got out of bed and pulled the curtains aside; his room faced down over the river. There was little air, but the sight of that breadth of water flowing by, calm, eternal, soothed him. 'The great thing,' he thought, 'is not to make myself a nuisance. I'll think of my little sweet, and go to sleep.' But it was long before the heat and throbbing of the London night died out into the short slumber of the summer morning. And old Jolyon had but forty winks.

When he reached home next day he went out to the flower garden, and with the help of Holly, who was very delicate with flowers, gathered a great bunch of carnations. They were, he told her, for 'the lady in grey'—a name still bandied between them; and he put them in a bowl in his study where he meant to tackle Irene the moment she came, on the subject of June and future lessons. Their fragrance and colour would help. After lunch he lay down, for he felt very tired, and the carriage would not bring her from the station till four o'clock. But as the hour approached he grew restless, and sought the schoolroom, which over-looked the drive. The sun-blinds were down, and Holly was there with Mademoiselle Beauce, sheltered from the heat of a stifling July day, attending to their silkworms. Old Jolyon had a natural antipathy to these methodical creatures, whose heads and colour reminded him of ele-phants; who nibbled such quantities of holes in nice green leaves; and smelled, as he thought, horrid. He sat down on a chintz-covered window-seat whence he could see the drive, and get what air there was; and the dog Balthasar who appreciated chintz on hot days, jumped up beside him. Over the cottage piano a violet dust-sheet, faded almost to grey, was spread, and on it the first lavender, whose scent filled the room. In spite of the coolness here, perhaps because of that coolness the beat of life vehemently impressed his ebbed-down senses. Each sunbeam which came through the chinks had annoying brilliance; that dog smelled very strong; the lavender perfume was overpowering; those silkworms heaving up their grey green backs seemed horribly alive; and Holly's dark head bent over them had a wonderfully silk sheen. A marvellous cruelly strong thing was life when you were old and weak; it seemed to mock you with its multitude of forms and its beating vitality. He had never, till those last few weeks, had this curious feeling of being with one half of him eagerly borne along in the stream of life, and with the other half left on the bank, watching that helpless progress. Only when Irene was with him did he lose this double consciousness.

Holly turned her head, pointed with her little brown fist to the piano —for to point with a finger was not 'well-brrred'—and said slyly:

"Look at the 'lady in grey,' Gran; isn't she pretty to-day?"

Old Jolyon's heart gave a flutter, and for a second the room was clouded; then it cleared, and he said with a twinkle:

"Who's been dressing her up?"

"Mam'zelle."

"Hollee! Don't be foolish!"

That prim little Frenchwoman! She hadn't yet got over the music lessons being taken away from her. That wouldn't help. His little sweet was the only friend they had. Well, they were her lessons. And he shouldn't budge—shouldn't budge for anything. He stroked the warm wool on Balthasar's head, and heard Holly say: "When mother's home, there won't be any changes, will there? She doesn't like strangers, you know."

The child's words seemed to bring the chilly atmosphere of opposition about old Jolyon, and disclose all the menace to his newfound freedom. Ah! He would have to resign himself to being an old man at the mercy of care and love, or fight to keep this new and prized companionship; and to fight tired him to death. But his thin, worn face hardened into resolution till it appeared all jaw. This was his house, and his affair; he should not budge! He looked at his watch, old and thin like himself; he had owned it fifty years. Past four already! And kissing the top of Holly's head in passing, he went down to the hall. He wanted to get hold of her before she went up to give her lesson. At the first sound of wheels he stepped out into the porch, and saw at once that the victoria was empty.

"The train's in, sir; but the lady 'asn't come."

Old Jolyon gave him a sharp upward look, his eyes seemed to push away that fat chap's curiosity, and defy him to see the bitter disappointment he was feeling.

"Very well," he said, and turned back into the house. He went to his study and sat down, quivering like a leaf. What did this mean? She might have lost her train, but he knew well enough she hadn't. 'Good-bye, dear Uncle Jolyon.' Why 'Good-bye' and not 'Good-night'? And that hand of hers lingering in the air. And her kiss. What did it mean?

Vehement alarm and irritation took possession of him. He got up and began to pace the Turkey carpet, between window and wall. She was going to give him up! He felt it for certain—and he defenceless. An old man wanting to look on beauty! It was ridiculous! Age closed his mouth, paralysed his power to fight. He had no right to what was warm and living, no right to anything but memories and sorrow. He could not plead with her; even an old man has his dignity. Defenceless! For an hour, lost to bodily fatigue, he paced up and down, past the bowl of carnations he had plucked, which mocked him with its scent. Of all things hard to bear, the prostration of will-power is hardest, for one who has always had his way. Nature had got him in its net, and like an unhappy fish he turned and swam at the meshes, here and there, found no hole, no breaking point. They brought him tea at five o'clock, and a letter. For a moment hope beat up in him. He cut the envelope with the butter knife, and read:

"DEAREST UNCLE JOLYON,—I can't bear to write anything that may disappoint you, but I was too cowardly to tell you last night. I feel I can't come down and give Holly any more lessons, now that June is coming back. Some things go too deep to be forgotten. It has been such a joy to see you and Holly. Perhaps I shall still see you sometimes when you come up, though I'm sure it's not good for you; I can see you are tiring yourself too much. I believe you ought to rest quite quietly all this hot weather, and now you have your son and June coming back you will be so happy. Thank you a million times for all your sweetness to me.

"Lovingly your IRENE."

So, there it was! Not good for him to have pleasure and what he chiefly cared about; to try and put off feeling the inevitable end of all things, the approach of death with its stealthy, rustling footsteps. Not good for him! Not even she could see how she was his new lease of interest in life, the incarnation of all the beauty he felt slipping from him!

His tea grew cold, his cigar remained unlit; and up and down he paced, torn between his dignity and his hold on life. Intolerable to be squeezed out slowly, without a say of your own, to live on when your will was in the hands of others bent on weighing you to the ground with care and love. Intolerable! He would see what telling her the truth would do—the truth that he wanted the sight of her more than just a lingering on. He sat down at his old bureau and took a pen. But he could not write. There was something revolting in having to plead like this; plead that she should warm his eyes with her beauty. It was tantamount to confessing dotage. He simply could not. And instead, he wrote:

"I had hoped that the memory of old sores would not be allowed to stand in the way of what is a pleasure and a profit to me and my little grand-daughter. But old men learn to forego their whims; they are obliged to, even the whim to live must be foregone sooner or later; and perhaps the sooner the better.

"My love to you,

"JOLYON FORSYTE."

'Bitter,' he thought, 'but I can't help it. I'm tired.' He sealed and dropped it into the box for the evening post, and hearing it fall to the bottom, thought: 'There goes all I've looked forward to!'

That evening after dinner which he scarcely touched, after his cigar which he left half-smoked for it made him feel faint, he went very slowly upstairs and stole into the night-nursery. He sat down on the window-seat. A night-light was burning, and he could just see Holly's face, with one hand underneath the cheek. An early cockchafer buzzed in the Japanese paper with which they had filled the grate, and one of the horses in the stable stamped restlessly. To sleep like that child! He pressed apart two rungs of the venetian blind and looked out. The moon was rising, blood-red. He had never seen so red a moon. The woods and fields out there were dropping to sleep too, in the last glimmer of the summer light. And beauty, like a spirit, walked. 'I've had a long life,' he thought, 'the best of nearly everything. I'm an ungrateful chap; I've seen a lot of beauty in my time. Poor young Bosinney said I have a sense of beauty. There's a man in the moon to-night!' A moth went by, another, another. 'Ladies in grey!' He closed his eyes, A feeling that he would never open them again beset him; he let it grow, let himself sink; then, with a shiver, dragged the lids up. There was something wrong with him, no doubt, deeply wrong; he would have to have the doctor after all. It didn't much matter now! Into that coppice the moonlight would have crept; there would be shadows, and those shadows would be the

339

only things awake. No birds, beasts, flowers, insects; just the shadows—moving; 'Ladies in grey!' Over that log they would climb; would whisper together. She and Bosinney! Funny thought! And the frogs and little things would whisper too! How the clock ticked, in here! It was all eerie—out there in the light of that red moon; in here with the little steady night-light and the ticking clock and the nurse's dressing-gown hanging from the edge of the screen, tall, like a woman's figure. 'Lady in grey!' And a very odd thought beset him: Did she exist? Had she ever come at all? Or was she but the emanation of all the beauty he had loved and must leave so soon? The violet-grey spirit with the dark eyes and the crown of amber hair, who walks the dawn and the moonlight, and at blue-bell time? What was she, who was she, did she exist? He rose and stood a moment clutching the window-sill, to give him a sense of reality again; then began tiptoeing towards the door. He stopped at the foot of the bed; and Holly, as if conscious of his eyes fixed on her, stirred, sighed, and curled up closer in defence. He tiptoed on and passed out into the dark passage; reached his room, undressed at once, and stood before a mirror in his night-shirt. What a scarecrow—with temples fallen in, and thin legs! His eyes resisted his own image, and a look of pride came on his face. All was in league to pull him down, even his reflection in the glass, but he was not down—yet! He got into bed, and lay a long time without sleeping, trying to reach resignation, only too well aware that fretting and disappointment were very bad for him.

He woke in the morning so unrefreshed and strenghless that he sent for the doctor. After sounding him, the fellow pulled a face as long as your arm, and ordered him to stay in bed and give up smoking. That was no hardship; there was nothing to get up for, and when he felt ill, tobacco always lost its savour. He spent the morning languidly with the sun-blinds down, turning and re-turning *The Times*, not reading much, the dog Balthasar lying beside his bed. With his lunch they brought him a telegram, running thus: 'Your letter received coming down this afternoon will be with you at four-thirty. Irene.'

Coming down! After all! Then she did exist—and he was not deserted. Coming down! A glow ran through his limbs; his cheeks and forehead felt hot. He drank his soup, and pushed the tray-table away, lying very quiet until they had removed lunch and left him alone; but every now and then his eyes twinkled. Coming down! His heart beat fast, and then did not seem to beat at all. At three o'clock he got up and dressed deliberately, noiselessly. Holly and Mam'zelle would be in the schoolroom, and the servants asleep after their dinner, he shouldn't wonder. He opened his door cautiously, and went downstairs. In the hall the dog Balthasar lay solitary, and, followed by him, old Jolyon passed into his study and out into the burning afternoon. He meant to go down and meet her in the coppice, but felt at once he could not manage that in this heat. He sat down instead under the oak tree by the swing, and the dog Balthasar, who also felt the heat, lay down beside him. He sat there smiling. What a revel of bright minutes! What a hum of insects, and cooing of pigeons! It was the quintessence of a summer day. Lovely! And he was happy—happy as a sand-boy, whatever that might be. She was coming; she had not given him up! He had everything in life he wanted —except a little more breath, and less weight—just here! He would see her when she emerged from the fernery, come swaying just a little, a violet-grey figure passing over the daisies and dandelions and 'soldiers' on the lawn—the soldiers with their flowery crowns. He would not move, but she would come up to him and say: 'Dear Uncle Jolyon, I am sorry!' and sit in the swing and let him look at her and tell her that he had not been very well but was all right now; and that dog would lick her hand. That dog knew his master was fond of her; that dog was a good dog.

It was quite shady under the tree; the sun could not get at him, only make the rest of the world bright so that he could see the Grand Stand at Epsom away out there, very far, and the cows cropping the clover in the field and swishing at the flies with their tails. He smelled the scent of limes, and lavender. Ah! that was why there was such a racket of bees. They were excited—busy, as his heart was busy and excited. Drowsy, too, drowsy and drugged on honey and happiness; as his heart was drugged and drowsy. Summer—summer—they seemed saying; great bees and little bees, and the flies too!

The stable clock struck four; in half an hour she would here. He would have just one tiny nap, because he had had so little sleep of late; and then he would be fresh for her, fresh for youth and beauty, coming towards him across the sunlit lawn—lady in grey! And settling back in his chair he closed his eyes. Some thistledown came on what little air there was, and pitched on his moustache more white than itself. He did not know; but his breathing stirred it, caught there. A ray of sunlight struck through and lodged on his boot. A bumble-bee alighted and strolled on the crown of his Panama hat. And the delicious surge of slumber reached the brain beneath that hat, and the head swayed forward and rested on his breast. Summer—summer! So went the hum.

The stable clock struck the quarter past. The dog Balthasar stretched and looked up at his master. The thistledown no longer moved. The dog placed his chin over the sunlit foot. It did not stir. The dog withdrew his chin quickly, rose, and leaped on old Jolyon's lap, looked in his face, whined; then, leaping down, sat on his haunches, gazing up. And suddenly he uttered a long, long howl .

But the thistledown was still as death, and the face of his old master. Summer—summer—summer! The soundless footsteps on the grass! 1917.

To the Student

This study guide has been designed to assist you in reading and in analysis of this novel so that you will gain a full understanding of and complete enjoyment from *The Man of Property*.

The first thing you should do is read the introduction to this book for the necessary background on Galsworthy, his times, and his writings. After reading this carefully, you will be ready for this study guide, using it as your teacher and you may decide. It is divided into four main parts, arranged chapter by chapter.

The first section consists of suggestions for discussion, in the form of challenging questions and statements to make you think, to act as a good check-up on your reading comprehension, and to provoke lively discussion.

Following this part is the vocabulary section, consisting of three main types of words or expressions. Each key word or expression is italicized in context with page references to the novel for each. Some of these words are ones you should already know and consequently are not defined. Others are more difficult words that should be in your working vocabulary; definitions, explanations or synonyms are given for this group.

The vocabulary section also includes words and expressions that are primarily British and are so indicated (Br.), with explanations or definitions provided. Many British words, with the same meaning and just a minor difference in spelling from their American counterparts, are not listed in the vocabulary section at all because they are so easily identifiable. The words and expressions in all three classifications are intermingled in the vocabulary section, and are listed in the order of their occurrence in each chapter.

The great number of words listed in the vocabulary section is due in large part to the fact that Galsworthy (as well as the British in general) so often uses words with meanings that are uncommon and unfamiliar to most Americans. Should you encounter still other words with which you are unfamiliar, be sure to consult a dictionary.

After the vocabulary section comes the Glossary, a catch-all of words and expressions not included in the vocabulary section. This glossary includes unusual, archaic or obsolete words, geographical references, and classical as well as foreign words or expressions.

The fourth part of the chapter-by-chapter study guide material lists some topics for wirting; perhaps you and your classmates will suggest others. These topics for the most part will have general applications, but some are restricted to observations on *The Man of Property*.

In the final part of the Study Guide, you will find a brief section of general topics and questions for discussion together with theme suggestions for the novel as a whole.

The Man of Property lends itself admirably to discussion, as does any great book. You will benefit most from it when you have exchanged ideas, observations, and opinions about it with your classmates and with your teacher.

Study Guide

Study Guide

THE MAN OF PROPERTY

Part I • Chapter I

DISCUSSION

1. Very early in the novel, you get a glimpse of "Forsyteism." Exactly what is it?

2. What do you learn about each of the brothers? In what ways are they alike and different? Apply the same question to the sisters.

3. The Forsytes lack sympathy among themselves, but they are described as having tenacity. Show evidences of this characteristic in this chapter.

4. Explain the phrase, "so clear a reproduction of society in miniature," on page 3.

5. What is represented by Aunt Ann's "inflexible back"?

6. How is death involved in Forsyteism?

7. The Forsyte family is described as living "on their guard." What accounts for this attitude? What is a Forsyte's reaction to a premonition of danger?

8. What picture of Philip Bosinney is given before you actually meet him? What does Bosinney's "soft grey hat" reveal about the Forsytes?

9. What is the first indication that all things are not going well with the Forsytes?

10. Is it admiration, envy, or contempt that is represented in James' comment regarding Timothy's great concern for his own health? Why does James keep repeating, "This isn't real old Worcester"?

11. What is Aunt Ann's most precious form of property? Discuss her position in the family. Why is she so particularly fond of Soames?

12. The Forsytes support certain charitable institutions. Which ones? Why?

13. What underlies the doubtful feelings of the Forsytes for Irene?

14. How does the author build up the picture of the Forsyte family in this chapter?

VOCABULARY

PAGE

3   family in full *plumage:* finest clothes
has *gleaned* from a gathering: slowly collected or gathered
something of *patriarchal* life: ruled by older people
a *paragon* of tenacity: a model or pattern of excellence
plants less *fibrous*
almost *repugnant* prosperity: distasteful, objectionable
the highest *efflorescence:* blossoming, flowering
buff waistcoats: yellowish brown, medium or dark tan
under the *aegis:* protection, sponsorship
surrounded by the *effigies*

4   *encroachments* on their property: quiet and slow trespassings
The habitual *sniff:* contempt, disdain
perfection of *raiment*
exuberance of family cordiality
a *burnish* on their armour: brightness, gloss
his permanent *stoop*

5   his *sardonic* jests: sarcastic, sneering
a *prescriptive* right to it: claimed by long use and enjoyment
the very *hall-mark*

348

6 in *pallid* strenuous Archibald: pale, wan
foppishly determined Eustace: lightly, weakly
ineradicable in the family soul: irremovable, indestructible
a *connoisseur* of such
was *bandied* from mouth to mouth: passed back and forth
her *imperious* brisk way

7 feathers were *vulgar*
If he were *sleek*
commodious red-brick residence: roomy, spacious

8 *make a bolt of it* (Br): suddenly leave (from an uncomfortable
  situation)
disconcertingly inattentive
sidle round: move secretly or slyly
lips, *sensuous* and sweet
this *passive* goddess

9 *exigencies* of social intercourse: circumstances that need prompt
  action
husbanding her aged voice: saving, not overusing
Putting the bowl *pettishly* down: crossly, peevishly

10 a kind of *incarnation:* human being or representation
committed the *imprudence*
aquiline old face: curved like an eagle's beak
quailed before her: lost courage, shrank with fear

11 *dapper* clean-shaven man
a *preternaturally sage* schoolboy: (1) abnormally, supernaturally,
  (2) wise, scholarly
in his *dandified* way: foppish, exaggerated
aspirating the 'h': using excessive breath when sounding the letter
in good case (Br.): in good shape, healthy

12 faded from James's *visage*

13 The thought *rankled:* festered
of the finest *lawn:* thin or sheer linen or cotton fabric

14   that little *flibbertigibbet:* frivolous person (usually a woman)

15   with a *mottled* face
a *buttressed* outer wall: supported, propped up
round that *estuary:* where smaller streams meet a larger one
the *primeval* Forsytes
small beer (Br.): ordinary, insignificant

16   some primitive *sect*
James was *musing*

17   forgotten his *spleen:* ill-humor, bad temper
to notice *phenomena*

18   father was *cement* (Br.): in the cement business
Each felt *aggrieved:* wronged, spiritually injured

19   *Cantankerous* chap Roger: ill-natured, quarrelsome

GLOSSARY

PAGE

3   pampas grass: South American grass growing in large clumps

4   Dundreary whiskers: long side-whiskers separated by a shaven chin
moustache (Br.): mustache (Am. sp.)

6   *mot* (Fr.): word

10   three per cent. consols.: British government securities at 3% interest
Worcester: English porcelain or china

11   thousand a year: British pounds (money)
thread-papers: very thin people

14   lustre: luster (Am. sp.)—a decorative art object

15   Madeira: a rich, strong white wine

15 Dorset*shire* (Br.) : equivalent to the American county
yeomen (Br.) : independent farmers

16 Metropolis: London, the chief city of England

17 barouche: four-wheeled, horse-drawn carriage
rumpty-too (Br.) : ordinary, commonplace
Underground (Br.) : subway
'lunar': observation, measurement

Suggestions for written work

A character sketch of Old Jolyon
First impressions of the Forsytes
People, as others see them, using illustrations from this chapter

Part I • *Chapter* II

DISCUSSION

1. How does the study of Old Jolyon now have "its revenge" on him?

2. Why, according to Old Jolyon, had James "always been a poor thing"?

3. In regard to June and Bosinney, what is meant by "they must cut their coat according to the cloth"?

4. Why does Old Jolyon call Soames "a cold-blooded young beggar"? Has Soames shown in other instances to deserve this description?

5. What does the business about Old Jolyon and the cigar, on pages 22-23, tell you about him?

6. Why does Old Jolyon wonder if perhaps he had been too careful of himself?

7. Comment on Old Jolyon's rationalization of his being refused membership at the Hotch Potch Club. Does this seem to be typical Forsyteism?

8. Why are impersonal thoughts so foreign to a Forsyte?

9. What caused the break between Old Jolyon and his son? How long ago?

10. What lies behind the first sentence in Young Jolyon's letter to his father? Behind the entire letter?

11. Why does Old Jolyon consider the child's name, Jolly, to be cynical?

12. What, to Young Jolyon, is so ironical about his father and his property?

13. Discuss the last sentence of the chapter.

VOCABULARY

PAGE

20   was *wont* to say: accustomed, used
    had always been *a poor thing* (Br.): not very smart or clever

21   taking up with *'lame ducks':* poor or unfortunate people
    harum-scarum unpractical person: reckless, rash
    in her *slap-dash* way: hasty, careless
    getting into the swim: doing much better, making more money

22   plain as a *pikestaff:* the shaft of a weapon without fancy carving or decoration
    this was the most *poignant*

23   outliving his *palate:* sense of taste
    had *got out of his shares* (Br.): had sold his interest in the company
    felt a sharp *chagrin*
    succeeded splendidly *at the Bar:* as a lawyer or barrister
    a *racketty* chap: dissipated, unhealthy

24   *well-constituted* Clubmen: established, lifelong
    being *'in trade'* (Br.): a merchant or dealer
    stockbrokers, *solicitors:* British lawyers who handle cases but usually cannot plead cases in court

25 the *piebald* decoration: having patches of different colors
put a spoke in the wheel of their marriage: done something to stop
The grim *remorsefulness:* lack of pity, absence of regret

26 *run with the hare and hunt with the hounds:* play both sides in an
argument or situation
proof of *rupture*
from habitual *proximity*

27 elastic-sided *patent* boot: hard, glossy, smooth leather

28 a social *pariah:* outcast, person generally despised
by courtesy, our *surname*

29 had *surreptitiously* brought them: secretly, stealthily
Varsities had never wavered: British universities

31 the *introspective* look: examining one's own thought or feelings
"Middling", Old Jolyon answered: fair, so-so
sort of *water* you're in: trouble, difficulties

33 to *inscrutable* ends: incapable of being known or understood

GLOSSARY

PAGE

24 shillin': shilling (British coin equal to 1/20 of a British pound)
guineas: British gold coin with value of 21 shillings

25 whitebait: young herring

26 hansom: a low, two-wheeled covered vehicle drawn by one horse,
the driver on an elevated seat behind
stall: a more expensive theater seat separated from the others

28 cheque (Br.): check (Am. sp.)

29 Lloyd's: large British insurance company

29 holland suit: children's cotton or linen clothes first manufactured in Holland
   Eton: a very famous British school

31 sovereign: British gold coin worth 20 shillings

32 spirit-urn: a closed vessel or kettle to make hot drinks
   manoeuvre (Fr.): skillful operation, maneuver (Am. sp.)

Suggestions for written work

The old generation *vs.* the new
What is really important in life
Show Old Jolyon as "a man of property" and also his traits which contradict this description

Part I • *Chapter* III

DISCUSSION

1. What provided Swithin with his most lasting happiness?

2. How would you describe "a regular Juley" today?

3. What comments can you make on Nicholas' scheme for employment in the gold mines of Ceylon?

4. Why do Forsytes resist any sentimental craving for beauty? (Keep this in mind for consideration at the end of the novel)

5. Why is the saddle-of-mutton at dinner of prime importance to a Forsyte?

6. What Biblical quotation had Mr. Scoles, the minister, reversed in his sermon (p. 42)? Why was Mr. Scoles a "humbug" to Soames?

7. What lies behind Irene's statement: 'Abandon hope, all ye who enter here!'?

8. Why does the fact that June had ideas of her own alarm James? How does June's attitude toward money differ from her uncle's?

9. What is meant by the "Forsyte 'Change"? What does this show about the family?

10. Why does Irene resent and dislike her husband? Who gets blamed for this resentment? Why?

11. What is Galsworthy's purpose or effect in using indirect discourse for some of the conversation in this chapter?

VOCABULARY

PAGE

35 with *crewel-worked* seats: embroidered with a worsted yarn
gold and *onyx* buttons

36 would *swill* water: drink greedily or to excess, guzzle
small, painful *oscillation*

37 *sterile* within her

38 with a *mauve* front: pale, bluish purple
esteemed very *chaste:* simple, dignified
bringing to *fruition*
prematurely of *damp:* excessive moisture or gas
an *effete* woman: tired, worn out

39 soft *pallor* of her neck

40 silent, almost *morose*
subsidence into their seats
into its *primal* element: of first importance, fundamental
its *succulent* solidity: juicy, full of flavor

41 being *remonstrated* with
they're a *cranky* lot
without a *joint* (Br.): roast of meat
making little *ramparts*

42 voice like a *courtier's:* one in attendance at a royal palace

355

43   air of an *inquisitor*
      he *ejaculated*
      with inexpressible *mortification*

44   all that *naive dogmatism*
      exact *pecuniary* possibilities: financial, monetary
      not *cognisant* of phenomena: cognizant (Am. sp.)—aware, in-
         formed
      emporium had been established: commercial center, trading center

45   a little timely *foreclosure*
      most lucky *hits* (Br.): strokes of success, breaks
      looked *furtively* at Irene
      face of these *exhortations*

46   had not *scrupled* to say: hesitated, been reluctant
      a *contingency* had occurred: possibility or chance based on uncer-
         tainty
      diffused an atmosphere: spread, sent out

GLOSSARY

PAGE

35   ormolu: an alloy of copper and zinc used to imitate gold

36   West India: sauce for the ham

38   bombazine: dress fabric, formerly much used for mourning

40   *hors d'oeuvres* (Fr.): appetizers, small bits of food served before
      dinner.
      saddle of mutton: the whole upper back portion of a sheep

41   German (Br.): mutton raised in Germany and sold at high prices
      in England
      guinea-fowl: a domesticated bird valued for food and eggs

43   freehold: an estate held for life or passed on through inheritance

46 farthing: British coin valued at ¼ of a penny

47 *vieux jeu* (Fr.): old-fashioned

Suggestions for written work

Character sketch of Aunt Juley
Can a family member evaluate a family better than an outsider?
Women should be seen and not heard
The "Forsyte 'Change"

Part I • Chapter IV

DISCUSSION

1. How do you account for the love Soames feels for his wife? Why was he fearful of someone finding it out? Why could he not accept the possibility that she no longer loved him?

2. Why did Irene marry Soames? In attempting to understand Irene's lack of feeling for him, what does Soames fail to consider? What type of things does he consider?

3. Comment on Soames' taste in paintings. Why, looking at them now, does he derive less pleasure than usual?

4. What is Soames' chief motive in building the house? What are some of his secondary considerations?

5. Do the Forsytes show any sentimentality in any way? Discuss this.

6. Soames feels sure that he can get the best of Bosinney in the deal on the house. Is this consistent with his character? Why?

7. What lies behind the unpleasant feeling Soames feels as he watches Bosinney? It disturbed Soames greatly that Bosinney, not he, has picked the site for the new house. Why?

VOCABULARY

PAGE

49 *manifestly* waiting for him: evidently, obviously

50 *adroitly* taking advantage
    with the dainty *capriciousness:* changing of mind for no apparent
      reason
    till it is *malleable:* adaptable, easily managed
    its *interminable* streets

51 *imperturbable,* enforced composure

52 *precluded* the employment: eliminated, removed
    a bit up in the air: having unusual ideas, extreme in thinking
    Soames reflected, *complacently*

53 the names and *epitaphs*
    church was *inexplicable*

54 though these *eccentricities*

55 road across a *warren:* a place where rabbits live
    Tussocks of feathery grass: tufts of grass or twigs
    a line of *downs* (Br.): small hills
    grizzled beard
    sorry if you *go off* (Br.): change your mind, don't buy

56 felt his spirit *daunted:* discouraged, dismayed

57 *Thistledown* floated round: feathery part of a dandelion
    serenity of the *ether:* clear sky, heavens
    caught the *promontories:* high points, projections
    build you a *teaser* here (Br.): something temptingly attractive

58 *overborne* his own decision: overruled, prevailed over

GLOSSARY

PAGE

53   swells (Br.): rich, elegant people

56   bracken (Br.): a large fern or clump of ferns

57   copse (Br.): thicket or grove of small trees (also "coppice")

Suggestions for written work

The effect of circumstances on a person's attitude
Is sentimentality in a person a bad thing?
Class distinctions
An analysis of the personalities of Soames and Bosinney in the light of
    Bosinney getting his way in the land-site dispute

Part I • Chapter V

DISCUSSION

1. Explain the title of this chapter. Discuss the second sentence in the
    third paragraph.

2. What essential differences in the personalities and characters of
    Soames and Irene are brought out in the early pages of this chapter?
    Of whose attitude toward the servants do you approve—Soames' or
    Irene's? Explain Soames' irritation at telling his wife about building
    a new home.

3. Soames' thoughts about his wife during dinner reveal more about
    himself than they do about Irene. What do you learn about the
    things bothering him at this time? Is Soames' attitude toward his
    wife realistic? How does Soames' feeling for his wife show an
    important flaw in the theory of property by which he lives?

4. What sentimental and illusory impressions has Soames absorbed from his reading? Can you name some novels that might have been among the group he had experienced?

5. Why does Irene show so little reaction to June's telling about Bosinney and the new house?

VOCABULARY

PAGE

59 A Forsyte *Ménage* (Fr.): household, family
filled with *fuchsias:* pink-purple flowers
with pink *hydrangeas:* large, showy, white flowers
parchment-coloured Japanese sunshade
two kinds of *fastidiousness:* daintiness, extreme carefulness
skin-like *immaculateness*
collar *unglossed*

60 like some *nymph*
woman had *gone to the wall:* lost the battle, been defeated
a conventional *superstructure*
play the *concertina:* a small accordion

62 had *imbibed* the belief: absorbed, received into the mind
Society *conjugal* problem: pertaining to marriage
perverse processes of Nature
It was an *axiom*

64 smoke at a *lady-bird:* ladybug

GLOSSARY

PAGE

59 First Empire and William Morris: styles of interior house decoration
Molière: French playwright (1622-1673)

62 savoury (Br.): savory (Am. sp.)—small, highly seasoned dish served at the end of a meal

360

Suggestions for written work

Account for the qualities in each that would have been attractive to the
other in a friendship between Irene and June.
What determines one person's opinion of another?
Can character be read from appearance?
Galsworthy's plot advancement

Part I • Chapter VI

DISCUSSION

1. When Aunt Ann heard the news of Soames' new house, she said,
"...it's rather .dangerous!" Exactly what does she mean?

2. What do you learn in this chapter about the route by which news
travels the Forsyte circuit?

3. What is meant about James in the line, "...his nose, like the nose
of a sheep, was fastened to the pastures on which he browsed"?

4. Discuss the relationship between James and his son, Soames. Is it
typically Forsytean? Contrast it with that between Old Jolyon and
Young Jolyon.

5. What is meant when James is described as the sanest man in
London?

6. Explain the last sentence in the first full paragraph on page 69,
beginning, "In him . . ."

7. Why is James so sure he would have a miserable time at the dinner
at Soames'? Describe James' attitude toward the family, and
distinguish in what ways his feeling seems deeper than that of the
others.

8. What effect does James' conversation with Irene have on him?

9. What do you learn about James in his continually stating that no

one ever tells him anything? What leads James to tell his wife that
things are not going well between Soames and Irene?

VOCABULARY

PAGE

66 *presaging* a rainy morrow: forecasting, foreshadowing
    with extreme *punctiliousness:* exactness, strictness

67 of whose *taciturnity*
    How *droll:* comical, amusingly queer
    waifs lying prone: children without homes or friends

68 *cheek by jowl:* cheek to cheek
    monotony of the *treadmill*
    ferule off the ground: metal tip on an umbrella

69 all his *'Jonah-isms':* actions or words that show a lack of respect
        for godly things
    Beneath the *adamant:* hardness, hard outward character
    shook his head *querulously:* peevishly, in a complaining manner
    young Street was *assagaied:* killed by a throwing spear of the
        African Kaffirs

70 *knell* of all prosperity
    influence of her *deference:* yielding, submission

71 not too *Frenchified* (Br.): rich in sauces and wine
    an excellent *liqueur*

74 *descanted* for half an hour: commented or talked at great length

GLOSSARY

PAGE

68 *Elysium* (Gr.): any place or state of perfect happiness

362

70   Baden-Baden: a health resort in Germany
     soirée (Fr.): an evening party

Suggestions for written work

The revelation of Irene's unusual inner strength
Character sketch of James. Compare him to Old Jolyon.

Part I • Chapter VII

DISCUSSION

1. What is Old Jolyon's "peccadillo"? Explain Old Jolyon's reflection that "new -fangled places were all humbug."

2. Why had no Forsyte entered St. John's Wood "without open disapproval and secret curiosity." What has driven Old Jolyon to it?

3. Old Jolyon does not like what he sees in Young Jolyon's house. What is the basic reason behind this? What lies behind Old Jolyon's reference to his son's family as "the enemy"?

4. What is Galsworthy's observation concerning the good in the Forsyte's way of life? Why does he call them and other members of the upper middle class "the core of the nation"? On the basis of the reasons he gives, do you agree with him?

5. Young Jolyon sees his father enjoying himself with his grandchildren. How do you account for his sudden desire to cut their pleasure short? To what in this whole episode does Old Jolyon think he has been false?

6. How does the youth in Old Jolyon's heart and his attitude toward the young serve to offer new hope at this point in his life?

7. Old Jolyon's butler wears a mustache. Why does this distress the other Forsytes?

8. Young Jo's wife remains somewhat of a mystery to the reader. What is suggested about her in this chapter?

9. Why does Old Jolyon hold in his heart a deep resentment toward society?

VOCABULARY

PAGE

75   Old Jolyon's *peccadillo:* small sin or offense
      had *taken a resolution:* made up his mind, determined what to do
      went to a *hydropathic:* a place that treats disease by the internal
          or external use of water, hydro-therapy
      bushes of the *acacias:* a tree or shrub native to warm regions

76   *funny little toad* (Br.): odd or unusual little person
      covered with *chintz*
      expressed it, *pokey:* small, cramped and shabby
      distempered rather a long time ago: painted with a certain type of
          paint, calcimined
      meandered a long crack

77   the *unostentatious* conduct
      offspring of a *liaison*
      tow-coloured hair: yellow, blond
      garden beds looked *'daverdy'* (Br.): withered, drooping
      smut-stained wall: the black powder of a fungus

78   *mesmerized* by this sight: hypnotized
      following her *cyclic* laws
      to the *treble* tongues

79   My wife's *not the thing today* (Br.): not feeling well
      a *ramshackle* lot: run-down, shabby

80   *basked* a crouching cat
      the *creepered trellis*
      was too *thin-skinned*

80 Society, *forsooth:* indeed (said sarcastically)

chattering *hags* and *jackanapes:* (1) evil and malicious old women, (2) impertinent and conceited men

to *ostracize* his son

the *backwater* of traffic: area of little movement of people on the road, back road

81 had been to *public schools:* endowed boarding school in England attended by the wealthy to prepare for entrance into English universities

the acknowledged *wag:* humorous person, joker

great polished *sideboard:* a piece of dining room furniture with shelves and drawers for table service

watched him, *feigning* sleep

rattling through his work: going quickly, moving rapidly

A *slug!:* slow moving animal

relentless and *stealthy*

unseemliness of being carried: improperness, impropriety

a piece of *chamois* leather: a goat-like European antelope

wine in the *decanters*

he appeared to *pore* over

was an old *buffer:* person of no importance

GLOSSARY

PAGE

81 *chef d'oeuvre* (Fr.): masterpiece

82 toureen (Br.): tureen (Am. sp.)—a large deep bowl from which soup is served at the table

Suggestions for written work

The Briton's idea of a great citizen

Qualities in a person that appeal to other people

Using Galsworthy's criteria for "the core of the nation," the British upper middle class just before the turn of the century, describe their counterparts in your own society

Part I • Chapter VIII

DISCUSSION

1. Do you agree with the value the Forsytes put on their "habitats"? Explain.

2. What similarities to the poet Byron might Bosinney's father have had?

3. What is explained about the Forsytes in Mrs. Small's statement: "We think—I mean Timothy thinks......"?

4. Why, at first, does Soames think that Bosinney's plans were made for an "odd" house? Is this a typical Forsyte reaction? Account for their dislike of "originality."

5. What did Bosinney mean by "In architecture, as in life, you'll get no respect without regularity"? Why does Soames think that architecture appears to have exhausted Bosinney's "regularity"?

6. Why does Bosinney state that Soames would not like to live in a house built for manufacturers? What are the specific reasons that Soames finally decided on the house?

7. What extended significance does the Forsyte family name take on in this chapter?

VOCABULARY

PAGE

83   without *habitats:* homes, abodes

to be an *anomaly:* something out of the ordinary

a private *annuity:* certain income at regular intervals usually for the life of the recipient

366

83 and *Byronic* tendencies: like those of the British poet, Lord Byron
(1788-1824)

84 all doing *capitally* (Br.): very well, excellently
in a *frock coat* suit: a man's close-fitting coat, usually double-
breasted, extending to the knees
quite an *original* (noun)
because they've no *method:* routine, set way of doing things
The good cause: the important thing

85 *out of countenance:* completely out of her mind and consideration

86 was instantly *compunctious:* regretful, remorseful
taking up her green *reticule:* small purse or bag
with little *mincing* steps

87 by a *gallery:* upper porch
You can swing a cat here: there's a great deal of room here
with decoration, *gimcracks:* useless trifles, showy things

88 look like a *barrack*
front door be sunk so that you may come up again (Br.): necessi-
tating a small flight of steps up to the inside door
made a *deprecating* movement: showing disapproval, protesting
his *innate* distrust
What the *deuce:* devil, dickens

89 He was *nonplussed:* completely puzzled, perplexed
nineteen to the dozen (Br.): rapidly and loud

90 a *chink* of sunshine: small ray or beam

GLOSSARY

PAGE

83 spirit case: a case for liquor

84 Indian Civil: British Civil Service in India

85 Barlow's extract of veal: medicine or tonic to improve health

Suggestions for written work

Narrow-mindedness, its cause and effect
Contrast Bosinney's living quarters with those of Swithin, described in
  Chapter 3.

Part I • *Chapter* IX

DISCUSSION

1. As Old Jolyon gazes at the body of Aunt Ann, what is on his mind?

2. Why does James show greater emotion than his brothers?

3. How do you account for the strong dislike between Soames and
    George?

4. At the funeral why does each man of the Forsyte family want to
    sit in order to hide "the emphatic blackness of his trousers"?

5. Galsworthy calls Aunt Ann's funeral "a proud pageant." Describe
    the qualities of pride and pageant evidenced by the gathering.

6. What is the Forsyte attitude toward death? How is this attitude
    related to their attitudes toward love, sentiment, and pain?

7. Explain the last paragraph on page 96, and also Galsworthy's state-
    ment about Aunt Ann: "She was spared the watching of the
    branches jut out beyond the point of balance."

8. How does Old Jolyon differ from the other Forsyte men when he
    takes his three nephews in his carriage after the burial? How do
    you explain his action?

9. At the end of the chapter, what two thoughts reveal Soames' self-
    interest?

VOCABULARY

PAGE

91   *prostrated* by the the blow
by the short *interregnum:* an interruption, interval

92   *counterpane* had been placed: bed quilt, coverlet
the *coif* banding the top: close-fitting band of cloth

93   they had no *gumption:* initiative, resourcefulness

94   who was sole *executor*
a *sallow,* fattish face: yellowish, sickly
that *incorrigible* commencement: cannot be corrected, unstoppable
something deeply *ingrained*
in men who *speculate:* engage in business involving risk
a carefully veiled *sprightliness:* gaiety, animation

95   bowing *precedence* to each other
settling his *stock:* collar, neck-cloth
casting an indirect *libation:* honoring words, a verbal toast

96   *diversity* of life

97   a woman, old, *angular:* bony, gaunt

98   some slow, *disintegrating* force

GLOSSARY

PAGE

92   gout: a disease characterized by painful inflammation of the joints

93   brougham: four-wheeled, closed carriage with the driver outside
imperial pint: a standard British liquid measure

94   claret: a red wine
R. S. V. P.: French abbreviation for *"Répondez s'il vous plaît"*,
meaning "Answer if you please."

369

95   *cortège* (Fr.) : procession, train of attendants

98   tram-line (Br.) : street-car line or track

Suggestions for written work

The effect of death
Keeping up appearances
The right to be different and its obligations
Pride goeth before a fall

Part II • Chapter 1

DISCUSSION

1. What goes through Soames' mind as he views the framework of his new house? What were the basic reasons behind the arguments between Soames and Boisinney over the cost of the "extras" for the house?

2. Irene seems cold-hearted to Soames. How do you account for this situation? Why was Mrs. Heron anxious to have her daughter married?

3. Why did Irene consent to marry Soames when she did not like him from the start? What do you learn about an agreement between Soames and Irene at the time of their marriage? Has Soames been true to this agreement?

4. Soames despises Bosinney. Why, then, does he at times feel baffled and ill at ease in his presence? Why is Bosinney so abrupt with Soames when the latter questions him about Irene's artistic qualities?

5. Acount for the "strange smile" on Irene's face in the last paragraph of the chapter.

VOCABULARY

PAGE

100 winter had been an *open* one

101 this not inconsiderable *discrepancy:* difference, inconsistency
to the use of *makeshifts*
to be off your bargain (Br.) : to break an agreement
make an open *breach*

102 an *ineffable* yearning: inexpressible, indescribable

103 an *unmitigated* bore: absolute, unqualified
acquaintance with *alacrity:* willingness, briskness
this desirable *consummation:* achievement, fulfillment

104 with her in an *embrasure:* an enlargement of a doorway or window
on the inside
an *enigma* to him
get an *illusive* look: unreal, deceptive
Soames smiled *superciliously:* scornfully, disdainfully

105 give him *askance* a look: out of the corner of the eye, sidelong

106 look of a *coquette:* flirt, one who tries to attract men's attention

Suggestions for written work

Parents determining their children's lives. Try to be objective.
From insignificance to importance. What happens to people, usually?

371

Part II • *Chapter* II

DISCUSSION

1. What is June's "treat" referred to in the title of this chapter? How does it disappoint her? What did June hope to gain by being antagonistic to everything said at the dinner party?

2. What lies behind Irene's interrupted remark: "If only it could always be spring!"

3. Account for the sneering smile on Soames' face as Bosinney and June leave the dinner party. What does Soames mean when he says, "I wish you luck!"?

4. Explain the statement on page 109: "New-lighted lamps were gaining mastery......"

5. What is the meaning of the paragraph on page 109 beginning, "Those countless figures..."

6. What lies behind Old Jolyon's statement that he had always known that June would have trouble with Bosinney? What does Old Jolyon mean when he says that Bosinney has no "method"?

VOCABULARY

PAGE

107 *swathed* round the neck
there's nothing coming (Br.): this is the last course of the dinner
with your *sweet* (Br.): dessert

108 Why can't we have the *Spanish* (Br.): olives from Spain rather than from France

109 *spurned* the pavement: kicked or treated with contempt (the horses were happy to be able to run)

he's a *poor stick* (Br.): poor actor

110 reward for her *subterfuge:* trick to avoid unpleasant consequences

112 with a foot on the *fender:* a screen or guard in front of a fireplace

a tone so *tremulous:* trembling, quavering

going to *jilt* her

his unerring *astuteness*

may not be a *scamp:* worthless fellow, rascal

he's a *queer fish:* odd person

as *glum* as a monkey

GLOSSARY

PAGE

107 charlotte: a pudding or dessert made of fruit and gelatin in a mold of bread, cake or graham crackers

Suggestions for written work

Obstinacy and its effects

The I-knew-it-all-the-time person and his popularity

Part II • *Chapter* III

DISCUSSION

1. Discuss the statement on page 114 that Swithin "looked too primeval for a Forsyte." What does Swithin mean by "....Mrs. Soames, he felt sure, had an eye!"?

2. What characteristic of Swithin's is brought out in his refusal to drive Juley a second time? Why does Swithin like being called "Four-in-hand Forsyte"?

3. Swithin, in reporting his drive with Irene, suddenly becomes very silent. Why?

4. Explain the last paragraph on page 118 and the first paragraph on page 119, beginning, "And asleep..."

5. What lies behind Swithin's statement to Bosinney that Soames' new house is too "new-fangled"?

6. What does Swithin mean when he refers to Bosinney as "quite a Monte Cristo"? Why does Swithin tell Irene about all his troubles?

7. Account for Swithin's race with the coster. Ironically, what comparisons can be made between Swithin and Irene and the coster and his girl!

8. How do you explain Irene's statement to Swithin: "I don't care if I never get home." Do her actions support her statement?

VOCABULARY

PAGE

114 *contemplated* his horses

around his *personable* form: handsome, attractive

they wanted the stomach of a horse (Br.): only someone with a strong stomach could smoke them

The new plaid *rug* (Br.): lap robe for riding in a carriage or a car

115 had been *welshed* by some *thimble-riggers* (Br.): (1) cheated, (2) crooks or thieves

Four-in-hand Forsyte (Br.): referring to one who drives a carriage pulled by four horses

forced into *land agency* (Br.): buying or selling land

the *cockaded* groom: having a knot of ribbon or a rosette on the uniform hat

The *equipage* dashed forward: carriage, vehicle

116 *languid* but permanent excitement

he *wheezed* out slowly

117 solemn pride came *portentously:* in an indicative way showing
    something about to happen
  a turkey-cock *preening* himself
  from falling *askew:* out line, awry
  guard against the *draughts:* drafts, currents of air in enclosed areas
  the *baronial* style: pertaining to the lowest grade of English
    nobility

118 a very *pooty* little cellar (Br.): pretty
  on the *nob* of his cane
  in *pagan* days

119 to stand *akimbo:* with hands on hips and elbows bent outward
  spring was running *riot:* in full bloom of trees, shrubs and flowers

120 his kiss; her *recoil*
  Damme! (Br.): an oath—shortened form of "Damn me!"
  looked precious *handdog:* miserable, wretched
  had got a flea in his ear (Br.): something was bothering him
    greatly
  moved it *spasmodically*
  giving him a *rub* (Br.): scolding him
  he said *tartly*
  a *bumpy beggar* (Br.): a most unusual and disturbing person
  of the calm *satiety:* complete satisfaction, extreme gratification

121 quite a *Monte Cristo* (Br.): an extraordinary, magical person (ref.
    to Alexandre Dumas' novel)
  which he afterwards *imparted*
  the *pink* of *discretion:* (1) highest degree, finest example,
    (2) good judgment, prudence

122 *immersed* in the still, green water
  frogs across the breast: an ornamental fastening (a button and a
    loop) for the front of a coat
  had *flogged* his donkey
  his *shallopy* chariot: resembling a small boat
  on his full *cravat*
  a *fly-blown boa:* (1) ragged and dirty, (2) a woman's long scarf
    of fur or feathers, neck-piece

375

122 Her *swain* moved a stick: lover, boy-friend
 he was being *guyed* (Br.) : jeered or made fun of

123 a little *fresh:* uncontrollable (referring to the horses that had not
  lately been exercised)
 with a *finickin'* feller: too fussy or particular

GLOSSARY

PAGE

114 pomatum: oil or ointment for the hair
 opopomax: an odorous resin used in making perfume (also spelled
  'opopanax')
 Sare!: Sir!
 phaeton: a light four-wheeled carriage, with or without top, with
  one or two seats and no sides

115 pounds (Br.) : a pound is worth 20 shillings, approximately $2.40,
  but the value varies
 Derby Day: the day of the famed horse race at Epsom Downs (a
  great English race track)
 Taglioni: an Italian ballet dancer, Marie Taglioni (1804-1885)

116 T-cart: small, racy carriage

117 Star and Garter: English pub or place of entertainment
 Malacca cane: made of the brown stem of the East Indian rattan
  palm

122 coster: one who sells fruit, vegetables or fish from a small wagon
  (also coster-monger)

123 thyme: an herb for seasoning

Suggestions for written work

The place of "challenge" in life
The Forsytes' revelation of their supremacy to Irene

Part II · Chapter IV

DISCUSSION

1. Explain the sentence in the next-to-the-last paragraph on page 124, beginning, "No one desired...."

2. Why did membership in the Forsyte clan demand candor and reticence?

3. Explain the meaning of the image of the wild flower as it is used in this chapter.

4. A Forsyte never forgets a house. How is this explained in the light of Forsyte thinking?

5. Why doesn't James put all the blame on Irene for the seeming failure of Soames' marriage?

6. When James blames all the trouble on the house, whom is he trying to protect? Why? With what one thing is he concerned as he views the new house?

7. Is Bosinney "slinking along the wall", as James puts it? If not, why does James think so?

8. Though the family gossip is resisted by some of the younger members, in what way does Galsworthy show that this prying into the affairs of others has often been of benefit to the group as a whole?

VOCABULARY

PAGE
124 with a *curt* handshake
all *tallied* too well
in visits of *condolence*
affording consolation to the sound

125 more certain *reticence*
    not only pleasant but *salutary*
    tales, reports, *surmises:* guesses, conjectures
    as the *prattling* babes
    it is *indubitable:* certain, unquestionable
    against the *perception*

126 the *purlieus* of Mayfair: neighborhood, environment
    the *prudence* of the match

127 a skin-tight *bodice* (Br.): a woman's fitted waist or dress body
    form *decourously* shielded: properly, in good taste
    dodging among the *palpable:* readily seen, easily recognized
    fate had *lurked* within
    very naked, sometimes *sordid*

128 so *recondite,* so *figurative:* (1) little known, obscure,
        (2) symbolic, emblematic
    through the *catch-word:* an oft-repeated word or phrase

129 there being no *'flies'* (Br.): no public carriages, taxis
    which was the *speckless* gloss
    the *drone* of talk

130 *tethered* by a string
    daubed each with a white patch
    anxious *rapt* expression
    a *flagged* terrace
    list of two or three inches to *port:* (1) leaning, tipping,
        (2) the left side
    with a *bevelled* edge

131 he *stifled* that curiosity

133 *By the by:* by the way, incidentally

GLOSSARY

PAGE
127 bitters: liquors in which bitter herbs are used

378

Suggestions for written work

Candor and reticence—can one have both?
Scapegoats. Are they necessary to everybody, or not?
Gossip and rumor, causes and effects

Part II • Chapter V

DISCUSSION

1. How do you account for Euphemia's judging Irene's character by her figure? What is Euphemia's judgment? Why, according to Euphemia, is the General, doffing his hat to Irene, an old fool?

2. Discuss the reference to the "eternal position of Art toward Property," on page 136.

3. Why is Soames considered by clients to be a "safe" man? Is Soames' poor opinion of his partner, Bustard, in keeping with the Forsyte character?

4. Explain Old Jolyon's dislike and distrust of newspapers. Is it true Forsyteism to be opposed to the Press?

5. Old Jolyon's chin comes under discussion. Why? Is this type of evaluation of a person's character common today? Can you cite examples?

6. What does "good, solid wives" mean to a Forsyte?

7. In the incident concerning the supervisor that comes up at the board meeting, what is revealed about Galsworthy's own sense of humanitarianism? Do you agree with the Board's decision against payment, as expressed by Old Jolyon? Support your views.

8. In discussing the cost of the house, what are Old Jolyon's feelings toward Soames? How do you explain this deviation from the "sticking together" for which the Forsytes seem to be famous?

9. How do the letters of Soames and Bosinney advance the plot? Which one has your sympathy? Why?

VOCABULARY

PAGE

134 piece of *prunella* silk: bluish-black
Euphemia's instinctive *propriety:* good taste, modesty
was *accosting* the lady: speaking to, greeting

135 an *eddy* in the traffic: a circular motion
caught out just (Br.): very embarrassed, very flustered

136 *counter* to my scheme

137 a *long-headed* fellow (Br.): sound, practical
he was a *safe* man: cautious and careful in business
his soul *abhorred* circumstances
mousing amongst *precedents*

138 *set his face against the Press* (Br.): gave no personal news to the
papers

139 old Mr. Bleedham, very *bland*
leading to a *working:* part of the mine where digging is taking
place
a *Jove*-like serenity

140 tendencies of his *cloth:* those who wear church robes, clergymen
within the ensuing *fortnight* (Br.): fourteen nights and days, two
weeks

141 thus *impiously* removed: wickedly, irreverently
so grave a *dereliction:* negligence, remission

142 his attention *tweaked away:* pulled away sharply, broke away
quickly

143 a parting *turn-up* (Br.): argument

144 somewhat mysterious *awe*
under their *non-committal* allusions

380

144 wide *asunder* as the poles
wounded to the *quick:* deeply, severely
owned with the *dispassion:* state of no emotion, calmness
He had a *presentiment*

145 *flurried* by that sharp look

GLOSSARY

PAGE
134 Paregoric: a soothing medicine, an opiate

135 *intriguée* (Fr.) : curious, intrigued

136 Tacitus: a Roman historian (circa 55-120)

137 Colliery: a coal mine, including all buildings and equipment

142 *in toto* (Latin) : completely, in every respect

145 Chablis: a French wine

Suggestions for written work

Good manners and success
Art *vs.* Property
Blood will tell?
The Forsyte idea of a good wife
Conservative middle-class stability *vs.* artistic individuality

Part II • *Chapter* VI

DISCUSSION

1. Is June's reaction to the Irene-Bosinney affair typical of her family? Is it a feminine reaction?

2. What does Young Jolyon mean when he observes: "It was good as a play to see his father with the children, but such a play as brings smiles with tears behind"?

3. Why do so many well-to-do people decide to go to the Zoo this day? In his picture of them at the Zoo, what does Galsworthy say about the "cultivated" Forsyte barbarity? Why is it ironical that this is shown from Young Jolyon's point of view?

4. Explain the attitude shown in the third paragraph on page 150 beginning, "In his eyes..."

5. Why does Old Jolyon find it impossible to discuss the situation of Irene and Bosinney with his son? With whom do you sympathize?

6. The term "Forsyte" comes to mean more than the actual family. Whom does it include?

7. How does the visit to the Zoo further your interest in the novel?

VOCABULARY

PAGE

148 an ordinary Board—*summarily:* directly and promptly, without ceremony

were left in *cabal:* plotting, scheming

He had an *assignation:* appointment for a meeting (usually of a questionable nature)

walked toward the *tryst*

149 a special *peep-show:* exhibition of objects through a small opening
     fitted with a magnifying lens
    had been a morning *fête*
    tawny, ravenous beasts
    in a white *waistcoat:* a man's vest
    and gold *nose-nippers* (Br.): nose glasses

150 to an *intermittent* contempt
    to *stigmatize* as barbarity: brand, mark

151 behaving *precious* badly (Br.): extremely
    meaning of Bosinney's *defection*

152 defended by *sunshades:* parasols

GLOSSARY

PAGE

152 equipage, landau, sociable, Victoria: types of horse-drawn carriages
    toilettes (Fr.): dresses or costumes of women

Suggestions for written work

Personal pride—its dangers
Similarities between humans and animals, using specific examples
A person's life is his own, or is it?

Part II • *Chapter* VII

DISCUSSION

1. Why does Old Jolyon find it so upsetting to have been seen in the park with his son and grandchildren?

2. With Old Jolyon, is it that he won't or doesn't believe any of the rumors about Bosinney and Irene? Explain your answer.

3. What does Old Jolyon think of his background and ancestry? Are his beliefs honest? Does he have any doubts about them? If so, what?

4. How do you explain the younger Forsytes' reluctance to use the family crest? Why did they use it?

5. Roger liked the idea of Frances dabbling in musical composition up to a point. What is the point? What Forsytean characteristic does Roger show in this instance?

6. Why is Dartie so reluctant to have Soames see him at his club?

7. What caused Dartie to believe that there is not a single "sportsman" among the Forsytes unless it is George? On what is his opinion of the Forsytes based?

8. In Old Jolyon's reply to James' statement: "Here, you've got a cat here," what was implied?

9. Why is Old Jolyon's arrival and behavior at Timothy's disturbing to the gathering there? What is the impending danger the Forsytes have begun to feel whenever June's name is brought up? Account for this feeling. Why does Old Jolyon want to give his brothers "another rub or two"?

10. Explain the meaning of the second paragraph of page 164 beginning, "The six women. . . ." What do these seven people believe is troubling Old Jolyon? Are they correct in their assumption?

11. Explain the difference in attitude between Hester and Juley in regard to doing something to help Old Jolyon. Exactly what brought about Juley's new feelings for Old Jolyon, as related in the last paragraph of this chapter?

VOCABULARY

PAGE

154 with some *sagacity:* sound judgment, shrewdness
    being in *gilt-edged* securities: of highest value or quality
    Bosinney was *maligned:* slandered, wronged by gossip
    June had *flown out at him* (Br.): "bawled" him out

155 as though in *conclave:* consultation, solemn talk
  torpid in a red satin chair: sluggish, lethargic

157 *Imperceptibly* the rest of the family
  recovered his *affability:* courteousness, civility
  a pretty little *pot* of pin-money (Br.): bit, sum

158 'a *Celtic* appearance'
  the *sonata* form: a form of musical composition

160 he told his *cronies*

161 *rusty* ever since that (Br.): cross, ill-tempered
  amongst the green *baize:* soft green wool fabric resembling felt
  borrow a *tenner* (Br.): ten English pounds
  this Buccaneer *Johnny* (Br.): fellow, chap
  the marble *chimney-piece* (Br.): mantelpiece
  His *advent* had obviously put

163 he had come to *scotch:* stamp out, eliminate
  to Old Jolyon's *clemency*

164 when he had *rapped out* (Br.): spoken angrily
  to *vent* itself

165 in the *muslin* curtains

GLOSSARY

PAGE
156 Heralds' Office: a royal corporation in England occupied with
    family trees and coats-of-arms
  dexter: situated to the right of the bearer in coats-of-arms
  sable ground gules: red on a black background in coats-of-arms
  pheasant proper: in natural colors in coats-of-arms
  crest: a figure placed above the shield-like part of a coat-of-arms

163 sciatica: a nervous disorder causing pain from the hip down the
    leg

385

164 *adieux* (Fr.): farewells, good-bys

Suggestions for written work

Is family background important?
Old ideas and young people

Part II • Chapter VIII

DISCUSSION

1. Comment on the following aspects of Roger's party: (a) decoration, (b) music and dances, (c) clothes, (d) guests.

2. Why does Roger object to a band for the dance? Why does Francie go to the pretense of having one? Why has Roger long since reduced his wife to chronic dyspepsia?

3. What is meant, on page 167, by "a number of Nicholases"? Is there any connection between this and previous references to "a group of Forsytes", which pertained to people not members of the Forsyte family?

4. What is the meaning of the reference to the young men at the dance as "the light brigade"? Discuss what goes through the mothers' minds as they watch their daughters dancing. Are these thoughts universal? Explain the likening of the dance floor to a battlefield.

5. Why doesn't Soames dance with his wife? On the balcony what are his observations, and what is Galsworthy suggesting through these observations?

6. Why did June really go to the dance? In doing this, is she a real Forsyte?

VOCABULARY

PAGE

166 a *parquet* floor: a wooden floor of inlaid design
those strange *appendages*
embowered in palms: sheltered, surrounded

386

166 that *tortuous labyrinth:* (1) twisting, winding, (2) confusing
    state of affairs, maze
    which must be *traversed:* examined carefully, thought out com-
    pletely
    with much *tulle:* a thin, fine silk or rayon

167 received her *effusively*
    socks with *clocks:* embroidered or woven ornaments on the sides

168 irresponsible, charming, *suave*
    without *pedantic* attention: excessive and tedious, dull
    chaperons *sitting up* along the wall (Br.): gathering in great num-
    bers, lining up
    the *volatile* element: frivolous, flighty
    with some *callow* youth
    life, its *pathos*

169 the *mazes* of the dance
    essences that women love: perfumes, fragrances

170 air of *stolid* watching
    the *refraction* of human needs: change in direction or scope
    gardens, mansions and *squalor*
    They looked *fagged* (Br.): tired
    the *languor* in her eyes

172 she would *knock herself* up (Br.): make herself ill
    to *countermand* the carriage: stop by a contrary order

GLOSSARY

PAGE

166 'rout' seats: light, movable chairs provided for a large, fashionable
    party
    cottage piano: small, as opposed to a grand piano

167 *infra dig* (Latin): beneath one's dignity or position

170 bobby (Br.): policeman

171 conservatory (Br.): greenhouse

172 Globular Gold Concessions: a company dealing in gold

Suggestions for written work

Putting up a good "front"
Wallflowers. Do they still grow at dances today?

Part II • Chapter IX

DISCUSSION

1. What has caused so many people to notice Irene and Bosinney? Is this a natural thing among people? Why?

2. Explain the meaning of the third paragraph on page 174, beginning, "There are moments . . .", in the light of what you know about the Forsytes and about people in general.

3. Explain the reluctance of the Forsytes to discuss the situation that involves Soames, Irene and Bosinney.

4. What does Winifred Dartie mean when she says that Bosinney is very *chic?* How do you account for her attitude toward "those two"?

5. Explain Dartie's idea that four little Darties were a sort of perpetual insurance.

6. Why did Winifred write to Irene?

7. Dartie is described as a "man of the world" because his first name is Moses and his second name Montague. Explain.

8. Discuss Dartie's idea that "to stint yourself is the mark of a fool."

9. How does the aftermath of the dinner advance the plot?

VOCABULARY

PAGE

174 *prodigal* of something

175 having lost *caste*
render him *bilious:* suffering from liver trouble
descendants undoubtedly *accessible*
only that *buffoon* George: one given to undignified poking, a poor
  joker
This *dictum:* announcement of authority, judicial statement

176 *Bowling* smoothly (Br.) : driving
were *of rare prime* (Br.) : unusually fine, magnificent
precincts of those gardens: walled areas with locked doors
vague sympathy *evoked*

177 *bye-ways* and hedges: out-of-the-way places
was *in good feather:* feeling exceptionally fine

178 didn't care a *cursh:* damn, hoot (Dartie is slightly drunk)
a bottle of Pol Roger to his own cheek (Br.) : the effect of wine
  added to his own natural boldness
nothing like *pluck:* courage, spirit
swop hansoms there (Br.) : swap (Am. sp.)

179 to be *much in the running:* getting anywhere
paying for things *vicariously:* through or by someone else
he should *stint* himself
profited by his *perspicacity:* mental keenness, discernment

180 a *concession* to the company: privilege, special right
and laugh, and *quaff:* drink large amounts with great pleasure

182 burst into *imprecations:* curses, foul language

183 He drowned Winifred's *rejoinder:* answer to a reply, response
ceased a *Jeremiad:* prolonged wailing or lamentation
Dartie at once *concurred*

389

GLOSSARY

PAGE

174 Titian: famous Italian painter (circa 1477-1576)

175 *chic* (Fr.): stylish, elegant

178 mucker (Br.): a vulgar person, a no-good

180 *mandoline* (Br.): mandolin, stringed instrument

181 satyr: a mythological woodland god, part human and part goat, that was noted for lewdness

Suggestions for written work

Names can indicate character?
Situations point up character. Illustrate by specific examples.
The modern Dartie (name no names)

Part II • Chapter x

DISCUSSION

1. Discuss the statement: "It is the nature of a Forsyte to be ignorant that he is a Forsyte." How does this apply to Young Jolyon? Does he have the Forsyte "sense of property"? Explain your reasoning.

2. Explain the comparison of Young Jolyon to a Chinese idol (par. 3, p. 185).

3. "My liver is out of order" is a common statement of many of the Forsytes. Just what does this mean?

4. In spite of his daughter June's unhappiness, Young Jolyon likes Bosinney on their first meeting at the club. Why?

5. How does Young Jolyon define "the Forsyte"? How does he identify himself as one? On what basis does Young Jolyon claim that the Forsytes are "half England . . . . . the half that counts"?

6. Why does Bosinney never think of Young Jolyon as a Forsyte? What does Young Jolyon mean by his statement that the world is full of Forsytes?

7. Explain Young Jolyon's statement that he is the "missing link" between James and Bosinney.

8. According to Young Jolyon, what two qualities are the real test of a Forsyte?

9. Why does Bosinney believe that Soames will never "blow his brains out"?

10. What warning does Young Jolyon give Bosinney about the danger of disregarding the Forsytes? What reasons does Young Jolyon give for his own survival in the face of having disregarded them?

11. Discuss the statement: "A man's fate lies in his own heart" in regard to the Forsytes and to people in general.

12. What is meant by the statement: "Bosinney had still to eat his pudding"?

13. How does the thinking of Soames and Young Jolyon differ on the subject of an unhappy marriage? Explain your answer.

14. Young Jolyon thinks it curious that all people who believe in the sanctity of property "are followers of One who never owned anything." What does he mean?

15. Explain the chapter title.

16. How does Young Jolyon interpret the real meaning of the Forsyte's "sanctity of the marriage tie"?

VOCABULARY

PAGE
185 the financial trouble, *slights*

186 a domestic *finesse*
stealing at him *unfathomable* looks

187 *to bring him up to the mark* (Br.) : to make him do and think as
     they do
     He looked *covertly:* slyly, so as not to be detected

189 disposed to *myopia:* near-sightedness
     the *cornerstones* of convention
     I catch your *drift*

190 It's *deuced* kind of you (Br.) : extremely, very

191 that indefinable *malaise:* condition of bodily weakness or discomfort
     time had *assuaged*

192 tasted to the *dregs:* the bitterest part
     wended his way home

GLOSSARY

PAGE

189 Royal Acadamicians are Forsytes: members of societies for promot-
     ing literature, art or science

192 *status quo* (Latin) : existing state, present situation

Suggestions for written work

Real tests of character, as shown in this novel
Blind followers. Cite examples from this book.
The perfect Forsyte
The Forsytes—the better half of England

Part II • Chapter XI

DISCUSSION

1. What is the *real* reason that Soames is upset when Irene brings up the question of his letting her go? From Soames' point of view what will make his marriage a success? What is Irene's view of the situation?

2. Why does Irene go with Soames to the Park when she obviously does not wish to go? Why does Soames invite Bosinney to dinner? In what way is this typical of a Forsyte?

3. Characterize Soames' behavior toward Bosinney in the Park and at dinner. Considering the circumstances, does this behavior earn your respect? What is typically Forsytean about it? What convinces Soames that Bosinney is in love with his wife?

4. Soames' memory goes back to a night four years ago. What effect does this have on him? What is the effect of the sound of the peacocks?

5. Explain the meaning of the chapter heading.

VOCABULARY

PAGE

194 went into the *drawing-room:* room for the reception of company

195 the *motley* hour: characterized by wide variation in color, people, etc.

196 *quartering* his ground: covering from one side to the other and back
exchange of those *platitudes*
put a strange *bravado*

197 out in the *farce*
     cleansing the *reek:* dirt and foul odor

198 a cry *writhing:* sounding painful and distorted

GLOSSARY

PAGE
195 Achilles: a Greek legendary hero

Suggestions for written work

Facing up to situations
What makes a successful marriage?
Soames Forsyte—husband

Part II • Chapter XII

DISCUSSION

1. Is it typical of a Forsyte not to want to "miss a Board"? Explain.

2. Young Jolyon comments that "The more I see of people the more I am convinced that they are never good or bad—merely comic, or pathetic." Why does Old Jolyon call this statement a rambling generality? Do you agree with his evaluation?

3. Galsworthy speaks of the Forsytes' "illusions and principles which they have cherished carefully for practical purposes but never believe in." What are some of these illusions and principles?

4. Why does Old Jolyon seem to be more understanding of the younger generation than his brothers?

5. Why does June decide to call on Irene? Is this a wise move?

6. When June is announced at the house of Mrs. Baynes, the latter's

first reactions are typical of a Forsyte. What are they, and what do they represent?

7. Why does Mrs. Baynes consider individual action to be immoral? Why is Mrs. Baynes referred to as "one of the principal priestesses of Forsyteism"?

8. The so-called altar of Forsyteism is inscribed "nothing for nothing, and really remarkable little for sixpence." What does this mean?

9. What distinguishes the society with a capital "S" from that with a small "s"?

10. Why does Mrs. Baynes seat June "opposite the light"? Discuss Mrs. Baynes' reluctance to question June. As far as Mrs. Baynes is concerned, what is the *real* issue involved here?

11. As a woman who believes strongly in "organization," why is Mrs. Baynes upset by her conversation with June? Why is June's visit with Mrs. Baynes not a success?

VOCABULARY

PAGE

199 which *permeates* all respectable
    baited by a ring: worried, tormented
    bereft of those illusions: cruelly separated from
    of all *corporeal* enjoyment: physical, bodily

200 too adventurous or too *foolhardy*
    the petty *precipices:* dangerous situations, uncertain events

201 can't have you *racketting* about: having a gay time, socializing
    that *pertinacity* of hers: persistence, tenacity
    dragooning her into temporary comfort: forcing, harassing
    Her *tremors* had passed
    the *touchstone* of Forsyteism: test, criterion

203 in *ecclesiastical* circles
    covered with *sequins*

203 had not a *double name:* hyphenated family names quite common in England, e.g., Ormsby-Gore

institutuions, *maxims,* and 'principle': general truths, strong statements

206 some *recompense* for the shame

G L O S S A R Y

PAGE

200 Baedeker: one of a series of guide-books for travelers

201 charring interest (Br.): housework done by the day usually by a woman not part of the home

202 morocco: goatskin leather originating in Morocco
embonpoint (Fr.): exaggerated stoutness

Suggestions for written work

Maintaining "face." Is it important?
A problem—Society vs. society

Part II · *Chapter* XIII

D I S C U S S I O N

1. Why does James like to dine at French's? Discuss the evolution of the Forsytes as exemplified by James tucking in his napkin at French's. ·

2. Why has Irene refused to move into the new house?

3. In the conversation with Irene during the trip to Robin Hill, James is asking for her obedience rather than attempting to understand her position. Cite evidence for this.

4. When Irene informs James that she does not love his son, why does

he show such slight reaction? When she refuses to argue with him, why is he at a loss for an answer?

5. Does anything lie behind Bosinney's remark to Soames: "Don't get caught in the storm!"?

6. In what difficulty does Soames now find himself with two properties: his wife and his new house? What is Soames' reaction to the extra four hundred pounds that Bosinney has spent on the house? What do you think Soames will do about this?

7. What is it about Irene that makes Soames so furious when he talks to her?

VOCABULARY

PAGE

207 after the tasty *fleshpots:* luxuries, good living
done away with the *cubicles*
have your chop, prime *chump* (Br.): the thick end of a loin of mutton

210 rather that of *acquiescence*
ruminating over his *rebuff:* (1) pondering, meditating, (2) verbal slap, abrupt check
the silence and *impenetrability*

211 spying the *tracery:* ornamental design, decorative carving or relief
the pattern of the *frieze:* usually decorated band just below the cornice of a stone or wooden column

212 have already been *chronicled*

213 and all the *rancour:* rancor (Am. sp.)—enmity, animosity
no notice of the *taunt*

Suggestions for written work

Revenge, its causes and effects
The eternal triangle

397

Part II · *Chapter* XIV

DISCUSSION

1. When Irene refused to open her locked door to Soames, what is the real reason he dismissed the thought of other women from his mind? Why is it incredible to Soames that his wife now hates him?

2. Explain Soames' inability to believe in the Irene-Bosinney affair. Discuss Soames' feeling of satisfaction that neither Irene nor Bosinney had any money.

3. Why does Soames continually think of Irene when she is away from him? Is there any element of love in this? Has Soames changed in any way?

4. Does Soames or Irene have your sympathy in this chapter? Explain your choice.

5. Point out the relationship between the ending for this chapter and the ending for chapter XI, part II.

VOCABULARY

PAGE

215 *sleeping-suit* laid out: pajamas
   in this *inexorable* silence: not to be broken, relentless
   like an animal *at bay*

216 but a *spectral* journey: unreal, ghost-like
   appetite for these *exploits*
   be *appeased* by his wife
   surly anger took its place

217 showered on the *plane-trees:* trees of southern Europe and the Near East

224 by no means the *neurotic*

225 the very *van* of Forsyteism: forefront, vanguard
neither surprise nor *disapprobation*
admitted as the *criterion*

226 in his *mooney way*
bitter, *derisive* smile
yellow-*ochre* walls: pigment used in making paint
its infinite *vista* of brown: long, narrow view
Such a *rattle!* (Br.): talker, gossip

227 a *pittance:* small amount for living, very small pension
° really fashionable *proclivities:* tendencies, inclinations

228 two lean *hacks* (Br.): saddle horses
they *cantered* up again: galloped easily
leaning over the *balustrade:* bannister of a staircase
the Alhambra *promenade*

GLOSSARY

PAGE
219 'Ultra Vivisectionist': magazine favoring extreme use of a dissected
human body

220 Q. C.: Queen's Counsel

226 chinchilla: small South American rodent valued for fur

228 Dromios: twin brothers in Shakespeare's *Comedy of Errors*

Suggestions for written work

The acceptance of the obvious
People as subjects of conversation
Snobbery, causes and effects

Part III • *Chapter* II

DISCUSSION

1. Why is talk of the Irene-Bosinney affair kept from Timothy?

2. James tells his wife that she is a "regular Juley." What does he mean? How does James account for Soames' difficulty with Irene?.

3. How does little Publius show that he has traits in common with both his grandfather James and his father, Montague Dartie?

4. In trying to place the blame for the scandal, in what way are Old Jolyon and James alike in their thinking? Is this similar thinking natural, or only natural to a Forsyte? Why does James' opinion of Old Jolyon drop a little at this time?

5. Explain the Forsytes' disapproval of the Park. What does Soames expect to accomplish by his nocturnal wandering through the Park? Is he successful?

VOCABULARY

PAGE

229 with her *infallible* instinct
   'the Buccaneer' was *'going it'* (Br.) : very much entangled in what he was doing
   In this *impasse:* position from which there is no escape

230 under his *lee:* watchful eye, protection
   to *pall* on little Publius: have a tiring effect
   little Publius knew a *sweet-shop* (Br.) : candy store
   over the *robust* child-figures

402

231 *probing* the blackness
with the *myriad* passions

232 like some *morbid* stimulant: unwholesomely gloomy
in her *draggled* blouse: soiled, bedraggled

GLOSSARY

230 *soubriquet* (Fr.): nickname

Suggestions for written work

Dislike of that which is "common." Of whom is this characteristic and
   why?
Jealousy, causes and effects
Solitude, assets and liabilities
Reaching for the moon, figuratively not literally
The role of Nature as a criticism of Forsyteism

Part III • Chapter III

DISCUSSION

1. What criticism of his work does the art critic give Young Jolyon,
   and on what is this criticism based? Do you agree? Did Young
   Jolyon?

2. When Young Jolyon changes his attitude toward his painting, is he
   a real Forsyte? Comment on the keenness of Young Jolyon's self-
   awareness by relating what he finds out about himself in relation
   to the series of watercolors of London.

3. Why doesn't Young Jolyon recognize Irene at first when he goes to
   sketch in the Botannical Gardens? Summarize his impressive description of her.

4. Discuss Young Jolyon's statement that "he had rowed in the galley himself."

5. The Forsytes think that they know what is bothering Irene so greatly. How does Young Jolyon's explanation differ from that of the others?

6. What lies behind Old Jolyon's disapproval of June's working with her "lame ducks"? In his thinking, is he really a Forsyte?

7. Why is June so calm when she first hears of Soames' impending suit against Bosinney? What lies behind Old Jolyon's suggestion to James that the lawsuit be settled out of court?

8. Discuss Old Jolyon's removal of James and Soames as trustees of his will. Why did he do this and, at the same time, make restitution to his son?

9. Discuss the sixth paragraph on page 242, beginning, "Slowly, surely . . ." What change in the basic Forsyte philosophy has come over Old Jolyon? How do you explain it?

10. When Young Jolyon knows that he would be the major beneficiary of his father's will, does any part of the Forsyte attitude become apparent in him?

VOCABULARY

PAGE

233 without having *prosecuted*
bit of faded *damask:* a reversible fabric woven with patterns

234 in her *staccato* voice: sharp and quick, rapid-fire speaking
his *impersonal* moods
sweet, *acrid* smoke: irritating, pungent
green and *russet* pattern: brown, reddish-brown

235 prepared his *easel*
in a cream *ruffle*
riveted by the look

235 professor of *horticulture:* the science of cultivating garden plants
face of a *sorceress*
and *neurasthenic* figure: exhausted from prolonged mental strain

236 of the autumn *rime:* ice formed on trees from fog or damp air,
hoarfrost
the *unhallowed* lover: wicked, irreverent
that wake up *ravening:* extremely hungry, ravenous
surfeited and asleep: satisfied to excess, satiated

237 with an *ingratiating* twinkle
brocaded up to the frieze: woven in elaborate fashion with the
right side having a raised effect
days of *degenerate* taste

238 trouble with the *chimney-sweep:* one in the business of cleaning
chimneys
had worn *night-socks* (Br.): bed-socks

239 *lugubriously* turning over: dismally, dolefully

240 a mass of *affidavits:* statements written under oath

241 answered *'Down-by-the-starn'* Hemmings (Br.): describing a person who is slow and non-aggressive

242 *testament* or testamentary disposition
and in *default,* etc.: absence, lack
in seven *folios:* sheets of paper, each folded to make four pages
in his *palmy* days: prosperous, flourishing
nature of *retributive* justice: done in a spirit of revenge
the *comely* edifice: pleasing, becoming

244 had been *baulked* (balked): deprived, stripped
mingled its *gall:* bitterness, rancor
can *cut your coat a bit longer* (Br.): live a little longer

GLOSSARY

PAGE
233 monkey-puzzler: a South American tree

405

241 realty or personality: (1) real estate, land, (2) personal property
   assigns: persons to whom property of another may be transferred,
     beneficiaries
   hereditaments: any inheritable estate or interest in property
   coverture: status of a married woman considered under the pro-
     tection and authority of her husband

Suggestions for written work

Misery loves company. Or does it?
Changing one's mind. Is this just a "woman's privilege"?
Effects of a sudden change in one's life. Cite examples.

Part III • Chapter IV

DISCUSSION

1. What is the meaning of the title of this chapter?

2. Of what significance to his personal situation is the list of "offences"
   that Soames notices in the paper en route to the city?

3. Justice Bentham is referred to as a "strong" judge. What did this
   mean to Soames?

4. Soames' attorney advises him to use "a little bluffness" at the trial.
   Explain what he meant.

5. Discuss Galsworthy's simile, on page 248, that compares people
   and rabbits.

6. A figure waits at the station door. Discuss the reactions that any
   Forsyte would have toward such a person.

7. Explain the last sentence in the sixth paragraph on page 249,
   beginning, "They helped him . . ."

8. On various occasions Soames retires to his picture room. When and
   why? Is this true to the Forsyte character?

9. Explain George's great amusement in a drunken man. Why does this amusement turn to sorrow when he realizes it is Bosinney?

10. George does a great deal of thinking as he follows and observes Bosinney. Are his thoughts those of a Forsyte, or do they come closer to being those of the average man? Why did the fog upset George?

11. Why does the conclusion that Bosinney was finally heading for Soames' residence appeal to George?

12. George associates with Dartie quite a bit. Explain this in the light of his considering Dartie to be "a bit of a cad." Is it George or Dartie who feels more sympathy for Bosinney? Explain your choice.

VOCABULARY

PAGE

246 not *deigning* to ask: condescending, stooping

247 to *con* the news: read carefully, study
seven *arsons*

248 a little *bluffness*
breach of promise
weird *excrescence* of the driver: unusual growth, disfiguring addition
haloed by a vague glow: surrounded, enclosed

249 he never *flinched*
any *narcotic* to such worry
'Grave *indisposition* of a Statesman'
at her strange *sortie:* going out aggressively, sally

250 putting the *high guard* (Br.): large fireplace screen
that unique *hostel:* lodging place, inn

251 the look-out for *fillips:* things to excite, stimuli
had 'taken *the knock'* (Br.): been severely hurt mentally
tall, *burly* figure

251 dodging *warily*
whistles *mocked* the sense

252 *put his 'two-penny' under a bus* (Br.) : committed suicide
wielded a *knout:* whip used for flogging criminals
remain *green* in his mind: fresh vivid
estranged and unwilling wife
shrouded in *cocoons:* coverings that completely envelop
come into view like *spectres:* specters (Am. sp.)—ghosts, phantoms
saw them *gaping* round

253 now his *quarry* again
victim to strange *qualms*

254 a *smirch* of doubtful *amours:* (1) disgrace, tarnish, (2) illicit love
affairs
there *stalked* to him: came slowly, returned gradually
failing at a *'jenny'* (Br.) : shot in pocket-billiards
'looked upon the drink when it was yellow' (Br.) : become a little
drunk

255 The *murky* blackness: gloomy, cheerless

GLOSSARY

PAGE
246 Inferno: hell, Hades

252 sphynx (sphinx): a mythological creature having the head of a
man and the body of a lion

Suggestions for written work

Birds of a feather flock together. Cite examples from this book.
Bluffing—who does it to whom and why?
George's character in comparison to the other Forsytes
The "image of the hunt", as Galsworthy uses it

Part III · Chapter V

DISCUSSION

1. Explain the last sentence in the third paragraph, on page 268, beginning, "The sound of their voices . . ."

2. What kind of relationship and understanding is there between James and his son, Soames?

3. What does Soames' lawyer give as his client's reason for bringing Bosinney to trial? What is his real reason? When Soames is on the witness stand, why is his father at that moment proud of him?

4. Why does the absence of Bosinney from court make James feel uneasy? What is Bosinney's lawyer's chief appeal for his client's case?

5. What does Galsworthy mean when he refers to Justice Bentham as a "somewhat ordinary Forsyte"?

6. Cite passages in this chapter that hint that Bosinney's reason for not attending the trial might be a tragic one. Did you expect the trial to resolve itself as it did? Explain.

7. Explain the phrase describing James at lunch, which reads, "eating two muffins not altogether in the intervals of speech."

8. Do Timothy's words at the end of the chapter indicate that he knows what has happened in regard to events at the trial?

9. How does the short description of Timothy at the end of this chapter belie the impression that his sisters have always tried to give of him? Coming when it does, what do you think might be the significance of this appearance of Timothy?

VOCABULARY

PAGE

256 *barristers* in wig and gown (Br.): lawyers permitted to plead a case
at the bar
emanation of a refined cheese: odor, smell
so *indissolubly* connected

258 given him his first *brief:* memorandum of facts or law for use in
conducting a legal case
to *go into the box:* take the stand in court

260 could not be limited, *fettered:* confined, restrained
by any *verbiage*
indeed *unprecedented* character
expression *nullified* itself

261 the *amplitude* of his robes: fullness, extent
broke the *nib* of a *quill:* (1) point, (2) goose feather made into a
pen for writing
a person *endowed*
disinter therefrom: dig out, unearth
wrote to the *plaintiff*

262 *defrayed* by the plaintiff
alleged by the plaintiff
importation into the correspondence: introduction, insertion

263 *assented* to a very clear proposition
ruddy brown face: healthy, fresh
had seen a *portent*

Suggestions for written work

The majesty of the law. What and why is it?
Should one always "put it in writing"?
Omens, good and bad
Galsworthy's foreshadowing of plot, as exemplified in this book

Part III • *Chapter* VI

DISCUSSION

1. Why, after unusual events, do the Forsytes seem to turn up at the home of Timothy? Discuss Mrs. Small's and Aunt Hester's feeling that the Forsyte family was breaking up.

2. Soames states, "Mrs. MacAnder is a cat!" Why does he answer Mrs. Small in this way?

3. Soames' intentions when he left Timothy's home are far different from those he held when he arrived. How do you account for this change?

4. Why does the thought of divorce appall Soames? Why does Soames go to his parents' home after failing to locate Irene or Bosinney? When Soames announces that Irene has left him, how do you account for the difference in the reactions of his mother and father?

5. Why does James despise and dread Dartie? Is this a phase of Forsyteism?

6. Would all the Forsytes, family and non-family, have agreed that Soames should get Irene back? Why, or why not?

7. Why is James delighted upon hearing that little Publius had given a bad penny to a beggar?

8. In the confusion concerning future plans concerning his marriage, what several conflicting attitudes does Soames consider? How can you explain his inability to know which to take?

9. What details of James' and Emily's marriage can be contrasted with that of Soames and Irene?

10. What is so pertinent about the painting, 'Sea Piece by Turner', being on the dining room wall when Soames and the others dine at the home of James and Emily?

11. What lies behind Irene's note that Soames found in her jewel box? What effect did it have on Soames? In his intense emotion upon realizing that Irene was definitely gone, how did Soames betray the Forsyte in him?

VOCABULARY

PAGE

264 He felt *disinclined*
he *'pished'* (Br.): expressed contempt

265 *emblem* of departure

266 Mrs. MacAnder is a *cat*
He would *tax* her with it: reprove, censure
so utterly at *variance*
jettisoning of his property: throwing away, casting off
seemed *uncanny* to Soames

268 *grope* out the meaning: figure, search
a greyish *tinge*

271 *endorsed* by that wider body

272 composed of *cordage:* cords and ropes of a ship's rigging

273 he had *purged* himself

GLOSSARY

PAGE

265 Barbizon school: a group of 19th Century French landscape painters
Corot: French landscape painter (1796-1875)

412

Suggestions for written work

A "Dartie" today in America
Seasons and life
Evidences of the breaking-up of the Forsyte family

Part III • Chapter VII

DISCUSSION

1. What is June's plan? Describe the behavior of each when June and Irene meet in Bosinney's room. When Irene runs quickly out of the room, why does June try to call her back?

2. What is Old Jolyon's plan? Does he really think it would work? If it were just a hope, acount for its entering his mind. On what basis does Old Jolyon re-evaluate his son's watercolor paintings?

3. Why does Old Jolyon now refer to Soames only as the "man of property"? How has his opinion of his nephew changed?

4. Why is June so sure that Soames will not be moving into the new house at Robin Hill? What is June's "victory"?

5. What combination of events and circumstances have suddenly made Old Jolyon feel old, tired and beaten? Could he be getting away from true Forsyteism?

6. What quality in June does Old Jolyon admire without knowing it? Why? How does buying Soames' new house appeal to Old Jolyon?

VOCABULARY

PAGE

274 with an *assiduity:* attentiveness, diligence
   to *hazard* her all
   passed in freezing *vigil*

275 its terrors were *discontinued*
buoy up her hope
disappearance *augured* happily: pointed ahead, boded

278 *I'm a Dutchman:* I miss my guess, I'm all wrong

279 *reincarnated* that tender love: gave rebirth to, put into real form again

280 at his *indomitable* grandchild

GLOSSARY

PAGE
278 Mrs. Gummidge: a character in Dickins' *David Copperfield,* who is always lamenting that she is a lonely, unhappy creature

Suggestions for written work

The scheming individual in life and in literature
Things that age a person ahead of his time
Giving in order to gain
Contrast the characters of Irene and June

Part III • *Chapter* VIII

DISCUSSION

1. The author refers to "the clasp of a Forsyte" when Old Jolyon and James shake hands. What is meant by this?

2. Discuss the bargaining tactics each uses in James' and Old Jolyon's arrangements for the sale of Soames' house.

3. To whom does Soames refer when, in regard to the visit of the policeman, he mentions that 'nonconformist' of Uncle Jolyon's? Is

this a true Forsyte remark? Why are James and Soames so ill at ease with the Inspector there?

4. Discuss the next-to-the-last paragraph on page 285, beginning, "For all men..."

5. The finding of the pawn tickets in Bosinney's flat directly connects with what previous episode in the story?

6. Old Jolyon sends for his son. Why? Is this betraying the character of a Forsyte?

7. What change in Old Jolyon's attitude toward James and Soames occurred as the three of them view Bosinney's body? Is this a natural thing?

8. Why does Young Jolyon feel that Bosinney's death will break up the Forsyte family? Young Jolyon compares the death situation to trees. Explain.

9. Young Jolyon feels that the Forsytes will consider Bosinney's death an act of retribution. Why could the Forsytes believe this?

10. Why is Bosinney's death so much more pitiful to Young Jolyon than to the others? In what way is Young Jolyon's rejection of the theory that Bosinney committed suicide different from the rejection that the others make?

VOCABULARY

PAGE

283 is a *white elephant*
not material to me

284 sell it at a *forced* sale
was a little *cowed:* intimidated, frightened by signs of trouble
his head in *dudgeon:* resentment, anger

285 has been *pilfering*
that final *renunciation:* voluntary giving up, formal abandoning
medley of his thoughts: varied mixture, jumble

286 *lynx-eyed,* taciturn: sharp-sighted (like a wildcat)
divining the league: perceiving by intuition, conjecturing

287 This is the *mortuary*

288 and of no *import:* importance, significance
breathless, and *prostrated*

289 *saplings* would take: young people, younger generation

290 *heyday* of his summer: highest point or stage
looked very *wan*

Suggestions for written work

A handclasp as an index of character
Nonconformity, its assets and liabilities
Foreshadowing of Bosinney's tragedy. Trace from earlier parts of this
story.

Part III • Chapter IX

DISCUSSION

1. All his life Soames has thought that wasting even a moment would
   be fatal. Account for the change in his thinking as he walks away
   from the mortuary.

2. Why does Soames tell Bilson that Irene is at the sea?

3. Why does George imply that an "act of property" has caused
   Bosinney's death? Why does George so dislike Soames?

4. What arouses Soames' anger when he finds Irene in his home?
   Why, and in what frame of mind, has Irene returned to Soames?
   What various attitudes does Soames consider taking toward this
   return? Why is he incapable of knowing which is his true one?

5. When Soames thinks that all this unhappy affair is not his fault, is he sincere? What feelings does the half-starved cat arouse in Soames? Is this consistent with his thinking? With that of a Forsyte? Even the man across the street from Soames' house affected him. How?

6. Why cannot Soames act on impulse? Why does this business of "surrendering" cross his mind? Does it solve anything?

7. What do you imagine was the message Young Jolyon said he had to deliver to Irene? Explain Irene's reaction to Young Jolyon's knock at the door. Why does Soames slam the door in Young Jolyon's face?

VOCABULARY

PAGE

291 the *inquest* was over: legal inquiry, concerning the cause of death
had taken the *first-post* letters (Br.): earliest mail delivery
was *closeted* with Boulter
Soames answered *stonily:* without feeling, without compassion

292 to run *amok:* wildly, without thought
so *cracked* with jealousy (Br.): out of his mind, insane
"That cat won't jump" (Br.): that story won't be believed

293 *fume* of the burning: odor, fragrance

294 *lull* him to indifference
ghoulish cries mingled

Suggestions for written work

Reactions of a loser
Impulsive actions—good or bad?
Memories die slowly
Implications concerning the future of the Forsytes

417

INDIAN SUMMER OF A FORSYTE

I

DISCUSSION

1. What changes have taken place since the end of Book I? How much time has elapsed?

2. How do you account for Old Jolyon's sudden attachment to the dog, Balthasar, that he formerly disliked?

3. To what drive of Swithin's is Old Jolyon referring on page 299?

4. Nature is having an effect on Old Jolyon, and he regrets his eighty-five years of age. Specifically, why?

5. At this point Old Jolyon is reverent in regard to three things only: beauty, upright conduct, the sense of property. Is this a significant change in him? Has he rejected the orthodox Forsyte philosophy? If so, how far? Of these three things he revered, which one is getting stronger in his thinking? Account for this.

6. Old Jolyon is deeply affected by the opera, *Orfeo*. Why?

7. Has knowing all the facts about Bosinney's death changed Old Jolyon's attitude toward Soames? Toward Irene? When Old Jolyon recognizes Irene sitting on the old log, his first thought is her beauty. How is this consistent with his changed philosophy?

8. Irene's greatest regret about the women she helps is that they almost all had some sort of beauty. How does Old Jolyon react to this?

9. Irene eagerly looks around the house at Robin Hill. Why?

10. What are the basic differences between Old and Young Jolyon's ideas of interior decoration? Is this natural between these two Forsytes?

11. Have any of the Forsytes kept up with the times?

12. "By the cigars they smoke, and the composers they love, ye shall know the textures of men's souls." Explain this statement.

13. How does Old Jolyon err in asking Irene to play selections from *Orfeo?*

VOCABULARY

PAGE

299 for the *midges* to bite: very small flies
earlier *Victorian* days
her *doleful* nose buried

300 Soames's *ill-starred* house
the *cackle* of Forsyte 'Change'
a delicious air, *sappy:* fresh, invigorating
'Open, sesame'

301 the *orthodoxy* he had won: beliefs, doctrines

302 had so *reprehensibly* become: inexcusably, blamefully
this *subversive* thought

303 *Have plummers got leggers, Mother?'* ⎫ a boy swallowing a snail, but
'. . . swallowed a sniley-bob' (Br.): ⎬ hoping it was something else
little boy's *'red lane':* throat ⎭
opened the *wicket gate* (Br.): a small gate in a fence
gambolled in front: gamboled (Am. sp.)—skipped about playfully
arrangements were very delicate: digestive organs

304 *Powers* above: Heavens

305 *Woa,* Myrtle: Whoa (Am. sp.)

306 trying to *conjure* somebody

419

307 over the *'prospect':* view or scene presented to the eye

    emanation of the long: a flowing forth of something that is intangible and cannot be seen

308 wine of perfect *bouquet*

309 the only *disconsolate* hour

310 for some *occult* reason: mysterious, beyond the bounds of ordinary knowledge

    festooned with pearl-grey: decorated, adorned

311 scent as of *snuff*

312 as panteth the *hart:* male deer, stag

    that precious *rip* (Br.): worthless person

GLOSSARY

PAGE

299 *eau de Cologne* (Fr.): a perfumed liquid, cologne

301 Meyerbeer (Giacomo): a composer (1791-1864)

    Golden Age: the finest age in the history of the world when art, music and literature flourished and mankind lived in innocence and happiness

    Ravogli: a character in the opera, *Orfeo ed Eurdice,* by von Gluck, first produced in 1762

    Orpheus: Greek mythological singer who lost his wife, Eurydice, to Pluto

306 Magdalenes: reformed prostitutes

    mangold wurzels: large coarse beets

307 Grand Stand at Epsom: large stand for spectators at the Epsom Downs racetrack

308 hock: any white Rhine wine

308 Steinberg Cabinet: brand name of a hock
nectarine: a form of common peach with no down on the skin
nectar: the drink of the mythological gods

310 Botticelli: an Italian painter (1447-1510)
lavender: small fragrant shrub with pale-purple flowers

311 Delilah: treacherous Biblical woman who betrayed Samson
'Che faro' (Ital.): the final, and considered the most beautiful, song
in the opera, Orfeo.

313 protégées (Fr.): those under the care and protection of another

Suggestions for written work

Time heals all wounds
Man and beauty
Man's attitude toward upright conduct
The effect music has on the listener
Keeping up with the times
The relationship between a man's character and his likes

INTERLUDE II

DISCUSSION

1. Winter is appropriately coming on when *A Man of Property* ends; summer has arrived in this interlude. In what way is summer just as appropriate here?

2. Does Old Jolyon really need boots, or are they merely an excuse? What leads you to your conclusion? Account for Old Jolyon's pleasure that Irene has taken her maiden name.

3. What lies behind Old Jolyon's decision to sit in Kensington Gardens rather than drive in the Park? Does he care what the other Forsytes might think?

4. What, to Old Jolyon, seems contradictory when Irene says that Bosinney loved balance and symmetry? Is his attitude typical of a Forsyte? Explain what Irene means when she says that Old Jolyon is of the Golden Age.

5. Has Bosinney been right in his appraisal of Old Jolyon in regard to beauty? Explain. Why, in spite of himself, is Old Jolyon pleased at hearing Bosinney's opinion?

6. Why cannot Old Jolyon understand Irene's interest in her "lost" women?

VOCABULARY

PAGE

313 *Stodgy* chap: dull, uninteresting

314 that little *whippersnapper:* a young person affecting importance

315 balance and *symmetry*

316 Was she *chaffing* him: ridiculing or teasing good-naturedly
unkempt young faces

318 shall be quite *cut up* (Br.): disturbed or upset
the flat was *impregnated:* completely filled, saturated
abashed by her quiet smile: embarrassed, somewhat shamed

319 so *paltry* an idea

GLOSSARY

PAGE
318 patchouli: perfume derived from an East Indian plant

Suggestions for written work

The lust for life
Love has its trials

INTERLUDE III

DISCUSSION

1. In a reference to a game of cricket, the statement is made that "Forsytes always bat". What does this mean?

2. Is Old Jolyon aware of the dangers of the pain that keeps recurring? Could anyone have influenced him to change his ways? Why, or why not?

3. Why does the thought of Irene's concern only for her lost lover bother Old Jolyon?

4. A great change occurred during the night between Old Jolyon's first thought of doing something for Irene and his actually doing it. What is it? How does it so well represent the change in Old Jolyon?

VOCABULARY

PAGE

322 *'A thin rum little soul'* (Br.): not much of a person, weak-sister type
certain *aromatic* spirituality

323 something *irreconcilable* about her
nature of sex *antipathies:* aversions, definite dislikes

324 an *insatiable* appetite

325 the *tenor* of his life: course, progress
things done in *dotage:* feebleness of mind from age, senility
future was *vested* in

326 Draw me a *codicil:* addition to a will indicating a change in the original contents

GLOSSARY

PAGE

322 eczema: an itching disease of the skin with sores

323 studies, mazurkas: (1) instructive pieces with a melody, (2) Polish dances
"...*Mais enfin—qu'est-ce que tu fais là—danser, le dimanche! Viens, donc!*" (Fr.): Come now! What are you doing there? Dancing on Sunday? Come now!

325 heliotrope: herb or shrub with fragrant purple blossoms
asp: poisonous snake

Suggestions for written work

The man who "must always bat"
Determination contrasted with stubbornness

INTERLUDE IV

DISCUSSION

1. Is it Irene's beauty alone that has brought about the increased admiration for beauty in Old Jolyon? How else can you account for it?

2. After his early morning hours of thinking about Irene, to what conclusion does Old Jolyon come? Do Old Jolyon's feelings about Irene bother him at all? In what way?

3. Is Old Jolyon's silence regarding his pain in consideration of himself or of others?

4. In the opera, *Faust*, the main character of the same name exchanges his soul for some fresh years of youth. This idea has crossed Old Jolyon's mind before. What does he think of it now?

VOCABULARY

PAGE

327 *Preposterous,* at his age

328 What a *cadaverous* chap!: like a corpse, ghastly appearing

329 enjoy an *infirmity*

330 another *aberration* like that: deviation from normalcy
    there was any *cupboard* love (Br.): love that is self-interested, selfish
    made *'jubey'* his drive (Br.): very happy, jubilant

330 an *asthmatic* feeling: labored breathing, pertaining to a chest constriction

331 didn't care a *dump* (Br.): half-penny, the least bit

GLOSSARY

PAGE

328 *sal volatile* (New Latin): smelling salts

329 Marguerite ... Mephisto: characters in the opera, *Faust,* by Charles Gounod, first produced in 1859.

Suggestions for written work

Beauty and age
Regaining the past

425

INTERLUDE V

DISCUSSION

1. Discuss the opening paragraph of this section of the interlude. How does Old Jolyon feel about this? Could this be a definition, in a way, of Forsyteism?

2. A Forsyte never lives on his capital. Explain this in the light of Old Jolyon's current thinking.

3. So many old people live in retrospection. Old Jolyon no longer does. What points up this fact very clearly?

4. Why, now, does Old Jolyon refuse to see a doctor? Why does he increase the consumption of luxuries that he had much earlier reduced?

5. In his room after the opera, Old Jolyon is haunted by the music of *Carmen*. What view of life does he explain here? Is it a true Forsytean view?

6. Old Jolyon becomes annoyed with sunbeams, the dog odor, the smell of perfume—things that never bothered him before. Why is he so affected by them now?

7. Why is the "prostration of will-power" so difficult for Old Jolyon?

8. Discuss the real reason for Old Jolyon's reluctance to have his meetings with Irene stopped. In this, is he a true Forsyte?

9. Is Old Jolyon in character when he writes the letter to Irene and does not say what he originally intended? Explain Old Jolyon's wonderment as to whether Irene had actually existed.

10. With everything of immediate value to him seemingly gone, why does Old Jolyon now send for a doctor? Explain the last sentence of the interlude. Why, on the last page, is there such repetition of the word "summer"?

426

VOCABULARY

331 *dynamos* of memory
peradventure he shall decline: possibly, perchance
which *transcended* Forsyteism: went beyond, surpassed

332 each throb *fretted*
shibboleths of the past: habits, customs
had always been *anathema:* a curse, something damned
so *gross* a phrase: indecent, flagrant
he *fidgeted* himself to death
not in *retrospection*

333 to one naturally *abstemious:* careful in diet, temperate
pet his frequent shortness of breath (Br.): pamper, indulge
was a priceless *boon*
with the pathetic *improvidence:* lack of foresight, thoughtlessness

335 *scruff* of the neck: back, nape
great *blunderbuss* of a town: large and stupid place

336 wonderfully silky *sheen*

337 *prim* little Frenchwoman
might have *lost* her train (Br.): missed

338 swam at the *meshes:* the threads surrounding the open faces of a
net

339 *tantamount* to confessing: equal, equivalent
forego their whims

340 It was all *eerie*
to reach *resignation:* patience, state of submission

341 *quintessence* of a summer day: most perfect state, highest form
'soldiers' on the lawn: flowers standing very straight in rows
cropping the clover: eating the tops off

427

GLOSSARY

PAGE

334 *entr'acte* (Fr.): interval between the acts of a play

335 Habanera: aria from Bizet's opera, *Carmen,* first produced in 1875

339 cockchafer: a beetle

Suggestions for written work

Living on "capital"
Difficulties in giving up what one loves
Retrospection
Living vs. existing
Will-power
Old Jolyon—then and now

General discussion of the entire novel

1. How is Galsworthy's realism portrayed in this novel?

2. Compare the various reactions and attitudes of the Forsytes toward beauty.

3. Do the Forsytes have a religion? Discuss this part of their lives.

4. Explain the quotation from Shakespeare on the title page of the interlude.

5. Which events, if they had happened earlier in the story, could have changed the outcome?

6. Is there "the man of property" today?

General suggestions for written work

1. Forsyteism

2. Vivid, colloquial dialect in *The Man of Property*

3. Major themes in *The Man of Property*

4. Parasitic qualities of the Forsytes

5. John Galsworthy—humanitarian moralist

6. Family ties

7. The Forsyte scale of values

8. True Forsyte, mongrel Forsyte, and non-Forsyte

9. Matthew Arnold's "Philistines" and John Galsworthy's "Forsytes"

10. A philosophy of life different from a Forsyte's

11. American vs. British attitudes

12. Beauty—a necessity for life